Mysteries of the GOLDEN STOOL

Ernest Nsiah Youngmann

Kofyoung Entreprise

Accra. Ghana

authorHOUSE®

AuthorHouse™ UK
1663 Liberty Drive
Bloomington, IN 47403 USA
www.authorhouse.co.uk
Phone: 0800 047 8203 (Domestic TFN)
+44 1908 723714 (International)

Published by AuthorHouse 09/27/2019

ISBN: 978-1-7283-9374-2 (sc)
ISBN: 978-1-7283-9373-5 (e)

Print information available on the last page.

Cover design: Mike Amon Kwafo, Design Consult.
Typset by: Osborn Tetteh & Kofi Antwi Boasiako
Typeset in: Adobe Garamond

Photos: Manhyia Palace Library and Museum, Yaw Owusu Amankwaa & Enerst Nsiah Youngmann

DEDICATION

I dedicate this novel,
Mysteries of the GOLDEN STOOL to the Monarch of *Asanteman*,
Otumfoɔ Osɛe Tutu II
King of the Asante Kingdom.
I also dedicate it to all his predecessors
Opoku Ware II (1970 – 1999)
Osɛe Tutu Agyeman Prɛmpɛ II (1931-1970)
Agyeman Prɛmpɛ I (Kwaku Dua III) (1884-1931)
Kwaku Dua II (1834-1867)
Kofi Karikari (1867-1874)
Mɛnsa Bonsu (1874-1883)
Kwaku Dua I (1834- 1884)
Osɛe Yaw Akoto (1824-1834
Osɛe Tutu Kwame Asibe Bonsu (1800-1823)
Opoku Fofie (1798-1799)
Osɛe Kwame (1777-1798)
Osɛe Kwame (Ɔko-awia) (1764-1777)
Kusi Obodum (1750-1764)
Opoku Ware I (1720 -1750) and especially,
Osɛe Tutu I (Opemsoɔ) (1680-1717) the sovereign Monarch,
Creator of the Asante Kingdom.
Also, I dedicate it to H. E. John Agyekum Kufuor,
Former President of Ghana (2001 – 2009), my mentor
with whom I worked as his personal Audio/Video Archivist
(1995 – 2009)

TABLE OF CONTENT

ACKNOWLEDGEMENTS

It is with great appreciation that I would like to thank the following people who helped me in the preparation of this book:

Madam Elizabeth Ohene, Grandma, my big sister, formerly, Editor of Daily Graphic, a BBC Correspondent, a Senior Presidential Staffer and Minister of State in the erstwhile President J. A. Kufuor Administration, who was the first person to see and read my manuscript. Her in-depth analysis and recommendations gave the story tremendous leap in its flow.

I am grateful to Rev. Dr. Philip Arthur Gborson and his team at the Department of Communications Studies at the University of Cape Coast who did the first review and evaluation.

Uncle K. G. Osei Bonsu, Mrs. Mary Krobo Edusei and the late Nana Kwadwo Agyemang, former Pampasohene (May he rest in peace) for their support and encouragement.

To Mr. Mike Amon-Kwafo, former Director of Ghana Television and an Artist in his own right, who designed the book cover and other images, I say thank you.

To Nana Kwadwo Fɔdwoɔ, *Kwadwomfoɔ* (praise singer) of Otumfoɔ the *Asantehene*, who assisted me in the translation of some of the appellations of the kings from its original *Twi* to English. Nana, *me da wo ase* (I thank you).

Special gratitude goes to Emeritus Professor J. H. Kwabena Nketia,J. H. Kwabena Nketia Foundation, University of Ghana who granted me special permission to use extracts from his book AYAN, an anthology of appellations in drum language of kings of Asante kingdom and other Akan traditional rulers to compose the appellations in the Mysteries of The Golden Stool.

Professor Esi Sutherland of Institute of African Studies, University of Ghana deserves great gratitude for her personal commitment to my finishing this work, editing and other content inputs.

Mr. Enimil Ashong, former Editor of The New Times, thank

you for the invaluable time you spent proofreading and polishing the content.

For the last minutes cleanup of critical errors and final proofreading, Mrs. Mercy Nsiah Sarfo-Antwi of Oil of Gladness Publishing, thank you for your time and efforts.

Working for close to 15 years with H. E. John Agyekum Kufuor, former president of Ghana, who is also a member of the *Apagya* Division of the Asante Royal family brought me closer to Otumfuo Osei Tutu II and the Manhyia Palace, the epitome of Asante tradition and culture. I learnt a lot that gave me a good insight into much of the traditional stuff I used as matrix on which the story of the Mysteries of the Golden Stool was built. President Kufuor, I am grateful.

Hon Kojo Yankah of African University College of Communications (AUCC), my greatest inspiration and wind in my sail, gratitude.

Finally, to my Nsiah Youngmann Family: my spouse Vida and all our eight children, Jeffery Cobby, Ernest Junior, Beatrice, Maame Efua, Nana Essie, Nana Afua, Papa Kwame and Awuraa Ama(Bibi), the quality family time you lost with me while I was working on the manuscript but tolerated and encouraged me to complete it at all cost, I am grateful.

Thank you all who assisted me in diverse ways I could not mention here.

Thank God.

ABOUT THE AUTHOR

Born, the last of ten children, to a Presbyterian school teacher/catechist father and a farmer mother at Bechem, Ernest Nsiah Youngmann grew up in Duayaw-Nkwanta. His deep interest in the theatre arts and entertainment led him into a career in the Arts. He joined the Ghana Theatre Club performing in plays like: "The Struggling Black Race" and "Back to Mau Mau." He later joined the Talents Theatre and became its permanent Stage Manager and Director of Business and saw it run its first ever Festival of Seven Plays in the 1987. The plays included: The Black Star; Mambo; The Trial of Kwame Nkrumah; Jogolo; Chaka – the Zulu, and Aikin Mata.

He had his first stint on screen playing the lead in "WALKING OUT", a NAFTI Graduate film production which led to his being cast in two NDR/Afromovies productions of "KUKURANTUMI – ROAD TO ACCRA" and "NANA AKOTO." He was also cast in Peter Bringmann's "AFRICAN TIMBER," Kwaw Ansah's "HERITAGE AFRICA" and Danny Glover's "DEADLY VOYAGE." He also directed and co-wrote two video movies "SHOESHINE BOY" and "POLICE OFFICER 1".

His greatest ambition was to become a filmmaker. He set up Movie Haus Ltd, one of the first private video production businesses in Ghana to build video archives, produce home videos, short documentaries, Corporate videos, Television commercials and cover events.

Ernest Nsiah Youngmann, worked as Video and Photo Archivist for H. E John Agyekum Kufuor, President of Ghana from 2001 to 2009. He was also a news correspondent and liaison for almost all the media houses of Ghana accredited to the Presidency. Currently, he owns Kofyoung Ent., audio and video archiving and publishing house.

His hobbies: Watching movies, cooking vegetarian food and traveling.

ABOUT THE BOOK

The "MYSTERIES OF THE GOLDEN STOOL" is an historical fantasy adventure story built around the Kingdom of Asante, its vibrant culture and its most sacred relic - the Golden Stool.

The ruler of this kingdom is very powerful. He derives his power and authority from his occupancy of the Golden Stool, the symbol of state, the spiritual soul of the kingdom of Asante, which holds the unity and strength of the Asanteman, the kingdom.

The story elucidates the journey of a thief of ancient relics whose decision to steal the Golden stool sets into motion a thrilling fantasy battle with departed kings and guardians of the Golden Stool in an ancient mausoleum.

A cosmopolitan Asante academic transforms into the reluctant hero who defends his heritage and finds the love of his life.

Ernest Nsiah Youngmann
Author

APPRAISAL

The story, “Mysteries of the Golden Stool” by Ernest Nsiah Youngmann is a good story well told, full of suspense and surprises, flashbacks, flash forwards and imagery. Particularly symbols, metaphors, similes and personification are highly appreciable.

The delineation of the entire story is simple for the ordinary reader to enjoy. It has good expression, a lot of humor and simplicity of language. Presented in a linear manner using the omniscient narrator, the story is very catchy and dramatic, with series of dialogues which make it come alive. It has appropriate style and technique that should attract a wide readership.

REV. DR. PHILIP ARTHUR GBORSONG DEPARTMENT OF COMMUNICATIONS STUDIES UNIVERSITY OF CAPE COAST

INTRODUCTION

The Golden Stool is an ancient ancestral relic some four centuries old. It exists in the Asante Kingdom in present day Ghana in Africa. Ghana, which until 1957 was called the Gold Coast, a unique country, west of the continent, closest to the confluence or the intersection of the Equator and the Greenwich Meridian, longitude zero degree and latitude zero degree, considered by scientists as the centre of the earth.

In the middle of Ghana is located the Asante Kingdom in an area very rich in gold and other precious minerals like diamond, bauxite and manganese. It is a Monarchy ruled by a very powerful king, who derives his power and authority from his occupancy of the Golden Stool, the symbol of state, the spiritual soul of the kingdom of Asante and that which holds the unity and strength of the *Asanteman*, the kingdom.

It is believed that the original Golden Stool was conjured from the heavens by *Okomfo Anokye*, a spiritual companion of the first Monarch of *Asanteman*, King Osei Tutu *Opemsuo*. With him, Osei Tutu I created what is now the Asante Kingdom, making the spiritual power of the Golden Stool a force, around which the survival of the Asante kingdom evolved.

The Asante kingdom has a very rich history of bravery and valour, culture and tradition, custom, art and industry. From 1680 A.D. to date sixteen monarchs have ascended the throne.

Every six weeks, considered the calendar month of the Asante Kingdom, Akwasidae is marked to celebrate the Golden Stool in pomp and pageantry. Nine of these are observed every year.

Attempts to dispossess the Asante of their sacred relic, the Golden Stool, are as old as the beginnings of colonial occupation of the sub-region. The British colonial authority, in their bid to take administrative control of the Gold Coast colony, from the coast to the northern territories, was halted by the strong and formidable Asante warrior kings and their kingdom. The British found the Asante an irritation, an empire impossible to subjugate and traced their strength, power and protection to their possession of the Golden Stool. For this, Asantes and the British fought many wars.

After the Sagrenti War (1873 -1874) had been fought and won by the British, they thought they had defeated Asante. But Asante rebuilt under Prempeh I. He refused British entreaties to subject his kingdom voluntarily to the British. He refused to come under British rule. They promised to pay him and his senior Chiefs, and Queen a monthly salary. He refused. So, they came back in 1896. There were negotiations, still, he refused to subjugate his kingdom under British rule.

At that point, all Asante knew they were going to take Nana Prempeh away. The governor arrived with an armed contingent, surrounded the king and his people, arrested them and eventually sent the king and some prominent councilors into exile in the Seychelles. Prempeh I surrendered and sacrificed himself rather than plunge Asante into another needless war. And he returned after 28 years to take back what he left.

In the aftermath of this diabolic betrayal, the British raided Kumasi, searching for the Golden Stool. It is believed though that they never found the Golden Stool.

This story, Mysteries of the Golden Stool, an historical fiction fantasy adventure, elucidates the journey of a thief of ancient relics, Abdul Ali who decides to steal the original Golden Stool for the significance of the power it possesses and all that it represents to the people of *Asanteman* and also for the fact that no foreign interest had been able to lay hands on it.

Abdul Ali kidnaps Kofi Nsiah, a lecturer in Anthropology at Kumasi University and an authority in the traditions, culture and life of the people of *Asanteman,* who had traveled to the United States on an invitation from a prominent University to hold an exhibition and to deliver a series of lectures on the theme: "The lives of the people of *Asanteman* and the relevance of the Golden Stool in the contemporary

Asante Kingdom." Abdul Ali brings him down from New York to Kumasi for his nefarious venture, consumed by his foolish pride and obsession to own the Golden Stool using modern technology and science to steal it instead of waging war with the Asante.

For what will happen to Abdul Ali and the thrilling battle with the legendary departed kings, guardians of the Golden Stool, in a tomb underneath the City of Kumasi, the seventeen chapters of the Mysteries of the Golden Stool unfolds. It will also reveal what the people of Asante go through in celebrating their king and the Golden Stool, in a festival they call *Akwasidae.*

Chapter One

AGENDA FOR A CHASE

A late spring morning broke with a drizzle after a heavy rainy night.

It was misty and the famous Manhattan skyline had disappeared into the clouds. As usual, there was traffic jam and the ambience was filled with tooting horns, running engines and intermittent splashes of little pools of water on the washed streets when the traffic moved till it stopped at the next red lights. The atmosphere, spiced with the sweet fragrance of the pollen of blooming flowers, yet mixed in there, was the intermittent punch of foul smell of leftover foods from the garbage bins of the many restaurants and eating joints along the street. Hot steam oozed out of grates covering the underground sewerage and the pavements were choked with people, many with umbrellas and raincoats, shielding them from the gentle droplets.

Downtown, Kruger was caught up in the traffic. He looked desperate. At the junction, he eased his car out of Canal Street onto West Broadway towards the Grand Hotel. He found a parking space a few blocks away and stepped out. Kruger, a short stocky man, wearing a gold necklace with a big pendant and gold rings on all his left fingers, in dark goggles, a leather jacket and brown khaki baseball cap over his bald head, he looked carefully around and rushed to the hotel, quickly headed directly for the lift through the lobby to the fifth floor. He took out from his pocket a piece of paper with 511 written on it, looked at it and pushed it back into his pocket.

When the lift opened on the fifth floor he stepped out, looking for door No. 511. Finding it, he brought out a screw driver-like piece of metal from his pocket and forced open the lock. A waiter appeared from the corner and saw Kruger standing at the door. The waiter called out, thinking it was their guest, Kofi Nsiah, a young lecturer and anthropologist from the University of Kumasi in Ghana who was in New York to hold an exhibition and a series of lectures on MYSTERIES OF THE GOLDEN STOOL.

"Golden man!" The waiter shouted as Kruger succeeded in opening the door, entered the room and shut the door behind him.

The waiter wondered why there hadn't been a response from Kofi. That was unusual of the Golden Man, he thought. He became curious and decided to crosscheck if indeed the person who had entered was the Golden Man.

Kruger looked around the room, not sure what exactly he was looking for. He spotted the small ring box on the bedside table. He picked it up, opened it and saw a gold pendant of an elephant inside it. He shut it quickly and dropped it into his pocket. He began a frantic search of the room. Suddenly, the door opened and the waiter peeped in.

"Golden Man, it's me, your friend," the waiter uttered as he pushed his head into the room. "Hey! You are not Golden Man!" The intruder stopped short in his search of the room and eyed him with a mean look. "Who are you? What the hell are you doing in his room? I'll call the security." The waiter said emphatically, moving towards the phone on the desk beside the bed. The door slowly shut by itself. Kruger dashed for the waiter, grabbed him by the neck from behind and flung him at the mirror, shattering the glass. The waiter's forehead gashed, oozing with blood. Kruger picked the helpless man up and threw him at the television. With the waiter passed out, Kruger began to tear up the room, searching everywhere, including Kofi's luggage.

Outside the hotel, Kofi Nsiah, the occupant of the Grand Hotel room 511 arrived in a taxi. He paid the driver for the trip but told him to wait to take him back to where he had picked him. Kofi rushed to the Front Desk to get the key to his room.

"Golden Man, you are quite early today," remarked the cheerful receptionist.

"My key, please." He responded with equal cheer and a smile. "I am picking up something. I'll be on my way back, immediately." The receptionist turned round, swiftly picked the room key and handed it to Kofi.

"Scuse me, sir!" A voice called from behind him as he turned to head for his room. Kofi turned. There stood a short and smallish Korean man holding a laptop computer to his chest. "Allo, sir," the Asian said, bowing to greet him. The sight of the man momentarily disoriented Kofi.

"What can I do for you, Mister?" Kofi asked as he recomposed himself. "My name is o, Jimmy Cho." The Korean responded, bowing again to Kofi.

"Yes, Mr. Jimmy Cho, what can I do for you?"

"I have o business to -o discuss o with you." He spoke with a typical Asian accent bowing intermittently. "What sort of business?"

"Business o withi internet o website."

"Look, I am not conversant with these gadgets and how you people juggle with them."

"A-so computer, internet o izi easy to do. I teach you."

Kofi felt the gestures were causing some embarrassment for him. He pulled Jimmy Cho aside to a corner in the lobby where there was a sofa. "Look, I am in a hurry. You sit down and wait for me. I am picking up something from my room upstairs. I will return with you to my exhibition venue where we can sit and talk. Alright?"

"Ah, so. I wait o," he responded and bowed as Kofi dashed to the lift.

Jimmy settled in the sofa in the lobby.

Tango and Don arrived shortly after Kofi. They had also made their way to the hotel lobby and had observed the encounter between Kofi and Jimmy Cho from a distance. They moved slowly towards Jimmy as Kofi waited for the lift. Jimmy flicked open the laptop he was holding, turned it on and set it on his lap. The lift delayed but eventually arrived. Kofi entered and headed for his room. Tango pulled out a small communicating device and pressed a few knobs and returned it into his pocket.

Kruger frantically searched but did not seem to find what he was looking for. The pager in his pocket beeped. He reached for it. Reading the message on it he dashed out of the room, jumping over the lifeless body of the waiter in the process. He opened the door and peeped to check the corridor. Finding it empty, he sneaked out towards the lift. The lift indicated it was moving up to the floor. It stopped. He also stopped. He hesitated a while, then changed his mind and dashed for the emergency exit.

The lift door opened and Kofi stepped out. He saw Kruger dashing away. The emergency exit door was locked and with a pass key Kruger attempted to open it.

"Hey, my friend," Kofi called. "Why don't you use the lift. It may be faster." Kruger turned to look at him as the door opened, then exited quickly.

The door to the room was not closed. Unsuspecting, Kofi walked to his door. He touched the door, it flung ajar and he was confronted with an unbelievable sight.

"Oh my God. Oh my God! Who the hell----?" he muttered, seeing how almost everything in the room had been strewn around.

Then he recollected meeting a man in the corridor. He saw the shattered mirror and the TV, then a man in a pool of blood. He screamed. "That man! Who-? Dead body? Dead body! Aaaahhhh!!!"

Kofi dashed out of the room to the lift, his heart pumping. His suspicion went immediately to the man he had seen in the lobby. He pressed the knob persistently. The lift was not coming so he dashed towards the emergency exit. He remembered the possible murderer went that way. He stopped short, turned round, slipped and fell to the floor. He struggled up, crawling and falling again as he went towards the lift. The lift arrived; he ran to it. As the lift's door began to close, he jumped and crashed into the lift door trying with his right arm and right leg to stop it from closing.

The lift's door opened again, he entered and it closed. He pressed the knob again and again. The lift began to move upwards. The lift stopped and the door opened. Kofi jumped out only to realize it was the seventh floor. He turned round to the lift but he was not quick enough. The lift door shut before he could get back to it. He turned and saw a door with a stairway tag on it. He opened it and ran down the stairs. Dumb-founded, he could not even scream.

Kruger appeared out of the emergency exit door into the lobby and walked briskly away without notice.

Meanwhile, Tango and Don reached Jimmy. He had opened a web page trying to create a website. He typed "THE GOLDEN STOOL OF THE ASANTE" in the search column.

"I see. 'The Golden Stool of the Asante.' You are interested in the stool.

Why?" Tango inquired.

He lifted his head to see who spoke and with a smile on his face, Jimmy responded without hesitation. "Yes. I wait -o Mr. Kofi -o. for Internet -o business -o."

"Well, let's see what you have there."

Jimmy, in his anxiety to impress the two, tapped the enter key on his computer. A 3-D image of the Golden Stool appeared, glittering and rotating. Don touched Jimmy on the neck and pressed his fingers heavily and deeply into the neck. Jimmy, startled, opened his mouth but was unable to scream. He sat frozen with eyes and mouth open. Tango snatched the laptop and the two men walked out unnoticed.

Kofi burst into the corridor of the ground floor, and dashed towards the reception. He ran into a couple holding hands and walking along the corridor which threw him off balance, sending him bumping into a waiter holding a tray with glasses and drinks. The tray flew, splashing the drink on him, spilling everything onto the floor and smashing the bottles and glasses. Without paying attention to the commotion, he ran on and crashed into the counter at the front desk. The receptionist looked at him, astonished by his disheveled appearance, while still panting and out of breath.

"Hei, Golden Man. What's up? You look quite frightened," the receptionist said.

Panting and unable to speak Kofi screamed the words out, "Murder!...

Murder! Call ...the Police. A dead man.... in my room .... upstairs." "Murder?" The receptionist re-echoed. This attracted the attention of

the guests and the people in the lobby who, out of curiousity, all began to move towards the counter. The head of the front desk staff pressed a button and two in-house security men showed up at the counter.

"This is our guest. He needs help in his room, 511. He says someone is dead in there."

The demeanour of the two security men changed immediately from cordial to a hostile one. One of them pulled out his revolver. "Man, put your hands on the counter where I can see them," the first security man ordered. Kofi put his two hands on the counter. The few people who had started to gather there backed away a little, at the sight of the revolver. He held up Kofi as the other one ran to check on room 511. Gradually, his shock at finding a dead man in his hotel room began to change to anxiety at what was going to happen to him should he be a suspect for murder.

The second security man ran to the lift and took it to the fifth floor. He could see the door of room 511 was open as he exited the lift. With his revolver in hand, he cautiously tiptoed towards the door. It was ajar. He peeped into the room, pulled out his walkie-talkie and radioed.

"Base One, this is 3 – 4," he spoke over the walkie-talkie. "Base One, go ahead," a response came over.

"We have a situation. Suspected homicide at my loco. Call 911. Require immediate backup support."

The message could be heard on the walkie-talkie of the first security man and to the hearing of all around.

"I said put your hand up where I can see them!"

"2-5, this is 3 – 4," it came from the walkie-talkie of the security man with Kofi.

"Yes, 3 – 4, go ahead," he responded.

"It is really bad here," 3 - 4 voiced on the walkie-talkie.

"Mister, you are in real trouble." 2 – 5 said harshly to Kofi still with his gun pointed at him.

Kofi burst out, "I am not the murderer! I said there is a dead man in my room!"

"Call 911," the security man instructed the receptionist. "I have. The police are on their way," she responded.

"Base One, did you copy the last message?" The walkie-talkie broadcast the message of the second security man in Kofi's hotel room.

"Roger, Roger! Support's on the way," Base One responded.

Kofi tried to turn to look at the security man behind him. He could feel the heaviness of the gun pointed at him. The first police patrol arrived with deafening siren and flashing lights. The men descended and ran into the lobby. The security man moved closer to Kofi and ran a quick check on Kofi's body.

"Over here!" He called the attention of the policemen who

quickly rushed to him. They grabbed Kofi without any provocation from him and wrestled him down to the floor. One of them pulled out his handcuffs and clipped Kofi's hands, one after the other, behind him.

"Awch! It hurts! What is wrong with you?" Kofi protested. The policeman ignored him. He made Kofi sit on the floor, watching over him as the other took a briefing from the in-house security man.

Lt. Croffy, the head of homicide unit of the New York City Police Department (NYPD) was driving down town when his radio came on.

"Calling all units! Calling all units! Grand Hotel reports homicide within premises of the hotel…."

Lt. Croffy did not wait for the message to end. He knew it was an emergency, so he switched on his siren, placed a blue flashing light on top of the car and whirled the car around 180 degrees in the middle of the road. Drivers of the two vehicles behind him hit hard on their brakes, swerved to avoid hitting Lt. Croffy's car and running into each other. He paid no attention to the commotion he had caused, and simply sped through the city, jumping the red lights.

Within minutes the frontage of the Grand Hotel was swarming with police vehicles and ambulances. They took positions and cordoned off the precinct of the hotel from human and vehicular traffic. Crime scene investigators arrived and paramedics moved up with their stretcher to the lobby and they were directed where to go. The detectives and other men began their work. The Detective Sergeant came and spoke to the two officers who had taken custody of Kofi. The whole scene looked like a well-rehearsed performance, with all the cast and crew moving in perfect harmony. Lt Croffy arrived. He was allowed through the barrier. He drove and parked his car next to the ambulance.

Inside the hotel lobby, the lift arrived with the mutilated body of the waiter on the stretcher. He was still alive but in pretty bad shape and the medics had oxygen and insulin transfusion on him. They wheeled the stretcher swiftly along the lobby. Just as they reached where Kofi was being held, Lt. Croffy also arrived there.

"Wait a minute," Lt. Croffy stopped the stretcher. He took a look at the helpless man who was struggling for his life.

Kofi also took a look at the man on the stretcher. "Poor soul. Thank God; he is still alive," he muttered.

The medics swiftly wheeled the waiter away as his condition suddenly changed and he began gasping for breath. Kofi strained and followed the stretcher with his eyes. They placed the waiter in the ambulance and it sped away.

"Lieutenant, the suspect." The Detective introduced Kofi to Lt. Croffy.

Lt. Croffy looked at Kofi. "I see. Have you read him his rights?" he enquired.

"No, sir," the Detective replied.

"What are you waiting for? Book him! And take him away from here. Comb the area inside out for possible accomplices or the real murderer. He may, probably, not be our prime suspect. The standard procedure: Screen everyone in here thoroughly. And, no exceptions."

"Yes, sir." The Detective responded.

"Have you ID the victim?" Lt. Croffy asked further. "Yes, Sir. He is a waiter here."

"I want to see all the security camera tapes. Let's get on with it." Lt. Croffy ordered and turned towards the front desk of the hotel. "Who is the In-Charge here? And where is the head of security?" He asked.

"Lieutenant, sir?" The detective called but Lt. Croffy paid no attention to him as he moved away.

"Aaah!" A sudden shrill scream came from the corner of the lobby where Kofi had asked Jimmy Cho to sit and wait for him. One officer rushed there with his gun drawn. The couple Kofi ran into a little while ago in the corridor had strayed towards where Jimmy's dead body sat on the sofa. The apparently frightened woman directed the police officer's attention to Jimmy's corpse as it sat there. The officer beckoned for support as he slowly approached Jimmy Cho's body. Lt. Croffy and a few more policemen rushed there too. The officer examined Jimmy. Another set of paramedics arrived with a stretcher. They took over from the officer and examined the body of Jimmy.

"He is dead," the paramedic pronounced on Jimmy Cho.

Lt. Croffy drew closer to the body and reached into the inner jacket pocket of the dead man. He pulled out a wallet. "Jimmy Cho," he read out almost to himself as he went through the personal information. "A legal immigrant, with work permit, green card and a driver's license." He rose, turned and spoke to the hotel manager who was joining them by Jimmy's body, "You know him? What was he doing here?"

"Oh my God!" the hotel manager exclaimed. "Is he dead? "Yes. Is he one of your guests?" Lt. Croffy asked.

"The front desk can confirm it." The manager led the way to the front desk. "A dead man has been found. You know him?" He asked his desk staff while Lt. Croffy showed Jimmy's ID. The receptionist saw the image and immediately identified Jimmy.

"I remember him," she said. "He spoke to the Golden Man when he came to pick his key here moments ago. The Golden Man walked with him to that corner. That's all I can remember of him." The lifeless body of Jimmy was lifted onto the stretcher and a sheet thrown over it. Lt. Croffy called for Kofi. He was brought to the stretcher in the corner.

"Do you know him?" Lt. Croffy asked

Kofi's heart missed a beat. "No, I don't know him." Kofi replied.

"You were seen talking to him minutes ago. Now he's been found dead.

And you say you don't know him?"

"Does that mean I killed him?" Kofi retorted.

"No one is saying so. Confirm or deny you've met before."

"Well, yes. For a couple of minutes. That's about all. That's as much as I know of him."

"Never known him before?"

"Never until then," said Kofi, emphatically. "Sergeant, book him.

Provisional Charge of murder." "What?" Kofi protested. "How? Why?"

"Read him his rights and take him away from here." Lt. Croffy ordered.

Kofi was beside himself with anger and complete disbelief. He could not understand why the police officer was bent on charging him with the crimes without first hearing him out. What was the haste in coming to that conclusion? Many questions ran through his mind. The more he thought about them, the more his confusion gained momentum and made him speechless.

The crime scene investigators got busier with Jimmy's body and the area around it, looking for any evidence that would help unravel what was gradually emerging as mystery crimes in the hotel. Kofi felt dizzy and all he could see, hear or feel were the flashes of the cameras, movements of those engaged in the investigations, several voices, police sirens in a cacophony of sounds over which he could hear the Sergeant speak and read him his rights and charges. "You are under arrest! You have the right to remain silent. Anything you say or do will be used as evidence against you in a court of law. You have the right to an attorney of your choice or the state shall provide you with one if you are unable to find any..." He could feel he was virtually being carried away through the corridors and lobbies of the hotel to face the cameras of the several media men and women who had converged outside the main entrance to the hotel, sending messages and broadcasting live to their various stations. The media dashed towards Kofi and the police with their cameras and microphones as they came out of the hotel, asking questions. The closest they could get was the barricade and crime scene tapes placed there by the police to cordon off the area.

"Officer, do we have a prime suspect?" "When is the press briefing?" were among the many questions that were thrown at them. To each of them, the simple response returned was, "No comment." Kofi was jostled into a police car and driven away.

Lt. Croffy moved up to Kofi's room. The crime scene investigators were busy with their meticulous work. He spoke to one or two of them and turned to go away.

Abyna Saah, a very pretty twenty-seven-year old lady who had come from Ghana to study law at the Yale University, came out of the City Hall to the frontage outside. She paced up and down, expectantly. She was very anxious, expecting Kofi Nsiah who had left her several minutes earlier with the promise to be back in a jiffy. She wondered why he was still not back. Was it another of his disappointments that seemed to have characterized all the dealings she had had with him in the last few days? She felt uneasy. She kept looking at her wrist watch intermittently, pacing up and down the doorway while people moved in and out of the exhibition hall past her. After waiting for what looked like eternity, she decided to cross the street to a coffee shop on the other side.

She bought herself a cup of coffee and began to sip. She kept her eyes on the entrance to the exhibition hall to make sure she would spot Kofi the moment he arrived. She had lost interest completely in whatever she was expecting from him. What could have kept him so long, she thought. The announcement of "breaking news" on a television set nearby attracted her attention. The many police vehicles with their red and blue beacon lights obviously suggested there was an emergency situation. She could not hear the beginning of the story but as she drew closer she could hear the reporter clearer.

"Two victims have so far been found. One dead and the other, in a very critical condition." A female reporter stood at a conspicuous position showing in the background almost all the activities at the precinct of the Grand Hotel. Saah's heart jumped. She became very alarmed and drew closer to the set.

"The first victim has been identified as a waiter of the hotel, currently struggling for his life at the General Hospital," continued the reporter. "His battered body was found in the room of the alleged suspect. The second is an immigrant of Korean or Chinese descent. He was found seated stone dead in a sofa in the lobby. It is not known, as of now, the real motive behind the incidents or whether they are related. An African Professor of Anthropology, holding an exhibition on the

Golden Stool of the Asante Kingdom at the City Hall has been taken in for questioning as a prime suspect or as a witness?" Saah screamed, dropping the cup of tea on the floor. She could not believe what she had just heard on air.

"It is possible," the news report continued, "the suspect could have been the target for the real murderer or murderers. We are anxiously waiting for the police chief to give us a briefing soon. This is Cleo Brew reporting from the crime scene at the Grand Hotel."

Saah, shocked by the news, dashed out of the coffee shop, muttering, "Oh my God! No! No!" as she raced towards her car. She carefully crossed the street, trying to keep her composure. Be strong, keep your head up, were a few thoughts that came to her mind as she dashed for her car. She sped off joining the traffic towards the Grand Hotel. Ahead, the traffic was blocked and the police had diverted the vehicular traffic away from the frontage of the Grand Hotel. She followed the diversion and found somewhere close by to park. She made her way to the Grand Hotel. She was astonished by the crowd and the scene. She moved closer to a TV reporter of another network making a live broadcast.

"It has been confirmed that the suspect has not yet been formally charged with the crimes. Information reaching us has also confirmed the first victim, a waiter of the Grand hotel who was taken away in very critical condition has died. We shall bring you updates as they unfold. This has been Felicia York reporting live from the Grand Hotel, the scene of the murders."

This is enough to calm me, Saah thought. She dashed back to her car and made for the NYPD 5th Precinct.

She arrived, but there was no space to park in front of the station. She drove to a corner almost behind the Precinct building. She got out of the car and hurried to the entrance, but stopped. "What am I going to do? What am I going to say? Who am I? What do I want?" Many more questions came to her mind. She returned to the car. She picked up her handbag and Kofi's files on her arm, raced to the building and up the steps to the front desk. She approached the counter to the officer on duty who was attending to some duties so she waited her turn.

"Hi, Officer," said Abyna to the officer. "I am Abyna Saah. I am here for Mr. Kofi Nsiah, the man you are holding for the Grand Hotel homicide case. I am his attorney. I want to see him."

"Speak to Lt. Croffy," replied the officer pointing to a door behind her. She turned and saw a glass door with the name tag "Lt. Croffy" on it. Saah walked to the door. She knocked and pushed opened the door. Lt. Croffy sat behind his desk working on his computer.

"Lt. Croffy?" She inquired.

"Lookin' at him." He responded without taking his eyes off the PC. "Hi, I am Abyna Saah," she continued nonetheless. "I am told you are holding my client here. I want to know what for and get bail for him."

"Who is this client of yours?"

"Kofi Nsiah, your suspect, or is it witness in the Grand Hotel homicide case I presume you are investigating? I am his attorney."

"When did he engage you?"

"Have you charged him? Did you read him his rights?"

"Of course, we have. But I am afraid you cannot get him bail."

"Why not?"

Lt. Croffy lifted his head and looked her in the face, "Look here, our investigations are going on. We are going to interrogate him to determine his charge. He has to make his caution statement. We have not yet established motive for the murders, now that the other victim is dead and all the circumstances surrounding the whole incident and …."

"Standard procedure," Saah cut in.

"Of course, you know that". He went back to attend to his work on the computer.

"May I talk to my client?"

Lt. Croffy lifted his eyes off the screen again to look at her. "Look here, Miss. We cannot grant him bail; not until the primary investigations are completed. And the D. A...."

"I want to see my client. It is his right." Saah cut in again.

"Very well. Come with me." Lt. Croffy got up from his desk and led her out of the office.

"Since your client has no current address now, and since the last one he had has now become a crime scene, it will be prudent we keep him here till our investigations are over and most importantly if he qualifies for the bail."

"You are not the one to grant bail. The D. A. and a judge will have to decide that. I thought you said so yourself."

Lt. Croffy immediately realized he had been outwitted by the young woman he had attempted to intimidate. He reaffirmed himself by challenging the locus of Saah. "Get him a good lawyer. I know practically every attorney in this city. Say, I've never met you anywhere before. You are not a registered practitioner in this state. You cannot represent him. For his own safety, he will be better protected in our custody." Lt. Croffy opened the door to the room Kofi was being kept. "You have ten minutes." Saah, befuddled, just looked at him as he walked away.

Chapter Two

HORNET'S NEST

Kofi Nsiah sat in the Police interrogation room with his eyes closed, thinking and trying to recollect the harrowing experience he had gone through a few hours earlier that day that had brought him to where he was sitting, tightly gripped in the arms of the law in a strange land. Perplexed and overwhelmed, the thrilling and breathtaking events from the morning played back to him like a movie.

Early that morning, as he picked his clothes for that day from his suitcase, he saw a small ring box. He picked it and opened it. It had a gold pendant of an elephant in it. He shut it and placed it on his bedside table. He quickly dressed up and pulled a kente stole and threw it around his neck. He picked his file and headed out. He stopped briefly at the door. He felt he had forgotten something he must do before leaving. He waited for a few seconds but could not remember exactly what it was. He slowly shut the door and rushed towards the lift as he heard it arrive at the floor. A couple of guests had arrived with it and were getting out so that gave him enough time to get to it. Luckily, the lift was going down.

At the front desk Kofi left his key to a very cheerful receptionist who wished him a great day. Responding likewise he stepped out.

He hailed a taxi to "City Hall." The driver nodded as he joined. The usual New York City morning traffic was heavy as the cab joined it and the drizzle of the morning. The City Hall, the building housing his exhibition and a series of lectures, was a few blocks away from the Grand Hotel, where he was lodging,

Kofi had arrived from Ghana ten days earlier on an academic and cultural exchange programme with Columbia University to hold these lectures and exhibition on the theme: "The lives of the people of *Asanteman* and the relevance of the Golden Stool in the contemporary Asante Kingdom," It took three days, after his arrival, to set up the exhibition. He had come along with a team of craftsmen comprising gold smiths, kente and adinkra cloth weavers, beadings and sandals, designers and salesmen for several artifacts such as gold, ornaments, trinkets, weights, and symbols of adinkra. The exhibition was to showcase and promote the Asante culture and traditions, centering it around the mysteries of the Golden Stool.

Since the exhibition opened two days earlier, he had delivered two out of three scheduled lectures and the artisans and salesmen in his team had engaged in considerable commercial activities, selling almost everything they had come with. As he sat in the cab, he thought about the last lecture he was going to deliver if the cab ever got him to the hall, he would then be free to do some sightseeing around this impressive city of New York and maybe even get some shopping done. He looked at his wrist watch. The time was half past eight.

"Damn!" he exclaimed, watching the people walking briskly on the pavement past the cars while he sat in the cab. He wore no protective clothing against the weather and had no umbrella. It was not so cold outside at that time of the year in New York. He was late and the traffic was not moving. He decided to make the rest of the journey on foot which seemed a better idea. "How much do I owe you, Mister?" he spoke to the driver. "I want to get off."

"Nine bucks," the driver replied.

"Nine dollars," Kofi almost shouted, "for this short distance, from the Grand Hotel?"

"That's what it says right here, Mister," the driver responded, pointing to the counter on the dashboard."

"Of course. We've spent more time stationary than moving." Kofi said, half to himself as he pulled a couple of bills out of his wallet for the driver. Without allowing the cab to pull aside, Kofi stepped out into the drizzle. He pulled up the collar of his jacket to cover the back of his neck, over a kente stole he wore around his neck. For an African who was not used to the weather, it felt cold. He raised his leather file over his head and rushed through the milling crowd of umbrellas and raincoats till he arrived at the lobby of the exhibition hall.

There was a crowd waiting. Some people were seated in the lecture hall. Others were going through the exhibits. At the entrance, Kofi shook the water from his wet clothes and walked into the exhibition hall. He tried to attract the attention of one of the curators of the exhibition who was standing a bit removed from his counter. Kofi caught his attention and tried to give him a message with sign language. He pointed to a big picture frame hanging high up on the wall. The curator did not get the message and indicated to Kofi that he could not understand what Kofi was saying. After a couple of confusing sign messages to each other Kofi gave up, walked up to the curator and screamed, "Put the big light on!"

The patrons of the exhibition were startled by the raised voice and looked around to see who had shouted.

"Oh, the light!" The curator whispered to himself, nodding his head in approval and turned towards the switch to put it on.

Kofi gave a sigh of relief. He walked off trying to make himself invisible among the crowd of people. With a flick of the switch, a golden light began to glow from inside the giant picture frame hanging on the wall, revealing a resplendent, glittering image of the Golden Stool, which, without the light had been a fuzzy representation. The sudden brightness attracted the visitors in the hall. They all turned to look at the glowing giant picture.

You could hear the "Ohs!" and "Ahs!" of admiration that came from the crowd as some of them moved closer to take a better look at the picture. *Akannnwomkro,* traditional music compositions of Emeritus Professor Kwabena Nketia, Kofi's former head of department at the Kumasi University, began over the loudspeakers in the exhibition hall. Quite a number of the patrons there were students from the Columbia University. They were doing various research projects related to Africa. Some wore African clothes to show affinity to the culture. There were also a number who believed in the African cause and had come to support the programme or show solidarity. Most of the students showed great curiosity towards the exhibits and the programme. It was a great experience as most there were highly impressed with being so close to true African cultural artifacts for the first time. They had only read about them in books and magazines or seen in television documentaries. Soon, a voice was heard over the loudspeakers.

"Attention, please! The final part of the Golden Stool Lectures will begin in ten minutes at the theatre. All interested persons should make their way there and take their seats. Thank you."

Some of the people drifted slowly towards the lecture theatre while others continued going through the exhibits, looking at or buying artifacts on show.

Kofi entered the lecture hall. It was not a very large hall. It had a lecture platform with a spot light on the lectern. The hall was half full. The audience was made up of people from diverse walks of life. Some were chatting, others were on the phone. The murmur of voices subsided with Kofi's entry. He looked at the sparse attendance, walked directly to the lectern in front and turned to face his audience.

A couple of young men and women rushed in and took seats near the front. They took out their note pads, laptops, other electronic gadgets, listening and recording devices, ready for the lecture.

Kofi placed the file he was carrying on the lectern, cleared his throat and began his address.

"Greetings, friends! Today's lecture is the last in the series of talks on the mysteries of the legendry Golden Stool, *Sika Dwa Kofi* - the soul of the Asante Kingdom. In the last few days, we have heard a lot of things about the Golden Stool. We've heard how it came into existence, how it inspired the Asante people and led them to many glorious victories in wars and how it has made them a most feared and powerful kingdom with the soubriquet: *Asante Kɔtɔkɔ, wo kum apem a, apem beba,* which literally translates as: Asante, the porcupine; you kill a thousand, a thousand more will come after you. We've also heard of the spiritual protection it has given to them as a kingdom or tribe: the invincibility and immortality of each occupant of the stool – the king, the *Asantehene,* who is also called *Otumfoɔ*, after his life as king. The kings don't die, they just go to the village."

The audience was attentive. Some took copious notes, others recorded with various gadgets.

"The Asante Kingdom has a museum situated within the King's Palace complex, *Manhyia*, where the history of the kingdom, the Golden Stool, the fifteen kings who have occupied the stool is documented. Indeed, all relevant information about the kingdom, from the 17th century to date, is stored there."

A door at the back of the hall opened and two men, Don and Tango, entered and sat at the back. They looked like strangers sneaking into a place in which they knew they were not welcome. Kofi spotted them but his attention did not linger on them and he continued with his lecture.

"Our focus today is on the current location of the Golden Stool and how the Asante Kingdom has been able to protect it and the powers it possesses. In the 19th century, the British colonial power exercised control over much of the territories in the West African sub-region. The colonies were the Gambia, Sierra Leone, the Gold Coast and Nigeria. The British began to find the Asante Kingdom to be quite an irritation as they could not subjugate the kingdom. Their strategic and sophisticated art of warfare, and the sheer show of bravery and courage bemused the British each time they met at war. Indeed, the British and the Asante kingdom fought several wars for much of that century. Gradually, the British began to realize the importance of the Golden Stool and the hold it had on the psychology of the Asantes. They decided, the only way to defeat the Asantes and bring them under the control of the Gold Coast Colonial Administration was to find and take control of, or destroy, the Golden Stool. There were several botched attempts at war against the Asantes, one of which was the Sagranti War in 1874 under the command of Sir Garneth Wosley.

They tried to capture the *Asantehene*, the great King of the Asante and the Golden Stool. The Asantes repulsed and beat the British mercilessly in that famous war. The Commander, Sir Garneth Wosley died in that war. The war came to be known as the *Sagranti Sa*, a coinage from the Commander's name in the Asante language. While the vanquished British Army was retreating after the humiliating defeat at the hands of the Asante Kotoko warriors, they decided to raze to the ground the Golden City of Kumasi, the capital of the Asante Kingdom. They destroyed everything in their way including the Royal Mausoleum, where the remains of all the great kings of Asante were kept, not buried, to begin their new life of immortality. Yet, much of the mausoleum remained intact as it was protected by the gods of the land and ancestral spirits of the kingdom. The Royal Mausoleum was also the sacred abode of the Golden Stool."

He paused and sipped a little water from the glass on the lectern. Kofi continued, "The Golden Stool possesses the power of immortality. Any mortal who sits on it obtains the power of immortality. He does not die. He becomes the soul of the people and the protector and guardian of the stool."

The door at the back opened again, this time, Kruger entered the hall. He walked straight to where the two strange men were seated. He was the leader of the group of three. He sat in between them and the two men proceeded to whisper to him, one after the other. He nodded and looked at a piece of paper they had given him with '511, The Grand' written on it.

Kofi shuffled through the sheets of paper in his folder. He pulled one to the top and continued his address: "On the Asante calendar, every six weeks or forty-two days, *adaduanan*, constitute one month. At the end of each Asante calendar month or *adaduanan*, the Golden Stool and its guardians, the departed kings, are visited, cleansed and purified with libations and blood sacrifices." As Kofi went on with the lecture, Kruger hurriedly walked out of the hall, into the car park and drove off in his car. His two friends stayed on and listened to the rest of Kofi's lecture.

Kofi's lecture went on, "I am sure I have been able to arouse your curiosity about the Golden Stool and what it stands for in the lives and history of the people of the Royal Kingdom of the Asantes, *Asanteman*. I hope this will attract you to start making plans to visit Ghana in the near future to experience a life with the people of the Golden Stool." The audience gave a thunderous applause. "Thank you all for attending these lectures." Kofi said to wrap up his lecture. "In fact, you've made my visit to this city and to the United States very enjoyable and worthwhile. The support, the encouragement and patronage have given me the impetus to come back again. I am carrying back home fond memories of all of you and what I have seen. I thank you." The crowd gave him a standing ovation. Kofi bowed to acknowledge the overwhelming support he had received from his patrons. Don and Tango rose and joined in the applause.

"Not so fast with your plans, buddy." Don whispered into the ear of Tango.

The two laughed and slapped each other on the back.

Kofi bowed to the audience again, picked his file and walked out to the exhibition hall. Some of the younger patrons of the lecture, mostly of African descent, ran after him as he moved along. He shook hands with a number of them who congratulated him for his work. They chatted with him seeking clarification on some of the issues he had raised in the lectures. The crowd had grown thicker at the exhibition hall. Kofi moved through the milling crowd, enjoying the support and patronage.

Saah arrived at the precinct of the City Hall. She rushed into the exhibition hall after parking her car at the kerb behind the building. She had tried very hard to come in early for the day's lecture but had not been able to. She spotted Kofi and started working her way through the crowd towards him. Kofi immediately recognized her as she approached him.

"Hei, Saah. It's you!"

"Kofi!" she said excitedly as she rushed forward to meet him. They embraced warmly and shook hands. "I could not come in early enough to hear the lecture, no matter how hard I tried. I guess it's over now."

"Yes, it is." Kofi pulled her aside out of the way of other patrons. "But never mind. The same old story you are familiar with. There was nothing I said there that you did not know before."

"How come you haven't called me again? Are you avoiding me because of one small gold pendant you promised me?"

"Oh my goodness! Your pendant?" He ran a quick check through his pockets. "I am so sorry. I swear I picked it up this morning."

"There you go again."

"You don't believe me, do you? I picked it up this morning. I don't know why I forgot it again."

"It's been a long time since I left Ghana. I miss everybody and everything. That's a good reason for me to come back to see you." She took a quick panoramic look around, seeing all the exhibits and the patrons doing purchases of the various artifacts on display. "Don't worry about the gift. Please, don't make it look like I only came here because of it. I am already excited with what I am seeing. There's quite a good patronage here."

"Oh, yes. It's always been like this since we opened the exhibition," Kofi said feeling disappointed with himself and trying to redeem himself from the apparent embarrassment. "All the same," he remarked, "you give me ten minutes. I'll dash back to the hotel for it."

"And the exhibition?"

"For you, everything else can wait."

"Forgive me for putting you under such pressure."

"You wait right here. I am going for it. It is sitting on my bedside table. Look, hold these." Kofi handed her his file. "It contains all my lecture notes on the Golden Stool, my reports on this trip, my passport and return ticket to Ghana. Take them. When I bring you the pendant, I'll take my stuff back. All right?"

Saah saw the genuineness in his plea and conceded to him. "I am sorry if I have pushed you this way."

"Never mind. Never mind. I'll be back before you know it." Dumping his documents in her hands, Kofi dashed out of the hall. She looked forlornly as he departed.

For a moment Tango and Don who had been observing Kofi Nsiah as he talked to Saah lost track of him.

"Where is he?" Tango asked Don.

"What do you mean where is he?" Don retorted. "Ah, there! He is moving."

"Who?"

"The nugget, dummy. Let's go." The two men dashed after Kofi as he waved down a taxi, sat in it and gave the destination. Tango and Don also jumped into another taxi.

"Follow that cab," said Tango to the driver.

Lt. Croffy led Saah to the interrogation room where Kofi was being held. Kofi was startled awake from his reminiscence of events of the morning by the sound of the door as it suddenly flung open. Kofi rose to his feet. He saw Saah and rushed to meet her halfway in the room. She embraced him and comforted him. He broke down in tears. "Saah! Get me out of here. Get me out of this. I have no hand in whatever has happened."

"I know. I know. Calm yourself," she comforted him.

"Sit down," Kofi ushered her to a second seat by the table. Saah placed her bag and the file on the table and took the chair. She looked straight into his eyes for a moment and shook her head, holding back her tears.

"How did you know I was here?" Kofi broke the momentary silence and inquired as they sat by the table.

"It's all over in the news. I hear the waiter too has died." "Has he?"

"Yes, the police chief has just confirmed it."

"I did not kill those two. I am innocent. How do they arrest me when I am the one who came to report the murder in my room? And especially after they found the second dead man?"

"Calm down. The system here works differently from the way we know it in Ghana. It is a process and until it runs through, one cannot do anything about it. All we need is patience. And, I need to get you a competent lawyer to represent you."

"Oh, I thought you were a lawyer, are you not?" "Yes. But not this kind."

"Oh!" Kofi sighed with grave disappointment as he sat looking, helplessly at Saah.

"Oh, Kofi. What have I brought on to you?" She controlled herself to avert breaking down in tears. She blamed herself for what had happened. Perhaps, if she had not insisted and pushed him so hard for the gift, Kofi would not have found himself in this trouble. She gave a heavy sigh, took Kofi by the hand and assured him: "I know a friend who can help. Give me an hour or so. I will get my friend who can handle this more confidently. I also need to contact the Ghana Embassy to see if they can give you diplomatic cover for immunity or whatever help they can come up with. First, let me get this friend to set your bail."

"The university, those who sponsored my trip, the exhibition, . . ." Kofi said with confidence, realizing they were making headway in decisions they were taking.

"Yes. Yes," Saah added.

Lt. Croffy stood in another room behind a one-way mirror that separated him from the interrogation room. He could see them and hear all they said. Saah pulled her mobile phone and dialed a number. She rose to her feet. As she walked, the door opened. Lt. Croffy walked to the doorway and told her her time was up. She picked her bag and the file from the table. She walked out of the room placing the phone to her ear. She led the way to the corridor in front of Lt. Croffy's office as he closed the door to the interrogation room. Coy sat behind his desk, packing and getting ready to leave the office.

He had the phone receiver to his ear, listening to someone with disinterest. "Yes. Yes. Thank you. Good evening." He banged the receiver. "Huh! This job will kill man."

He rose from his seat, shut his briefcase and picked it up to move. The phone on the desk rang. He sighed with great frustration. He looked at the phone, but turned to go away. After a few steps he returned reluctantly to the phone. He pressed the speaker and began to talk harshly. "I have told you the deal is closed! I am not, simply not, interested! Period!" "Coy, it's me. Saah," said the voice from the speaker.

His briefcase dropped from his hold to the floor. He picked up the receiver. "I am sorry, my dear. Look, where have you been all day? I have been looking for you everywhere."

"Coy, I've gotten myself in some serious trouble. Please come and help

me."

Coy could immediately perceive that this was a distress call he must respond to without hesitation. "Where exactly are you?" He inquired.

"At the 5th Precinct."

"5th Precinct? What sent you there? Just hang in there. I'm on my way."

"Ok."

He felt there was no point talking on the phone. All he needed to do was to get to her. Coy dropped the handset, grabbed his briefcase and dashed out.

Chapter Three

THE SAFE HOUSE

Downtown, somewhere in a warehouse, Kruger in baseball cap and his hoodlum friends, Tango and Don, were waiting. A black limo pulled

up outside at the gate. The gate opened and the limo drove in. The limo parked at the center of the big warehouse and the door opened. Abdul Ali descended. He was dressed in a cream suit and hat. In his left hand, he carried a short black staff. Kruger and his friends approached Abdul Ali with Jim's laptop computer.

"I am told you botched a courtesy call on our special guest," Abdul Ali said in a harsh and authoritative voice.

"Yet we found nothing." Kruger replied as if he was completing Abdul Ali's statement.

"Nothing?" Abdul Ali retorted.

"Yes, except this." Kruger collected the laptop from Don and turned it on. He presented it to Abdul Ali. A 3-D image of the golden stool appeared on the screen, rotating. "That's all."

"That's all?"

"Yes, that's all," Kruger turned the laptop off and passed it back to Don. "Do you have him?"

"No, we were late."

"How come?"

"The exercise at the hotel went a bit out of hand. The police were one step ahead of us."

"You were to capture him and bring him to me."

Realizing Kruger could not come out with any convincing reason Tango cut in, "He moved earlier than we'd expected …"

"… throwing all our plans out of gear." Don concluded

"I am not interested in excuses." Abdul Ali burst out. "I want the man.

You don't have him. That's all. Do I get someone else to find him for me?" "No. We will bring him, sir." Kruger responded apologetically as Abdul

Ali walked away from them.

"Alive!" Abdul Ali stopped, turned and emphasized.

"Alive. Yes, sir." Kruger confirmed to him. The three exited the warehouse, sat in Kruger's car and sped off.

In New York, it was long past midday. In the City of Kumasi in Ghana where Prof Kofi Nsiah hailed from, it was just before dusk, about four hours ahead. Three gentlemen in their late fifties met around a table at a club house they thought was discrete. They sat a little away from the main bar which was very active and lively, where many more people, men and women, also sat, drinking, eating and chatting away. The three were so engrossed in their discussion that the high-pitched music, shouts, giggles and laughter which were blended into a cacophony of noises seemed no distraction to them. They often went to the club house whenever they wanted a discrete place to attend to very pertinent issues. Their presence there today was no exception. As councilors at Manhyia, the court of the King of the Asante Kingdom, their lord had tasked them to investigate a dispute over succession where two royals of one of the sub-divisional clans were fighting for ascension and inheritance to a vacant stool.

The three, very well educated professionals, like their other thirteen or so colleague councilors at the King's court at Manhyia, had a pile of files in front of them and Nana Mawere, a legal expert was leading them through. The other two, Nana Akyempem, a surgeon in his own right and Nana Apagya, a certified accountant listened attentively as Nana Mawere ran them through the history and ancestry of the disputing family. Though they had covered a lot of ground in their research, they were still a long way from concluding on who was the rightful heir to the stool. But their seeming solitude in the mist of the noisy atmosphere was broken by the entry of Nana Kyerewaa, queenmother of the feuding family who was lobbying for one of the prospective heirs.

"Good evening, gentlemen." Nana Kyerewaa burst out as she stood over them from behind. The three men, startled, turned. She smiled at them, a middle aged woman, very pretty and attractive. She sighed. "Thank God, I have found you at last," She looked them in their faces. "I am sure you remember me. I am Nana Kyerewaa."

"We know who you are," Nana Akyempem cut in.

"What do you want?" Nana Apagya asked, obviously, very upset, wondering how she could find them.

"Oh, nothing so serious. May I…" Nana Kyerewaa attempted to pull a chair to join them.

"No, you may not!" Nana Apagya vehemently repulsed her. Nana Kyerewaa turned sharply, shocked by the response. "We do not want you near us," Nana Apagya further informed her.

At that point Nana Akyempem's mobile phone began to ring. He picked it and looked at the number and shook his head. "Guys, I have an emergency. There's a surgery I have to supervise." The rest of his colleagues rose with him. They gathered the files on the table and in no time left Nana Kyerewa standing in awe, desolate.

In front of the NYPD 5th Precinct, Saah stood waiting for the arrival of Coy. She paced up and down feeling uneasy. A police car arrived. Two men in police uniforms emerged and made their way into the main building. They passed by Saah as she stood at the entrance. Saah looked at her watch. She followed them into the building.

As Lt. Croffy got busy on his computer, studying the video footage of the CCTV from the hotel, the two policemen walked past his door towards the investigations room. Saah turned towards Lt. Croffy's door. Suddenly, there was a great deafening explosion, accompanied by a vibration that shook the building like an earthquake. The police car that dropped off the two men exploded. The wreckage was thrown up high in the sky and came crashing to the ground. Saah was thrown off her feet; Lt. Croffy dashed for cover behind his desk. The impact shattered glasses and shop windows nearby. The explosion caused extensive damage to the frontage of the police station. Car alarms triggered off, and the exploded car lay burning. Everybody was thrown off. Lt. Croffy pulled himself together and pulled out his revolver from its holster. Cautiously, he dashed out to see what had happened. Other men and women around recovered slowly from the tremor and began to run helter-skelter. Lt. Croffy got to Saah and helped her on to her feet. One frightened officer hiding behind the counter sent a distress message of the blast and called for support.

"Code red! Code red!' The officer spoke on a communicator. "5th Precinct calling. A big explosion in front of the 5th Precinct. We are under attack. Repeat, we are under attack. Calling for back up and support services. Immediately, ….over."

Kofi, perplexed by the impact of the explosion and the commotion, rose to his feet. There was no way he could see outside and wondered what was going on. The two men who had come in the exploded car walked around in the midst of the commotion and confusion as if nothing had happened. They searched from room to room and eventually made their way to the room where Kofi was being kept. They saw Kofi standing behind the table.

"FBI," one of them said, showing an FBI badge.

"Let's go," said the other. "We're moving you to a new location where it is safer."

Kofi joined them. For a moment, he stopped at the door and hesitated. He thought that could not be right. Addressing the two, he asked, "Where is the officer in charge of my case?"

"We've taken over the case," replied one of the men. "Now, let's go!" "And, my lady, where is she?" Kofi probed further.

"We are the FBI. We do not answer to the local police and their command. And as I said we've taken over the case."

"Oh, she," the other interjected, "she is off duty today."

Kofi immediately realized that was a wrong answer and that the men may be fake FBI. He returned quickly into the room and attempted to close the door. With greater force the men pushed their way into the room and grabbed him by his upper arms. He screamed for help and struggled with them as they tried to take him away. In the process one of the men dropped a device in Kofi's pocket. Apparently, that was what they were supposed to do: attempt to capture him, and if that failed, to tag him so he could be tracked wherever he went.

Lt. Croffy saw the destruction outside. "Good gracious! What happened?"

A large contingent of support services and extra security began to arrive. As they cordoned off the area, Saah overheard the screams of Kofi, as the fake FBI agents pulled him out of the room. Saah rushed there. She screamed at the men and demanded why they were struggling with Kofi. One of them flashed a badge.

"FBI."

"But where are you taking him to?" she demanded. "You can't take him from here without prior notice to Lt. Croffy."

"We do not answer to him. Now back off. You are interfering with FBI duties."

"Lieutenant Croffy!" she screamed.

Realizing her interference could create problems one of them pulled out his gun and pointed it at her to scare her off. Lt. Croffy who had heard the screams of Kofi and those of Saah dashed back into the building.

"They are taking him away!" Saah yelled further as the two intruding men jostled Kofi, holding him by the waist band of his pants and pulled him along. "You have no right to take him anywhere!" Saah continued to scream at them.

Lt. Croffy arrived and ran past Saah. He pointed his revolver and shouted: "Hold it right there! Release him! You two!!"

"FBI," one of the intruding men let go of Kofi and pulled out his badge. "FBI has no hand in this case. Back off!!! I said back off! Or I'll put bullets in your skulls." Lt. Croffy pointed his pistol at them. Seeing they were in no mood to obey him he fired a warning shot to the ceiling. A couple of other policemen with rifles arrived on the scene and gave support to Lt. Croffy. Hearing the cocking of weapons, the men surrendered. Kofi struggled out of their hold to free himself and fell to the ground. The supporting officers rushed in and apprehended the men from behind, disarmed them and pushed them into an empty cell. The two men struggled with other policemen making it difficult to lock them up, but eventually they succeeded in subduing them.

"Lock them up," Lt. Croffy ordered. "ID them and charge them; impersonation, abduction and interference. I will deal with them appropriately when we sort ourselves out." Lt. Croffy was outraged and wondered how the two could intrude without any notice. He reached out to Kofi to raise him to his feet. Kofi ignored Lt Croffy and got himself up. He staggered towards Saah. He crouched in pain, unable to walk straight. Saah rushed to his aid and walked him into the investigations room.

"Lt. Croffy, I don't think your precinct is safe. I don't think my client is safe here." Saah said to him.

"Look, Miss. We are under attack. We have a great task ahead, unraveling what's behind this car bomb attack on us, whether it's a terrorist or a freak bomber. I told you to get him a lawyer. You haven't. What I don't need now is further distraction from you. Right now, he is hurt. He needs medical attention." He ordered one of his subordinate officers. "Call in one!"

"Yes, Sir!" The officer took the order and called in paramedics.

Lt. Croffy ordered his men to increase the security and vigilance at the station and, particularly on Kofi and Saah.

Coy arrived to see the chaos. He parked further away and walked in to the frontage of the 5th Precinct. He spoke to a couple of investigators on duty and they allowed him into the station building. He saw the damage caused by the explosion and cautiously walked through the debris into the building.

Saah picked up her bags and the file. She grabbed Kofi's hand and led him out of the investigations room. They met Lt. Croffy as he was returning to the investigations room.

"What do you think you are doing? Where do you think you are going? You cannot take him out of here on your own, you know that." Lt. Croffy pointed out to her and restrained her from leaving.

"Why not?" Saah responded. "Your station is under attack. You said so yourself. How can a helpless man protect another helpless man? You have too much on your hands. I don't. If faceless assailants can enter your station and attempt and nearly succeed in abducting your suspects or witnesses, then you have lost the moral right to hold my client in this station. I can provide better security for him myself."

"I am sorry, madam. You have to return to the investigations room or I may have to place you too under arrest."

"What for?" Coy entered and burst out in his deep baritone, "You know you can't do that until you've proved to me why. What's her crime? What's your charge?" He was not new to the 5th Precinct and Lt. Croffy and his criminal investigations. Saah gave a great sigh of relief. Coy stretched forth his hand to Lt. Croffy. He took it and shook it warmly, "What's happening here, for God sake?"

"I can't understand what is happening. Nothing makes sense to me."

An investigator entered holding a flash drive. "Sir, you've got to look at this. Footage from the CCTV."

"Coy, go ahead. You can talk to the suspect in the investigations room while I attend to this now and join you soon." Lt. Croffy directed an armed officer to escort Coy, Saah and Kofi and stay around while he entered his office with the investigator. He took the flash drive and plugged it into the computer. It was a video of the sequence of the two intruding fake FBI operatives as they drove in, leaving the car and after a while, the car blowing up. "Those two idiots. That was a decoy," he concluded after reviewing CCTV footage. Then he ordered, "Get their full IDs and if we could trace them anywhere. Find anything about them, who sent them and if they have any connection with our suspect and the deaths in the hotel. Get the move on!" Lt. Croffy ordered with his eyes glued to the screen. The investigator responded, saluted and marched off.

Saah sat down on one of the chairs. Kofi sat too as Coy stood with his arms folded across his chest. Saah introduced Kofi and tried to give an account of what had happened between her and Kofi. "This is Kofi, Kofi Nsiah, my countryman. He is a Professor at a University back home in Ghana and is holding an exhibition and lectures on the Mysteries of the Golden Stool. He has been arrested for double homicide."

Coy stopped her and demanded: "I thought you said you had run into trouble and wanted me to rescue you."

"Yes, more or less," she explained. "I got him to do something for me that has gotten him embroiled in this homicide. I cannot leave him locked in for my sake. So, I am also locked in more or less. I want to get him out. As an intern at your office, there is no one else I can call on but you. I cannot also represent him without your authority. Even if I do, you're my boss I need to report to you. That is the trouble I am in and want you to get us out. More, I feared if I left him the police might twist his case and implicate him in a way we may find too difficult to get him out. And my fears were confirmed with the explosion outside a few minutes ago. If I had not been alert, some strange men would have abducted him right under our noses."

"Really? Here?" Coy asked.

"Yes, right here, by some phony characters posing as FBI agents. They are locked up in the cells"

"I see." Coy was convinced Saah was right calling him in. "Has he been formally charged?"

"No," Saah responded. "I am not privy to any such thing." "Mr. …" Coy turned to address Kofi.

"Kofi, just Kofi," Kofi said while stretching his hand for a shake. Coy took it and so powerfully it almost took his arm out of his shoulder socket.

Kofi felt his strength, and that bolstered his confidence in Coy as a man capable for his case.

"Well, Kofi," continued Coy, "Did you kill anybody?"

"No."

"Did you know the victim?"

"Yes and no."

"Meaning?"

"I do not know the first dead man but I may have known him."

His answer did not seem to have been clear to Coy. "Wait, wait." Coy cut in and demanded. "Did you say a first dead man? How many more were there? How did you know and not know them?"

"There are two dead men. The first victim was confirmed to be a waiter at the hotel. I may have met him as they tended my room every day. Those who do are very nice with me. That's about all I know of him."

"And the second?"

"I did not know him. Never, in my life before then." "How is his death connected to you?"

"I met him at the reception counter as I received my key from the front desk staff. I turned and there he was. He may have been a Chinese or Korean. He said he wanted to do some business with me on the computer or internet. I did not pay any particular attention to him and told him to sit and wait for me. I got to my room. I saw the mess and the waiter in a pool of blood. I did not know of this second death until the police found him in the lobby where I had asked him to sit and wait for me."

"Was he alive when you left him," asked Coy. "Very much alive."

"Is that the truth?" Coy sought confirmation from Saah who had sat listening attentively, making short notes on a pad she took from her hand bag.

"I am hearing this for the first time," she replied. "Have you given any statement to them?"

"No," Kofi answered. The door to the investigations room opened, Lt. Croffy entered with photos and information on the two fake FBI agents. He threw the photos on the table towards Kofi and enquired: "Do you know them?"

"No," he replied. "You're sure?" "Never, in my life."

"Why were they here to pick you up if you don't know them?"

"Don't answer the question!" Coy intervened. "Lt. Croffy, I demand the unconditional release of my client. You cannot continue to hold him here. I believe you are holding him to help you in your investigations. My client cannot play a pawn in your activities here at this precinct. It seems you are engaged in a never-ending twist of sequence of events that I cannot understand why you should involve my client. He is an innocent man going about his life cautiously. He is a victim of circumstance. He may have gotten to a wrong place at a wrong time. He should not be made to suffer unduly for a crime he has not committed. You have also shown gross negligence in his protection and his rights by allowing hooligans into your station. They nearly succeeded in his abduction and kidnapping. He may also be a target of an assassination attempt." The statement shot Kofi with an adrenalin of confidence. His face began to beam with smile. Yes, he thought, this is a lawyer, a good one at that.

Before Lt. Croffy could attempt any comment, an officer ran into the investigations room and whispered into his ears that there was an emergency. The two fake FBI men had suddenly been seized with fits and were dying. Lt. Croffy ran to the cell where they were being held. The two were lying lifeless in the cubicle. A set of paramedics arrived. The cell was opened for them. They entered to examine the two bodies and pronounced them dead, cause: poisoning by cyanide. Lt Croffy returned to the investigations room looking very distraught. He pushed the door open and entered.

Coy turned to look at him. He could see he was greatly disturbed. "Hey, man. You look like you've seen a ghost." Coy said.

"Yes, two of them." Lt. Croffy responded. "Too much is happening. I am beginning to..."

"...Sound too much superstitious." Coy completed the statement. "That is the word. Too much is happening today. I cannot predict what's going to happen next. I must change the strategy. We have not even commenced investigations on his case. And from one incident to the other, too much is happening here today." Lt. Croffy turned to Kofi. He looked him in the eyes for a moment without saying a word. He looked intensely at Kofi as if he did not know what to ask him. In fact, he did not know what to ask him. He was worried and confused. Then he burst out in anger and leaned towards Kofi. "Who are you? What is wrong with you? What have you done? Why did you come to the United States?"

"Do not answer any question, Kofi. Do not answer." Coy cautioned. Kofi felt frightened by the aggressive composure of Lt. Croffy. He nodded in affirmation looking back at Lt. Croffy in the eyes.

For a short moment, Lt. Croffy looked more piercingly, deeply into Kofi's eyes. There were more questions to ask, he seemed to say with his eyes. He eased back and looked away, then walked away. He did not say anything but one could see from his demeanour that he regretted his outburst on Kofi. He stopped at the door and turned to talk to them.

"We've got to leave here right now." Lt. Croffy said to them in a sober tone. "This station is no more safe. We cannot release him as he currently has no known address. We cannot also release him to you at this point if we are not convinced of his personal safety. He is a very critical witness in unraveling all that has happened today." Lt. Croffy returned into the room and turned to Coy. "This is what we are going to do. There is a safe house, a discreet place we can move him to for his personal security and protection while the investigations go on. We can go now. There's no time to waste."

"Are you charging him with any offence? If not, why are you not considering a bail for him," Coy requested.

"That is out of the question right now. We have not even completed the docket for the case for the DA's consideration, so how can you talk about bail. For all you know he may be the prime target in all that is happening. I don't want to draw that conclusion yet. For now, his personal security must be our prime concern. Let's get out of here first. You can continue your briefing in the vehicle."

"Not with you breathing over our necks. Client and counsel privacy."

"Unfortunately, we've got to evacuate now. Too risky we're still here. Please come with me. This way." Lt. Croffy did not give them any chance to decide, he moved them out of the investigations room.

"Do we follow in our cars?" Coy demanded.

"No. We don't need to attract undue attention."

Saah picked her bag and Kofi's file. They hastened out slowly, following Lt. Croffy through the back to the car park at the basement, escorted by heavily armed security men. They joined a bullet proof van and pulled away with one armed escort car following. It was an executive van with heavily dark tainted glasses and a centre table and four seats around. The driver's area was separated from the main cabin. Lt. Croffy rode with the driver in the front passenger seat leaving Coy, Saah and Kofi in the main cabin. Both vehicles were unmarked. They quietly eased into night traffic without fanfare or siren. The traffic flowed slowly but consistently.

The three sat quietly for a while. Then Saah broke the silence. "Our cars, what happened to them?"

"We'll not spend all night there." Coy answered. "Whatever happens, we shall come back to recover them. Kofi, is the exhibition over?"

"Looks like it is, now," Kofi responded.

"Pity, I couldn't see it. I heard a couple of commentaries on my car radio about the lectures on the Golden Stool and the people of the Kingdom of -."

"Asante," Kofi added

"Yea. Sounds like it was great."

"It was great," Kofi confirmed. "My first ever solo exhibition on something I know best. It did, indeed, go well."

"Until I got in," Saah added.

"What are you talking about?" asked Kofi.

"I feel like all that's happened was all my fault."

"Don't be silly. You have nothing to do with the murders at the hotel."

"Of course, I don't."

"Why blame yourself, then?" Coy asked.

"If I had not pestered him with the demand of a present he had promised me, he would not have gone back to the hotel at that time, got connected to the murders and subsequently got arrested."

"Preposterous!" exclaimed Kofi. "Childish!" added Coy.

"How can you concoct such absurd scenarios to blame yourself in this crime," Kofi demanded.

"That's how I feel," she replied. "Your feeling is wrong."

Coy realized the two were going off into a banter. He burst in to bring them back on the substantive issue. "Kofi, are you a member of any secret organization, cult or human rights group fighting for a cause on any issue?" he asked.

"No, I am not."

"Any member of your family, close relatives and friends?" "None that I know of."

"Involved in drugs and drug business and the cartels?"

"Drugs? The closest I have come to drugs was in high school. I tried some myself. Never liked it and I've never gone any closer ever since."

"Kofi," Saah intervened. "I don't know. But if what I saw on TV and the reports are anything to go by, then I will say the murderer or murderers were after you, Kofi or looking for something you are connected with."

"Me, what have I done? I don't know anybody. I can't think of anyone I could have offended. A poor innocent lecturer, going round the world, telling tales of my native clan, living off the culture of my ancestry, whom could I have offended?"

"The spirits and gods of Asante," Saah responded and they all laughed. "Perhaps."

"Did you notice if you had lost any of your belongings?" Coy demanded.

"I can't tell now," Kofi responded. "I had a good look at the room, although I could not identify the dead man immediately. I think I can easily say there was a struggle: the room looked ransacked. The other man found in the lobby is a Korean national. I spoke with him. He might be some computer genius or something. He wanted to do business with me on the internet about the Golden Stool. He had this laptop computer with the image of the Golden Stool on it."

"Where is the computer?" asked Coy.

"At the hotel or with the police, I guess." Kofi replied

Coy sat quietly for a while, thinking. Several possible reasons for those murders and subsequent events ran through his mind. Possible conclusions he could draw at that time were that: definitely, Kofi was not the murderer; he could, himself, be the target; he had been lucky his assailants were unable to reach him. Then what was the motive, he wondered? Who was behind it all? What were those behind looking for, from him, through him and to whom? He shook his head in disbelief. But then, he was definitely convinced there was no case against Kofi for murder. He also concluded he could be more a witness than the accused. And, if he was not the target he could only be used as a bait to get to the real target or any object being sought for by the perpetrators. Also, he thought, this would help to track the mastermind behind the plot.

The van made a sharp turn off the main road. The convoy exited onto a dirt road. This was a few miles out of the city into the countryside. Ahead of them was the safe house, a single storey building in about a four-acre woodland. The trees had grown tall into the sky hiding the house among them. The driveway was a narrow path that had been created by the tracks of the vehicles that frequently went there. The van approached a gate deep into the acreage. Lt. Croffy picked his mobile phone and placed a call. After a short exchange he hung up the phone.

There were a few lights that were lit around the house. Then a few more came on inside and outside to brighten the area. The driver of the van honked at the main gate, which opened to reveal a gentleman in sleep clothes opening it. He unlocked the gate and the two vehicles drove in to park in front of the house. The middle-aged man ran back to meet his guests, after locking the gate. He was the caretaker of the safe house. He had lived there for a few years and ran the place like his own home. Four weapon-bearing men descended from the escort vehicle, ran and surrounded the van. Lt. Croffy opened his door and stepped out the van and met the caretaker. Smart was his name. He welcomed Lt. Croffy and led him into the house while Coy, Kofi and Saah remained in the van. Lt. Croffy and his men did a quick check on the compound, satisfied themselves of the security and safety of the facility. The van was then opened and the occupants were led out and escorted inside the house. The security men returned and positioned themselves at vantage points to protect the house. Smart settled his guests comfortably into the house and served them some refreshments. Kofi and Saah sat away from Coy and Lt. Croffy. She got up and approached Smart. After a short exchange Smart pointed to the wash room where she proceeded to.

"Don't worry about food, Smart," Lt. Croffy announced. "I've ordered dinner. We shall all eat something good soon."

Coy demanded, "I hope we are also not being held prisoners as well." "Not at all, Counsel." Lt. Croffy explained. "I am waiting for the reports on the investigations so far. Afterwards, you can excuse us. From what has happened so far this is the best protection we can offer as of now."

Saah returned from the washroom, sat by and held Kofi's hand and inquired, "What are you going to do next?"

"I am confused. I am tired of being here. I want to go back." "To Ghana?"

"Yes," he affirmed. "I am even scared to go back to the exhibition hall. My hotel room, I don't know what I am going to pick up from there. My passport and tickets are here, aren't they?" Saah opened Kofi's file she had been carrying. The tickets and the passport were in there. "That's all I need, anyway, plus the exhibition and the exhibits. You can check the rest of my things and dispatch them to me. I have return shipment, fully paid, with UPS. You'd do me that favour, won't you?"

"Of course!" Saah assured him.

"Members of the team I came with will handle the packing of all the exhibits. I hope they are not drawn into this as well."

"Well, I cannot tell what can possibly happen from now." Saah cautioned. "The systems here are a little complex. They do not work that simply. The preliminary investigations and the legalities will take a couple of days to work out. I am afraid your men may be drawn in. The investigators may call them in for questioning if they need them in the preparation of a prima facie case."

"Huh!"

"Well, you just have to condition yourself and your mind for some of these things. You don't understand," she tried to explain further.

"I don't care whatever they want to do." Kofi dismissed her intervention. "There has been an attempt on my life. You want me to wait here till I am ready to be dispatched to Ghana as 'an unprofitable cargo?' I want to go back now." Saah could not hazard any response. She sat and just stared at him. "I need to go to the washroom."

"It's over there." She pointed it out to him.

Outside, at the sentry, the security guards lay alert, their weapons concealed underneath the overcoats and watched out for any intruder. One of them was constantly on a pair of binoculars with night vision capabilities. In a distance, a van approached the safe house. The other guard by him picked up his walkie-talkie and spoke on it to Lt. Croffy announcing the approach of a van.

"Our dinner is here," Lt. Croffy announced to the rest inside. Smart pulled a drawer and brought out a pack of plates. He commenced laying the table, spreading a table cloth on the table first.

"Come on, guys. I am hungry," Coy said confirming his eagerness for the food as he and Lt. Croffy moved towards the dinner table.

The van came closer to the house and stopped at the gate. One of the security men at the gate opened the closed gate and swung it ajar. The van drove through. The security man at the gate pulled it to close again. The door at the back of the van opened. Six heavily-armed men were inside. They wore bulletproof jackets and night vision cameras attached to headsets for their communication. Two of them dropped out one after the other. One of them shot down the security man at the gate with a silenced gun. The Security man with binoculars noticed that his colleague had fallen. He burst out and yelled that there had been an intrusion on the safe house. He instantly dropped to the floor and engaged the intruder in an exchange of gun fire. The other security men immediately took cover and joined in and fired weapons to repel the intrusion, firing on the van as it approached the house. The rest of the armed men in the van dropped out and launched a fierce assault on the safe house. They ran behind the van using it as shield to get them closer to the house. One guard got hit and he fell. The others returned the fire from their positions. One of them using a sniper rifle aimed and shot at the driver of the van. The bullet hit the driver, making him lose control of the van. It crashed into a wall.

When Lt. Croffy got the information from outside that they were under attack he immediately ordered those with him inside to lie on the floor. “On your bellies!” he ordered. “We are under attack!”

Saah screamed at Lt. Croffy: “I thought you said this was a safe house!” The glass windows began to shatter as bullets began to fly into the sitting area. Saah went down and pulled Kofi off the seat to join her. Smart, returning from the kitchen with a tray of drinking glasses ran into the firing. The glasses were hit as bullet flew through. Smart ducked sending the tray of glasses flying and crashing on to the floor.

“Jesus Christ! What the hell ---!” screamed Coy as he ducked behind the sofa. Objects in the room were hit indiscriminately. Lt. Croffy also ducked. He was extremely perplexed. He wondered how anyone could trace them to where they were. He had not mentioned to anyone bringing Kofi to the safe house. He tossed the heavy dining table down and used it as a shield. He pulled his revolver as he also ducked behind the table and began shooting in the direction where the bullets were coming from. Smart pulled a drawer nearby where he lay and brought out two pump-action rifles. He tossed one to Lt. Croffy who immediately changed to the pump-action gun and fired out. The gun fire went on fiercely. Some of the assailants were felled, reducing the intensity of their fire power. Smart crawled to a door. He opened and signaled to Kofi, Saah and Coy. “Come, over here,” Smart beckoned them. “On your bellies!” he warned.

They moved with difficulty as the shattering of the widows resumed and other objects fell off from shelves and the wall. The door opened to a stairway descending down into a bunker or basement. Smart signaled to Coy to lead the way. Saah and Kofi followed.

“I thought you guys said this was a safe house.” Kofi hushed at Smart as he passed him into the basement. Smart did not respond but shook his head in disbelief. Lt. Croffy fired his pump-action gun till he ran out of ammunition. He screamed for more bullets. Smart did not have any more at that instant but he screamed out for Lt. Croffy and beckoned him to come in to the basement.

It was dark on the stairway down. They hastened cautiously as they descended. "Damn! It's dark in here." Coy muttered.

"Keep moving!" Saah hushed at him.

"I can't see nothing, man."

"Feel your way with your hands! Keep moving!"

"Wait a minute. I got a lighter." Coy said as he went into his pocket to fetch it..

Lt. Croffy ran toward Smart. Smart saw grenade breaking through one of the glass windows. "Grenade! Hurry!" He screamed as Lt. Croffy dashed for the basement door. The grenade rolled after Lt. Croffy. He passed Smart but it blew up before he could go through the door. The impact of the explosion hit Smart, killing him instantly. Lt Croffy was thrown down the steps. He crashed into Kofi and pushed him onto Saah. She also tripped and fell on Coy. All four screamed as they tumbled down the steps to base. The blast of the grenade lighted and set the room upstairs ablaze. The brightness of the fire flares illuminated the basement to show a passage. It goes further forward. They all struggled up on to their feet.

"Let's go!" Coy said as he helped Saah to get to her feet. Kofi joined them. Lt. Croffy was unable to get on to his feet. He had broken his leg as he fell and crashed from the impact of the blast.

"Aw! My leg! I can't move it," Lt. Croffy screamed.

"Oh my God!" Saah exclaimed and ran toward him. Kofi and Coy joined her in an attempt to lift and help him up along. A series of gun fire rained at the door at the top of the stairs. Saah screamed again. The two men rushed and picked the wounded officer who was in a very bad shape. He screamed in pain as they touched him. They dragged him along deeper into the tunnel. Coy reached for the cigarette lighter and flicked it on. He handed it over to Saah and asked her to lead the way. The brightness of the lighter identified an oval shaped steel door a few feet away.

"My shoulder!" Lt. Croffy yelled as he could no longer bear the pain. He had a broken shoulder also. They laid him down as they got to the door. Saah reached the door and turned a big ringed knob. The door opened. Two rats emerged. "Rats!" she screamed, jumped and grabbed hold of Coy, losing hold of the lighter in the process.

"The lighter?" Coy inquired. Lt. Croffy responded that the lighter had hit his head. Kofi felt his way around Lt. Croffy and found the lighter and flicked it on again. Kofi handed the lighter back to Saah and went down to help Lt. Croffy. Coy joined up but Lt. Croffy refused and asked them to move on without him. He insisted he was going to be alright. Saah held up the lighter again and walked behind them as the two men virtually dragged the wounded officer past the door. Lt. Croffy groaned as they pulled him along. The shooting resumed as they shut the door and braced it with some wood planks. With his condition, Lt. Croffy realized he would slow them down. Pointing the way, he asked them to move on. "No! We can't leave you here to die." Kofi protested, particularly, as he was so wounded and needed immediate medical attention.

"Oh. I will be alright. You go on," Lt. Croffy told Kofi. "What do we do now?" Coy demanded.

"Don't worry about me." Lt. Croffy said as he lay helpless. "This passage will lead you out of here. Hurry out and get help. My walkie-talkie is upstairs. I can't call backup for rescue."

"My phone!" Coy called out.

Then Saah also shouted: "My phone!"

"My passport and documents!" Kofi too recalled. They all realized they had left them as they fled.

"Get the move on. Go! Get out of here. Ah!" Lt. Croffy groaned. "I'll be fine." He pulled himself up and rested his back on the wall.

"Help from where? If you can't help us now where else can we go?" Coy knelt beside him.

"Go. Just get out of here. I'll take care of myself. And, take care."

Lt. Croffy insisted and urged them to take advantage and get out to gain time ahead of their assailants. This concluded the fact for Kofi that the officer had lost the battle and could no longer protect him. He felt his fate was then in his own hand. The police and the law had failed to protect him. What would he do? Where could he go? Was he then a fugitive, running away from the law? He wondered.

Coy took over the lighter and led the way out of the tunnel. Lt. Croffy heard steps running down the stairway; there was an attempt at the door to open it. There were bangs at the door, heavy bangs, but the wood planks kept the door in place. There was a short silence; then a deafening explosion took away the door sending a big ball of fire through the opening. The flare swept through the tunnel at Lt. Croffy; he crawled but could not make any distance before the fire reached him and consumed him. He screamed as the fire torched him to death. There was another explosion at the door. The roof caved in blocking the tunnel completely as it crashed on Lt. Croffy.

The three ran faster as the flare, heat and smoke of the explosion surged after them in the tunnel and died off soon after. They reached another door. This one was like that of a vault. Coy turned the levers and pushed out the door to open. They exited on to a hillside. Above them, a few feet to climb, was a road and they could see vehicles passing. They could also see smoke and flames of the safe house in a distance. Kofi dropped to the ground out of exhaustion. Saah went to him and inquired whether he was hurt. He responded in the negative. He sat up on the dirt ground. Coy screamed at them to get up and get on the move. No one could guarantee that they were safe from there on. Kofi asked what next they were going to do.

"I am getting out of here." Coy responded harshly. "How? And to where? What about us?" Kofi questioned.

"You? Go to hell!" The harsh response of Coy hit Kofi and Saah like a bomb. The shock and surprise of Coy's answer were felt heavier than the explosions some few moments ago.

"Don't say that, Coy," said Saah, pleading. "You cannot say that." "I have had enough of both of you and your problem."

"Are you dropping the case?"

"I have and I don't want to have anything to do with you, your friend and this goddamn case anymore. I am done with you. Thank you for all the troubles, and good bye." Coy began to climb up the hillside on to the road.

Saah followed him. "Are you leaving us here? You can't leave us here." Kofi saw the desperate move of Saah. He also followed her.

Coy stopped and turned to Saah. "I made a mistake by responding to your distress call. It was a mistake to have agreed to take your case. This case stinks. It could kill me; it could kill me anytime if I follow you. Stop following me!" he yelled at her. She felt it like a shock from an electrical power volt, sending her dumbfounded.

"What are you talking about?" Saah managed her words with tearful eyes. Kofi had frozen in his motion. He looked at them speechless.

Coy descended closer to Saah. "Can't you see? Can't you understand what is happening?"

"What's happening?" Kofi retorted

"I can smell it. The underworld peoples."

"What do you mean?" Saah tried to understand. Coy looked sternly at her.

"What?" Kofi asked seeking better explanation.

"You are crazy, Coy!"

"Yes, I am!" Coy raved with rage and anger. "I am crazy not to have recognized that until now. Can't you understand what is going on? Within the last twelve hours or so of your life, a man is brutally murdered in your hotel room; another, who spoke to you is also killed a few minutes afterwards. You are chased into your police cell to be abducted by phony characters posing as FBI agents. These phony characters are later found dead in their cell; you are discretely sent away for safe keeping, you are followed there and chased out of the secret safe house with bullets, bombed and smoked out like a rat, escaping by a hair's breadth. Think! Think of all the people who have had to die associating with you or trying to protect you! Lt. Croffy and his selfless men? How many more are going to die because of you? Who are you, eh? Who are you? You ain't nothing, you know! You ain't shit!"

"Coy!" Saah screamed, telling him it was just enough.

"Maybe," Coy turned to her, "you could be the next to die. I don't know. It could be me. I don't want to die, certainly, not for him. Fuck!"

"Mr. Coy, please, calm down." Kofi attempted to intervene to console Coy.

Coy burst out with vociferous anger; "Calm down! I'll tear your heart out first. Fuck you!"

Coy ran past Saah and attacked Kofi and engaged him in a fierce scuffle. The two men fell to the ground and rolled down the slope. Saah stood helplessly, looking at the two men wrestling on the ground. Coy, being bigger and the stronger one, held Kofi by the throat and tried to squeeze the breath out him. Saah saw the development as precarious and followed them down. She grabbed a branch of a tree and ripped it off the stem. She rushed on to the two men, Coy lying on top of Kofi, pinning him to the ground. She whipped them with the branch.

"Break it up! Idiots! Break it up!" She whacked them with Coy taking most of her strokes till they separated. The two men broke apart, each panting profusely, with Kofi coughing as a result of the strain on his throat.

"What is wrong with you, idiots?" She screamed at them. "Instead of you two uniting your minds and energies into looking for ways and means to get us out of here and the trouble on our hands you prefer wasting them to destroy each other. What the hell is wrong with you? This is the last time -." "Shut up! Shut up!" Coy yelled at her. "You got me into this. Get me

out. I want out. Right now!"

"You better sit down and use your brains instead of brawling!" she yelled back. "You suck!"

"I am tired! I am - fucked!" Coy sat up and held his head, tears dropping from his eyes. Kofi tried to rise to his feet but gave up and sat on the ground.

"Do you know what I am thinking?" she asked.

"Leave me alone!" Coy brushed her off with a wave of his hand.

"Coy, I think you were right. I suspect there is something behind whatever is happening."

"Who do you think is behind all this?" Kofi asked her.

"Looks much to me like one of those movies. Coy, I agree with you. Think of all that has happened in the last 18 hours or so, from the deaths at the hotel, to the attack at the police station and to here. And our escape."

"How could they track us to the safe house? That's what beats my mind." Coy who had then calmed down, wondered. He looked at Kofi with suspicious eyes and walked to him. "Can I take a look?" He tried to touch him. Kofi brushed him off. "Cool it, man. I thought we were square now."

Saah intervened. "Come off it, Kofi. There is no point dragging this. Allow him."

Kofi relaxed and allowed Coy. He ran a search on Kofi. He noticed something inside Kofi's jacket pocket. Coy retrieved a small device. "Shit! They've tagged you."

"And they are following you wherever you go," Saah added. "What are you talking about?" Kofi asked with a shock.

Coy dropped the device on the ground and smashed it with his foot.

Inside Abdul Ali's warehouse, down town, on a scanner screen, where the signal from the device was being received, the light indicating the location of the device went off. A man behind the console alerted his colleagues:

"Guys, the beacon is out and off radar. I've lost him."

Saah went close to look at the smashed device. "That is how they traced us to the safe house."

"Someone is behind this. Someone is after you; someone is looking for you. Who? And why? This is the work of the members of the Family, the underworld." Coy pronounced, confirming his suspicion.

"Underworld? You mean it has some spiritual or voodoo influences?" Kofi asked showing his ignorance and naivety.

"No." Saah tried to explain. "It is like what we call the Mafia in Ghana."

"It is possible there is a contract on you." Coy added.

Kofi, petrified, began to tremble. "What? Mafia? What contract? What have I done? They are going to kill me? I have done nothing. I don't know anybody here. Apart from you whom do I know? Who else? Oh my God. Oh my God!"

A police car appeared in the distance with its siren blurting, flashing its blue and red lights. Kofi got hysterical, turned and ran towards the road side. "Police car! Come on. They can get us out of here." Coy and Saah ran after him, grabbed him and pulled him to the ground just in time as the police car whisked pass. Kofi struggled with them in an effort to break loose from their hold. "I don't want to die! I don't want to die!" He screamed.

"Shut up!" Saah yelled at him. "Shut up!" She whacked his cheek with a hefty slap and Kofi went numb and silent, nodding persistently in compliance.

"Are you mad? Where did you think you were going?" Coy asked him.

He shook Kofi hard enough to wake him up from the hysteria. "What did you think you were doing?" Saah asked further.

Kofi broke down weeping. "The Mafia, they are going to kill me. I don't want to die." Saah held him to console him. Coy broke into uncontrollable laughter.

"This is not funny." Saah rebuked Coy.

"Yes, it is funny. A moment ago, I was the one under pressure. Now, it is him." He laughed himself to tears. Then he stopped and started walking up the slope towards the road. "Seriously," he said.

"What's it?" Saah asked, leaving hold of Kofi. "Come. Follow me," Coy waved, beckoning to them.

"Where to?" She got on to her feet pulling Kofi up too.

"I need a phone. When you are pursued by a force, you need another force of equal or greater measure to repulse or crush it."

Saah and Kofi hurried to catch up with him. They walked by the road side till they saw a phone booth. Coy looked around and made sure they were not being followed. He asked them to wait, out of sight. He walked to the phone and placed a call. From where they waited Saah and Kofi could only see Coy making gestures with his hand as he talked.

Down town, Abdul Ali, seated on a sofa with a phone receiver to his ear, gave instructions to his subordinates. "Guys, we are back on line. Not too far away from where we lost them. Relay to our men on site to pick him and his company up and bring them home."

Satisfied, Coy replaced the handset and joined them. "I have some solution now. I have contacted a friend with great connections with the underworld. I did him a favour before, handling a couple of his cases. Time to return the favour. Glad to say I spoke to him personally. He has sent a ride for us. It will be here soon. Before then, you have to tell me all the truth, nothing but the truth; all about yourself. Who are you?"

"Who? Me?" Kofi asked as if the question was not meant for him.

"Yes. My guy will not take you in and protect you if he does not know what is chasing you. I must vouch for you as well."

"I am just a common University lecturer." Kofi said about himself. "I teach anthropology. I am only lucky to have studied the way of life, history, traditions, culture and customs of my people, and I am trying to inform the world."

"Do you do drugs?"

"No. I don't even take coffee for caffeine. But I drink cocoa for chocolate."

"The true Ghanaian." Saah said looking at Kofi. They burst into laughter.

"Do you have any links with drug dealers? "

"Absolutely not. But you've asked me these questions before?"

"Just answer the question. I am only refreshing myself. So, why are you being pursued by this unknown force? Who is after you? And for what? When you look behind, within the last 24 hours, the carnage and the destruction, the loss of lives, all in trying to protect your life; one man, you should be very special or you must be possessing something special that someone, so powerful, needed, to hunt you down for. Have you met any group of people or individuals or cartels, drug dealers and gun runners?"

"Questions, questions, questions! Look, I don't know anybody: cartels, drug dealers and gun runners, like you are talking about. I don't know anybody. I can't think of anyone I could have offended. I am only a poor innocent lecturer going round the world telling tales of my native clan, living off the culture of my ancestry. I don't know whom I could have offended doing that."

"If you have not offended your ancestors then you're being chased here by witches from home." Saah interjected again and they burst into laughter again.

"*Ofie Abayifo*! (Witches from home!) Absurd." Kofi retorted. "I couldn't think of anything else." Saah observed.

A black van drove in to a stop. The lights were flickered twice. Coy emerged out of the bushes where they had been hiding. He walked to the van and spoke to the driver. He screamed to call Kofi and Saah. Kofi and Saah emerged and joined him. Coy assisted them to quickly board the van. The van sped off.

Chapter Four

THE DEVIL YOU DON'T KNOW

The warehouse gate opened. Inside, one part of the big but empty storage had been set up as a big operation centre with computers, monitors and CCTV. This was Abdul Ali's operations center. The command centre where he issued commands and monitored his operations; his set up was configured for video, audio and data with satellite and internet connectivity for access to any network system to receive and transmit messages and information; monitors of all sizes, those with multiple split screens were fitted. He could see anything anywhere in the world that was of interest to him. He had the capacity to hack into any electronic and security-controlled system if that was of any interest and relevance to him. He had men with high cyber knowledge and facilities that could crack into high sophisticated security networks and systems, to intercept confidential and top secret information. Strangely, he never used his capacity to rob banks or interfere with any institution. He considered them jobs for amateurs in the art of thievery. His interest was in ancient relics and artifacts and very valuable treasures of historical antecedent. Indeed, for every eccentric, there was a peculiar passion. Like any clandestine organization, he had operated out of notice or view of the law enforcement agencies, walking the thin line lest he be led into temptation. Of course, Abdul Ali had run into some trouble and had a brush with the law before. Coy legal brilliance rescued him, for which reason he had called on him for a turn.

The van drove into the big warehouse. That was the warehouse Kruger and his friends Tango and Don went to meet Abdul Ali. Abdul Ali was seated on an arm chair. He could see them from where he sat inside a huge glass cubicle. The van stopped right in front of his cubicle. The side door slid open for the occupants to descend. Coy stepped forward. Kofi and Saah stood behind him. The warehouse was very big but empty apart from Abdul Ali's set up. It was more like a hanger. Abdul Ali used only a small area. He sat on his command seat. By him were his three partners in crime, Kruger, on his left and Don and Tango on his right hand side. There were many other people there, guards, computer engineers and operators, cyber technicians and analysts, drivers and others of several uses to him. The visitors were ushered into the cubicle. Abdul Ali wore a neatly cut black suit. He rose to meet them.

"Welcome, my friends, welcome." He stretched forth his hand for a shake.

Coy took it and shook it, smiling: "Hi, Ali. Long time."

"Well, you see, I've kept myself out of trouble." Abdul Ali returned to his seat.

"That's true," Coy said confirming it had been long since he earned money from him defending him in some of his unlawful activities.

He, clasping his hands in front of him, tried to look at Kofi and Saah from behind Coy. "What brings you here, my friends? Why did you call for my help?" Don leaned towards Abdul Ali and whispered to him. Abdul Ali nodded. "And who are these with you?"

"She is an intern at my office, I am sure you've met her before. This is my friend." Coy turned and pulled Kofi forward and closer to him. "He has run into some trouble. We want your help."

"I thought you were America's top legal brain. No case can pass you without your resolution. Are you dried up?"

"Yes, I am dried up. I am bereft of clues. In this area, I am aware you're an adept, and we require your expertise."

"Don't flatter me, my friend. You, rather, are the master creator, shaping our fate with your masterful mind, and our lives with the law."

"I am honoured," Coy bowed in appreciation. "But today, it's not me. I called in here for help from my friend, for a dear friend in need." Kofi acknowledged being introduced and also bowed slightly with a little smile on his face.

Saah followed the proceeding from behind them with rapt attention. She looked at Don and Tango. Their faces looked like she had met them somewhere before but could not remember where.

Coy placed his hand on Kofi's shoulder and continued. "You know, I..."

"Yes. I know," Abdul Ali interrupted Coy. "I know your friend very well. I've followed him since his arrival here for whatever he came here to do. I have been interested all along. It's rather unfortunate we have found it too difficult to meet each other. Mr. Kofi, you are welcome."

"You know him?" Coy and Saah both said almost together, astonished. They looked at each other and then turned to look at Kofi who appeared perplexed. They all wondered how Abdul Ali could know Kofi and even call him by name.

Abdul Ali stretched his hand to Kofi with a smile, "Yes, I do."

"You know me?" Kofi asked as he stepped forward to Abdul Ali to take his hand, looking at Abdul Ali with an inquiring eye then pulled his hand quickly from his hold.

"Of course, I do, Mr. Kofi. I have details of your activities here." Abdul Ali pressed a button on the console next to him. A large monitor screen behind him illuminated. It showed several scenes of activities of Kofi in a multiple split screens to the amazement and awe of the three visitors who are looking for his refuge and protection. He flipped his fingertips twice; a forklift brought in a huge wooden crate to the entrance of the command centre. Abdul Ali led his visitors to the crate. The lid on top of it was lifted away by four men in uniform. Inside the crate was an equally huge metal chest or box like a safe. Abdul Ali pressed the key combination of numbers and a knob on the box. The box opened to reveal two hard suitcases lying within. He opened the two suitcases. Inside the first case was a brass mask, neatly packed, padded with foam to protect it. It looked like a well-preserved artifact of antiquity.

"This is the Mask of Alata." Abdul Ali pointed to the mask. "It is over five centuries old. It possesses the power to transcend into ancestral world when it is worn on a full moon night. It is now my property." He touched the second case. "This also is the Stallion of Yenega of the Mosiland. It is one of my priceless collections. It is also about six centuries old and made of Abyssinia gold. I love these artifacts of antiquity. As a child, I was greatly fascinated by the adventures of one Dr. Henry Jones and his son, Indiana, in their many quests and searches for lost relics and artifacts like the lost ark, the holy grail and the silver skull. As I grew up, my desire to follow the steps of my greatest inspirers and mentors grew up with me and pushed me to follow my dream to also search for others that were yet to be discovered. Your being here today with me commences my next adventure: the quest for the Golden Stool."

"What are you talking about?!" Kofi asked, confused by what he had heard.

"What?!" Coy exclaimed.

"Relax, my friends. Relax." Abdul Ali tried to calm them down. "I may sound stupid. But I know what I am about. I have followed you and your activities since you arrived here, my friend, Mr. Kofi. I am highly convinced that you are the one who can lead me to it."

Kofi was more confused and could not make any understanding of what Abdul Ali was blabbing about.

"I shall not confuse you any further. Just relax. I want you to know that my collections of the Mask of Alata and Stallion of Yenega, and now my desire to undertake the quest for this Golden Stool have not come by accident. I thank you, my friend Coy, for bringing my friend here to me easier than other associates who had tried earlier." Abdul Ali closed the cases and boxes. The wooden lid was brought in to cover the crate. The forklift turned and sent the crate away. "While you ponder what you have just learned," he continued, "I shall attend to other pressing matters elsewhere. Kruger!" he called out, "please find a comfortable place of rest for my guests. They will need some time to condition themselves to assimilate what shall be unfolding to them later. Ah, please, make sure no harm comes to them."

Kruger signaled to two guardsmen with automatic rifles who had shown up after Coy and his company entered the cubicle. They stepped up beside the three visitors and escorted them away.

Shocked, Coy shook his head in great disbelief. "What?!" He exclaimed in grave disappointment. He wondered what he had done. He bowed his head as they were escorted away.

Kofi tried to look at Coy, trying to catch his eyes, but he looked away. The perplexity of the circumstance was overwhelming and too shocking for the three. Coy began to sweat from his clean shaven head dripping on to his forehead. Saah almost collapsed and had to hold on to Coy and, Kofi, dumb-founded, and feeling like a succumbed lamb tied to a sacrificial altar.

"Coy, what have you brought us to?" Saah screamed, tears dropped from her eyes as they moved along. "You drove us to the 'temple of doom?'"

"How could I have known?" Coy said, shocked and wet with sweat; so devastated that a man with his physique could not muster energy to generate any muscle to resist.

"Kofi, I am so sorry. I didn't know…" Saah tried to console him. "Well, what can I say? If this is my fate, I leave it in the hands of the almighty, the gods and my ancestors."

"As for you," she turned to Coy, "I'll tell what's on my mind when we get out of this."

"Alive, if we would ever," concluded Kofi.

Coy looked at her forlornly with apologetic eyes. He felt so sorry for himself.

Two more men with arms led them to a corner in the warehouse where there were two rooms. One guard tried the first door. It was locked. He attempted to force it open but to no avail. The second guard tried the second door. It opened. They were all shoved in and the door closed behind them.

"Damn it! Damn!!" Coy exclaimed, cursing himself. He looked around. The room was bare like a prison cell, but large like an office. He was not unfamiliar with places like that. He had spent time in a couple of them years ago when he was in the army. The door was the only entrance but it had no handle to open from inside. It was like an empty storeroom, or was it a guardroom, with a very high ceiling. Kofi moved to one corner and squatted with his back against the wall and faced the door. A bulb hanging overhead was the only source of light. Near the bulb was an air vent which brought in air, cooling the place. Coy paced up and down thinking what to do next. Saah leaned forward against the wall. She had covered her face with her palms, frustrated. Coy moved to Saah with a view to console her. She reacted violently and attacked him.

"Leave me alone! Don't touch! Don't!" "Cool it, Me Lady. Cool it."

"What? What?"

"Help me think like you always do." Coy tried to coax her to get her to calm down. He could recall the many times Saah had helped him to think out strategic solutions to some very pertinent issues that seemed insurmountable to win that opposing counsel marveled at the end how Coy could beat them to it. Strangely, his attempt to get her mind to concentrate was futile. "Me Lady? Help me; like we always do."

"What do you want me to do?" She knew very well that without any effort, they had walked through the day. Now, Coy had brought them back into the precipice or the trouble they were running away from, into the hands of the very force they were fleeing from. How could she bring herself to think; to strategize? Coy approached her again, this time, cautiously and grabbed her by her upper arms from behind. She struggled to free herself from his grips. She turned to face him, hitting Coy in his torso and temples.

She struggled until she broke down, crying. Coy pulled her to his chest and consoled her. Kofi watched them, then turned to look away. He noticed a cctv camera high up in a corner of the ceiling.

"They are watching us." Kofi's voice startled them as if they had forgotten his presence with them. "They can see us."

"Who? What? Where?" Coy asked turning to Kofi. "There. A camera. Up there."

"I'll be damned!"

Coy broke hold from Saah. He walked to where the camera was, looked at it up in the ceiling. He removed his shoe, aimed and threw it at the camera. He hit the camera. He threw his shoe again and hit the camera again. The camera twisted from its axis and the signal went off. He slipped back his shoe on his foot.

The guard who was monitoring them from a screen called for attention to the room when he noticed that no video signal was coming on to the screen monitor. Two guards moved towards the room.

Without knowing what was happening outside, Coy suspected a reaction and called his colleagues: "Now, guys, let's get ready. I have a hunch. If my suspicion is right, follow me. I am getting us out of here. "

"Huh!" Kofi remarked with great anxiety and rose to his feet.

Saah reacted and suddenly became aware of herself. "What? How? How are you going to do that? The guards out there are armed."

"Don't worry." Coy responded confidently. "When the going gets tough…"

Kofi drew closer and responded to Coy's riddle, "The tough gets going." "No! You use your head and do the unexpected. That's how we say it."

Saah intervened.

"We are breaking out."

"Huh!" Kofi and Saah exclaimed.

Coy moved closer to the door. He called them to him. "Get behind me. All I need is to get out of this room. I shall figure out the rest from out there. I am a war veteran."

"A veteran?" Saah uttered as she rushed to stand behind Coy. Kofi followed closely.

"Yes, and I used to play football too. Come behind me. Quick!" They lined up behind Coy who had knelt down on one knee. He seemed to have been possessed by some power and energy. Just then the door flung open. A guard, unarmed, popped his head into the room. Coy grabbed the guard by his clothes and threw him to the floor, crashing his head on the wall and broke his neck in the process. The guard passed out.

The second guard seeing what had happened raised the alarm. "Break out! Break out!"

An emergency alarm went off with an announcement of the public address system: "Break out! Break out! Prisoners breaking out at the arrival area."

Coy hit the second guard in the face with his fist, so hard that it broke the guard's nose. He grabbed the dazed guard and used him as a shield and exited the room. Gunfire started with bullets flying towards them. They hit the guard. Kofi and Saah, their hands covering their heads, walked closely behind Coy.

The public address system went off again, "Cease firing! Cease firing! Prisoners must be captured alive!"

The gunfire ceased. Coy threw down the bullet ridden body of the guard and faced four others who approached him. He dispatched the first two with ease; the third, he engaged in a little wrestling and broke the arm, dropping him to the floor as he writhed in pain. The fourth guard hesitated to approach him. Coy beckoned to Kofi and Saah. They joined him. Together they ran to the van that had brought them to the place which was a few metres away. Two more guards confronted them. Kofi and Saah took cover behind Coy. The two guards were heavily built, tall and stout. One wielded an iron bar and the other, a baseball bat. The guard with the iron bar threw it at Coy. Coy grabbed it. Kofi and Saah backed away from Coy. The other guard with the baseball bat hit Coy in the leg. Coy toppled to the floor. The two guards began to beat him with their weapons. Saah pulled off one of her shoes from her foot and hurled it at the guards. It hit one of them in the facedazing him and causing him to whirl his weapon off Coy, and in the process, hitting the other guard in the face. The two guards fell to the ground. Saah and Kofi went to the aid of Coy to bring him to his feet quickly. The big gate of the warehouse slowly began to draw open. "To the van!" Coy yelled out, limping as they raced to the van.

Saah took the wheels. Kofi joined the van on the seat behind her. He pulled Coy on board. The keys were still at the ignition. Saah kick started the van and sped off towards the opening gate. Just as she got close to the opened gate, a big articulated truck appeared at the entrance driving in at top speed. Saah swerved the van off to avoid a head-on collision. The van missed the crash narrowly. It tilted and rolled on two side wheels for a distance and then tipped over and somersaulted.

The truck entered the warehouse and stopped in the centre of the space. Kruger, who was at the wheels, jumped down and raced towards the van. Other guards joined him. They surrounded the wreckage and allowed Kruger to approach the damaged van. He pulled the door open and Kofi helped himself out of the wreckage of the van as he was not hurt. Tango and Don took custody of Kofi. Saah was injured behind the wheel. She struggled to free herself as she was trapped in there between the steering wheel and the seat. Coy pulled himself up. He was restrained by a couple of guards holding rifles. Kruger joined

Don and Tango to bring Kofi to the truck. Abdul Ali who had been seated at the passenger seat jumped down. He wore a white military camouflage suit with an accompanying cap.

"Why my friend," Abdul Ali accosted Kofi, ignoring the attempt to escape as if nothing had happened, "you don't like the reception I am giving you, do you? I do not have to harm you. You are very precious to me. Do not make it too difficult as we have a very long journey to make." He turned to Kruger, "Bring him along. We have to evacuate now."

A Rolls Royce car was pulled out of the forty-footer container on top of the articulated truck. The forklift carrying the crate they had looked at earlier brought its cargo and offloaded it into the container. Kruger took the wheels of the Rolls Royce and brought it closer to Abdul Ali who joined him in the front. Tango and Don jostled Kofi and seated him in between them in the back seat. The big gate of the warehouse opened again and Kruger drove the Rolls Royce out at top speed. One of the guards took over the truck, turned it round and left the warehouse with the crate to a different location. The rest of the guards in the warehouse scattered and joined other vehicles out of the warehouse leaving Coy and Saah, groaning in pain, stuck behind the steering wheel in the van. Coy turned to her and tried to free her from the entrapment.

"What do you want from me?" Kofi asked as the sight of the warehouse diminished in the background. "Where are you taking me to?"

"Don't worry; nobody will miss you," Abdul Ali said without looking back at Kofi. "No one will be looking for you. You have caused enough trouble here that all the jackals and scoundrels will be happy you were gone. And that is exactly what I am doing for them. I am taking you back home where you are welcome, among your kith and kin, those of whom you make a living by telling tales."

The sarcasm of his statement hit Kofi. "Who are you?" He asked. "What do you want from me?"

"Oh, as I told you before. My name is Abdul Ali. I am German by birth and Russian by citizenship but live in the United States. My parents were very staunch members of the Nazis in their youth. They had to live under cover after World War II. I had to find my own way out of their lives because I became bored with their way of life. I am neither a Muslim nor an Arab. I adopted the name and lifestyle so I could move around freely without let or hindrance. Do not get me wrong. I have no fundamentalism in me. I do not fight for anyone nor for any cause. In fact, I hate religion; all religions." He sounded too confusing for Kofi's understanding.

Kofi ignored Abdul Ali's statement and did not even attempt to make any sense of it. And to galvanize himself to build some confidence and courage in him, he also responded: "Well, I am also Kofi Nsiah. I am a Ghanaian. I do not have rich parents. I don't work for the UN. I have no superpower behind me nor do I have any famous friends and associates who would need me so badly that you can go to for a ransom, that is, if you are kidnapping me."

"Ha, ha, ha!" Abdul Ali burst into laughter. "Kidnap? Ransom? What will that give me? I am content with what I have. And there is nothing in this world I cannot have, if I want."

"Then, just let me go. I will sort myself out with the law here. I don't know you and I will swear I never saw you."

"Why did you come here to give your lecture and the exhibition?"

"Well, it was an academic and cultural exchange programme between my faculty and its counterpart in the host university."

"And the ultimate purpose is selling your story to the world?" Abdul Ali asked, and without waiting for an answer, he continued. "You don't have to worry. I am one big client. I will buy anything you have offered. Name your price."

"I have nothing to sell, please."

"The history and the powerful ancestry of your tribe and kingdom interest me. I want to learn more. Take me there. Take me to your people."

Kofi ignored Abdul Ali. As their sedan joined the freeway, his mind went on to Coy and Saah whom he had left behind. "What happens now? My friends, what happens to them?"

"Gone up in smoke, that is, if they are not quick enough to leave the storage before now." In a distance the warehouse exploded in a big ball of fire, smoke and rubbles into the skies.

"Huh?" Kofi became worried for his friends, Coy and particularly Saah, realizing now that they could be killed in a possible blow up of the warehouse. He tried to look back for anything to confirm if really Abdul Ali would carry out his intention. Of course, he did not doubt Abdul Ali would. He felt very uncomfortable and helpless. The road took a long bend to the right. Through the window, Kofi turned, and to his shock he could see the fire in the skyline of the city. He sank deep into his seat, very disturbed and worried for his friends. If they died, it confirmed that everyone who had tried to help him had to die.

"That's a big bone for the scoundrels and the jackals." Abdul Ali said. "By the time they realize, we would be long gone, out of their jurisdiction." Kofi sat quietly. The sedan took an exit from the freeway and went on for a couple of miles. They soon arrived at a small airport.

The Rolls Royce drove into a hanger at the end of the airport runway. A 16-seater executive jet was parked in the hanger. Its engine was running. A number of boxes and chests were loaded onto the aircraft from the Rolls Royce. Kofi was escorted to join the aircraft. It had only six seats more fitted beside those of the crew. The rest of the seating space was converted to hold the many pieces of luggage of chests and large boxes, containing equipment and accoutrements Abdul Ali was traveling with, some of which were already loaded on board before they arrived. The three-member crew assisted the occupant of the sedan to board the aircraft. Kofi was seated beside Abdul Ali on the second executive seat while Kruger, Tango and Don sat directly opposite them on a four-seater settee. Within minutes the aircraft was coasting on the runway and it took to the air smoothly.

Abdul Ali unfastened his seat-belt when the sign came on to do so. "Feel free and relax," he said to Kofi leaning towards him. "Not even NASA nor the FBI will be able to detect your whereabouts or track you. I have already seen to that. There is a total media blackout on you in the homicide at the Grand Hotel. No one would know you were ever associated."

"The blast at the police station and the assault on the safe house?" Kofi asked astonishingly.

"Ha ha!" Abdul Ali chuckled. "Don't you worry. No one will miss you. Nothing can be traced to you." He paused and looked at Kofi, expecting a response from him. "Do you still doubt my prowess? Forget it. Please bring our guest here something to eat and drink. You must be very hungry, my friend."

Kofi sat quietly, thinking: Who is this crazy man? Is he just crazy or eccentric? He thought.

"I'd like to go to the washroom," Kofi requested. It has been over twenty- four hours since Saah set him running and the unfolding drama had been breathtaking. He could feel in his muscle that his body was yielding to the call of nature. He was tired and hungry. He had not had a wink, nor food all the while. He was shown the way. Tango saw him enter and stood guard at the door. Inside, as Kofi refreshed himself, washed his face and rinsed his mouth with water. He observed himself in the mirror, ran his hand over his head. After wiping the water with tissue paper, he turned to open the door. Tango stood waiting at door. Tango stepped aside to allow him pass to his seat. He slumped into his seat. He looked at Abdul Ali with a large tray of food spread before him.

"I am sure you will be wondering what this crazy man is about." Abdul Ali began to speak as Kofi settled in his seat and his meal was spread on the table next to him. "I feel so incensed," he continued after he had swallowed a morsel of food and washed it down with wine, wiping his wet lips with a napkin, "by the mere mention of the Golden Stool, the *Sika Dwa*, that's how you call it, that it is so well protected by its people that no one can get access to it. Ha! Your sentimental attachment to your Golden Stool is grotesque. And I'll prove it to you. I have possessed the Stallion and the Mask without great effort and I am sure it will be equally easy with the Golden Stool. I hope you'll assist me in my quest."

Kofi watched him, completely lost on what to do, and offered no response. He felt guilty for being the one through whom the security of the Golden Stool had come under threat. The scent and aroma of the food overtook his senses and anxieties. He quickly turned to the food and set himself to eat, munching seriously to show how hungry he was.

Tango watched him as if he must not let him out of his sight for a second. Abdul Ali watched him and felt he should let him be, at least for a while.

After satisfying himself, Kofi went for some wine. He adjusted himself comfortably in his seat and strapped on his seatbelt. His mind was tired and he did not care anymore whatever was going to happen. He felt his fate was no longer in his hands and looked forward to whatever was to come. Seconds later, he was overtaken by sleep, knocked out by the wine that was laced with a strong sedative. After a few minutes, Tango checked on him. Kofi's shoe was removed from his right foot, Tango inserted a tracking device and fitted the shoe back on his foot.

The aircraft flew for hours, which gave them all a bit of time to take well needed rest. Kofi and all on board were jolted awake by some turbulence. He looked around and saw he was still on the aircraft. He looked at the travel map on the aircraft wall. The time read 13.48. It was day. The aircraft hit another turbulence for a few seconds. He looked around; Tango was still staring at him as if he had not had a blink since he dozed off. He looked away and looked back at Tango. Their eyes met. He turned away from him. His sly look made Kofi feel very uneasy. Abdul Ali was not around. Kofi saw a curtain drawn to cordon off the cockpit of the aircraft. He satisfied himself that Abdul Ali might be there. He rose to his feet. Tango rose too. He sat, and

Tango sat again. Kofi burst into laughter and pointed his finger at Tango. "Oh, you are to look after me?" Kofi inquired looking at his face. Tango nodded slowly. "Don't worry. I won't make your work too difficult for both of us. I just want to go to the loo again." Just at that moment Abdul Ali appeared from behind the curtain.

Tango showed Kofi the way and followed him. Kofi spent only a few seconds. As he exited the loo the aircraft hit another turbulence. This time it was a big one. Kofi took hold to keep his balance as the jet made a sharp dive. Kofi rushed to his seat and fastened his belt.

"Where are we?" Abdul Ali asked as he fastened his seat belt and held on to his seat.

"Just over the Bermuda," responded Don who sat a little away from him.

"The Caribbean. No wonder." Abdul Ali observed, with the look of a man who was no stranger to geography of the world.

The aircraft stabilized. Kofi sat up and looked at the flight map. "Bermuda! Did you say Bermuda? As in Bermuda Triangle?" Kofi curiously enquired.

"Yes. We're closer home, aren't we?"

"I am sorry we are not. Definitely, way out. We are lost." Kofi said as he watched the flight map again.

"In the skies?"

"Yes, we are. From where we took off, we should have been going eastward, not south. Accra airport is east of the United States from where we took off. Get me a map. I'll show you."

"I'd be damned." Abdul Ali muttered.

With a remote control Kruger brought a google map of the world on an LCD screen near Abdul Ali. Kofi turned to face it.

"Find Accra. Ghana. West Africa. Greenwich Meridian. Equator. That is where we should be going." Kofi directed

Kruger typed in the information on a cordless keyboard he had put on his lap, "Google earth," zoomed in to Accra and showed the location and coordinates.

Abdul Ali picked up the intercom. The pilot came on line. "Jim. New destination."

"What? We're changing course? Where?" Jim asked. "Africa."

"No more South America?"

"No. The new destination is Ghana; spelt G H A N A; not Guyana in South America. We are going to Accra, Ghana, longitude 5.36 degrees North and latitude 0.11 degrees West, precisely. Let's go."

"Right, sir." Jim responded.

Jim turned on a device and inputted the new coordinates he had received from Abdul Ali. At the press of a button, the aircraft made a smooth turn.

"Accra, here we come. Accra, Ghana." Jim said to confirm his change in direction and destination.

"Any refuel plans? Do we have enough fuel for the distance?" Abdul Ali asked.

"Enough to keep us in the air for the next 8 hours." Jim confirmed. "How much flight time do we have?"

"Approximately, six – three – quarter hours."

"Flight path and overland flying problems?"

"Do not worry, sir. We shall deal with them when they come. Our main route now is over international waters. We'll pick an altitude that will cause no problem to ground controls until we are close to landing."

"Go ahead, then." "Yes, Sir!"

Abdul Ali sat back as the aircraft leveled up, heading toward the new destination. "Kruger, who are our collaborators and associates there," he enquired. "Get on to it. I need to know what help they can give us: discrete alternative routes, landing sites and on-ground transportation out of the view of and detection by local authorities."

"I have already done so, Sir." Kruger had been searching since the information for the new location came up. He was familiar with the area. It was not too far from where they undertook their last two expeditions to Nigeria and Burkina Faso. "You'd be surprised to know it is around Alata land and the Mossi land, the sites for the Mask and the Stallion."

"You don't mean it!" Abdul Ali exclaimed.

"I do. We have three collaborators close by: one in Nigeria, one in Burkina and the other in Ivory Coast."

"What about Ghana?"

"We don't have any there. The Ivory Coast agent has jurisdiction there. He can give us equally very reliable details we can work with. You would need to instruct him directly and personally as to what we would need. Here." Kruger passed on the communication device he was working on to Abdul Ali. It looked like a big size laptop with a headset attached to it. It had powerful transmission and receiving capabilities linked to Abdul Ali's communications system on the ground. With this he could access any radio, audio, data and video to and from any of his contacts via existing communication systems. Within no time, Abdul Ali had had a quick interaction with his Ivorian agent who in turn had passed on vital information, directing them to an airstrip in the centre of Ghana precisely near Tarkwa, a mining town which has a very short runway.

He gave the coordinates to the pilots. They also inputted the information and returned with estimated time of arrival. It was also confirmed that on- ground transportation was going to be ready as well to quickly whisk them away without detection. After a number of back and forth information and communication, the parties agreed on a ground plan. It was also concluded that with Kofi Nsiah in their company who knew where the Golden Stool was and had been a willing collaborator so far, the expedition was perhaps going to be the fastest operation. It was anticipated that the mission was going to take a few hours and by the time the authorities in Ghana would realize, they would have already taken off and gone with no trace.

The enthusiasm in the aircraft was great with very high expectation. Kofi felt very uncomfortable and very disappointed that he was the one who was going to facilitate the stealing of the *Sika Dwa*, the soul of *Asanteman*. While the expression of optimism within the ranks of Abdul Ali and his team was high, Kofi sat quietly and watched as the clouds moved backwards through the aircraft window.

Chapter Five

FORCED LANDING

The *Sumankwaahene,* the spiritual advisor of the *Asantehene*, King of the *Asanteman,* his role as the spiritual head of the kingdom was to divine and consult oracles and deities which protected the kingdom and the Golden Stool. The soul of the Asante Kingdom was under his personal control and direction. All processes for regular visitation, cleansing and purification of the Golden Stool for it to hold its power and protection of the Asante Kingdom, as well as the occupant of the Golden Stool and all the subjects of the stool derived and rested on him. He had the capacity to forecast coming events and messages from the ancestral world.

Nana Sumankwaa, he was resting in a lazy chair in his patio next to his bedroom. It was late afternoon. The house was the usual traditional Ghanaian compound house, and across the compound was the kitchen where Auntie Yaa, Nana's wife and a teenage girl were preparing a fufu meal. On a coal pot beside them was a pot of soup, boiling. In the centre of the house was a shrine erected with a pile of boulder stones around a post. The post was a stem of a *nyamedua* or an umbrella tree with a fork at the top. Inside the prongs of the fork was placed a black pot decorated with talismans, parchments and other things to present it as a spiritual soul of the house.

Nana Sumankwaa was dozing off when he was suddenly startled up. He looked deep into the skies. Suddenly, there appeared a large swarm of flying bats. A group of these flying bats began to encircle around the roof of the house high up in the sky. A chilly feeling ran through him which made him move to the centre of the compound to observe and interpret the symbolism of the spectacle. A heavy dark cloud began to gather above the circling bats. From the expression on his face one could easily read what was to come. He hushed at the women preparing the meal who obviously appeared oblivious of what he was experiencing. "Hey!" He pointed his left forefinger at them, placed it to his lips and then flashed it at them. They understood him and stopped what they were doing. They quickly covered the meal they were preparing and disappeared into a room nearby.

Walking backwards, Nana Sumankwaa retreated into his room but quickly returned with a double barrel shot gun and a bottle of schnapps. He slowly walked to the middle of the house where the shrine was. He placed the shot gun on the floor and opened the bottle of schnapps.

"I call you, *nananom,*" he made a libation.

"I bear witness of what I have seen.
This does not seem to be a blessing.
If it is evil send it far, far away from us.
Bring us what is good and progressive.
The evil one who sent this,
He does not wish us well.
Let every evil he sends return to him manifold."

He placed the bottle down and picked the shot gun, took an aim at the pot on top of the *nyamedua* and fired. This caused pandemonium in the sky among the bats. They rapidly dispersed in all directions. Right in front of him, one dead bat dropped. He picked up the dead bat and threw it on the shrine. Within a few minutes, the house was besieged by some youth in the neighbourhood, numbering about twenty, men and women, chanting war songs.

"Osee yei, yee yei!
Yee yei, yee yei!
Ɔsɛe wo yɛ hwan ni a?
Yɛnyɛ wo dɛn ni o
Ɔsɛe aa na yɛ som no o
Sika Dwa aa e yɛ som
Osee aye!"

The youth frantically demanded interpretation. Nana Sumankwaa presented them with some bottles of alcoholic drink. "Go out and hoot at the evil one," he urged them.

The group departed onto the streets. As they paraded up and down chanting war songs and dancing, a car pulled up in front of Nana Sumankwaa's house. Nana Kyerewaa, the occupant of the car got out. She was dressed in a colourful traditional attire in dansinkran style and wore a pair of dark goggles. Her exquisite makeup and poise exposed her as a very stylish person. She slung her hand bag on her left arm and slammed the car door, locking it with her remote key. The young men and women parading the street caught her attention as she made her way into Nana Sumankwaa house. Nana Sumakwaa had returned the rifle into the room and was returning to his chair when Nana Kyerewa rushed into the house. The fufu meal team had resumed in earnest.

"Nana, what is happening? Why have the youth besieged your street?" Nana Kyerewaa asked curiously.

Nana Sumankwaa was surprised to see her. "They are only hooting at the evil one," Nana Sumankwaa replied as he offered her a seat. "Have a seat. You are welcome."

"Thank you. Anything amiss, man with eyes that see the beyond?"

"I am only doing my sacred duty as assigned me by the gods and our ancestors."

"Well done."

"Now, to what do I owe this courtesy?" Nana Sumankwaa tried to bring her to the purpose of her visit.

"Oh, nothing, really. You know since my brother died several years ago my family has been bothering me over my choice of his successor. They won't accept my son as his heir. You are one person who knows me and our family very well. You knew my brother before he died and you also know my siblings and our children one of whom must ascend the stool. Why are you not helping me resolve this issue once and for all, by backing me on my choice?"

"Stop! Nana Kyerewaa," Nana Sumankwaa interjected. "We've been here before on this matter. And I gave you my position. Let Otumfoɔ's eminent men settle it in order to bring tranquility among you."

"Does this mean you do not support me in my choice?"

"No, I do not say that."

"Then, why do you not veto the process? A word from you would have ended this matter long before now. Why?"

"I – I," Nana Sumankwaa hesitated, baffled by her accusation. "Oh, you disappoint me."

Nana Sumankwaa felt embarrassed and could not gather himself together to redeem himself. He had had a soft spot for Nana Kyerewaa ever since they knew each other. And he almost always buckled under her charm whenever the two met. But their current meeting was an exception. He had never felt like that before in his life. Because of how she spoke to him, he sat quietly and could not utter a word.

Nana Kyerewaa sensed his frustration but could not imagine what the reason was. "Why, are you not saying anything? Look, I came to see you to help me reach the sub-committee handling our case. I want to petition them. This is my drink."

"Stop!" Nana Sumankwaa shouted before she could pull out an envelope of cash from her bag. He gathered courage to chide her. "Must you always influence everything and everybody in anything you do?" She stopped short with her hand stuck in the bag, shocked at his reaction. "Look, I am going to confess to you today. And I am doing so with great pain because of the respect I have for your late brother and the friendship that existed between him and me. I am doing so, again for the respect I have for you and your family, and also for my own integrity."

Nana Kyerewaa straightened up and looked at him, perplexed and curiously wondered what he was going to say next. "Yes, I sat in the same classrooms with Nana Kwame from my first day at school till we finished our university education. He became more of a brother to me than a friend. My involvement in your family is far deeper than you know. I was one of the first eminent persons Otumfoɔ selected to sit on your petition. I stood down and recused myself because I am compromised in your family. I am too involved. And my conscience, I – hm. Don't make it more difficult for me than it is already." Nana Sumankwaa paused and sighed. What are you trying to say?"

"I - I am finding it hard to decide which -."

"But it is only between my son and Janet's son? What is your difficulty then?"

Nana Sumankwaa sat, gazing, confused. The suspense got Nana Kyerewaa more curious. Then in a flash she recollected. "Were you involved with Janet too? Did you date her too? Answer me."

"Look, I – I. She was mature. You were a little kid. I was scared I'd get into trouble getting intimate with you at that age."

"So, you took Janet. Why were you patronizing me then? You slept with me, on my sixteenth birthday?"

Nana Sumankwaa stammered and could not hazard any tangible response. "I just could not resist your charm."

"You are an idiot!" Nana Kyerewaa said angrily as she sharply rose to her feet, whacked Nana Sumankwaa in the face and stormed out on him. The slap was so loud that it took the attention of the fufu making crew for a moment. Bemused, Nana Sumakwaa's hand touched his face where the slap had landed. Helplessly, he watched her storm out.

It was quiet on the flight bringing Kofi Nsiah to Ghana. Everything seemed calm. Darkness had come to them quite fast. Most of the passengers had fallen asleep. They had flown at high altitude and outside the territorial waters of countries within their flight path. As they approached Ghana on the Gulf of Guinea, the pilot dropped altitude to prepare to land. It was getting to dawn of the next morning. Flying to the east they had gained almost six hours in time. Morning had come early. There was a large cloud that appeared before him that he could not avoid. They ran into it but it turned out so rough that it shook the aircraft waking up those who were sleeping. Jim and his co-pilot put on their communication headsets.

The flight assistant fastened his seatbelt. The aircraft was virtually fluttering like a leaf, swinging, dashing and dropping anywhere the storm would take it. Kofi Nsiah gripped his seat with both hands, dancing to the swing of the aircraft. His heart was in his mouth. He was sweating. One man, however seemed unmoved. Despite the tempest in the air, Tango sat with his eyes locked on Kofi, observing him without a blink. Jim and his co-pilot were nervous, very anxious and sweating. They watched a weather screen that indicated the size of the storm as the aircraft pierced through the thick clouds. He maneuvered and directed the aircraft out of the cloud that had generated the storm. This made him veer off the flight path that he had taken to elude detection by aviation scanners. Slowly, the storm weakened and the aircraft stabilized.

Checking on their location, Jim announced that they had just entered the territorial airspace of Ivory Coast and by the speed at which they were traveling they had about an hour to reach their destination. He asked the co-pilot to search for the frequency to contact the control tower for landing procedure. "This is Special Flight GJ 403 T requesting permission to land at Accra Airport, over." He waited for a response. Nothing came through. He tried again for contact; but again, no response came through. Then, a sudden beeping sound like air missile locked on an aircraft and then an air force fighter jet whisked past them in a dangerous maneuver that shook their aircraft for a few seconds.

"What the hell was that!" the co-pilot asked.

"I think we've got company," Jim said. He looked out of the side windows.

Two more air force jets pulled beside them at the same speed as their aircraft. Then from the speaker in the cockpit came an announcement in French: *"Un aéronef non identifié qui viole notre espace aérien. Vous* êtes *invité* à *revenir immédiatement. Nos missiles sont formés* à *vous. Nous allons vous abattre si vous ne reculez pas. Je répète. Un aéronef non identifié qui viole notre espace aérien. Vous* êtes *invité* à *revenir immédiatement. Nos missiles sont formés* à *vous. Nous allons vous abattre si vous ne reculez pas."*

The message was heard by all on the aircraft. Abdul Ali got alarmed. He looked out of the windows too. He saw the two air force jets. He became very disturbed and hysterical. "What is happening, Jim?" he inquired.

"We've got unexpected company. I will handle it." Jim responded to the warning: "Station hearing me, we have an emergency. May day, may day. We have an emergency and request emergency landing."

The announcement came on again in English with a French accent: "Unidentified aircraft violating our airspace. You are ordered to turn back immediately. Our missiles are trained on you. We will shoot you down if you do not turn back. I repeat. Unidentified aircraft violating our airspace. You are ordered to turn back immediately. Our missiles are trained on you. We will shoot you down if you do not turn back."

Jim again responded with a distress message. "May day, may day! Emergency landing requested, do you read me?"

The radio responded: "You do not have permission to fly our airspace. You do not have permission to land anywhere in our territory. Turn back or we will shoot you down."

Realizing his camouflage message could not make any impact he alerted his passengers and crew to brace up for the worst. "Guys, we have a situation. Sit tight, we'll go for the run."

The two Ivorian jets broke off from beside the intruding aircraft. Jim quickly turned the aircraft and directed it out of Ivorian territory but was not fast enough. Suddenly, fired bullets started hitting them.

"We are under fire!" Jim shouted. His co-pilot turned left and right in an effort to locate the aircraft. Jim remembered his days as a jet fighter pilot in the US Air Force. He suddenly commenced a maneuver to extricate them from the Ivorian Air Force attack. He reduced speed at once and instantly dropped the aircraft to a lower altitude in a free fall. The aircraft dropped very fast; the two fighter jets zoomed past above them. Suddenly Jim lifted the aircraft about 75 degrees into the sky again at high speed. He turned the aircraft towards Ghanaian territorial waters as they were very close.

"Hi hooo!" Jim jeered. "We lost them, yes! We lost them."

But before Jim could stabilize the aircraft, he received another barrage of bullets. He turned the aircraft in several maneuvers in a great effort to elude his pursuers. Jim sped on but the engines began to jerk. "Wow! Wow!"

"What was that?" Abdul Ali asked.

"We've been hit! We've been hit! This is for real. We are going down." Jim alerted. The aircraft began a sudden fast descent again. Abdul Ali shifted in his seat and sat up straight.

"Engine one is on fire. Shut engine down!" Jim ordered his co-pilot.

"Shutting engine one down," the co-pilot responded to confirm executing the order. The Ivorian fighter jet turned away as Jim approached Ghana territory with heavy smoke streaking behind him. It was definite the plane was going down. It was getting warmer inside the aircraft and Jim and his co-pilot began to sweat in the cockpit, doing everything they could to avoid an imminent crash. They turned and pressed switches and levers, one after the other but to no avail. The pilot and his co-pilot initiated emergency landing procedure communicating between them in the cockpit.

"Dump fuel." "Dumping fuel." "Engage landing gear"

"Landing gear engaged" But the landing gear did not respond. The hydraulics have malfunctioned; the landing gears could not engage; the wheels did not move into position. The wings had stretched out half way.

All the passengers sat, tense, expecting the worst. Kofi, though in his seat belt, had grabbed on the seat to keep his balance, his heart pounded heavily. At that point, he felt only God's miracle could save them from crashing. He was sweating profusely. His shirt was drenched. He closed his eyes when the aircraft made a sudden long drop in altitude for almost a minute. His conclusion was that the end had come, anticipating in his mind how it was going to feel when the aircraft finally hit the ground. Would it explode, disintegrate into pieces, tumble or catch fire?

"Mayday, mayday!" Jim called out. "We are going down. One engine is out, the second is going up in flames."

The aircraft fluttered with twists and turns in the sky and was dropping down fast. They had barely half an hour left to reach their anticipated destination. With only one engine alive and a trail of smoke following it Jim managed to control the aircraft to glide down. They were well inside Ghana territory. The final engine conked out when the aircraft was a few feet above water level. Out of the window they could see it was at an area close to a shore with coconut trees along the beach towards lagoons and mangrove or marshland with water patches and small trees and bushes. Also, ahead, about a mile away was a town called *Nzulezu*, the coastal town almost on the Ghana - Ivory Coast border built on wooden stilts on the mangrove and lagoons. The aircraft crashed into the shallow waters with a big bang, splashing water and quenching the enflamed engine. It skidded on the water surface. The momentum helped it to slide on top of the water like a boat, slower than they had thought. With the engines out, Jim could not control the aircraft. He could only watch as the rudderless vessel took them wherever it might.

The aircraft slid for about half a mile with its wings whipping the shrubs and plants in the mangrove. Two men, throwing nets in the water standing in their canoe saw the aircraft approaching. They stopped their activity and tried to paddle the canoe away. But they were not fast enough. The wing of the aircraft hit their canoe and tossed then into the water. The aircraft moved directly towards the village. The impact and its associated noise attracted the attention of some residents who turned and saw the strange object coming fast, approaching their homes. Those who saw the craft approaching took to their heels, screaming and alerting fellow residents of the imminent disaster.

Then, the momentum began to reduce. The aircraft smashed a few canoes that had anchored in the water close to the village. The canoes were the only means of transport for the inhabitants of *Nzulezu*. The aircraft floated till it finally crashed into *Nzulezu* shaking the whole town awake. The nose of the aircraft rammed through a couple of houses before it finally came to a halt. The aircraft sank half way into the shallow water, its tail submerged but from its wings up to the nose protruding through the debris of the houses on stilts it had ran into and on top of the water.

In the cockpit, Jim yelled with delight as the aircraft safely came to a halt and they all escaped unhurt. He burst into loud laughter of great relief and shook the hand of his co-pilot, hugged him and patted him on the back. They quickly engaged the emergency evacuation procedure.

The rude entry of the flying bird shocked the residents. The few that were already out saw the aircraft. They screamed at the sight and this brought out a few more. Some of them were in their night dresses, others half naked with cloths wrap around them. After a short period and seeing there was no explosion and fires, and most importantly, seeing that the occupants had begun to emerge from the wreckage, some of the residents ran to the crash site. A couple of them held fire extinguishers. Pilots of some powered canoes in the water also appeared around ostensibly to help rescue the occupants.

The occupants of the crashed aircraft followed the emergency exit process and evacuated the wreckage. Overwhelmed, Kofi could not stand on his feet. He crawled out onto a platform that served as ground and streets for the 'on water city.' The town's people came to his rescue. They helped him to regain his strength. They thanked God and their gods and ancestors for their survival. The excited town's men were very pleasant. They cheered them, shook their hands and congratulated them for their safe crash landing. Jim and his crew stayed by the craft and the luggage.

Abdul Ali was not comfortable. "Where are we?" he asked Kofi. "You know these people?"

From the signpost, Kofi recognized that they were at *Nzulezu.* He was feeling better and relaxed from the trauma and shock of the ordeal they had gone through. "Not really," he replied. "But we are in Ghana territory. This place is called *Nzulezu,* meaning, 'on water' in the local language of the people here. This is a coastal town about 240 miles from my hometown to the north, in the heart of the country and it is about the same distance to the capital, Accra to the east."

Kruger ran in and showed Abdul Ali the location on a map on the laptop. "This is where we are. This is Accra. We are supposed to have landed here at Tark-wa and this is Ku-ma-si."

"Alright, no time to waste; we leave now."

Kruger returned to the wreckage with the laptop. The people were very helpful. They assisted in fully evacuating them and their luggage. They also provided them with some of the powered canoes and loaded the luggage on by tying a couple of canoes side by side to form a floating platform. As they made a move to the canoes, one elder shouted: "Nana is coming. Please don't go." The chief of the town, some men and women presumed to be the chief 's elders showed up. They lined up on the wooden platform street. Abdul Ali and his companion were led to them to shake hands. They held bottles of alcoholic drinks ready to welcome them with a libation and thanksgiving to the gods and the spirits of their ancestors for the safe crash-landing. Kofi went closer to the chief and addressed him directly in *Twi*, a Ghanaian language.

"*Nana, Me kyea mo*!" (Nana, greetings!)

"*Ɛyɛ* Ghana *nyi a*?" (Are you a Ghanaian?)

"*Me fri* Kumasi." (I am from Kumasi.)

"Oh that's good news. *Motsri nkwa*." (Congratulation for your safe landing.) The chief added.

Don quickly went in for Kofi and shoved him off. Kofi obliged without any resistance. The crowd reacted in displeasure of Don's treatment of Kofi. They saw it as a sign of disrespect to the chief; it also gave them the impression that all was not well with Kofi in their company. Don sensed a possible repercussion and confrontation as a result of his uncalculated reaction on Kofi. He pulled out his sub-machine gun concealed under his jacket and fired into the air, a few rounds of bullets. This stopped the ceremony abruptly. For a couple of seconds all was quiet. Then one young lady screamed as she saw Tango also pulling his sub-machine gun and Kruger also running in, brandishing his. There was pandemonium. The sudden outburst of the rifles sent the frightened townspeople assembled there fleeing or scrambling for cover. Some took to their heels running helter-skelter, in all directions. Others sought cover in the shanty wooden buildings and behind objects while the daring jumped into the water and swam away to some of the mangrove nearby for safety. The brave chief and a couple of men stood their grounds watching the men wielding the weapons.

Kruger handed Abdul Ali an envelope containing cash. Abdul Ali burst out apologizing: "Sorry, folks. I am not interested in your silly jokes. I have broken down some of your houses and structures. I'd like to make some restitution. I'll pay for them. It was not our intention to cause you any unpleasantness. We do apologize. Forgive us for our rude behaviour. Thank you for your unwanted hospitality." He stretched his hand with cash to the chief who just watched him with indifference. He dropped the cash on the floor and turned away.

Kruger grabbed hold of Kofi and dragged him along to the wreckage following Abdul Ali while Tango and Don held their sub-machine guns giving them protective cover till they arrived on the canoes. The people watched them from their hideouts as they boarded the loaded powered canoes piloted by one of the local people. A second person who tried to join was hurled off into the water as they rolled away. The townsfolk watched as they disappeared behind the grove with the large pile of boxes and chests. Jim and his crew had tried as much as they could to bring out all the luggage and as much of the moveable parts of the aircraft as were useful to them.

The native canoe pilot sat quietly as he steered the floating platform with Abdul Ali and his men and their luggage. One could easily tell his heart was in his mouth. After a short distance, Tango who sat by him pulled a wad of dollar notes and handed it to him. With a move of his head, the pilot understood Tango's order. He rose and took a jump into the water. The flight assistant came in and took over the boat. The security on Kofi Nsiah was tightened. He was not allowed to move freely or alone. He sat in the canoe with guns pointed at him. They travelled on the water for a while and took one of the many tributaries of rivers that brought fresh water into the marshland and the lagoons. Ahead, they saw a wooden structure, more like a barn on the bank of the river. On the shallow part of the river was a rice plantation. They manoeuvred the canoes to a point that was dry. In front of the barn was the trailer of a tractor. Tango and Don managed to get out of their water vehicle onto dry land and quickly checked the barn and the surrounding. Behind was parked the tractor. It was jacked up with one of its front tyres removed.

"Damn!" Don exclaimed. "One wheel off."

"No sweat. I bet this thing can run on the three wheels, won't it?" Tango remarked.

"You think so?"

"Let give it a kick and see."

"Wheew! No battery. Hard luck." Don gave up.

But Tango persisted: "This is a diesel engine and can run without battery. Go call the others to help give it a push." Tango ripped off the ignition wires as Don rushed out and called out. He beckoned them.

Abdul Ali signaled to Kruger to go and check on them. Kruger went in. He also came out and beckoned for more hands. The co-pilot and the flight assistant got off the canoes and joined them.

Abdul Ali sat wondering what was happening. His men were not coming out from behind the barn. After a short while the tractor popped out from the back of the barn with Kruger driving it on three wheels and the others running behind it, laughing and cheering. Abdul Ali stood up, amazed. He got off the canoes and ran to them as Kruger parked it by the trailer to get it coupled.

Abdul Ali shook Kruger's hand to congratulate them. "That's a surprise."

"Out of the blue." Kruger added.

The men ran quickly to their luggage and carted them onto the trailer. In no time they were done and were on their way. Kruger was driving, Abdul Ali sat by him on the mudguard of the back wheel with the luggage and the rest of the men packed in the trailer.

They drove on a rough and dirt road for some thirty minutes before they reached a good road which was tarred. With a smaller laptop in hand Abdul Ali used the GPS to navigate and gave direction until they reached a town. They enquired and were directed to a fuel station nearby. All who saw them watched with curiosity: white men driving a three-wheeled tractor with a mountain of luggage in its trailer! Kruger turned into the fuel station and requested for the tank to be filled. The attendant waved his hand to indicate there was no diesel. He checked and the quantity in the tank was so woefully low that they could run out in no time. Kofi stood up on the tractor with his arms folded across his chest and watched them, wondering what they would do next.

From nowhere, an 18-seater American Ford van with only two occupants, a man and a woman, turned into the station for fuel. The driver asked the fuel attendant to give him a few gallons. Abdul Ali walked to him and asked him to request for the tank to be filled.

"Why, sir? I can afford only a few gallons, that's what I am buying," said the driver of the van wondering what the motive of the stranger was.

"I said let him fill the tank," emphasized Abdul Ali. "How much will that be?"

The driver who could not understand what Abdul Ali was about stood speechless.

"An equivalent of sixty dollars will fill it." The fuel attendant answered for him.

"Okay, here. Hundred. Pay for it." Abdul Ali pushed two fifty-dollar notes into the driver's palm and walked away towards the tractor which had been moved a distance away from the pump.

After filling the tank, the driver moved the van towards Abdul Ali to express his gratitude. He pulled beside him and saluted him saying: "Thank you, sir."

"You're welcome."

"I am going towards the border. I could give you a lift if you're going in that direction."

"No, we are going to Kumasi."

"Oh, I am sorry. Or your driver can come. We could check the next station for some diesel."

"No thanks. We don't need fuel. I need a van like yours. If you will rent it to me or sell it. I'll buy it, right now."

The driver was taken aback. "I am sorry, sir. I cannot sell my van. I bought it just two weeks ago. And it is just what I need for my work."

"How much did you pay for it?" Abdul Ali persisted.

The driver hesitated.

"Twenty thousand dollars? I'll double your price." Abdul Ali pushed further to the surprise of the driver.

"What?" The driver screamed. "No, no, no." At this point, the driver was getting irritated by Abdul Ali's ridiculous prepositions. "No. I cannot sell the van. I will not."

"Okay, I'll make it better. Fifty thousand."

"No, I think I must be going now. Thank you for your kind gesture." As they were talking, Don sneaked into the van through the rear door, unnoticed. The driver stepped on the accelerator and sped off. About half a mile out of town, Don crawled closer to the driver. The driver got a hunch that there were movements in the cabin. He tried to look through the driving mirror. His lady companion asked what his apprehension was as he kept looking behind him. Before he could express his intuition, Don leapt and grabbed his neck from behind and tried to strangle him. They screamed at the surprise attack on them. The vehicle began to swerve from left to right as the driver struggled with Don. It veered off the road into the bush missing a tree narrowly. The lady companion screamed as she was tossed along. The driver, gasping for breath, managed to slow the vehicle down to a stop. He tried to release himself from Don's grip. His lady companion gathered courage, after regaining her composure and grabbed one of Don's arms and bit hard on it to help free her man. Don pulled his arm away from the lady and swung it hard at her temple, sending her into sudden coma. He managed to release the seatbelt and pull the driver from his seat into the main cabin and squeezed his neck till he passed out. Don sat back on the seat near him to regain his breath, examining his bleeding arm. After a short moment, he pulled the two bodies out and searched through the vehicle for all their belongings and threw them away. Don drove the vehicle out of the ditch onto the road.

With top speed, he raced back to his colleagues. He came to a screeching stop by the loaded tractor. Surprised as they were, they could not ask any questions but hurriedly commenced loading.

"Jeez! You're bleeding!" Jim exclaimed seeing his blood-soaked sleeve.

He called his flight assistant who brought in an emergency kit to dress the wound and bandaged it neatly.

While Don was receiving attention, Kruger and the others had three out of the five seats in the cabin dismantled to make room for the luggage. Piece by piece they carried them in and they fitted perfectly. Kruger took the wheels, Abdul Ali joined him in the front excited as everything seemed to be moving on smoothly. They tried to put behind them the harrowing emergency landing. Jim and his crew took the available seats at the back while Tango and Don sat Kofi in between them in the middle as they drove away.

More to three hours had passed since Abdul Ali and his team left *Nzulezu*. From nowhere, a fleet of coast guards arrived in their patrol boats. They inspected the wreckage, took photographs and talked to a couple of town folks who pointed their fingers towards the direction Abdul Ali and his party took. One party set out to chase them. Half way on the waters, the coast guards found the local boat pilot floating and clinging onto a plank. He was exhausted, but trying to use it to reach safety. They rescued him and followed the direction only to find the abandoned powered canoe platform they had built at the shore near the farm house.

The Ford van drove along the coastal road with coconut trees on the sandy beaches, past the Elmina Castle. After the Cape Coast Castle, the van made a turn towards Kakum Park.

About half a mile to the park, the van made a turn at a bend and ran straight into a large herd of cattle moving in the middle of the road. The Fulani herdsmen tried to move the cattle off the road but the animals came back filling the road again. Kruger struggled to bring the van under control and to a stop. There was no way to pass. Abdul Ali ordered the road to be cleared quickly. Tango and Don jumped down to assist the herdsmen.

Kofi, realizing all attention had gone to the road and the cattle, seized the opportunity and also jumped out of the van and took to his heels into the bush. He ran without looking back. The flight assistant saw him leaving and raised the alarm.

Jim who was half asleep was awakened: "But where is he going?" He asked.

Abdul Ali turned to him, asking "Who?"

"The man.," the flight assistant said pointing to the direction Kofi had fled.

"The man?" Abdul Ali retorted. Then it came back to him it was Kofi they were referring to. "Hey! Shit! Get him! Don't let him get away! After him!" He screamed calling his men to pursue Kofi.

Kruger jumped out from the steering wheel. He whistled for Don and Tango. The two saw Kofi as he disappeared into the woods. They abandoned the cattle and joined Kruger to chase after him into the bushes.

"Bring him back! Alive! Do not harm him!" Abdul Ali yelled to them.

They disappeared.

Kofi brushed through the thickets until he got on to a trail. He looked left and right. He turned left and ran along the trail climbing up a hill. There was a wooden structure ahead that looked like a hut on stilts. He ran past it but turned back, climbed the short wooden steps on to the platform. He entered a small room with an exit at the opposite side. He passed through it and appeared at the other side. He was startled as he came upon a long canopy walkway made of ropes and flat wooden slabs. It ran seven stretches in between tall trees high over a canopy of forest below that also ran along a hill side into a valley over one hundred and fifty feet deep.

The forest below inhabited many spices of wild life of birds, butterflies, reptiles, rodents and tree-climbing mammals like monkeys of several kinds. There were other animals like antelopes, duikers and grass-cutters.

Kofi touched and took a step onto the walkway. It began to swing from side to side. His heart began to throb heavily. Where does it lead to? How safe is it? He thought. He backed away from the walkway. As he turned to look for a place to hide, he heard the footsteps of the Kruger and the others as they ran in. He became confused, whether to go on it or not. He braced up and took bold steps on to the walkway. He stumbled after a few steps as it swung him left to right. He struggled up and moved along. Halfway on the first stretch he heard Kruger's voice: "Hey! Stop there!"

Kofi froze. Tango pointed his sub machine gun at him.

"Turn round and come back here!" Kruger said in very distinct voice.

Kofi turned momentarily but resumed his walk, briskly away. Don pursued him on the walkway. The walkway began to swing vigorously. Kofi was knocked off his feet. He struggled up and hastened away as Don drew closer. He fell again and crawled on the slabs, quickly away. As he got closer to the end of the first stretch Tango aimed and fired a few shots, hitting the slabs underneath Kofi's feet. Kofi hurried off the first stretch onto a landing or resting area and continued to the second stretch. He increased his steps to gain some distance away from Don. The second stretch went on a tangent that exposed him to his pursuers. When Don also got on to the second stretch, it began to swing vigorously. Kofi was thrown off his feet. He crawled away faster.

Don ran faster towards him. Tango aimed and fired more shots with the intention of preventing Kofi from moving ahead. The shots blasted away the slabs in front of Kofi. Some of the shots hit the ropes that had been used to weave the walkway into position as well, causing serious damage to the stretch. The ropes began to snap at Kofi's feet where he stood. Kofi looked back and saw Don closing in on him. Every step don took made the walkway weaker, capable to break at any time. Kofi hesitated but gathered more courage as Don drew closer to him. Just as Don stretched his arm to grab him from behind Kofi heaved himself over the area that Tango had shot the slabs away. His foot missed the slab he had wanted to land on. He slipped into the gap in the walkway. He grabbed the ropes. The impact gave a heavy strain on the already weakening walkway. Suddenly, the ropes began to snap and break the walkway stretch into two. He struggled to keep his hold on the ropes to prevent him from falling off into the valley below him. He held fast onto the ropes his fingers could hold. His struggle caused the weakened ropes to sever more quickly. Don recognized the danger coming. He quickly backed away when he also realized he could not grab Kofi and the walkway was breaking into two parts. In the melee, the pressure the two of them exerted on the already weakened stretch, forced the stretch to finally give way and snap into two; one part took Kofi away. Don had almost reached the last landing area. He grabbed the slab as he dropped. He struggled to climb up. Tango and Kruger rushed to the landing or rest area to rescue him. Tango stretched his hand, Don also stretched and pulled himself up until he reached Tango who grabbed him and pulled him up to safety.

The part that took Kofi away swung him into the canopy of forest below. He screamed, hanging on precariously as the ropes swung him away. He held onto the ropes to keep him from dropping. But they loosened, dropping him, in a free fall as if he was taking a scuba drop through the canopy of leaves and branches. He fell through the foliage, breaking branches of trees and finally landed on a spread of thicket like a canopy. He struggled slowly through the thicket and descended onto the ground a few metres below. He had scratches and bruises. He felt pains all over his body. He trotted away in pain through the bushes.

A hunter who was doing illegal poaching in the forest heard the fall through the foliage and wondered what it was. Then he saw movement of the bushes and thought it was game. He held up a homemade gun. He had a little dog with him. He tapped slowly on the top of the dog's head until it lay quietly on the ground. He perched himself at an obscure position and waited for the game he anticipated. He took aim and followed the movement with the nozzle of the gun. Just at the point he was ready to press the trigger, Kofi emerged out of the bushes. The gun went off just at the same time as Kofi dropped to the ground out of exhaustion. The hunter was startled. He screamed out of fright, thinking he had hit Kofi. His little dog leapt forward to where Kofi fell. He rushed there to check on Kofi. Kofi was too weak to respond.

"Pl-ea-se! H -elp me!" Kofi could manage a weak groan to show he was still alive.

The hunter was quite petrified but managed to pick him up and carried him away hoping to save his life. He waded through the bushes with Kofi Nsiah on his shoulder, his shot gun slinging on his other shoulder and his little dog at his heels.

As he sat on the slab panting and waiting to get back his breath, Don asked: "So, what do we do?"

"We lost him." Kruger replied. "And that's it?"

"What can we do now? We just go back and inform the boss."

Abdul Ali was seated with the aircrew in the van. He looked at a monitor of a GPRS device. It indicated the movement of Kofi. And just as his men were deliberating, he wondered why it had taken them so long to apprehend Kofi. He picked up the radio and called to Kruger. "Where are you guys?" he asked.

"Boss. We lost him." Kruger responded.

"I can see. Get back here quickly before he gets too far."

"He has fallen badly. He could be badly hurt or dead."

"No, he is not dead. He is still moving." Abdul Ali said as he watched the monitor. "I can see; he's still moving. He won't die. He is a survivor. Come back quickly. We must get some fuel for our ride and some food for ourselves. He can't go too far. He will take a rest when night falls. We will pick him up then."

Kruger, Tango and Don walked down the trail that led them to offices of the management of the Kakum Park. As they hurried on, some of the tourists and patrons of the park, who were on their way to the walk-way, looked at them with some suspicion. They stepped away from the trail to allow them to pass.

Chapter Six

LOST IN THE WOODS

The hunter entered his hut deep in the forest carrying Kofi on his shoulder. He laid him gently on the earth-beaten floor. In one corner was a hearth where he cooked and used as source of light. He tended the hearth and got the fire burning with more pieces of firewood put into it. He looked at Kofi as he lay unconscious. He examined him thoroughly and realized there were no gunshot wounds or broken bones. He heaved a sigh of relief, but seeing how badly Kofi was wounded, he ran out into the bush with urgency and alacrity, as it was getting dark. He returned with several species of shrubs, mixed them together, pounded and ground some into a very thick green soup or paste. He carefully removed the blood-soaked clothes off Kofi till he lay naked. He fetched broad banana leaves, warmed them on flames in the hearth till they were tender. He lay them on the floor like mats and smeared on top of them a great deal of the green paste. He lifted Kofi who was still unconscious and placed him on the paste. At last, Kofi began to stir. The hunter poured the rest of the green mixture on him and smeared his whole body with it until he was completely smeared up. The hunter went about his "surgical operation" systematically and meticulously and wrapped up Kofi into one fine banana leaf bundle like a cocoon, leaving his face uncovered for him to breathe.

The hunter looked at what he had done and nodded with satisfaction. Suddenly, Kofi went off with an excruciating painful scream, twisting his body in reaction to the effect of the treatment he was receiving, as the concoction got into his wounds. His screams forced sleeping birds and bats into flight out of their nests and hideouts. The little hunting dog began to bark and howled into the night. The screams went on for a while and gently faded away. All was quiet. Night fell. The hunter went on to prepare some soup and chopped in some cocoyam. When the food was done, he served himself and left some for Kofi. He ate and also fed his dog, settled into a lazy chair at the entrance of the little room where Kofi lay. The little dog lay beside him to sleep. He also slowly dozed off.

Hours passed. Then, there were some movements. Kofi's pursuers were continuing their search for him, tracking him with GPS, spotting him to a location. Three of them - Kruger, Tango and Don were dressed and equipped with rifles and communication systems, though not in full gear like special SWAT squad, marines or the US troopers at war in Iraq or Afghanistan. They raced through the forest following the direction the tracking device indicated.

Kofi Nsiah stirred slowly to wake up as if he had been shaken off sleep. He realized he was tied up in a bundle. He felt choked up by the smell of the concoction he was stewing in. He coughed. This startled the hunter awake. He rushed in to see Kofi trying to struggle up, seriously frightened.

"Huh! Where am I? Who are you? What have you done to me?" Kofi burst out as the hunter entered the hut.

The hunter gently tried to restrain him; "No. No. Stay down."

"Who are you?"

"You are hurt. You need a couple of hours more in this and you will be healed. In fact, in three days, you will not see even a scratch or scar on your skin."

Kofi was thrown aback restrained himself.

"Are you hungry," the hunter asked? "I have made you some vegetable soup."

"No. No. No." Kofi protested. He immediately recollected the last few moments before he passed out. He felt he had regained his strength. "Thank you, good friend. But cut me out. I don't have the leisure to wait for the skin tone. I must be on my way right now."

The hunter knelt beside him. "Who are you? And what were you doing in the forest with all these cuts and bruises?"

Kofi tried to break the tied-up with his own strength but could not. "I am a teacher. Please, untie me."

"Oh. You came to the park?"

"Will you please cut me out?" Kofi politely screamed gently.

"Sure, sure. If you insist." The hunter pulled a knife from a pouch lying by. He began to cut the strings to release Kofi Nsiah. He loosened his arms and the upper part of his body, so slowly that it began to irritate Kofi. Kofi kept his cool and went along releasing himself at the hunter's pace.

The little dog raised its head, sniffed, rose and trotted away into the bush. It had sensed the pursuers of Kofi in the distance as they got closer.

Kofi increased the pace of the removal of the wrap on him, pulling the leaves to free himself.

"When I saw you," the hunter resumed talking, "my gun went off. I thought I had killed you, because you fell, right in front of me. I thought you were dead. When I checked, you were still alive. I decided to bring you home to heal you. Where are you from? Where are you going? What happened to you? Why all the bruises?"

"You ask too many questions. Hurry up, please!" Kofi pulled the leaves away.

The hunter's dog tracked Kruger and his party, followed them cautiously as they closed in on the hut from a distance. After a while, the dog begun to bark.

They hunter heard his dog bark in the distance. He paused and listened. Then, he also heard sounds like the cracking of pieces of wood. The little dog howled and wailed. Another cracking sound; the dog went silent. "My dog!" The hunter lamented; he was alarmed. He had reached up to Kofi's knees. He abandoned Kofi. Slowly, he rose and with his forefinger signaled that he won't be long.

"Stop! Don't go out there!" Kofi cautioned him as he peeled of the last bits of the concoction and leaves stuck on him.

"My dog. I think he is in trouble. I must find him."

"Yes, there is danger out there, where your dog may be," Kofi warned. "Please, listen to me. Get me my clothes. You and I, we must disappear from here right now. Get me my clothes!"

The hunter persisted: "My dog. It is in trouble out there. I must rescue him." The hunter exited the hut. Kofi followed him out as he continued to strip himself out from the rest of banana leaves bundle. With a piece of leaf, he held his groin.

"Please," Kofi pleaded, "listen to me. I appreciate what you have done for me. I am not well but I feel fit. What is coming is not pleasant. Let's run now before we are chased out of here. Please, come. Listen to me." The hunter looked at his face with great awe, confused and not knowing what to do or say. In the distance, Kofi Nsiah spotted flash lights of the search party. "There is serious danger out there. It won't be funny at all if you know what's coming. Please."

"Who are you?" The hunter curiously asked as he slowly and reluctantly conceded to Kofi. He cautiously retreated towards the hut. "Who are you? It seems you were being chased. Who is after you? What have you done? Are you a fugitive?" He felt frightened and kept his distance away from Kofi.

"Please, fetch me my clothes." Kofi pleaded as he held on to his groin with leaves. The hunter went past him and brought his clothes. He held the knife he had used to cut the tie on Kofi at a visible distance, indicating that should Kofi make any attempt on him he would not hesitate to drive the knife through his stomach. Kofi picked up his blood-stained clothes and began to dress up hastily. He wore them on his pasty green body.

The hunter watched him with eagle eyes. "What are you running away from? Justice?"

"My shoes!" Kofi ordered without an answer to the hunter's question. The hunter fetched Kofi's shoes and placed them in front of him. He wore a pair of sandals cut out from old lorry tyres. As he sat on the lazy chair to wear his socks, the hunter pestered Kofi with more questions. "Some people are after you. Those people have tracked you to this place. How could they know you were here?"

Kofi was amazed at the hunter's line of questioning and wondered how such a simple hunter living deep in the forest could push him with such intelligent interrogation. Before he could finish lacing his shoes and hazard any answer, bullets began to fly into the hut. The thatch roof lighted up in flames.

"Oh my God, what is this?" The hunter screamed out of fright and shock.

"Which way can we go?' Kofi inquired in hysterics.

The frightened, shocked and confused hunter pointed: "This way!" "That's where they are coming from. Which other way out here? We

need to get to the main road where I can get transport to Kumasi."

"Then, come this way! Follow me!" Without any further prompting the hunter recognized Kofi was being chased by something not pleasant; fair or foul, he needed help to get away. The hunter dashed to the back of the hut. Kofi jumped on his tail. Without care or caution they brushed through the bushes on a trail or bush path and ran as fast as they could.

Three men, holding sophisticated weapons with silenced nozzles and flash lights on top of the rifles like US marines emerged from the bushes to the precincts of the burning hut. They looked carefully around, convinced there was no one. Kruger looked on the monitor of the tracking device he held. He saw Kofi as a spot of light on it, moving. "He is moving! He is going south-east". He uttered.

"Was he here?" Tango asked.

"Yes," they saw, strewn around, the leaves and a blood-soaked under-pant of Kofi. He wore his trousers in haste without it. He did not have time to search for it.

Tango and Don took to the back of the hut and identified the track Kofi and his hunter friend took. "There is a track here. He must have passed here" Tango spoke on a communication system set fitted on the head gear that held the night vision camera.

"Let's go green!" Kruger ordered as he moved to the back of the hut to join Don and Tango. They set on their night vision lenses and followed the trail. "C'mon, let's roll".

Kofi Nsiah and his friend reached the bank of a big stream. They ran along the bank till they got to a point where it gorged a little. The area had some rocks. There was a tree that had fallen to almost halfway or a greater part across the river that was going to make crossing a little easier there. The hunter leading the way, tested the safety of it with his foot, how they could walk on it to cross. He warned Kofi to be careful as it was slippery on the tree. Kofi followed him closely as they crossed.

"There is a major road about half a mile ahead. If we can get there, we will meet those trucks that are loading foodstuffs for the market centre. One of them can send you somewhere you can find help; may be the police."

"That will be fine for me." That was good news for Kofi. All he wanted was a vehicle to move out of the area. This is Ghana, his home country. He can never get lost.

They inched their steps away slowly on the stem of the tree till they were over halfway in the stream, to the branches of the tree, almost submerged in the waters. The hunter stepped from one branch to the other as Kofi followed cautiously. He jumped from one more branch to yet another; Kofi followed same. But the next branch Kofi stepped on broke, slipping him into the water. This threw the hunter off balance. He also fell into the water. He quickly surfaced but Kofi did not. The water was breast level deep. He quickly looked around; Kofi was still nowhere. "Where are you?" He shouted.

Quickly, he dived into the water. Kofi was helplessly struggling for his life under the water with one foot stuck between two tree branches in the water. He grabbed hold of Kofi by the collar of his jacket and pulled him out, just enough so that his head could be out of the water. Kofi gasped for breath, holding on to the hunter to stay stable in the water.

"My foot. I can't move. It's stuck."

"Yes, I saw it." The hunter said as he also gasped for breath.

"I am stuck. I can barely keep my head above the water"

"Ok. You know what we're going to do? We'll take a deep breath at the count of three. Then we'll both take a duck and I'll take a good look to see how to free your foot. Alright?" The hunter suggested.

"Alright.,' Kofi agreed. "Here we go, 1…2…3!"

They both took deep breaths and ducked at the same time. The hunter reached for Kofi Nsiah's stuck foot. He tried to release it from the hold but it was too tough to pull away. They surfaced again, both panting and gasping for fresh air. The hunter asked Kofi if he was alright. He answered, yes. He asked again whether the pressure on the foot was hurting. He answered in the negative. In fact, he intimated that the pressure was on the footwear rather than his foot! The hunter thought that he could release Kofi's foot if he had a way to use a wedge to open the gap between the two logs. He asked Kofi to manage to hang on and keep himself afloat. He dived into the water again and picked a short staff. He tried to use the staff to wedge but it broke into two. He dropped the pieces and resurfaced. Kofi struggled and got hold of the hunter to keep his balance. "Look, could you hang on for just a moment while I get you something to hold on to keep your head above the water? I don't know but it will be safe when I get down there to untie your foot." He did not wait for a response from Kofi. He let go of Kofi in the water and waded out of the water to the bank to look for a stronger staff. Kofi decided to make an effort himself. He ducked into the water. He gently went for his foot. He untied his shoe lace, pulled his foot hard until it slipped out of the shoe. This threw him to the currents of the river and he was swept away. He struggled to keep afloat but he was swiftly drifted away. The hunter found a staff he thought was firm enough for the job and dashed back to the river. From behind him, the three flash lights appeared from the darkness. They saw the hunter run to the river and began to shoot at him. The bullets flew around him hitting everything including the stick he was holding. He ran towards the river. A bullet hit the hunter as he took a dive into the water. The currents carried him away.

Kruger looked at the search device. The light they were following on the device had stopped moving. "Hurry!" He ordered as they rushed to the river. "Looks like he's been hit. He is not moving. Hurry, before he drowns." Don pulled off his headgear and weapon and took a dive into the water. After a moment he surfaced.

"He's gone!" He said spewing a mouthful of water.

"What are you talking about?" Kruger impatiently reacted. "He is still there. Look again."

Don ducked again and resurfaced after a few seconds. "There's nobody." Tango took a look at the device as the light flashed but it was stationary, beeping very high. He also took off his gear and jumped into the water. The two ducked in the river together. Don surfaced. Tango came out after him with Kofi's shoe.

"Yeah. He is gone. This is the shoe I put the device in. He's left it behind." Tango said as he waded out of the water.

"Shit! How are we going to find him?" Kruger pulled out his Thuraya phone and called Abdul Ali. "Boss. We lost him again. He left the device behind…… Ok……..Ok…. We'll join you soon." Reporting to Abdul Ali, Kruger, Don and Tango retraced their way back to base.

The flow of the river brought Kofi Nsiah to a shallow area where the rapids were slow. He dragged himself out of the water, exhausted from the battering he had taken. He struggled to keep afloat and, more importantly, alive; his first time in water of that magnitude and flowing at that speed. The part of the country he hailed from was not close to big water-bodies. The closest he had come to large volumes of water was a bath-tub filled with warm fresh water for bathing. He would never forget the volumes of water he had gulped down. He thanked his stars as he got out of the water to dry ground. He turned to look at the water as the river flowed. He wondered what might have happened to the hunter who rescued him and helped him to get away. He prayed for him to escape from those heartless men chasing him. He heard the sound of vehicles passing. He lifted his head and saw a bridge over the river, just a short distance away, but too far to call any to stop. He quickly climbed the embankment and rushed through the bush about his waist high to the road side. "Ouch!" he screamed and jumped as a sharp object pierced his foot that had no footwear. He remembered he had lost his shoe to the logs in the river. He checked. He was not badly hurt. His clothes were wet and he looked scruffy as he walked in one shoe and a sock. He stood briefly by the roadside contemplating which direction to go; left or right. He had lost his bearings. The sky was overcast with clouds and it was very difficult to know his bearings or which was north so as to decide where to go. Rivers flowed south, so downstream was south. He turned to look upstream and concluded that was north, so he turned and moved right. "This will definitely take me somewhere," he said to himself as he walked briskly away, hoping he would soon get to a town or village to seek help; or better still, a vehicle would come by to save him from walking one bare footed.

The three men joined the main team; Kruger took the wheels again as Abdul Ali navigated their way. It was still dark, with morning just a few hours away. With Google map on the laptop, he directed Kruger from a minor road onto a major road. The van moved on with its bright lights beaming through the darkness. They drove on for a while; then Abdul Ali asked a question, more or less a riddle, "If you were Kofi what would you do, now that you are in your home country, Kruger?"

"I -. I'd find somewhere to hide. Yeah!" "Tango?" Abdul Ali turned to Tango. "Yeah. I'd hide," Tango too responded.

"Don? Or Jim, any of you, what would you do?"

Jim was not sure what to say: "I don't know. Well, may be. Well…"

Don cut in and said: "I'd go home. Every dog, no matter how long the night is or how far away he goes bitch chasing will get home before dawn."

They burst into laughter, making his answer sound like a useless comment. Don looked at Abdul Ali who did not laugh. They all turned to look at Abdul Ali and stopped the laughter.

"That was a clever one," Abdul Ali commended Don, to the surprise of the rest. "He will definitely go home. Let's go home: Kumasi. That's our next destination. Turn left at the next junction. This is the route to Kumasi." Kruger turned as Abdul Ali directed and followed slowly behind a timber truck loaded with heavy logs.

Kofi had walked for close to two miles in the darkness. No vehicle had come by since the last one when he was getting out of the water. Then he heard the sound of one that was very heavy. It might be a truck, he thought. He hailed the vehicle when it came by. It was a tipper-truck but carried no sand. It stopped a little bit away. The driver waited till Kofi ran up to him. He climbed by the side and spoke to the driver through the opened window. "Hello, I am trying to get to Kumasi," Kofi said, looking straight at the driver. The driver looked at him with deep suspicion. He saw through his bright curious eyes that Kofi did not know what he was talking about.

"Get down!" The driver shouted at him.

With great fright and shock, Kofi jumped down as the driver engaged the gears and tried to speed away. Kofi fell in the process. After about twenty metres or so, however, the truck stopped again. The driver honked the horn; ostensibly, he had had a change of mind. He honked again; Kofi slowly pulled himself together on to his feet. He hastened to the truck and climbed to the window again cautiously, wondering what was going to happen.

"I am sorry," the driver tried to apologize when Kofi's head popped at the window again. Obviously, he had been frightened by the sight of Kofi, looking scruffy. He feared it was an armed-robbery trick. The driver's direction was into the deep forest, coming from a major road that would take one towards Kumasi; he wondered again why Kofi should stop a vehicle that was going into the bush to ask for a lift to Kumasi. But the driver was hit by compassion as he quickly thought: how could someone be wandering in the forest asking for a lift to go to Kumasi which was about 160 kilometres away? He concluded that such a person may have lost his way; that was why he stopped again, and he was right in guessing so. "You don't seem to know these parts; you are obviously lost, aren't you?" The kind driver's statement comforted Kofi.

"Yes, I am lost. I've lost my bearing. I don't know where I am. Please help me get to some place from where I could continue to Kumasi."

"Get in." The kind driver stretched his hand to unlock the door. Kofi settled himself in the seat. The driver turned the truck around to face the opposite direction and drove on. They came across the bridge over the river. Kofi looked as the truck drove past. A quick flashback of his ordeal in the water ran through his mind. "Mankesim is just ahead." The driver's voice startled him back to consciousness. "I'll get you there. You can continue from there."

"I'd be most grateful," Kofi said as he sat with his two palms clasped and stuck between his thighs, his eyes were getting heavier, but he did not sleep. Then, he felt the truck slowing down. Kofi blinked and there, he could see lights. They had arrived.

The driver looked at Kofi critically as he turned to the lorry park at Mankesim. "I am sure you have no money on you," the driver observed, as he brought the vehicle to a stop. Kofi nodded. The driver reached into his top breast pocket of his shirt and pulled out some bills. "Here, take. This will pay your way to Kumasi. This is what I can do for you."

Kofi could not believe the gesture of this kind driver. He was so overwhelmed with emotions that he broke down in tears as the bills were stashed into his palm. "Thank you, my friend. Thank you, so much."

"Thank God. Don't worry. Don't cry. Safe journey." "God bless you. Thank you. Bye."

"Bye and good luck." Kofi jumped down from the truck and waved as the driver took off. He asked around and he was shown the bus to Kumasi. He boarded the bus which was filled with travelers of all walks of life. It was not long before the bus took off and got on its way to Kumasi. It was quite dark on the bus so no one observed him well. Most of the passengers were asleep or dozing off and his clothes had by this time dried.

Chapter Seven

GOLDEN CITY BLUES

The van carrying Abdul Ali and his men sped on the highway to Kumasi.

It was getting close to morning and the sky was getting brighter. With the aid of Google Earth and GPS systems, he navigated as Kruger drove. At a junction, the van turned left towards Obuasi, one of the few gold mining cities in Ghana. After a few more minutes of driving, they entered the city of Obuasi which was slowly waking up. The mining infrastructure showed up on the landscape and skyline. They drove through the virtually empty streets and soon got on to the highway again, driving through a typical tropical African forest zone with greenery and vegetation that ran several kilometres beyond what meets the eye. Some of the landscape showed several acres of natural forests with big and tall trees; cultivated lands with many different crops in plantations; farms with crops like cocoa, oil palm, coconut, plantain, pineapple, oranges, cassava and maize, among others. They drove past many small towns till they arrived in the city of Kumasi through a route with various landmarks: Offices of the Kumasi Metropolitan Assembly, Komfo Anokye Teaching Hospital, Kumasi University, Kumasi Central Market, Kejetia Lorry Station and the Golden Tulip Hotel.

It was already day on the highway from Mankesim to Kumasi with Kofi Nsiah on the bus. He was jolted awake as it turned towards Obuasi. The bus also drove through the city on the same route Abdul Ali and his group had taken. It was busy as the vibrant mining city had woken to a very active morning. The driver had to honk on his horn several times to warn off pedestrians and other road users. It was quiet on the bus as most of the passengers were still sleeping or just waking up as the bus made its way onto the highway out of Obuasi towards Kumasi.

After a number of turns, Abdul Ali directed Kruger to make yet another turn. They ran into a one-way lane going the opposite direction. It was a very fast lane, busy with a lot of traffic. In the confusion, with on-coming vehicles almost driving directly into them, amidst the blowing of horns, braking and screeching of tyres, Kruger swerved frantically to avoid near collisions. Then, the expected happened. He lost control of the steering and ran into a stationary sedan in a parking lot in front of a food joint. The owner of the sedan was Ohenenana, a middle-aged man, heavily built with a little pot-belly that had grown, obviously due to lack of exercise and too much food and beer. He was a popular member of the royal family of the kingdom, well known in the city for his extravagant and ostentatious lifestyle. He had come to the joint to have breakfast with a bevy of girls. Where he sat overlooked the road so he saw the crash. He screamed and rushed there to confront Kruger. His girls, in their hot pants and skimpy skirts, some with overdone make-ups, hairdos and manicure, followed him there screaming and swearing, ready to confront whoever the culprit was in support of their man, Ohenenana. Abdul Ali and Kruger immediately got down to inspect the damage.

"Who the fuck are you?" Ohenenana asked, ranting in fits of anger. "See what you've done to my car with your fucking truck. 'Know how much I paid for this bird? 'Know how much? Fifty thousand US dollars! Are you fucking blind? Or you were sleeping? Or are you high on something?"

"What a welcome! Ha ha ha!" Abdul Ali could only laugh and admire the tantrums Ohenenana was throwing.

"Sorry, Mister. Sure, this little accident should not cause a stir." Kruger tried to intervene for an amicable settlement.

Ohenenana freaked out: "Call this little accident? Do you know how much it's gonna cost me to fix?" He pulled his mobile phone and dialed a number. The girls shouted and screamed at the top of their voices, pointing their fingers in a rude and unruly manner. "Hello, Commissioner," he spoke on the phone. "This is Ohenenana. Can you send some of your boys to the joint now. Yes, the joint. Some idiot has crushed my sedan. Yes….. yes. Right away."

Abdul Ali watched the drama in utter amazement. A little crowd had begun to gather. He leaned towards Kruger and whispered into his ear. Kruger turned to Tango and Don who had also descended from the vehicle and positioned themselves at vantage points, ready to intervene should there be any mob attack on them. He whispered to them too. They slowly retreated near the van, still keeping their vigilance. Abdul Ali stepped forward to Ohenenana. "Gentleman, can I speak with you privately?" He spoke calmly to him.

"Why? What for?" asked Ohenenana in response with a very high and angry voice.

"Please, my friend?" Abdul Ali persisted, looking sternly at him.

"Eh? Ok, come with me." Ohenenana softened and moved towards Osei, the operator of the joint. "Osei, please can I use your office for just a moment?"

"Sure. With all pleasure." Osei willingly obliged and ushered them to the office.

It was not a big place; it had a desk and two chairs in front. On the desk were several receipts strewn, not properly arranged; a telephone set sat at the left corner close to the manager's chair. A metal cabinet stood beside the manager's chair with a heap of files on it. Ohenenana sat on the manager's seat while Abdul Ali sat in front of him. Kruger stood by his boss as Osei shut the door behind him.

After a short silence, Abdul Ali began to speak, "It is rather unfortunate that on my arrival into this lovely city I am getting such a welcome. I find it quite exciting. It may not be a coincidence but a true way of meeting good friends. I want my short stay here to be very fruitful and beneficial to all I come to meet. I work for an international organization affiliated to the United Nations which is involved in research and retrieval of lost artifacts and relics. I may need collaborators and people who know their way around to guide and support me while I undertake my venture. It will come with very attractive rewards dependent on how much you put in. I will need your cooperation and support on the way forward and I start with first paying for the little scratch on your bird. What I have for you is in manifolds that can afford you more than a few more up-to-date versions of 'the beast.' For now, please accept my apologies."

Abdul Ali winked to Kruger who pulled out a wad of fresh US$100 bills. desk.

"This is ten thousand dollars," Kruger said as he placed the wad on the Abdul Ali pushed the wad of notes towards Ohenenana. "Please accept my apologies," he said. "This is just the beginning; let's look forward." Abdul Ali added.

Ohenenana's eyes widened. It had been a while since he came by such an amount in dollars at a go. His hostile mood changed suddenly to a more receptive one; but he controlled his emotions and suppressed his excitement, not to give himself away. The two men looked each other in the face. Ohenenana looked at the notes in front of him again; a little smile began to form on his face as his lips stretched. He looked back at Abdul Ali and then to Osei who nodded in approval. He picked the wad of notes, stood up and slipped it in his pocket. Ohenenana stretched his hand to Abdul Ali. "It's a pleasure meeting you. We put everything behind us, do we?"

"We're square?" Abdul Ali shook hands with Ohenenana.

"Square." Ohenenana shook his hand warmly and turned to Kruger and shook hands with him too.

Osei leaned forward and joined in the handshakes.

"My name is Ohenenana. You can call me Nana. Look, whatever you want in your expedition, I am at your service. Call anytime." Ohenenana pulled out his wallet from his back pocket and fished out his business card. "My card," he said presenting one to Abdul Ali.

"I am Abdul Ali. Now, to business," Abdul Ali switched the topic, seeing he had made a good impression on Ohenenana. He recognized he was amenable to exploitation. He sought a way to bring him closer. "We just arrived. We don't know our way around. Right now, we are tired and hungry. We would need some food and a discreet place of abode."

"Of course! Of course! Consider it done. You are my guests. I shall take care of you."

Osei saw his opportunity, "My kitchen and bar are at your disposal. Shall we?" He opened the door. The four men exited laughing and backslapping to the amazement of the girls who were still shouting and screaming, and other onlookers who had gathered there.

Ohenenana raised his arms. "It's ok. It's ok, girls. The issue's been resolved."

"What!" Pommaa, the leader of the girls could not believe her ears. Nana ignored her and asked her to organize her girls back to the table for more fun. She reluctantly backed down and went to the girls. They all felt disappointed but followed her to join the men.

Osei ordered his staff to organize and get the place ready to receive their new guests. "Hei, pull these tables and chairs together. Bring more drinks. Bring food and everything that's available. The restaurant is closed to the public now for a private function. No more guests, please." He joined a few tables and ordered that all food available should be brought and served. The joint was turned into a big welcome feast for Abdul Ali and his men. Tango and the other colleagues were invited to join. The van was parked at a secure place but at a point where Tango and Don could have a good view. Jim and his crew joined the party.

Ohenenana placed a call on his mobile. "Hello, OPK. Hello. Do you hear me? OPK, eject all the guests from their rooms. The guesthouse has been booked from now. No new guests. Throw everybody else out. Clean up the place very well. I have some special visitors from abroad coming there right now. Do you hear?" Ohenenana hung up and shook his head in excitement. It had just dawned on him that his luck was about to shine. He wondered: to be paid ten thousand dollars for no more than just a scratch on his sedan! That meant that there was more to come, in fact, the best. His demeanour changed. Pommaa had been watching him from the corner of her eye. She joined him when he went in to fill his plate with food.

"Nana, what is going on?" Pommaa inquired with high curiosity.

"What is going on? I think my pay day has come early." Ohenenana

responded and walked away, humming to the music from the loud speakers and swinging his head to the tempo of the beat.

The taxi cab entered the campus of Kumasi University of Science and Technology. It stopped in front of one of the staff bungalows. Kofi Nsiah dropped off. He waited for the taxi to get out of sight. He looked round to make sure no one was watching him and then lifted a flower pot standing by the door to fetch a key to the house. He entered the house. He went round to check all the doors and windows. Satisfied that everything was in place, though he left the house some twelve days ago, he went to the bath room, took off his clothes and took a long, warm shower, shaved his beard and moustache he had allowed to grow since he undertook the trip. He checked the fridge; there were fresh foodstuff. He prepared himself a quick meal, settled down, ate and retired into his favourite chair to relax with a glass of fruit juice. He tried to recall what he had gone through in the last few days. No sooner had he touched the seat than he fell fast asleep.

"I have enough ladies for you for as long as you will stay," Ohenenana said as he beckoned Pommaa to come closer to him. "This is Pommaa, my right hand woman. She'll organized all of them for you. Just make your choice."

"Hello, Pommaa," Abdul Ali shook her hand but turned to Ohenenana. "Not yet, good friend. We shall have time for that later. Right now, we need to settle down and commence work without delay. Could you take us home."

"Of course, of course! Ready, whenever you are."

Abdul Ali signaled to Kruger. They wound down their feast and got into their vehicles. Ohenenana led his guests in his sedan with only Pommaa by him, leaving the rest of the girls behind. They drove to the guest house. Ohenenana showed Abdul Ali around. The visitors liked the place. He ordered his men to off-load and set up.

With lightning speed, the team off-loaded the boxes and chests, chose one of the rooms and set it up as the operations room. Several pieces of electronics equipment were installed; one could not believe they had carried them along with them in those containers. Jim and his air crew served as the technical and communication controllers, supervised the installation and took charge of the base equipment to serve as the control base. The whole operation was to be controlled from there. Don and Tango fixed a closed-circuit system with wireless cameras around the compound. A long telescopic pole with a small dish attached was installed outside. They switched on the system and tested it. They were satisfied.

Abdul Ali, followed by Ohenenana and Pommaa, entered the control room. "How are we doing?" Abdul Ali asked.

"We have eyes all round," Jim replied. "The satellite system will be up and running soon. In half an hour, you can reach the whole world from here."

"Good." Abdul Ali affirmed his satisfaction. He turned to Ohenenana: "Now, we will take a short rest. We shall alert you our next line of action in due course."

"I leave you now," Ohenenana said, took a hand shake from Abdul Ali and left with Pommaa tailing behind him. From the control room, they watched him on the closed circuit system till he exited the vicinity.

Kruger entered with a metallic briefcase which was the 'command controlled unit' (CCU) and laid it on the desk. That served as a console.

Abdul Ali opened it. It had an interface with the setup. He pulled out a cable and plugged it into the system laid up by Jim and his crew. He turned on a few switches on the CCU and the whole satellite system came alive; screens and monitors showed images of various sites and location in other continents and cities. He scoped and lined up the coordinates and zoomed in to Kumasi on one of the screens. A flashing light appeared on one of the screens accompanied by a beeping sound. "Bingo! We are in business." Jim and his crew cheered and slapped their palms. Abdul Ali was happy, "Well done, guys. We all take a break and reconvene when the sun goes down." They all concurred and deserted the operations room, leaving Kruger and Don behind.

Ohenenana drove through town with Pommaa by him in his sedan. He touched his pocket into which he had slipped the bundle of dollars. He pulled it out and threw it to Pommaa. Her eyes widened.

"Is that what you charged them for the rent of the guest house?" She inquired from Ohenenana.

"No," he replied. "That was for the scratch on the car."

"Eh! For just the scratch? Then they came with a lot of dough."

"I am perching. Whatever they came to do, I will make sure there is nothing that they will do without passing it through me. No transaction goes on without me. Every cash must be paid through me. No one gets to them without passing through me. By the time they leave I should be richer with half of the dough they have brought."

"I can trust you, Nana. Wo yɛ guy! (You're the man!) I believe you." "He does not know me."

"Nana, I am with you all the way. What will be my share if I play along?"

"I'll make sure of that."

"I'll always love you." She jumped to him at the steering wheel. That made Ohenenana lose control of the car momentarily, missing a collision with an on-coming vehicle. He brought the car back under control and sped away into the late afternoon traffic.

It was late in the evening when Abdul Ali and his men reassembled back at the control room. He issued out instructions to each one of them, spelling out their responsibilities in the special operation. "I did not expect we were going to get things done so easily and smoothly. But we must all do our best, stretching beyond normal limits to get everything done. We've identified the object which is about a mile or two from here. We shall go to the city to search for a possible access to it. Jim, you and your crew will, as usual, be in charge of communication systems at the base. Kruger, Don and Tango, you'll join me to do some reconnaissance now." Abdul Ali and his team moved out as Jim and his co-pilot got busy. They tested their communication system to make sure they could talk to each other without hindrance. The van carrying Abdul Ali and his team drove through the city of Kumasi. A revolving antennae with a small satellite dish was fixed on top of the van. Abdul Ali sat in the first passenger seat as usual with an electronic device searching. A red light flashed with a beep, tracking on an LCD screen with some images. They entered the Central Business District. The streets were empty. The van moved slowly, made a left turn at the street corner and made yet another turn at the next corner and stopped. Abdul Ali pressed and skewed a knob. The image expanded on the screen, zooming in to enhance the image.

"Move ahead," Abdul Ali instructed Kruger who drove the vehicle. "Turn right at the next junction and stop there."

Kruger pulled off the road to the side and parked with the engine still running and turned out the head lights. The image became clearer and revealed a realtime image of the specific spot of the city area as it appeared on google earth. The images zoomed in again to seismic level. A bright object appeared. "That is it," Abdul Ali said. "Yes. This is it. But it is underneath the next building approximately two hundred metres below. We need to find the access to it. It seems like it is in a cave. Or a tomb?

"Cave? How do we get to it?" Kruger asked.

"No entrance is indicated. The only way then is digging our way to it."

"Tunnel?" Kruger demanded.

"Yes, a tunnel," Abdul Ali confirmed. "The building on the left here is sitting right on top of it. This house will not be suitable. Looking at the size, we can't have access through it. We must approach it from a gradient. The possible choice is perhaps through here. This house. It looks smaller. We need to bring in drilling equipment, pronto. The project will be delayed a few days. Let's get back to the guest house to assess the situation to quickly draw out the logistics we shall require and from where, quickest."

Kruger turned on the headlights, but before he could press the accelerator for the van to get into motion, lights and flood lights and the police emergency red and blue flash lights mounted on several police patrol vehicles were turned on simultaneously, blinding and trapping them in the centre. There were also several men and women with weapons aimed at them standing at points ready to shoot at the signal of the commander. The team broke into a panic.

"Wow, wow, wow!" Tango exclaimed.

"Fuck, shit!" coughed Don.

Kruger wailed, "What the hell?"

"I'll be damned," swore an astounded Abdul Ali.

The commander of the police squad spoke on mounted speakers on the police car. "This is the City Police. You are surrounded. For your own safety, slowly come out of the vehicle with your hands over your head where I can see them."

Abdul Ali and his team were shocked and perplexed. Don reached for his sub machine gun: "We've been double-crossed."

"By whom," Tango demanded

"Our host, that Nana, I'm sure," replied Don. "Seriously."

"I'll squeeze the shit out of him." Don muttered angrily.

"Everybody, stay calm. I'll handle the situation," Abdul Ali warned his men as he opened his door. He handed over the scanner device he held to Kruger and dropped out of the van with his hands raised over his head. There were cracks of the cocking of rifles. He looked around 360 degrees. They had been surrounded by police vehicles and men in arms.

The Commander bellowed: "All occupants of the vehicle, come out now, slowly and gently!"

Abdul Ali shouted: "We are not armed."

The Commander ignored him and sounded again. "This is your last warning. All occupants must come out of the van now with your hands up in the air where I can see them."

Abdul Ali gave a signal to his men to come over and join him where he was. They responded one after the other. Kruger shut the engine, turned off the light and came out of the van. Don concealed his weapon by wrapping it in his jacket on the seat and joined his colleagues out of the van. About eight armed men in full police riot gear, wielding weapons, ran in and surrounded them and escorted them away from the van. A towing team drove in, jerked the van and towed it away. Abdul Ali and his men were forced into other vehicles and whisked away in a police vehicular convoy with motorcade.

Abdul Ali and his men were jostled and hustled into an office at the Regional Police Headquarters. They were seated behind a broad table in an interrogation room. The commander and two other men entered the room.

"Erm, Mr.?" the commander inquired. "Ali, Abdul Ali."

"Yes, Mr. Ali," the Commander continued. "This is my jurisdiction. Where you were arrested was a restricted area, not permitted for loitering at that time of the night. My conclusion is that your presence there was for something very suspicious and clandestine. Men of your kind have been arrested there before for their involvement of mercenary and other nefarious activities."

"We are not mercenaries. We are researchers, archaeologists, archivists." "Your coming has not been communicated to me by National Security. Besides, you have no indigene as your escort, how could I trust you. You are going to be kept here till morning when we shall call in the forensics to investigate your vehicle and all the accoutrements and gadgetry after which I shall take a decision about your fate. Surrender all your travel documents

now. Bring out all phones and all other communication gadgets."

Abdul Ali felt devastated by the commander's statement. His accomplices were overly beside themselves. Don felt he could take them on and single- handedly deal with the entire platoon that came to arrest them. He fidgeted and wished he had his weapon with him.

"Well, Officer," Abdul Ali attempted some explanation. "We are from the International Organization for the Research, Discovery, Retrieval and Restoration of World Heritage Properties, an affiliate of UNESCO. We are here on official business to enable us track objects and relics of archival relevance to our research and excavation. We chose this time because this is when there is less vehicular traffic and human movement."

"Do you have any documentation to attest to your accession?" The commander demanded. "Show me and I'll let you go. Without that, I am sorry, there is very little I can do now. We will wait till tomorrow." Thus saying, he turned away from them. "Detain them!" he ordered.

"Hold!" a voice broke out from behind them before they could continue.

Ohenenana appeared.

"Huh? Ohenenana." The Commander exclaimed on seeing him. Abdul Ali and his men were also surprised to see him, but Don was still skeptical of him.

Ohenenana spoke to the Police Commander with an authoritative voice: "These men are my guests. They are here on the bidding of the Monarch, His Royal Highness, the King and the ruler of *Asanteman*. Your authority to detain them is revoked. Release them at once."

"Shall we confirm it from the Palace, Ohenenana?"

Ohenenana took great objection to the comment from the Commander and flared up. "You are insulting me and for that matter

His Royal Highness. You want to wake him up at such an ungodly hour? By the authority of His Majesty, the King, I order you to release these men at once. You are, therefore, summoned to appear before His Royal Majesty tomorrow at 11.00 am. Failing this I shall personally see to it that you are transferred from this city and the kingdom."

The Commander realized his error, buckled under the pressure from Ohenenana and profusely apologized.

"My apologies. I oblige to your royalty." He ordered his men, "Release them! Quickly! Release their vehicle too!"

Abdul Ali and his men were astonished by Ohenenana's eloquent intervention. "Thank you, Commander. His Majesty appreciates your cooperation. You will receive the commendation of the monarchy promptly. Let's go, gentlemen."

They hurried, following him out of the police station. The commander supervised for the release of the van.

Ohenenana joined them in the van. "I saw your distress SMS and knew something wrong had happened," Ohenenana commented as they drove out of the precinct of the police headquarters.

Abdul Ali confirmed that on their way to the Police Headquarters, he managed to send a text message to Ohenenana's number. The message was very simple: "Police arrest" and he knew where to go. He felt that if they were arrested by any divisional command he would need help from the regional headquarters to get the subordinate division to succumb. But as it turned out, headquarters was the ones holding them. Dropping names was the easiest of Ohenenana's strategies of getting round people and things; and, that was a classic example and situation.

"Thank you, my friend." Abdul Ali expressed. "I really appreciate your timely intervention."

When they arrived back at the guest house Ohenenana was led to the operations room which had been completed. There were setups of equipment, computers and monitors; there was also a 3D seismic image of rock formation shown on a screen. He was very impressed.

"You came with all these?"

Abdul Ali nodded.

"Wow! You are a very serious guy."

Abdul Ali took Ohenenana through a process of identification of objects detected beneath the earth surface. He was cautious what details he had to give out and did not mention the Golden Stool at that time. "This is the earth. Zoom to Africa, 6 Degrees 41 Minutes North and 1 Degree 37 Minutes West to Kumasi. This is the city. Zoom in further." The geological structure of the earth beneath appeared. Ohenenana watched and listened with keen interest. He drew closer and leaned forward to look at some details on one of the monitors. In the process he left his mobile phone on the desk as he pointed at the screen, asking Abdul Ali for further explanation on what he was saying.

Tango picked up the phone, quickly dismantled it and took out the sim card. He inserted the sim card in a device, turned it on for ten seconds, removed and placed the sim card back into the phone and put it back where he took it from. He typed some information on one of the computers and pressed enter. By that, the details of Ohenenana's phone were lodged in Abdul Ali's GPS tracking system; anytime, and as long as the phone was turned on, Ohenenana could be traced to anywhere he would go.

Ohenenana followed Abdul Ali as he took him through a few details. There were several flashes of light on one of the screens in different colours. "The lights indicate the presence of precious metal or objects," Abdul Ali illustrated. "I am not interested in any of these." He probed through the flashing lights. There was one which appeared stable. He zoomed in to it. The light glowed bigger. "Yes, this is it. Now let's reverse the vision. This will reveal the location." The vision zoomed out again to the earth surface and took an aerial view to reveal an area in Kumasi. "This is where we are" he continued, pointing to the screen. "But this is where what we are looking for is. This is where the police came to meet us. What we are looking for is buried under here and we are going to get it."

"How are you going to do that?" Ohenenana inquired. "We'll see that in the morning," was his simple answer.

"Alright, we wait to see," Ohenenana said as he took Abdul Ali's hand. After the handshake, he spotted his phone and picked it up. He realized it was off. He turned it on and, suddenly, there was an instant notification on the computer Tango was on, indicating the bugging process had been effected. Tango smiled. Ohenenana slid the phone into his pocket and left.

Chapter Eight

WORK FOR THE IDLE HANDS

The day broke to a fresh morning. There had been a little drizzle hours before. The lawns and the flowers looked very fresh. Kruger was out in the front of the house. He had taken a walk round the house to make sure everything was in good order. He had met Ohenenana who had arrived to set up another breakfast feast in the garden of the guest house. Pommaa and her bevy of beautiful girls had also assembled in their resplendence, assisting in the setting up. Tango and Don were still sleeping in one of the bedrooms, each with his weapon in hand. Jim and his crew also had spent the rest of the night in one of the bedrooms. They had woken up and were getting themselves ready for the day. Abdul Ali had not had a wink since they returned from the night after the scouting and the encounter with the police. His conclusion from the surveys and probes he had done in pursuit of access to the Golden Stool was that: his systems had detected the Golden Stool as it lay in the belly of the earth, below the city; no known access had been detected. The option available to him was to dig his own way to the stool. How? He had spent the night speaking to the whole world searching for solutions. His contacts had located almost all his needs closer to him than he had imagined.

They were all in Ghana. Some of the multi-national mining companies were associates and affiliates of his cartel and network of collaborators. They had confirmed to him that one of the mining firms was going to supply him a power generator. Another was going to supply him a team of security personnel. There was going to be a team of geologists and engineers. The last communication he had was with one of his agents who was still searching for one and the most important special piece of machinery that was going to do the digging. In the meantime, he had settled for some excavators to start the digging. He was satisfied but felt very tired. Jim entered the ops room; that was good signal for him to also take a break. Jim took over from him. He rose and headed for the bedroom reserved for him, undressed and took a refreshing cool shower. He changed clothes and came out to the compound. There were a couple of Ohenenana's friends there. Ohenenana introduced them to Abdul Ali. In the background, Kruger had gone to awaken the sleeping duo and sent them out to escort Abdul Ali and provide him security as he mingled with his guests. Abdul Ali was not comfortable with so many people around his operational centre. He had preferred a quiet, discreet ambience without the noise and the crowd with its associated distractions. But there he was, his benevolent host who had saved his almost scuttled operation, seriously running the show.

The Police Commander arrived. Abdul Ali and Ohenenana received him warmly. He was invited to join the breakfast. Ohenenana picked his mobile phone and dialed a number. He walked away from the crowd and the noise. "Chairman. Hello, Chairman. I have some very important guests and need wheels. Don't worry about the cost. Two executive status. Unmarked. Now. Yes, deliver now to my guest house at Nhyiaeso. Good. Owusu and Agyei, are they available? I need them. Let them deliver the vehicles." Satisfied, he returned to join the feast.

Kofi turned on his bed. He opened his eyes and noticed his surroundings. For a moment he wondered where he was. He sat up quickly and looked around. Then the recollection came to him and he recognized where he was, in his bungalow at the Kumasi University: the harrowing experiences that he had gone through in the last few days, those who had died associating with him or trying to help him. The most painful deaths were those of Saah, Coy and Lt. Croffy. Then he started recounting in his mind what he had gone through from their escape from the Ivorian airforce, the crash landing at *Nzulezu*, his escape from Abdul Ali and then the hunter who saved him to his wonderful swimming he had in the river, not forgetting the amount of water he had gulped and his final arrival home. It sounded quite unbelievable to him but it was true that he had gone through all those. He sighed heavily. He looked around again, got up to the window and surveyed the immediate surrounding of his home to make sure no one had noticed him enter or followed him home.

He did not also notice any one around the house to indicate he was being watched or tailed. He concluded: perhaps his adversaries may have abandoned their expedition. He shrugged. What do I care; he thought and dismissed the thought. But he remembered one thing, Abdul Ali had always tracked him and found him whenever he got away from him. He became alarmed. He rushed to where the clothes he wore home were. He grabbed them and ran a quick search through them and the half pair of shoe. He went through them again and again to convince himself there was no bugging device in them. He sat down on the floor holding the clothes to his chest. He looked up and sighed. Tears started running down his cheeks.

Somewhere in the city, the doors of a garage opened. Two Sport Utility Vehicles (SUVs) of high specifications drove out. They took a route along some important landmarks in Kumasi and soon they arrived at the guest house. On seeing them Ohenenana called the attention of Abdul Ali and pointed to the vehicles, "I've got legs for you so you can be mobile all the time; discreet and unsuspecting."

"Impressive. Good." Abdul Ali acknowledged, surprised though he was, but very appreciative. He beckoned Kruger closer and whispered to him, pointing at the vehicles. Kruger called Don and together they received the vehicles. They took them out of the view of the guests and swept them with scanners and anti buggers. They frisked the drivers as well and certified that they were all clean.

Ohenenana and Abdul Ali joined them. He introduced the drivers. "Here are my two dedicated security drivers. They are professional, experienced and very reliable. You are safe with them. They will take you wherever you have to go. They know every part of this city and how to get there and out quickest."

With a pump of hands, Abdul Ali welcomed the drivers. Ohenenana then dragged him into the guest house. The Police Commander was called and escorted to a room.

The movements of the men attracted the attention of Pommaa who watched them from a distance. She walked away from the girls she was chatting with. She followed them and entered a washroom next to the room Ohenenana and his guests had entered and eavesdropped on them.

The Police Commander was made to sit and wait. Soon, Ohenenana and Abdul Ali came in followed by Kruger with a briefcase in hand.

"Well, Chief," Ohenenana addressed him. "We called you here to express our gratitude for the way you handled the little incident last night. We'd like to bring you into the picture of what is going on so that we can cooperate while His Majesty's guests are here to undertake a special operation. His Majesty requests a discreet, smooth operation without any hindrance or interference. Your full cooperation from now on will be tremendously appreciated and very rewarding to your very self. In the meantime, here you are. A small token of gratitude."

Ohenenana handed him a small briefcase. The Commander flipped it open. The briefcase was full of one hundred-dollar bills to the brim. The commander was visibly mesmerized and almost fainted at the sight. Ohenenana was also taken aback seeing the amount of money in the briefcase. The Commander trembled and stuttered. "T –

T -Thank you. Thank you. You can always c – c- count on my absolute co - co -cooperation." He shut the briefcase and exited the room. From the cctv the Commader was seen walking briskly away through the crowd, he did not look back till he disappeared.

Ohenenana turned to confront Abdul Ali over the money. He complained that the amount was too much for one person and particularly, that commander in that instance. Abdul Ali answered simply:"Well, in Africa, money talks; money buys everything." Ohenenana looked sternly at him to establish his displeasure at the statement as an indictment on himself. Abdul Ali recognized Ohenenana's displeasure and immediately rephrased his statement: "To whom much is given, much is expected. There is a lot he will be doing for us and we need to keep him happy from now."

"What about me?" Ohenenana lamented.

"Come," Abdul Ali pulled him along. "You and I are in this together," he said as they walked to the ops room. "Whatever we are going to do here is under your control and command. You will run the show." They entered the ops room. All the men were assembled there.

Pommaa tiptoed out of the washroom, following them as they entered the ops room. She tried to listen from the door.

"So, everything here is yours. Take it." Abdul Ali continued. He signaled Kruger who pulled up another briefcase and brought it to him. He in turn flipped it open and presented it to Ohenenana.

Ohenenana's eyes glowed at the sight of the cash. "Wow!" "So long as you will take me to what I came here for." "And, that is?"

"The Stool." "Which Stool?" "The Golden Stool."

For a moment, Ohenenana could not get the import of the statement. As he stretched his hand for the case, he was hit by the mention of the Golden Stool. "Eh! The Golden Stool?" He asked.

"Yes!" Abdul Ali responded. "Your Golden Stool. The Si-ka D-wa." "What? *Sika Dwa* Kofi?.....Why?" Ohenenana asked with shock and

great surprise.

"Why?"

"Yes, why! Is that what you came here for? Is it?... Why?"

"Whatever it stands for; to you, your people and the monarchy." Abdul Ali arrogantly uttered.

Several thoughts ran through Ohenenana's mind. He could not bring himself to reconcile with the demand Abdul Ali had made on him. For a while he was speechless. He looked at the briefcase, looked at Abdul Ali and back to the briefcase again. He shook his head. "So, what is this for?" he burst out, angrily pushed away the briefcase, spilling the cash on the floor as it crashed.

"This is for you alone. There is more for you and enough to go round everybody including your monarch."

"You can't be serious." Ohenenana rebuffed. "What do you take me for? You want to buy me off. Me, Ohenenana; a royal of the state, son of the court of His Royal Majesty, you want me to sell my conscience to you for pittance so you can gain access to the Golden Stool, the soul of my Kingdom? How insulting can you be? I don't blame you. I have encouraged this foolishness and I am stopping it now. I am walking out of here. By the time I return, you and your cabal would have vacated my property or you leave me with no alternative than to throw you out myself."

Don reached for his revolver in his pocket. Kruger grabbed his arm to restrain him.

Pommaa dashed away and ducked behind a sofa when the knob to open door was turned as Ohenenana stormed out. The party outside was going on. He walked through to his sedan and drove off.

Don, quite upset with the situation burst out his emotions. "What do we do, boss?" he asked.

"Let him go," replied Abdul Ali calmly. "Let him go?"

"Yes, let him go."

"What if he brings the police or the natives to attack us?" Tango joined the inquest.

"We will fight them." Kruger replied

"It will not have to come to that." Abdul Ali reassured them. He seemed to have figured everything out. "He won't do that. What will be our crime: that, we are inducing some influential people in the community with money to help us gain access to information on the legendary Golden Stool? Huh?

The most important thing is that I have located the Golden Stool. If they don't show me the entrance to the tomb, I'll have to make my own way to reach it by the shortest possible means. Relax. Go out enjoy the party as much as you can, with your eyes and ears wide open, though. Soon we shall be very busy. I'll make some contacts now. I need more muscles to flex."

Pommaa felt it was time to exit from her hiding corner as no one was in sight. But just as she pulled out of the corner Don appeared from the ops room. He eyed her with great suspicion. She pretended she was up to nothing and was just walking away. He followed her and grabbed her by the hand. "What were you doing there?" he queried her.

"Why do you have to ask me that?" she braved herself out and struggled to free herself from Don's grip.

"You were supposed to be with the other girls. Why are you here?"

"I can be anywhere I like, anytime. What is your problem? Leave me alone!"

As Pommaa struggled with Don, there sounded Police sirens. He paused and looked. A contingent of armed squadron led by the Commander arrived in a convoy. He gave orders for his men to surround the precinct of the house. Don released his grip on her and rushed back to the ops room where Abdul Ali was. "Boss. Boss. Police. Armed policemen led by the Commander. We've been double crossed."

Pommaa looked round and realized Ohenenana was not around nor was his car. She could not make sense of what the armed police were coming to do. She dashed away, out of the guest house as the police deployed and took positions. She stopped a taxi and asked the driver to get her out of there as quickly as he could. The taxi driver complied and sped away.

The music had stopped and all was quiet and tensed. Pommaa's girls and the other guests watched the police wondering what had gone wrong. The Commander walked briskly across to the ops room. Abdul Ali and his men could see him on the CCTV. There was panic. Tango, Krugger and Don scrambled for weapons ready to attack. Jim and the air crew also picked their weapons.

"Stand down. Calm down! Let's hear what they want. Put the weapons away." Abdul Ali instructed his men and moved to meet him. He opened the door and there stood the Commander. "Commander, is anything the matter?" Abdul Ali asked as he forced a smile.

Curiously, the commander was beaming with smiles and excitement. "I can imagine the importance of your project," he said. "I am here to offer you my full support and protection till your mission is accomplished."

"Really, I did not expect it so soon. I am grateful," Abdul Ali said with great relief. He was more surprised than relieved as he hugged the commander. Kruger and his colleagues relaxed inside and quickly concealed their weapons. Abdul Ali dragged him into the room. The Commander looked round and noticed that Ohenenana was conspicuously absent. He enquired about his whereabouts. Abdul Ali told him that Ohenenana had had to step out for a while.

Pommaa's taxi sped on. She put out a call to Ohenenana who was also struggling through heavy traffic in the centre of the city honking in desperation and speeding.

"Nana, Nana, where are you? Where are you?" Pommaa asked frantically as Ohenenana picked the call.

"That guy is a rogue. He must be stopped." Ohenenana replied. "There are armed policemen all over the guest house. What have you done?"

"What? I have not called any police."

"They are all over the guest house. The Commander brought them in himself."

"Good. He should take over the place and arrest them. I am on my way to Manhyia. I am also reporting him to Otumfoɔ. How utterly pig-headed can he get?"

"What? Manhyia? Have you gone out of your mind? Have you forgotten what they did to you when you went there the last time? What are you going there for?"

"I have to stop him before he causes any damage."

Pommaa tried to persuade him not to go to Manhyia but as adamant as he was, Ohenenana refused to listen to her and insisted on going, damn the consequences. He lost concentration and almost crashed into another car. The phone dropped out of his hand and slipped below the foot paddles beyond his reach as he tried to bring the car under control.

"Nana. Nana." Pommaa called but there was no response. She ordered the driver to take her to Manhyia.

Ohenenana meandered through the heavy traffic at high speed to Manhyia. He came to a screeching stop. He descended and made his way towards a section of the palace complex, the ceremonial grounds. It was a large courtyard, with half of it roofed, where Otumfoɔ would sit in court on a raised platform with his linguists, chiefs and courtiers arranged beside him, left and right. It was used for ceremonies like durbars for visiting dignitaries, swearing ceremonies for his paramount chiefs, among others. On this occasion, Otumfoɔ was sitting in court over some litigation of some sort; a common feature of the king's palace. Over his head was a smaller black umbrella. He was casually dressed in black cloth and wore no headgear and no ceremonial expressive decoration of ornaments, except a leather amulet on his right wrist. All appearing before him were also dressed in simple black clothing. The court was in session with litigants before Otumfoɔ. Nana Kyerewaa and some of her family members were there waiting for their turn before the King. There were also observers or those whom one would call spectators who had come to watch the proceedings, and other litigants awaiting their turn for Otumfoɔ's counsel.

There were also journalists and tourists who had come to experience the rich culture of *Asanteman* and their king. One of the courtiers (*nhenkwaa*) of the palace spotted Ohenenana outside as he approached the palace. The *ahenkwaa* ran into the court and whispered to one of the linguists. The linguist also whispered to one chief and another chief to the other and to the Adumhene. They turned one after the other to look at the entrance in anticipation of the entry of Ohenenana. Otumfoɔ also turned to look in the direction of those who turned. The figure of Ohenenana caught his eyes. The proceedings came to an abrupt halt. The set up was thrown into confusion with some of them murmuring at the sight of Ohenenana.

Pommaa's taxi arrived. She also headed for the court.

Adumhene rose to his feet and pointed his forefinger at Ohenenana as he approached and ordered him, "Ohenenana! Stop wherever you are! What are you doing here? Have you forgotten you are banished from this court and Otumfoɔ's Palace. Turn round and leave. Any step you take forward is a direct challenge to His Majesty, an assault on his throne and to his personal security; that is tantamount to an insurrection against his crown and the *Sika Dwa* Kofi (Golden Stool). It is treason! You are a traitor! You are not welcome here. For your own safety and freedom, turn back and leave at your own will and no one will harm or impede you."

Ohenenana attempted to make a statement.

"Do not force me to invoke Otumfoɔ's *ntamkɛseɛ,* the great oath of this kingship on you." Adumhene warned.

Ohenenana stopped where he was and responded to Adumhene in a remorseful tone: "Nana Adumhene, Otumfoɔ Akyeame, I know the consequence of my presence here and I plead with you to give me ear. I come in peace. I need to speak to Otumfoɔ on a very delicate matter."

Akyempemhene quickly rose to his feet and shouted him down. "What effrontery! You should have been executed the minute you entered here. Do you know that? Have you forgotten what happened the last time you were here? Well, then let me remind..."

I remember vividly," Ohenenana responded, "and you don't need to remind me. But please listen to me. The exigencies of the time and the magnitude of what is at stake is what has compelled me to contravene the banishment placed on me. When the rat is seen racing in broad daylight, it means there is something chasing it. I am here because I have news that the Golden Stool is under serious threat. I risk my life here to report to the occupant of the Golden Stool. As I speak to you, at this very minute, a group of men have gathered to…"

"Shut up! Otumfoɔ won't listen to you." Akyempemhene shouted him down. "All you are doing is just a lame attempt to worm your way back into Otumfoɔ's favour and magnanimity."

Apagyahene rose to his feet and intervened on behalf of Ohenenana. "Otumfoɔ, I show no disrespect to your Majesty and the oaths of *Asanteman*. Please, give him ear; or allow some of us to meet him and assess whatever it is that he has brought to your feet to see if it is of any value at all. The viper is a poisonous snake, very shy of humans but when you see it running towards you it means it is being pursued by a predator. I am sure he is very much aware of the consequences of the action that he has taken by venturing into your court from which he has been banished ..."

"Nana Apagyahene, you are out of order," Akyempemhene cut in. "A traitor is a traitor, whether he comes with good news or not. Otumfoɔin his good wisdom banished him for his treacherous acts against the state. And now you want us to receive him with open arms? So long as he is under Otumfoɔ's banishment and has not received any reprieve, he is forbidden to enter here. The leopard never loses its spots." He turned to Ohenenana, "You are a traitor! You have been banished from here. Your presence in and around the Manhyia Palace or near Otumfoɔ is considered as an act of aggression and threat to the throne and the *Sika Dwa*. You do not deserve any audience with Otumfoɔ. Otumfoɔ, with your permission: Adumhene, monkyere no dedua." (Adumhene, arrest him for contempt, immediately.)

Adumhene ordered his arrest, "Abrafoɔ, monkyere no dedua! (Guards, arrest him for contempt!")

Pommaa had meandered her way through the thick crowd on to the scene just in time to hear part of the encounter and the order. Ohenenana recognized then that he had made a mistake going there though his intention was for a good purpose. He attempted to flee. The abrafoɔ, palace guards, surrounded him. They closed in on him. He punched the first to grab him and attempted to fight his way out. He grabbed the next man who approached him and hurled him at a group of men who were coming at him. Seeing the confrontation was getting out of hand the king rose. His handlers quickly whisked him away through an alternative passage back to the main palace.

The assembly was thrown into a state of pandemonium with the chiefs, linguists and others running helter-skelter. Ohenenana's fruitless effort was soon overpowered by the numbers of abrafoɔ who joined in the scuffle. They seized him, tore his clothes and stripped him almost naked and tied him in a typical *sepɔ* fashion with sticks and ropes. Ohenenana was carried away.

Pommaa, petrified, fled from the scene and stopped a taxi outside the palace. She sat in it, panting and weeping, and directed the driver to the Nhyiaeso guest house. The driver focused his driving mirror on her, wondering why she was weeping. When she arrived she ran to the guest house gate. She was very desperate and anxious. She was stopped at the entrance to the compound by armed policemen posted as security men when she tried to enter.

"Yes, what can I do for you?" The police officer on duty asked her.

"The Commander, where is he?" She demanded.

"He has left already." the officer replied.

"We are on guard duty here under strict instruction not to allow anyone in. Anything the matter?"

"Yes, the white people, where are they?"

"They are in there."

"Are they?" she asked, baffled, hearing they were still around.

"Yes."

"Can I see them, the white people."

The police man looked at her and shook his head.

"Oh, I am with them. I just left here a little while ago." She pleaded desperately.

The police officer looked at her with some scorn but allowed her to enter. She looked round; the compound was deserted. The funfare that was going on when the police arrived had disappeared. The men, the women, the food and music were all gone, except the two SUVs which were parked in the compound with the drivers seated at the wheels. She rushed into the building. Abdul Ali and his men were in a meeting. Pommaa rushed in.

Don rushed to her. "What do you want here again?" he asked. Pommaa ignored him and addressed Abdul Ali directly, "Excuse me, sir. There is a situation. Nana has been arrested."

"By whom and what for?" asked Abdul Ali.

"The King, at the palace," replied Pommaa, almost in tears. "I followed him when he left here. I got to the scene just in time to see him being arrested. I did not hear or see exactly what he did. There was nowhere else I could go. I thought I could find the Police Commander here. Maybe he could help him. I know where he is and how to get you to him."

"And what do you think we can do under this circumstance?"

"Please, help him; they could kill him," she said as she broke down in tears.

Abdul Ali sat up looking at her. He threw the issue to his compatriots

whether they should follow up to rescue Ohenenana as Pommaa had pleaded for their intervention. The response was not favourable.

Don dismissed it: "Wait, wait, wait. What has this got to do with us." "This smacks of blackmail, pure and simple." Tango rubbished it.

"We came here on a treasure hunt and not to rescue kidnapped adults," added Don.

But Kruger went in favour of it, "Well, Nana has been good to us. He's been a good host so far. If he is in trouble, we must go to his rescue."

"You were here when he turned us down and stormed out on us. Who knows what he is up to? Who knows what's got him into that trouble for which we must rescue him?" Tango vehemently challenged Kruger. "We don't need to get ourselves embroiled in a local feud to distract us off our main objective and mission here."

"One good turn deserves another." That was a good endorsement from Kruger.

"Prepare for the rescue," Abdul Ali vetoed. Pommaa was relieved as the men accepted to rescue Ohenenana. She looked round quickly and saw the set up. She tried to configure in her mind what the purpose was for. She looked at one monitor showing images of the CCTV. She saw visuals of the immediate surroundings of the guest house. She wondered. They asked her to wait in the living room as they prepared for the rescue.

Evening fell. Ohenenana sat at a corner of a small cubicle he was being held in. His torn clothes had been bundled and placed beside him. He dozed off. He heard his phone ringing within the folded clothes but he could not reach it. Then he heard footsteps. The steel gate to the cubicle squeaked open. A group of abrafoɔ dressed in traditional camouflage apparels with black painted faces to disguise themselves, stood at the door. They were led by their commander, the Abrafoɔhene. He ordered his men: "Bring the prisoner."

Two abrafoɔ entered and lifted him by the wood he had been neatly tied to. Ohenenana struggled helplessly to free himself. He asked them where they were taking him to. They shouted him down, hitting him and pinching him as they carried him away. They took his clothes along with them, He frantically struggled to free himself but alas, it was a useless effort.

At Nhyiaeso Guest House, Kruger, Don and Pommaa waited to get aboard one of the SUVs. Pommaa was startled by the men's appearance. She looked at them and felt like she was in a different world. The two men were dressed in a gear similar to what they used to pursue Kofi Nsiah in the forest. They carried their night vision camera and communication equipment. In addition, Kruger had the hand held detector fashioned to locate the whereabouts of Ohenenana. Owusu was called in. He drove his SUV where the rescue team was waiting.

Frightened by the sight, though it was for her benefit, Pommaa braced herself and felt encouraged that her intercession had been upheld. The men were ready to go to rescue someone dear to her. She joined them to board the vehicle out of view of the police. Kruger sat at the front while Pommaa and Don sat at the back. The police men at the entrance opened the gate for the vehicle to leave the compound.

"Take us to where your man is." Kruger directed Pommaa.

She also instructed Owusu: "Owusu, Manhyia. I hope he is still there."

Don demanded to know why she hoped he was still there. She explained they could move him to another location to hold him until they decided what to do with him. Manhyia had many secret facilities dotted around the city which were used for many purposes, she added.

The rescue team moved very fast through the traffic. Kruger turned on the hand scanning device with vision screen. The router began to flash a red light and beeped. Owusu followed a route to Manhyia. The frequency of the beeping increased.

"We are not too far away." Pommaa commented.

The abrafoɔ dumped Ohenenana into the back of a twin-cabin cargo van. They jumped into the back passenger area. Abrafoɔhene was already seated in the front. The van took off. It showed on the scanner held by Kruger that the object was in motion.

"They are on the move." Kruger lamented.

"Then they are moving him to one of the secret locations. Owusu, hurry." Pommaa screamed out of fear they may lose track of Ohenenana.

The van carrying the abrafoɔ approached the main gate to the palace. The heavy gate was opened for the vehicle to exit. It drove slowly to join the main street in front of the palace. The rescue team was about a quarter of a mile away when the prisoner van joined the road. A taxi cab in front of the rescue SUV stopped suddenly, causing the vehicle to screech to a halt. The few seconds of manoeuvring gave the van more distance ahead. A few more vehicles joined in the traffic ahead of them. But by the scanner Kruger could spot the van.

"That van! Catch up and follow the van. He is in that van." Kruger urged the driver. Owusu pressed on the accelerator. After a few smart manoeuvres they caught up with the van. "Cut him off! Now!"

Owusu sped up to overtake the van and suddenly cut in front of the van, forcing it off the road to a stop. With a sub-machine gun in hand, Don quickly jumped down and raced to the van. Pommaa followed him. Don pointed the gun at the men. The men raised their hands up over their heads. Kruger, seated in the SUV with weapon in hand, gave Don cover.

Don looked at the men in the back seat but could not see Ohenenana. "Where is he, Ohene-nana?" he demanded. The Abrafoɔhene and his men froze. The sight of a white man wielding a gun at their faces frightened them to their bones.

"Who are you? What are you looking for?" asked the petrified Abrafoɔhene.

"Ohenenana? Where is he?" Pommaa screamed at them from behind Don. The Abrafoɔhene looked sternly at the gun without a blink. The visibly frightened men behind him give the game away by looking in the direction of the bucket of the van. Don moved to the back of the truck. The door was loosely tied with a weak rope. He ripped it off and opened the gate. Ohenenana, sweating, frightened, obviously oblivious of what was going on outside, blinded by the flash light on top of the sophisticated weapon Don carried. "Nana!" Pommaa screamed again. Ohenenana heard the voice of Pommaa which gave him some comfort.

"Po…Pommaa!" Ohenenana responded. He struggled and rolled himself towards the door with difficulty.

"Come on. We have come for you." Pommaa jumped in and helped him to the edge of the van door where Don pulled out a pair of pliers and cut away the tie up. "Where are your clothes." Pommaa saw them in the bucket. She grabbed them and jumped out of the bucket. The operation was quick, crisp and neat. Within minutes, they all rushed into the SUV and sped away leaving the Abrafoɔhene and his men dumbfounded. They were mesmerized by the Hollywood style rescue played on them without the notice of the people who walked around.

"Guys, thank you. Thank you very much." Ohenenana showed his appreciation as he put on his torn clothes in the SUV. They soon reached the guest house. Ohenenana descended from the SUV. He was very angry. He walked to the main building, beside himself with fury. He burst into the living room and hysterically began to knock off things, yelling and screaming. "Hey! ..... Hey! Me, Ohenenana? Me! Odehyeɛ! A royal! Is this how Manhyia would treat me….? Humiliate me? Like a common criminal? Bundled and thrown away like a rag? Manhyia has dared me. They have bitten more than they can chew. They've crossed the line. They've touched me. And I will hit them where it hurts most. 'When trouble sleep,

yanga go wake am.
Wey tin ede find?
Palava ede find.
Palava ego get!'"

He sang the first stanza of Fela's afro beat song "Palava" pacing up and down, pounding his chest, yelling and screaming.

Chapter Nine

A CALL FOR ACTION

Prof. Kofi Nsiah got out of his bungalow on the university campus. He looked round to check if he was not being watched; that Abdul Ali was not still on his tail. He walked for a distance to join the main boulevard. He flagged down a taxi cab and asked the driver to take him to Ash Town in the centre of the city. He had decided to visit his uncle who was the *Sumankwaahene* to Otumfoɔ. In his position, Nana Sumankwaa had been a great store of knowledge upon which Kofi had relied as source of information for his research. He was the only member of the family that he felt closer to. Unmarried as he was, Kofi spent much of his free time, besides academic work, with this uncle of his. He was the last person he spoke to before he left for his trip abroad.

Kofi felt he must visit his uncle to warn him of the presence of the man with the evil intention of stealing the Golden Stool; whether Abdul Ali was going to be successful or not was a different matter. His first trip out of the house was to just do that. He was very cautious of himself as he walked to pick the cab. He arrived at the Nana Sumankwaa's residence. He checked once again to see no one was following him and descended from the taxi in front of the house. He paid the driver who moved swiftly away. He walked to the main house. Nana had lined up a few pairs of native sandals that he was redecorating with black polish. The sandals were of different designs. He had finished polishing one more pair. He stretched and placed them in line with the rest. As he sat up he heard footsteps and lifted his head to look. Kofi was walking towards him.

"Hello, Wofa." Kofi said with his arms outstretched.

Nana Sumankwaa was surprised to see him. "Kofi, are you back already?" He knew Kofi had traveled to the United States of America and was not due back until after one more week. "Since when? I thought you were not due till a few days more."

"Yes, but by strange circumstances ...." Kofi reached him and shook hands with him. "Nevertheless, I am here. Home, sweet home."

"How did your trip go? The demonstration you went to do abroad; did it get good reception? Sit down." He showed him to a chair. "Bring that chair."

"Hmmm. Wofa. Everything went well but did not end well." Kofi said as he brought the chair closer and sat by Nana Sumankwaa. He took the polishing brush from his uncle and continued the redecoration.

"What do you mean?" Nana Sumankwaa asked.

"Oh, I did a very impressive exhibition, by all standards. The lectures were also good. Thanks to you for all the family history and advice you gave me. You should be a senior professor in anthropology. Of course, you are an authority when it comes to our culture and traditions. You are the repository of the history of the Asante Kingdom. You are the ones who should be given the title Professorship in Anthropology. For us, we are just tell-tales, parroting the wisdom passed on to you from the ancestors. You are rich in knowledge and wisdom."

"I am honoured," Nana Sumankwaa said in appreciation of Kofi's acknowledgement.

Kofi had stopped the polishing and was gazing at the object in his hand, as if lost on what he was saying. The silence attracted Nana Sumankwaa who tapped his knee. Kofi snapped out of the reverie. "Erm, sorry, Wofa."

Nana Sumankwaa could easily read from his demeanour that something was amiss. "Kofi, is anything the matter?" he enquired.

"Oh, no. I am okay. I just lost track of what I was saying."

"But you don't look fine for me. You went off a little while ago. I know you. That is not you."

"Oh, I am fine, I am fine." With a smile Kofi tried to assure him all was alright but Nana Sumankwaa looked at him sternly in the eyes. That was sufficient to tell Kofi to come forth with what was bottled up in him. He hesitated. He did not know how Nana Sumankwaa was going to take the news of what had happened and why he had arrived earlier than he expected. He did not want to stir up anything to send the old man panicking. "I was kidnapped here," he continued.

"What! By whom?" Nana Sumankwaa exclaimed curiously.

"Wofa, you are the first person in Ghana I am talking to since I came back. I was kidnapped. I am lucky to have got away for now."

"And you got away?"

"Yes, Wofa. But the evil that took me is here in Ghana." "I saw the sign, three days ago. I saw the sign."

"You did?"

"Yes. It came to me, in broad daylight. But I have dealt with it. What is pursuing you is not from the spirit world. Our ancestors will take control. Fear not. You are well protected."

"Wofa, thank you for the assurance. I know you've always supported me. But this thing is not as simple as we may see it. Somebody wants the Golden Stool, fair or foul."

"What did you say? Sika Dwa!?"

"Yes. I don't know the kind of information they have about it. They are determined to take it. I don't also know who they are and their capacity. My encounter with them was very brief, but I can say that they are a cartel with a wide network and connections all over the world. They operate like what we know here as 'the mafia'. They are dangerous and ruthless. They run with a 'no holds barred' policy. They will go to any length to get whatever they set their minds to, no matter the cost. I will want us to take this as a very serious warning and stay alert. They can strike at any time and pick anyone they find useful to their cause and, of course, dispense with him or her when they are done with you. Wofa, I know what I have gone through in the last few days from America to here today. The trail of deaths that I had left behind me, of friends and innocent people who had come in diverse ways to assist me; they all have been killed, one after the other. I missed death by hair's breadth. I fear to report myself to any security authority. The evil is always ahead of them and they will kill; will do anything to have their way."

"You need protection."

"From whom? I can't go to the police. I am not safe anywhere. Now I am an international fugitive. Don't be shocked to hear in the media tomorrow that the National Security, Interpol, CIA or any other security agency of that kind should put a price on my head and announce that I am a wanted man."

Nana Sumankwaa sat quietly and pondered. "What do they want from you?"

"They want me to lead them to the Golden Stool. How could they conclude I am the one to lead them to it, I can only guess that it is because, perhaps, I am so proficient in the knowledge of the history of the Golden Stool and the Kingdom they think I have clues to the location of the stool. How could they conclude I would oblige to lead them there even if I knew? The impudence of a cockroach."

"But you know you have already."

"How, Wofa? Besides what you have told me about the Golden Stool, I don't even know how it looks like or where it is. How could I possibly lead them to it?"

"Where did you say these people are now?

"Here in Ghana. They brought me in their own aircraft which crash landed at *Nzulezu*, somewhere in the Western Region."

"You've brought them close enough."

"But how, Wofa. I escaped from them somewhere near Cape Coast. They haven't seen me since and will not see me again. I don't think they even know I am back at campus."

Nana Sumankwaa chuckled, "If they could find you in America out of the several millions of people there how could you think they would not be able to find you here. Don't be naïve."

Kofi shook his head, "I am scared."

"Kofi, no harm will come to you. Trust me. Our ancestors who have protected us and the entire kingdom till now will never forsake you. Believe me, *Sika Dwa* Kofi…no one can have access to it….no one. You know the history. The many times white men have botched attempts to steal it! A whole empire with a King and his army with sophisticated weapons and bombs waged relentless wars just to get it. Were they successful? What can one man with perhaps a handful of men do now? If they could not take it away during the time of my forebears, how can they do it now?"

"Huh! I am scared, Wofa. With the sophisticated gadgetery and the technology available now, they are capable of anything. I am scared. I am also worried for the many innocent lives that could be lost. They will kill any and all who will stand in their way. Otumfoɔ must hear this. Perhaps he might direct a better way of dealing with the situation. We will need to mount security on the Golden Stool, 24/7, to make sure no one gets close."

Nana Sumankwaa dismissed Kofi's suggestion of mounting a guard on the Golden Stool, "I don't think that will be necessary. Nobody knows where it is. And it must remain as such. There is no need to draw unnecessary attention to it now. We will be on our guard, yes; we'll put our ears on the ground. I shall consult a few of my colleague chiefs to plan how to break such news to him, now that nothing serious has come up." Nana Sumankwaa picked up his mobile phone lying on a side table by him. He dialed a number. It rang but no one picked it. He tried another number. It went through but no one answered that too. "Ah, this is strange. Nana Akyempemhene and Nana Apagyahene are not answering their phones. Let me try this one." He called Nana Adumhene. It rang for a while then Nana Adumhene picked it.

"Hello, Nana Adum. It's me Sumankwaa. Please speak louder; I can't hear you."

"Sumankwaa, where are you?" Adumhene spoke in a suppressed tone but with a commanding voice. "We are in council with Otumfoɔ. Why aren't you here?"

"When was that decided? I have no idea." Nana Sumankwaa lamented. "Well an issue came up yesterday at the court concerning Ohenenana.

It has developed into a serious matter where he was snatched away from the hands of Abrafoɔhene by strange men wielding weapons."

"What? How?"

"Oh, so you have not heard? Then you better hurry here. There is a full council meeting now."

"I am on my way." Nana Sumankwaa got on to his feet as he switched off the phone. "Kofi, I must go to Manhyia now. There is a council meeting with Otumfoɔ."

"I'll return to campus, then." Kofi also got to his feet. "I will call when I get back."

"Ok, Wofa. I'll wait for your call."

Nana Sumankwaa entered his room. He took off his shirt and picked up a black cloth. He wore a pair of shorts. He spread and threw the cloth over his back and left shoulder and wore it in the Akan traditional fashion as he returned to Kofi who waited to see him off. He slipped his feet into one of the pairs of the sandals he was decorating. The two walked out of the house. A taxi cab was called for Nana Sumankwaa. Kofi stopped another for himself after Nana Sumankwaa had taken off.

Chapter Ten

PLANS FOR THE EXPEDITION

The Golden Stool "recovery team" assembled at the ops room. Abdul Ali addressed them on the strategy to search for it. His men - Kruger, Tango and Don - together with the aircrew, Jim and his two assistants, listened attentively. Ohenenana and Pommaa were also there. The city map of Kumasi was spread on the table with certain spots marked out. The Police Commander entered the room in some sort of a hurry. He went in and stood beside Abdul Ali. A google map image also showed on a monitor in a cluster of screens, some of which also showed other images of the various closed-circuit cameras.

"Guys, our purpose of coming down here begins now." Abdul Ali commenced. "By the statistics of UNESCO, there is a world heritage relic lodged underground, somewhere near here." With a pointer in hand he indicated on the map spread on the table. "Our task is to get to it and recover it. We have not been able to trace any existing access to the relic; therefore, we'll have to find our own way of reaching it - dig to it. Nana, we will need a spot to commence digging. You will take us to the location and assist in acquiring the property. Now, let's roll. My equipment for excavation and drilling has all been arranged and are already on their way here.

We move out now. Any other activity required will be discussed as we progress."

They exited the ops room and, joining the two SUVs, they followed the Police Commander's car to the Central Business District; a very congested area with human and vehicular traffic. Hawkers and vendors were busy plying their trade. They moved to the location where they were first accosted by the police on the night of their arrival. They looked for a convenient place and parked. Abdul Ali and his team got out. He took out and spread a site plan on the bonnet of one of the vehicles.

"This is where we are," Abdul Ali indicated as the men surrounded the map, "and this is the location of the relic. It is approximately 500 metres from here to there and almost the same distance deep in the bowel of these hills. The rock type is such that we shall require a particular type of earth moving equipment. Fortunately, Ghana abounds in many mining firms that have exactly what we need. I have consulted widely and have already located the machinery and ordered them. Our digging will take a gradient for a slow descent into the bowel of this hill where our object is lodged. This spot is the easiest point of access. We shall have to acquire this house. We will dig from within the compound. Some of the logistics we will need will include 50 dumper trucks and about two hundred workmen which will include technicians and artisans. The equipment, operations and construction of the tunnel have been outsourced to some professionals who will arrive with the various types of machines. The geologist who will be in charge of the digging will arrive tonight and will advise accordingly. This project should be completed in three days. After three days we will be out of here. But for now, Nana, you will lead me to the owners of this property."

Ohenenana immediately reached for his phone and placed a call. "Hello, this is Ohenenana. I am at Adum, on the 7th Street; in front of *Agya pa yɛ* house. Can you do a search for me? House number A32/12. Yes. A32/12 on the 7th Street. I want the owner. Who owns it? Aha!

Who? Okay. Please get all the details; I am on my way. Thank you." The call from Ohenenana was to an official of the Town and Country Planning Department.

The team returned quickly to the guest house. Ohenenana and Pommaa departed in one of the SUVs back to town. They arrived at the Town and Country Planning Department. They went into the building and met the official Ohenenana had spoken to on phone.

The official of the department who sat behind a desk pulled a folder from a drawer onto the desk, flipped a few pages to the site plan. He indicated a location on the plan: "This is *Agya pa yɛ* house. Which plot are you interested in?"

"Directly opposite, A32/12" Ohenenana said.

"A32/12." The official encircled the spot on the plan. He stretched and pulled a large ledger book and dropped it on the desk over the folder they were working on. He opened the ledger book and it covered the whole desk. A32/12 was traced in the book. The official ran his finger on the various house numbers till he reached A32/12. The details of the certified owner of the plot were written there. The official picked a piece of paper and scribbled the details on it and handed it to Ohenenana who in turn pulled cash from his pocket and handed it to him. The two men shook hands and Ohenenana left with Pommaa. They joined the SUV and it sped off from the Town and Country Planning Department.

Ohenenana looked at the details on the piece of paper he had received and read it out: "A. Asafu-Adjaye. Does it ring any bell?" he asked Pommaa. "Asafu-Adjaye, Asafu-Adjaye," Pommaa ran the name through her mind. "Not immediately. But I know one Asafu-Adjaye. Okay, driver, take us to Asafo Market. Yaa Achiaa, my friend may know some of the people who

own properties in the area."

The SUV arrived at the Asafo Market and stopped in front of a shop. Pommaa got out of the vehicle and entered the shop. It was a small clothing store. Yaa Achiaa, the owner, was a very pretty young woman who was current in fashion. She rose to meet Pommaa. They were friends. Pommaa brought her to Ohenenana in the SUV. The glass window by Ohenenana's side rolled down.

"Nana, this is my friend Achiaa." Pommaa introduced her. "I think she can help us locate the owner."

Ohenenana read from the piece of paper, the name, "Asafu-Adjaye, A Asafu-Adjaye. I am looking for this person: owner of a property opposite *Agya pa yɛ* house, Adum."

"Those houses," Pommaa added. "Don't you know some of the owners who may know who this is?"

"Not immediately," she shook her head. "No names come to mind immediately. Give me some time. I'll ask around."

Disappointed, Pommaa returned to her seat as Achiaa also walked away. Then Achiaa stopped and turned to the SUV again. "Wait!" she called out to them and walked briskly back to the vehicle as Pommaa sat down beside Ohenenana. "You said Asafu-Adjaye, A. Asafu-Adjaye, right?"

"Right." Pommaa responded. "Then it is Adelaide."

"Which Adelaide?"

"Lady, Lady. Her husband was Asafu-Adjaye?"

"Yes, yes. Lady" Pommaa recalled.

"I think their family owns a lot of the properties in that area."

"That's true. You have her number?"

"I am sorry, no." But she instantly recollected, "I know she lives behind the Odeon Cinema. She moved back to her mum's place when her husband died."

"Thank you, Achiaa." Pommaa said and waved her as she stepped back for the vehicle to move.

"That was good lead." Ohenenana acknowledged. "Let's go to Odeon, then." Pommaa ordered the driver.

The SUV joined the traffic and moved swiftly through the heavy evening rush to Bantama, a district of the city. The SUV parked in front of Adelaide's home. Ohenenana and Pommaa got out and approached the house. She knocked at the door. Adelaide's mother, an eighty-year old woman opened the door

"Good evening, mum." Pommaa greeted her. "Good evening."

"Please, we are looking for Lady."

"Who are you, and what do you want from her?" Adelaide's mum asked in her gentle slow voice.

"Erm -, mum, she is a friend." Pommaa said. For a moment she was confused and could not come up with any answer. She looked at Ohenenana who instantly came in to her rescue.

"I am Ohenenana. I want to have a small business discussion with her," he intervened.

Adelaide's mother looked at him for a moment and then slowly returned into the room, shutting the door behind her. After a few seconds the door opened again; Adelaide stood at the entrance and beckoned them in. She quickly settled them down and got them to business.

"What business did you say you have for me?" she asked.

"I am doing some project," Ohenenana began. "I need a specific site and from my search at the Town and Country Planning Department that property belongs to you."

"I don't own any property. Which property are you talking about?"

"Number A32/12, 7th Street." Ohenenana told her.

"I don't own that property. And I don't want to talk about it." Adelaide got up and began to walk away from them. She had lived with her mother after the mysterious death of her husband. Her husband's family took away all his property and drove her out of their marital home. The only property that was held in her name was the number A32/12, 7th Street house. Even that, she was still in court with her in-laws fighting for it. They had rented it out without her knowledge and for over a year, they had been collecting rent for it. The frustration she had endured with the property had got her so upset and disinterested that she would not want to have anything to do with it again. She stopped and turned to Ohenenana: "If you want it please go to Sam's family."

"Who is Sam?" Ohenenana asked

"Her late husband," Pommaa answered.

"Madam, but your name is still on the documents as the legitimate owner. Why are you walking out on it? Look, I could have ignored you and gone ahead to do whatever I wanted on the property the moment you said you are having a pull with your in-laws. But I feel you deserve better than the raw deal they are giving you. I want to help you. I have some foreign investors coming to do this project and I think you rightly deserve the compensation they are prepared to pay." Adelaide turned to look at Ohenenana and Pommaa. Ohenenana pressed his advantage. "Just do me a transfer document to say that you've sold it to me, that's all. I'll get you your money. As for your in-laws, leave them to me to deal with them for you."

"No, I am not selling it. That property is mine. They are cheating me for it. I lost my husband and all other properties due me. This is the only one left. I can't lose this too. No, I will fight them for it." She brushed off the offer and walked towards the bedroom door.

"Adelaide," Pommaa called as she rose to her feet. Adelaide stopped at the bedroom door. "What if you lose the court case, you would have lost everything, wouldn't you? Let it go. Give it to us. This is a golden opportunity you should not walk away from; at least, you would have gotten something out of it for all your troubles. You could then start a new life with this, build something your own. Lady, don't think about this; just do it. You can't live bitter forever."

Adelaide stood speechless, obviously confused. "I – I – am – I; how much were you going to offer for it?" she asked sarcastically with a snort in her tone.

"One hundred Thousand dollars," Ohenenana offered. "What!" Adelaide exclaimed in amazement.

"I know the value of properties in that area. It is a good offer."

"Where is the money?" Adelaide demanded in more

remorseful tone. "Go ahead, do me the transfer document. I'll return in an hour with your cash." Ohenenana assured her as he rose to his feet. "Pommaa, let's go." As they left Adelaide's place, Ohenenana called Abdul Ali on his mobile phone: "Hey, Ali. Guess what? Got a deal for the site. The owner will accept One Hundred and Fifty Thousand Dollars. We pay now, we move in straight away. Alright? I am on my way back." Abdul Ali agreed to the deal and asked him to come and pick the cash.

In less than an hour, Ohenenana returned with the one hundred thousand dollars. Adelaide had quickly got on to her computer and prepared a short sale receipt and notice of transfer of full rights. They settled down and signed the relevant portions, witnessed by Pommaa and Adelaide's mother. They exchanged documents and the cash exchanged hands.

"Don't forget my commission; ten percent." Pommaa said as an over- excited Adelaide followed them to see them off.

Adelaide was amazed and dumbfounded. She looked down into the large brown envelope with the cash of dollar bills. She stood with her mouth wide open, tears started running down her cheeks. She hugged her mother and wept while her mother consoled her.

Later that evening, Ohenenana moved to the No. A32/12, 7th Street, the targeted house. He arrived with armed policemen.

"Out! Out! Everybody, out!" Ohenenana shouted when he commenced the ejection of the tenants. "This house has been sold. I am the new owner. Everybody, out!" From one flat to the other, Ohenenana screamed, pounding his fist on the metal gate and some of the wooden doors as he walked the corridors of the two storey house.

There was great confusion and panic. They broke into rooms and forcibly threw tenants and the properties out. There were about 10 families, some with children. One young lady had her boyfriend visiting. They were in the middle of a serious love making session. The door was pounded open on them. She screamed as she and her mate scrambled for their clothing to cover their nakedness. Some were sleeping and were rudely woken by the bangs at the door. Children began crying. Women wailed, screamed, swore and insulted them. Some of the men struggled with those throwing their things out.

Ohenenana tried to calm down the frightened and agitated tenants. "Gentlemen. Ladies. I am sorry for whatever is happening. I am not so callous. I know you have paid rents. I am here with a very simple deal. I am giving to every family, three thousand five hundred dollars. This should be enough to pay for another three years of rent anywhere in the city. It will take care of a night at a hotel and for transportation away from here. If you have any difficulty in any way, I am ready to help you to move out now smoothly. All damaged property will be paid for. We apologize to you all."

The property was about three acres, sitting at the base of a small hill, with the main house built in the middle. It had a beautiful garden in the front stretching about one hundred and fifty metres away from the main gate with a thoroughfare driveway that had separate entry and exit gates. The bungalow was originally made of seven bedrooms but the Asafu-Adjaye family had reconstructed it into ten apartments of various sizes to suit their rental plan.

A fleet of trucks arrived in the driveway in front. The families were loaded onto them. Ohenenana handed them envelopes of cash. One old lady, with a hand bag slinging on her left arm, approached him. She snatched her envelope with her left hand, stomped on his foot and slapped him in the face with her right palm. Ohenenana screamed and reacted to the pain he had received from the old lady on his cheek and foot spontaneously. "Stupid man! You should have come earlier than now. I needed this money yesterday. I would not have sold my wedding ring." She walked away angrily, trying to stuff the envelope into her hand bag. Other tenants picked their envelopes, joined their packed trucks with their families and were driven away.

As those trucks left, another set carrying equipment for the drilling, prefabricated materials for construction and accompanying workmen also arrived. They off-loaded their materials and began building a canopy and a front covering to conceal the house from public view. A huge generator was set up to light up the area and provide power for them to work throughout the night. The structure looked like a huge warehouse or hanger with two huge gates.

Abdul Ali and his crew had dismantled and packed up all the set up at the guest house to relocate at the new site. They moved in with their equipment and set up their new command office in one of the rooms of the main house. They fixed wireless CCTV cameras to give them 'eyes' to oversee whatever was going to go on there.

By the next morning, the plot with House Number A32/12, 7th Street had been transformed into a huge hanger or warehouse with two huge gates through which heavy trucks could easily enter and exit without any hindrance. From the outside it looked like an ordinary factory or a warehouse; inside, both local and expatriate engineers and technicians set to work; geologists began micro drilling to check soils and rock structure.

Abdul Ali received a call. He signaled Kruger who immediately stopped what he was doing to follow him. They arrived at the frontage of the big warehouse just as a low-loader carrying a mobile drilling or boring machine with a huge drilling bit in front nicknamed, "The Worm," arrived. It could make a three-metre diameter hole. The Worm was downloaded, rolled on its metal tracks into the designated area to commence its work.

Excavators, graders and rollers began to work, clearing and leveling to set the place for "the Worm," The debris was loaded onto dumper trucks and driven away.

Abdul Ali went and stood at a very conspicuous place where he could oversee what was going on. Tango stood beside him as his personal security. Jim and his air crew sat behind the monitors watching the whole operation. Kruger and Don were in the thick of everything, fixing lights and wireless CCTV cameras as the work progressed. The many workmen and engineers brought in also got to work on various tasks that they had been assigned to.

The Worm mechanics who came with it quickly fitted it with all the accessories it required to make it fully functional. The geologists, with their equipment, had immediately assessed the seismic information. They identified a specific spot and earmarked it for the commencement of the drilling of a tunnel into the belly of the earth. They directed the drilling team which moved the Worm to the marked spot. The Worm was a specially-designed equipment with a conveyor belt fitted to it. In no time the Worm was ready and began to bore into the earth in front of it. The debris it created rolled onto the conveyor belt which rolled them onto a series of conveyor belts until they dropped into dumper trucks which also carried the debris away. Soon the tunnel began to take shape. It went into the belly of the earth at a gradient so low that one would not notice the depression while walking down or up the tunnel. The technical team that came with the equipment worked very efficiently with precision, well-tailored and coordinated.

Abdul Ali moved into the control room. He inspected the systems and monitors. There was one monitor that showed the position of the Worm and how far away they were from the targeted object. He felt satisfied with work so far and commented: "The way we are going we should reach there in a few hours," pointing to the anticipated location of the Golden Stool on the monitor.

"Yes. We are on course." Jim confirmed Abdul Ali's expectations. "Open your eyes. Don't let anything pass without your notice. Alert me

of any distraction without delay." Abdul Ali tapped Jim's shoulder. "I will, Sir." Jim responded.

Ohenenana joined them, excited, seeing everything working in unison and in harmony as if it were an activity planned and long rehearsed over and over again to achieve perfection and smooth running. "I have just resolved the issue of the dumping site." He told Abdul Ali. "I have also set in motion a process for free flow and a smooth movement of our trucks."

"That's very thoughtful of you." Abdul Ali commended Ohenenana. "I will need more cash. I now have a fleet of tipper trucks lined up out there. I am paying them as they go, trip by trip, and a little more for our commander friend and his traffic controllers." Abdul Ali signaled Tango who pulled out a parcel and handed it to him. Ohenenana stepped out of the office. He beckoned Pommaa and passed the parcel of cash to her. "Find somewhere safe for it. This is the beginning of our pay day."

Pommaa attempted to open the parcel. Ohenenana hushed her and with his finger, cautioned her to be careful. Pommaa quickly disappeared with the parcel.

The bustle of activity in the tunnel intensified. A lot more hand men were brought in. Almost all of them wore an orange workmen's over-all with reflective patches, gloves and hats with flashlights fitted to them like deep shaft miners. Only the specialists wore their own cloths.

Chapter Eleven

THE WORM, THE CAVES AND DISASTER

Frema was a journalist writing on environmental issues for a national daily newspaper. She was their correspondent based in Kumasi. A single parent, she had a daughter but due to pressures of work, she had left the 5-year-old in the care of her mother who lived at Owabe, an outskirt township of Kumasi. At 4.30 a.m. her alarm clock screamed. She struggled out of her bed in her two bed-room apartment in a plush residential area at Nhyiaeso. It was a block apartment of seven floors. She lived on the fifth floor. She dragged herself out of bed wearing a loose sleeping shorts and a sleeveless top and headed for the washroom and to the sink. She turned on the tap but the water was not flowing. She sighed in disgust. It was not surprising to her though; perennial water shortage was a daily occurrence. She turned to the fridge and pulled out a bottle of water. She returned to the sink in the washroom, washed her face, rinsed her mouth and drank a bit of the water. She ran her hand through her short dreadlocks and wiped her face with a towel. Returning the bottle to the fridge she opened her wardrobe and searched through her clothes.

She settled for a pair of jeans trousers and a neatly cut blouse made out of local fabric and a pair of sneakers. She had to endure this unusual dawn reveille because her mother had called to tell her of her daughter's poor health. She picked her hand bag and a shawl and threw it around her neck. She took her car keys and made for the door and left her apartment. She literally flew down the stairs. It had the good effect of shaking off the sleep she still wore. With the remote control she opened her car, a small but sleek saloon car, parked among others on the street in front of her apartment block. She dropped into the seat; flipped down the sun shade above her to use the mirror behind and the inside light to touch up her face with ponds and lipstick; and freshened up with a body spray. She started the car and took off. She fixed her seatbelt as she drove along.

The streets were virtually empty of traffic or any activity. She could see a few people still asleep in front of closed shops. Some had wrapped themselves in cover cloths and there were others who slept in mosquito nets. The headlights spotted someone having a bath by the roadside. He was lathered up with soap and was throwing water on his body. Frema shook her head and laughed.

Out of nowhere, she heard the deafening blur of a siren. That startled her. She quickly dashed off the road to a panic stop to make way for the blue lights flashing from behind her. A police motor bike whisked past, ahead of a convoy of large and out-of-ordinary size dumper trucks, which also flashed yellow lights on top of them. Wow! Good reason to keep her eyes on the road, she thought.

She pulled herself together and rejoined the road after the trucks and continued her trip. After a few minutes, another batch of trucks led by a police outrider appeared in front of her. She parked again to allow them to pass. When she rejoined the road, her curiosity as a journalist kept prodding her: Two convoys of dumper trucks, where are they going or coming from? What are they carrying that they require police escort? Of course, for the size of vehicles meant for use in open minefields they would require police escort to move within the city;

and the best time to work was when everyone was out of the streets; no big deal. But her instincts pushed her to follow those ahead of her.

She increased her speed till she caught up with them. She followed the trucks at a distance till they turned at a junction towards Owabe dam where she was also going. The trucks passed through the town towards the dam, the reservoir from which the city of Kumasi is supplied water. The truck turned and stopped by the edge of the dam. She stopped. Morning had broken so from a distance she could see the trucks turning, tipping and offloading the contents in the huge buckets into the dam. "Ah!", she exclaimed. "Why should they do that? Polluting the water?" She was surprised. She decided to find out more later. She swiftly turned round her car and sped off. She arrived at her mum's house and saw her sweeping the compound. She parked and quickly ran up to her mum.

Maame stopped sweeping to meet her. "Frema."

"Maame," Frema embraced her. "How are you? How is Bibi?"

"We are fine; But she is the one who has temperature." Maame turned and led the way to the house.

Frema ran to catch up with her. "Wait, Maame."

"Oh, you are not coming in to see her?"

"She is still sleeping; allow her."

"You've driven all the way here. Just one minute in to see her." Maame was not the least pleased.

"Maame, something has come up right now. I must follow now."

"You haven't seen her in days. Take a minute to see her."

Frema opened her bag and took out an envelope; without reacting to Maame's plea and she pushed it into her palm. "I hope this will be enough for now. Please, take care of Bibi for me." The trucks from the dumping site drove past in the background with the siren. Frema pulled Maame to herself and hugged her. "Sorry, mum. I've got to go now. I'll be back as soon as I am through with it. I'll be here for the weekend with you, right. See you," she said as she rushed to her car and took off leaving Maame disappointed.

Soon, Frema caught up with the convoy of trucks. She kept her distance behind two vehicles away from the last truck. With the police escort leading, the truck moved freely through the traffic. She began to plan in her mind the story she was going to send which she thought was definitely going to make the front page. As she followed the returning trucks, she met another convoy loaded with debris, going out of town. She cautiously followed the convoy ahead of her till they got to the Central Business District. The city had awoken to very brisk activities. With the heavy traffic there she was cut off as she was unable to beat the traffic lights. But ahead of her she saw the trucks had made a turn.

Number 32/12, 7th Street had been encased like a hanger. The roof was covered with transparent roofing sheets which allowed more daylight in. The huge generator was tucked away in the corner providing adequate power to run the machines and sufficient ventilation and additional lighting. From outside it looked like a big warehouse or an industrial set up, away from public view. Strangely, the neighbours did not pay any particular attention to what had sprung up in the neighbourhood. Much of the activities took place at night, which did not inconvenience them in any way. Typical of city dwellers, they never cared to even enquire what was happening. Occasionally, they saw the trucks move in and out and heard the police sirens. Once what was going on there never interrupted their activities in any way, they did not bother to interfere. The presence of the police there, perhaps, also made them feel all was well or above board.

Inside, Abdul Ali and his bunch pursued their diabolical agenda to steal the Golden Stool by boring their way to it. The drilling went on smoothly. In the ops room, Abdul Ali went through the set up assuring himself that all necessary precautions had been taken to make the venture go on without a hitch. The communications systems, CCTV, security, engineers and technicians and their equipment, all ran smoothly. From the console he flipped from camera to camera and was satisfied that all was well.

Kruger also coordinated the activities of the geologists, engineers and their staff in the tunnel area. The debris coming out from the drilling dropped on the conveyor belts and was transported into the waiting trucks. The Worm had bore a tunnel large enough for the heavy trucks to drive in without hindrance.

Frema's car moved when the lights turned green and followed the truck where it had turned a few minutes earlier. She slowed down but could not see the trucks or any activity. She drove past the sealed up digging site but did not notice any activity. The road ended up in a cul-de-sac. She stopped, turned around and sat in the car, wondering where those heavy trucks had vanished to. Just as she got past the site again, she saw the other convoy of trucks coming. She parked and watched the trucks drive past her.

Through her driving mirror she watched as the big gate opened for the trucks to drive in. Ah, so that's where they went! Frema quickly picked her mobile phone, came out of her car, locked it with her remote, slipped the key into her pocket and ran behind the last truck as it slowed down to enter the structure. She slipped past the security, unnoticed, by the side of the truck. She ran along the truck to a parking lot. She looked around to figure out her next move. She saw the police bikes, other trucks as they lined up in a queue, the tunnel and the conveyor belt as it brought out dug-out earth into the trucks' huge buckets.

Frema saw Abdul Ali lead a group made up of Ohenenana, Pommaa, Tango and the expatriate geologist, Antonio, and his men who came along with the equipment. They stopped at the entrance of the tunnel to inspect progress of work. A semi-circular tunnel about ten metres in diameter had been dug, running a fifteen degree depression into the belly of the earth.

Abdul Ali turned towards Antonio as he observed the roof of the tunnel. "How safe is it going to be, the tunnel?" he asked. "Will it not cave in on us? How are we going to support the overhang from dropping on our heads?"

Antonio confirmed the safety of the tunnel. He showed Abdul

Ali some rock samples. "You see these? Very hard rocks. They have granite properties. They run about half a mile into the hill ahead. The only thing that can disintegrate them is a volcano or maybe a powerful earthquake; which is not going to happen as we are here right now." Antonio laughed. He showed a 3D seismic image of the rock formation on an ipad screen monitor. "You see, this is where we are. This is the possible loco of your object. It is protected in the structure here. We need to get into the cave. We will figure out the rest from there. For now we are safe."

A batch of trucks were filled and ready to leave. The police dispatch rider mounted his bike and took the lead, followed by the three-truck convoy. They exited out of the big gate which was shut immediately after them.

With her phone Frema began taking pictures. After a couple of shots, she dispatched them via e-mail to her office address. She changed her location and picked another spot and took more shots. She tiptoed towards where Abdul Ali and the team had moved to and took more pictures. As she sent those pictures the truck she had hidden behind moved forward, exposing her. Pommaa spotted her as she tried to look for another safe spot. Pommaa became suspicious and decided to track her.

"Hey, you there. Stop!" Pommaa yelled at her as she caught up with her, out of hearing of her companions who had moved ahead further into the tunnel. Pommaa approached Frema from behind her. Frema froze and raised her hand above her head at Pommaa's voice. "Who are you? How did you get in here?" Pommaa got closer to her. "How did you get in here?"

"The gate was ajar." Frema answered.

"You liar. This gate is never left ajar. What do you want here? Who sent you?"

Frema turned and with her thumb on the knob she snapped a picture

of Pommaa when she got into frame. That annoyed Pommaa.

She now confronted Frema directly. "You are taking pictures. Give me the phone. Give me the phone!" Pommaa attempted to snatch the phone. Frema resisted. A scuffle ensued with the two women struggling over the phone.

Jim noticed them on one of his monitors in the control room. He raised the alarm to Abdul Ali on a two-way communicator. "Boss, there is a problem at the main yard. Our lady seems to be confronting a possible intruder."

Abdul Ali, Ohenenana and the rest, including some of the guards in uniform holding weapons, ran in to the yard to respond to the distress call. Frema had then overpowered Pommaa, pushed her down to the ground and had taken to her heels, attempting to flee the premises. Tango and one other guard went in and accosted her. They brought Frema before Abdul Ali.

Pommaa who had then got to her feet moved in on her in an attempt to slap her but she was restrained. Pommaa fumed and struggled, throwing her legs, in an attempt to kick Frema.

Abdul Ali looked at Frema for a moment. "Who are you? What do you want here? Who sent you here?" He asked.

Frema looked away not answering anything.

"Her phone. She's been taking pictures." Pommaa yelled as she shrugged herself from her hold.

Tango snatched the phone from Frema, scanned through the pictures and showed them to Abdul Ali.

"You. I know you." Ohenenana burst out after he had watched her for a while trying to recollect where he knew her.

Abdul Ali looked at her and then turned to Ohenenana: "You do?"

"Yes, I know her. She is a journalist."

"Yes, I am a journalist." Frema confirmed confidently. "Why are you arresting me? What are you doing here that you don't want the world to know?"

"None of your business. Shut up." Pommaa yelled at her.

"I mean no harm. I am only a journalist looking for news. The movement of your trucks in town raised serious cause for concern for curious minds like me. What did you expect?"

"And it called you to poke your nose into somebody's soup, didn't it?" Pommaa demanded.

Frema looked at her. She did not bother to respond to her question, but turned to Abdul Ali. "Well," she said, "this is just a simple act of trespassing, as you can see. Give me my phone and I'll be gone. You can even erase the pictures I took."

But Ohenenana disagreed. "No, don't allow her to go. She's seen too much to start a storm. I know her pretty well."

"You are going nowhere till we are done here." Abdul Ali told her and asked the security men to lock her up.

The boring machine, the Worm, continued to drill through the rubble of soil, rocks and mud; the conveyor system also continued to carry them into the bucket of the dumper trucks at the loading area. The soil and rock formation had changed from broken rocks and dust into more of wet soil, rocks and boulders. Suddenly, the earth ahead dropped off into a big hole. The Worm drill had perforated the soil into a gaping space ahead; the force with which the Worm grinded the soil compelled it to surge forward a little and stopped in a softer soil area.

"A tunnel!!!!!!!!" The Worm operator shouted.

"A tunnel?" Kruger, who was supervising the drilling process moved forward to observe. He could see that the soil ahead where the Worm was drilling had dropped off. There was a vast space ahead. It was possible that there was a tunnel. In their excitement they lost concentration on the nature of the soil and where they were. The operator of the Worm suddenly felt that his machine was dangling. It had lost its equilibrium and was standing precariously on the edge of the opening. He tried to back it away from the edge of the tunnel but the more he tried, the more the Worm slipped forward. The operator got frightened.

"The Worm is slipping!" he shouted.

Kruger looked and noticed the precarious position in which the Worm was and asked him to stay still and not to rock the machine while he arranged a solution. He shouted and called all hands on deck. Kruger and his team moved forward to aid the operator to save the Worm from falling into the pit. There was a bit of confusion as to what to do. Some of the men came in and with bare hands, held on to the worm to exert more weight at the end part to tilt its balance away from the pit.

Don and some of the men brought in ropes and tied them to the Worm and pulled. This stabilized the situation. The operator tried to back away again. The Worm began to slip again, slowly.

"Stop! Cut the engine! The vibration is making it worse." The operator cut the engine and sat motionless in his seat. Kruger noticed a wrench on one of the dumper trucks. He ran for it. He ordered the driver, "Start the engine to release the wire." The driver of the truck obliged and released the wrench wire with a hook at the end. Kruger lifted the hook and pulled the wire but it was slow. He beckoned the driver to move the truck forward after him. The men holding the ropes were straining hard yet the Worm slipped slowly. The ground was wet, muddy and slippery. Gradually, Kruger pulled about twenty metres of the wire and reached the Worm. He hooked up the wrench wire. He signaled the truck driver to engage the wrench to begin to pull. The wrench began to wind up slowly. But before the wrench could tighten and pull, Don and the men with the ropes lost hold. The Worm surged forward into the pit below. The impact pulled along the truck with the wrench. The truck driver engaged the reverse gear and hit the accelerator but the force was not enough to hold the Worm from falling. The weight of the plunging Worm dragged the truck along. The truck swerved from left to right crashing the wall of the tunnel to the left and smashing the conveyor belts to the right, destroying them completely. Don and some of the men around screamed and dashed off as the truck trailed the Worm. It missed them narrowly.

Kruger and a couple of his workmen got caught in between the hole and the truck. The wrench broke off from the truck, taking along the bumper of the truck on which it was fitted. With the truck coming at them and they having no way to escape, the broken wrench and the wire caught them and dragged them into the pit. One after the other the three workmen were swept away after the Worm in an avalanche of mud and rubble as it went crashing into the pit. Kruger was also caught in and dragged along into the pit. He was lucky. He fell on an area with mud. But the other men were not. Two of them fell on the Worm and died instantly. The other fell on a boulder, cracking his head in the process. Kruger lost consciousness and collapsed. The truck, because of its size, could not go through the small hole the Worm had broken through. It got stuck, blocking the entrance completely, making it impossible to get access to Kruger and the others.

The impact of the accident with the accompanying clashing of metal and shouts and screams of the men around created a loud noise that reached Abdul Ali and his team interrogating Frema.

"Shit!" Abdul Ali swore and took off towards the tunnel. Ohenenana and Pommaa and the rest of them were alarmed and followed Abdul Ali. The guards got hold of Frema, handcuffed her and held her at gun point where they were.

Kruger lay unconscious, partly covered by the mud and rubble. The Worm was in a ditch, lying by its side. Its driver had died from the impact of the crash.

Don ran in closer to the truck and realized Kruger had been swept along. He tried to reach Kruger on the communicator, but there was no answer. Abdul Ali arrived at the scene. "What happened? Where is Kruger? Where is the Worm?" he enquired as he beheld the scene: the wreckage and the remains of the conveyor belt. They stood helplessly. Slowly, they recovered from the trauma.

"Swept away; swept away into the pit." Don answered him. He could not hold himself together. He wept. "He is in there. He did not answer his radio. He was swept away with rubble after the Worm.

Kruger! Kruger! Do you hear me? Over."

"And the Worm is also gone?"

"Gone. The worm is also gone in there." Don replied wiping tears from his eyes with the back of his hand. Abdul Ali was astonished and speechless, thinking of the next line of action. Tango went to console Don.

Ohenenana, Pommaa, and the rest arrived at the scene and were awed by the way the metal structures were mangled and the hysteria of the other men who were busy seeking ways to reach the men down in the pit.

Abdul Ali turned to Antonio, angrily, "How come? Can you explain? Didn't you see this coming? Huh?" Abdul Ali grabbed him by the throat and hauled him up.

"Yeah, it was in the data I gave you. But I did not expect it so close and so soon." Antonio, visibly frightened tried to explain himself as he struggled to free himself from Abdul Ali's grip.

"You want to fuck up with my expedition, eh?"

"No, no, no! I - I saw there was a cave but the data did not specify how close we were to it."

Abdul Ali dropped him to the floor. Antonio struggled to get back unto his feet. Without paying any attention to him Abdul Ali called for rescue of the men in the pit to commence. "Alright, all hands on deck. Let see what we can do to save the men in there and figure out how to proceed." Abdul Ali called out to his men. Some tried to move the remains of the conveyor belt. Others began scraping and digging the mud and moving rocks and boulders with their bare hands and anything they could lay hands on. The truck had blocked the entrance of the tunnel. The only access to the pit behind was through the driver's cabin. A couple of them went into the truck. The wounded and bleeding driver was helped out and given treatment.

"Wow, wow, wow! This adventure is fucked up," an astonished Ohenenana burst out as he watched the wreckage.

Don tried to reach Kruger again but there was no response.

Ohenenana in his hysteria started shouting, "Call off the expedition. Let's wrap it up and get the hell out of here."

"You can't be serious," Pommaa reacted to him by pulling him aside.

"Why not?" He defended his position in subdued voice between himself and Pommaa. "See the wreckage. I don't know what is beyond and what is yet to happen. I cannot commit any more men to risk their lives. Those in there may be dead. What we've lost is enough." Then he burst out to the hearing of all, "Let's close, guys, we're done here!" There was a sudden silence. The men working their heads and hands out to rescue their colleagues froze.

Before the men could decide to abandon the rescue, Tango pulled out a shotgun and cocked it. The sound reverberated in the tunnel. Frema could hear it from where she was being held.

"Nobody moves anywhere," Tango screamed out to counter Ohenenana's order, "until the men down there are rescued, dead or alive! Let's get back to work. Let's go on digging. Am I clear?" After a short silence the rescue activity resumed in earnest.

Pommaa confronted Ohenenana. "I am disappointed in you" she attacked him. "They said Kruger is in there. That man down there was the one who rescued you from Manhyia. Is this the way you pay him back?"

Embarrassed, Ohenenana bowed his head. "You suck!" Pommaa snorted at him and walked off.

Kruger came round. It was dark. The worm lay in a ditch. Its lights were still on so, he could see around. Slowly, he struggled to his feet, still in a daze. Slowly, he regained his focus. He was wounded, bleeding in the palm. He tried to remove the torn glove soaked with blood. He looked at the cut. It was not too deep but it was painful. With his flashlight, he observed the structure of the space he had fallen into. He looked round and saw his companions lying about. He rushed to check on them. They were all dead. He saw light from above him about 30 meters. He could hear the clanging of metals as the men worked above. The call for him came up again on his communicator. Kruger picked up his communicator lying a little distance away. "Kruger, here. Can anyone hear me? Over."

Abdul Ali snatched the communicator from Don who had been trying to reach Kruger and responded to the call: "Kruger! Kruger! Do you hear me?"

"Yes, Boss."

"Kruger is Alive!" Abdul Ali announced and there was a yell of jubilation by the rest of the men. They all stopped whatever they were doing to listen in to the communication with Kruger. "Are you alright?

"Yes, Boss. I am alright."

"Good. Can you see anything? Are you in the tomb?"

Kruger looked around. The interior of the tunnel was like a cave, amorphous and had no specific structure. "No. There is no tomb here, Boss. A tunnel. Just a tunnel or something like a cave I can see."

"A tunnel? I could not see anything like that on the scanner." "It's true. Looks like a cave. I'll need more light to see well." "Right, right. The Worm?"

"It is in a ditch now." Kruger went close to examine the driver. "The driver is dead. So are the other men, three of them."

Frema strained to listen but could not figure out what the exercise was all about. Abdul Ali was very disturbed and disappointed and it was visibly written all over him. He did not seem to be bothered by Ohenenana and his miscalculated effusion. "We'll figure out a way to reach you soon." Abdul Ali concluded with Kruger. He turned to the workmen. "Kruger is alive and ok. Let's get to work. Clear the blockage and let's get on with it. Quick, quick! Bring the lights into the hole. I need eyes in there as well. Quick! Quick!" He handed over the communicator to Tango who continued the communication with Kruger.

"Kruger! How many of you are out there now? Over," Tango asked. "No one else." Kruger responded. "I am the only one alive.

Ohenenana had wandered away out of embarrassment. He stood

far off as the rescue continued. He felt he had lost face with the rank and file. He also felt slighted by the way he was rebuffed by Tango who got the men back to work. Pommaa drew closer to him. He moved away from her. She followed him. They got closer to where Frema was being held.

Frema was thinking of how to get herself out of the trouble her investigative journalism had pushed her into. She thought about what could happen to her. How could she get herself out? She thought about her daughter. She recalled her mother insisting she should take a moment to see her, and she did not. She would not see her daughter again. How foolish she had been; not listening to her mother. She had allowed her work to displace her love for her daughter – of course, that was what she had always done to put food on the table. But there she was, arrested and held at gunpoint, not knowing her fate; not knowing how dangerous these men there could be. Could she escape, and how? Would they let her go? Would they kill her? These and many more questions ran through her mind. Then she overheard the confrontation between Ohenenana and Pommaa and eavesdropped on them. Frema could hear them clearly though they spoke undertone.

"Nana, Please, listen to me." Pommaa was trying to persuade him. "You! Are you on my side or you are with them?" Nana queried her.

"What have I done?"

"You are siding with them against me. That is what you have done." Nana confronted Pommaa. "When I say this, you say that, opposing me, embarrassing me before all these nincompoops."

"No, Nana. I was only asking you to be fair with the situation.

That man who had fallen in there was the one who led the operation to rescue you when Manhyia caught you *dedua*. It was only fair to also go to his rescue if he was also caught up in harness. One good turn deserves another." "Fine. But you didn't have to do that to me in public; to slight or ridicule me."

"I am sorry, okay. I am sorry." Pommaa apologized.

"Look, these people don't care about us. They don't respect us. They are here to steal. That's all. And they will do whatever they can to achieve that purpose. I must also protect my interest."

Frema strained to hear them.

"What do they want? What do they want you to do for them?"

"Huh!" Nana hesitated, wondering whether to tell her. He looked around to make sure no one was within range of hearing. "They want the Golden Stool. They want me to help them steal *Sika Dwa*."

"Eh!" Pommaa exclaimed loudly.

Frema was alarmed by the revelation but did not react. Pommaa, realizing she had overreacted, now brought her voice down. "What!"

"Ha! He's asked me to help him steal my own heritage. How swollen headed can he get. That fool. I may be fighting Manhyia. But I will not sell my conscience. He thinks they can buy anybody or anything with money. 'In Africa, money talks; money can buy anything,' that's what he said. The idiot. How pig-headed can he get? He thinks he is wise. I will show him I am cleverer. And I want you by my side; all the way."

"Ok. Ok. I am with you."

"Clever, aren't you!" Frema muttered to herself. "So, that was how he disappeared from Manhyia; rescued by these mercenaries? And what are they doing standing right on top of the royal tomb? Digging a tunnel. What for? So it can lead them to the tomb and the Golden Stool. That's what they're here doing? Is he not the one who wants to steal the Golden Stool himself to embarrass Otumfoɔ and Manhyia because, as he says, he is fighting Manhyia and Otumfoɔ? Traitors to the Asante Kingdom."

Tossing all these over in her mind, it became clearer to her what the whole expedition there was about. It gave her an idea and a scenario to plot her way out of her current predicament. Frema saw Tango going to the ops room. She broke off and ran towards Tango. "Hey, guy. I want to speak with the boss." The guard who was looking after her, chased her to catch her before she reached Tango. She looked towards

Ohenenana and Pommaa. "I want to speak to him. It is urgent."

Pommaa saw her and became alarmed. She followed her. "Where do you think you are going? You bitch." Pommaa tried to intercept and cut her from meeting Tango. She had a feeling she might have eavesdropped on them and was going to report them to Abdul Ali.

"I want to see the boss, please."

Pommaa realized that from all that had happened Frema had been a negative intrusion. Her continued stay around would not work to the good of her and Ohenenana; the earlier they got rid of her the better it would be for them. She grabbed Frema by her arm.

"Let me go." Frema tried to break from her hold but her cuffed hands inhibited her. "You did not bring me here." Frema shrugged off Pommaa and approached Tango. "The boss, Please?"

"What about?" Tango demanded.

"I have some information for him that will be useful to your project here."

"What information."

"For his ears only." Frema insisted.

Tango hesitated. "Ok. Come along." He led her to Abdul Ali who was supervising the rescue as Don, Antinio and some men brought in the welding torch and cut off the conveyor belt that had entangled the truck. The door of the truck on the near side was chopped away. Ohenenana and Pommaa followed Frema there.

Frema started speaking as she got closer to Abdul Ali.

"Mr. Boss. Your friend here is a member of the royal family. They are the custodians of the Golden Stool. That's what I hear you are here for."

"That, I know already." Abdul Ali said dismissing her information as irrelevant.

"They know where what you are looking for is and know how to get you to it. Why don't you let him take you through the main entrance but have chosen to let you to it through the back door. This will get you nowhere."

"Shut your mouth! You fool." Ohenenana tried to shut her up.

He realized Frema had set off on a course to betray him; that, things he had kept away from Abdul Ali were gradually being revealed by Frema. That would spell doom for him and his plans to exploit Abdul Ali and to benefit from the expedition.

Frema ignored Ohenenana's interjections. "You are wasting your time," she went on. "He cannot tell you he does not know there is an entrance to the tomb. If he does not know himself, he knows people who go there. Yes. They go to it every forty days; so, he cannot tell you he has no idea how to get you there."

"Not one more word!" Ohenenana vehemently warned her to stop talking.

"But I knew that already." Abdul Ali said to the shock of Frema and to the surprise of Ohenenana too.

"You do?" Frema was lost as to what to say again seeing as everything she had said did not impress him. Out of shock and disappointment she added: "He is also a fraud?"

"Yes, but I also know what anyone can do for me. I don't care whether he is a fraud or a police commander as long as he provides results."

Frema got hysterical. She had realized her attempt to discredit Ohenenana could not work so she had to put in anything to substantiate her allegations. She was like a drowning woman clutching at straws, thus making a fool of herself. "You are wasting your time here, Mister. This is all a fraud. Your friend here has set you up to rob you. You know he has not been truthful with you; why are you allowing him to go on?" Pommaa dashed in and gave Frema a blow to the jaw shutting her up before she could end her statement. Frema fell to the ground. Ohenenana ran in and grabbed Pommaa to restrain her. Of course, it was a good revenge she had longed for since their first encounter. With her two hands tied, Frema could not easily help herself up. Tango picked her up with one hand. "Awwww! She hit me." Frema felt her painful jaw and spat out blood.

"That's enough!" Abdul Ali shouted out to restore order.

"See? She wants to stop me from telling you the truth." Frema added as she shrugged off Tango's hand.

"Truth. What truth?" Abdul Ali asked. Frema eyed Ohenenana. Pommaa attempted to break off to attack Frema again but Ohenenana restrained her. Realizing the tension, Abdul Ali invited Frema. "Come with me and tell me more. Untie her."

"What?" Ohenenana felt betrayed. He conferred with Pommaa as the guard removed the handcuffs.

Abdul Ali then instructed Tango to take over the rescue operations, "See to get to Kruger and those down there while I assess this new subject to see if she has anything substantial worthy of my attention." Abdul Ali was greatly disturbed but he tried to calm himself. The disaster was a major blow to the expedition. He could not envisage how long the rescue was going to take for operations to resume, even if it would at all. The information he had relied on from his geologists had let him down. Antonio could not detect the condition of the rock formation in order to prevent the disaster. Acrimony was the last encounter he would want to dabble in, nor to make enemies of his friends. He knew what Ohenenana could do and had done and at that point he felt he had reached the end of his usefulness.

He could not dispense with anyone; no, not when he has not finished the work. He did not know if the Worm was going to come back into action again and if it did not, how he was going to continue to meet his time before everything came crashing down on him. He also knew perfectly well that so far, he had not gone on to the radar of the security agencies for them to come at him. He must finish quickly so that by the time his welcome ended he would be long gone. In his strategy, he did not want to discard any information, no matter how small it was, for he could not know which would come in to save the situation. So, he decided to explore what Frema had. "Come along, Miss…"

"Frema. Frema is my name," she heartily said as she felt a sense of freedom, trotting behind Abdul Ali. She wringed her freed wrists, touched her bleeding lip and spat out blood again.

"Yes. Yes. Miss Frema."

For whatever it was, Frema felt her strategy had hit the tracks. She would endeavour to stay on course to see if it might yield her any results, she thought. Abdul Ali brought her to the ops room and sat her down. He offered her water. It was past midday and lunch was being served. Frema was served some pastry.

Tango called in more armed men. They were needed to strengthen the security and to prevent a possible revolt. Apart from the truckers who moved in and out carrying debris from the tunnel no one was allowed to leave the facility. Everything they needed had been provided. Abdul Ali had made sure of that so that everybody was comfortable.

By the time the damaged conveyor belt was removed the debris clear they had tried to remove the truck to make way to see behind it and fashion how they would enter the cave from where they were. After a couple attempts to remove it, they realized the truck was stuck; it had blocked the entrance of the tunnel into the cave below. Perhaps, it would be better they left there and used it to devise a way into the cave. Don went in and checked the safety of the truck at its current position. He confirmed it was safe. The way it was stuck there, it was better the truck was left to stay. Yet some of the engineers came in with some chains and hooks to clamp the truck firmer to hold additional weight and accommodate movement through it. Don opened the door to the driver's side giving him access to the pit and what was below. With a brighter flashlight he surveyed the tunnel. He carried a backpack with some logistics and first aid. He also wore a helmet fitted with a small powerful camera. As he moved, its images were transmitted onto a monitor at the ops room for Abdul Ali to view what was down in the tunnel.

"Kruger!" He screamed out.

"Yes! Over here!" Kruger responded as he saw the light. He waved his flash light to indicate where he was.

A rope tied to a firm post was brought to Don. His first attempt to descend through the driver's cabin doorway, he slipped and almost fell. He had to grab the driver's side door to save him from falling. Cautiously, the men who were aiding him to descend managed and dropped him through the driver's cabin doorway down into the pit; with the rope he cautiously climbed down. Kruger was there when his feet touched the ground. The ops room team saw Kruger. They cheered with satisfaction. Don let go the rope and grabbed Kruger who was smeared all over with mud. He hugged him with sincere affection. Don examined Kruger, saw his wounded palm. He gave him water. Kruger drank some, washed his face and the bleeding palm. Don applied some treatment to it and bandaged it. Kruger felt better. Don took another headset from his knapsack and gave it to Kruger to wear.

"Hi, boss." Kruger spoke as he stood in front of Don's camera.

Abdul Ali leaned forward to a microphone and responded as he saw Kruger well and strong. "Yes, Kruger. I hope you are okay."

"Yes, I am."

"Glad you are. Now you guys take a quick tour. Let's see what is there.

We've already lost a lot of working time."

More men followed the rope down and more lights were also brought in to improve the visibility there. They examined the bodies of the three that fell before Kruger and the operator of the Worm. The corpses were moved out of view to a corner. Kruger and Don walked for about 50 metres further into the belly of the earth in the new tunnel.

Ohenenana and Pommaa took their lunch pack and strayed off to an obscure corner out of the view of everyone. Ohenenana was completely beside himself with anger. He dumped the food aside, kicked the wall and punched his fist to the wall and screamed. He felt lost on what was going on and wondered what Abdul Ali was going to do with them from then on. He could not envisage what to do next. He felt betrayed, aware that Abdul Ali was sidelining him gradually from the centre of activities. He thought he had lost out on his expectations. The thought of it sent him berserk. Pommaa restrained Ohenenana and tried to calm him down. Ohenenana was at a point of breaking down in tears. Pommaa cuddled him in a more romantic way. He responded positively and the two engaged in a passionate romance, caressing and kissing. Ohenenana tried to reach into her jeans trousers from her waist and behind her with his hand. She grabbed his hand. "No. You can't go there now. I – I am not clean there. I am sorry." She looked him in the eye and kissed him. The passionate romance had come to an abrupt end. Ohenenana slowly disengaged from her and picked up his food and settled down to eat. He told himself that there was nothing more to do than wait, wait to get to the end and collect his dough.

Frema had finished her lunch and was also watching the visuals from the tunnel as the men in the tunnel prepared to descend into the cave. They commenced designing a safer way of descending in there with more men and logistics. Abdul Ali drew a chair to sit closer to her, his eyes still on the monitors. He apologized for the last encounter she had with Pommaa.

"What do you do for a living?" Abdul Ali commenced conversation with her again.

"I am a journalist. I write for the national daily newspaper. I am their local correspondent." Frema spoke freely as she felt relaxed.

"Yes, I recall now. You seem to have a fair idea about what we are doing here. How did you get to know?"

"I have no idea whatsoever you are doing here."

"Why did you come here then?"

"Your conspicuous activity attracted my attention. Any inquisitive journalist will certainly be attracted to those huge trucks driving through the centre of the city, heavily loaded with earth soil escorted in convoys by police motorcade out of the city. So, I followed the trucks to find out what was going on here and blah, blah, blah."

"I see."

"Why did you decide to dig instead of searching for the main entrance to the tomb if that is where you were going?"

"Searching for the entrance was not an option for me."

Frema enjoyed her encounter with Abdul Ali. It was like getting the opportunity to interview a high-profile underworld personality. It made her feel like trying to get into the mind of a sophisticated criminal like Abdul Ali. "What did you know about the Golden Stool that got you attracted to it?" she asked.

"Little. But, enough to bring me here."

"Well, for your information, the regular spiritual visit to the tomb is due in a few days. Why don't you wait and gate-crash on them? The royal spiritualist and his team do the regular 40-day visits. They will be going to make libation and offer drinks and food to the ancestral spirits and souls of the departed kings. They would certainly reach the stool which would offer you the easiest opportunity to pluck it without effort instead of this wasteful expedition that is costing lots of money and lives of your men."

"Thanks for the education but I have no time. Besides, I need no confrontation with anyone nor do I want to attract unnecessary attention to myself and what I am here to do. I want to be far ahead of them. Now, as you can see, your gods and the dead kings are at rest. What better time to go in through the back door, discreetly without stirring their quiet rest!"

"You failed then. You stirred the porcupine out of its hole."

"How?"

"You woke me up."

"Who are you? You are but one person."

"With enough quills to make you go green and your plans, up in smoke. I have a mouth wide and loud enough for a thousand. If I know, everybody else knows."

Abdul Ali sat up and watched her for a moment. Obviously, he had underestimated her intelligence. "That is very clever of you. What do you intend to do? Pop my balloon with your quill or blow it up in your tabloid?" He asked her.

"Well, I've not thought of that, seeing I am now a prisoner. I could not even chance on any info before I was caught in your snare."

Abdul Ali heaved a heavy sigh. "These few minutes with you have been very useful to me, educative. You've impressed me. I think I will need you by my side. Give me the right information to lead me to the tomb and to the stool faster, I shall pay you handsomely and release you unconditionally."

Frema felt warm within her. She had made a good impression on Abdul Ali but she still felt obtusely confused. Was he making her a deal? She was not sure. "Do you want to bribe me or trick me to join you?" she asked, wanting to know if he was making a genuine offer.

"I have not said that. But it's your choice. I am making you an offer."

She still wondered why he was making her an offer instead of coercing her or using force and pressure to induce her. "And that is for me to join you in your clandestine exercise?"

"No." He realized that her proposition would add some momentum to the work. "Lead me to one native who has access to the tomb."

"What about those two, I told you of their links to the kingdom."

"Each one for his purpose and relevance to me. I did not get here by

chance. Someone before them got me attracted to the Golden Stool and was leading me here."

"And, where is he?"

"I lost him on the way." "Who was that?"

"Prof. Kofi Nsiah. He visited the US recently to give a lecture and an exhibition on the Golden Stool.

"Oh, him."

"Did you know him?"

"Not intimately." Frema remembered Kofi Nsiah. "I covered one of his programmes."

"Oh, I see."

"You seem to know your way about then. Why don't you go look for him?"

"I said I lost him on the way here." "You killed him?"

Abdul Ali turned sharply. He did not like to be reminded that he had had to kill Kofi Nsiah and she seemed to be accusing him of Kofi's death. "I did not kill him." He protested vehemently. "I don't kill people. He took a dive in a river and did not surface again." He calmed down and went on in a very serious tone. "Look, nothing is impossible for me to achieve. I always find a better way out in every sticky situation. There is always a better way. You seem to give me the inclination that you're a better choice in my way forward now."

"I am highly flattered. But as I said I am not from the royal kingdom family. This is as far as I can help you.

"You are of a better use to me now. You have a better idea for my way forward. As I said, get me the native person with access to the stool, I'll give you your freedom and a reward."

"Immediately?"

"Immediately and unconditionally." "Sounds too sweet to be true."

"You have my word. Deal?" He stretched forth his hand. She took his and shook it.

"Alright...Deal."

Down the tunnel some more men had joined Kruger and Don. After the dead persons, including the operator of the Worm, were retrieved and placed away, automotive and mechanical engineers teamed up in an effort to see if they could recover and salvage the Worm.

All the handy men were quickly mobilized down the pit which had become the new area of activity. They brought in hand tools and began digging round the Worm. Within a short time, they managed to put it back on its tracks. After a few checks and trials here and there on the Worm they tried to restart it. From Kruger's camera Sam saw that the Worm was ready to be started.

"Guys, what's up now with the Worm?" Sam enquired as one of the engineers jumped into the driving seat and fired the engine.

"It's alive!" Kruger exclaimed as the men down cheered for their achievement.

Sam relayed the information to Abdul Ali. "Boss, the Worm is alive!" "Good." Abdul Ali received the message with satisfaction. "Let's get back to work at once. Come, my lady." He came out with Frema from the ops room. He called and met Tango. Ohenenana and Pommaa saw them and joined them. Tango handed over Frema's phone to Abdul Ali. As they walked towards the entrance of the tunnel Abdul Ali presented it to her.

"Yes, here, your phone. My number is first on fast dial. Call me immediately you come by anything." He gave her the terms of reference of the task she was going to do and explicitly warned her what she should not do. "Don't disappoint yourself. Don't try to play heroine with me or play smart by alerting the security people to attack us or to stop us. Let me warn you. Nobody can stop me. I have a small contingent of an army with enough fighting power to quell any assault or repulse any attack on me, I have enough to hold them till I am done here and leave. I don't want any trouble here and don't want to start one. I want to trust that you would do what we've just agreed to. Any trouble you bring will be on your own head and you will suffer for it," he warned.

"I'd do my best," Frema said.

Abdul Ali turned to Ohenenana. "Nana, there are new developments that require new directions."

Pommaa snorted at Frema, "You, snake. You've sold us out, eh?"

Abdul Ali cut in, "No recriminations. We are back in business and no hard feelings." He turned to Ohenenana; trying to make amends. "Miss Frema is going to handle one aspect of the process. Tango, she is yours. Take a couple of guys with you. She will go to town. Accompany her to bring here some folks." Tango beckoned one of the SUVs. Two armed security men with rifles joined the vehicle before it drove in. They wore dark goggles and long dark jackets which concealed their weapons. Abdul Ali pulled Tango aside. "Be careful with her. Do not let her out of your sight, come what may. Bring her back even if you are not successful with your mission. Do not let her come to any harm."

"Yes, sir."

"Her code name, Hummingbird. If she tries to double cross us, you know what to do. Call for help to be rescued if you run into any trouble. You should be back immediately. Now, you go!"

Tango took Frema by her upper arm and dragged her to the SUV and sandwiched her between the two armed men in the back seat while he sat at the front. The SUV slowly moved out of the compound meandering its way through the many trucks that were parked in the yard. From when the Worm stopped working, the soil evacuation had also halted. The truck drivers sat in their trucks and waited while the police dispatch riders hung about their bikes. They were served with their lunches which they ate with disinterest.

"Nana, we're square, aren't we?" Abdul Ali said as he pulled Nana along to the tunnel. He knew what he was talking about when he said he was done with Ohenenana. After his rescue, Ohenenana had become a fugitive and would not dare show his face anywhere. The tomb was the best succour for him.

"I do not know what you want me to say." Ohenenana followed Abdul Ali reluctantly. "You have a new friend now. Is she the one calling the shots now?"

"I don't have any new friends. You are my partner. We'll go on as such and finish the operation. Come with me, partner. The Worm is back in action. We are all going down there to supervise the activities. The stool is just a finger away. In the meantime, while we are getting ready to move down there, call off the truckers and the police escorts. We shall not require their services any longer. Make sure everyone is happy. There is more to do before we are done. Here," Abdul Ali received an envelope full of cash and handed it over to Ohenenana, "this should be enough to settle everyone there." Ohenenana received the envelope. "Express my utmost gratitude to them. It's been a pleasure working with them." As Ohenenana turned to leave with Pommaa, Abdul Ali called him. "Nana, I am waiting to go down there with you."

"Okay, I will not be long," Ohenenana responded.

With a hand-held scanner Abdul Ali probed. He could now see a network of tracks or tunnels crisscrossing the underground area. He pressed a button and the monitor screen split into two; one side showed live video and the other an infra-red image of the rock formation and also indicating the position of the Golden Stool.

Later, a more reliable mechanism for lowering men down the cave was put in place. One after the other, Abdul Ali, Ohenenana and rest of them were lowered into the cave. They joined the rest of the team who were busily going about their activities. The Worm rolled into a more leveled ground. The cave-like nature of the pit had a large area to deposit the output of the Worm. The engineers had managed to build a small-size conveyor belt out of the residue of the original one they were using above that dropped with the Worm into the pit.

"Our object is just behind this wall. Get the Worm working this way. Get the move on," Abdul Ali ordered.

Antonio came in. He looked frightened and there was a slight tremor in his voice as he assured Abdul Ali of the safety of the rock formation in the cave. Antonio directed from where the Worm should start drilling again.

The Worm began to work, drilling into the walls of the cave. As the soil came out at the rear, men and women with carrying pans and shovels moved it away.

Chapter Twelve

RACE WITH THE HUMMINGBIRD

Agyei, the driver, took a turn and drove through Adum, the Central Business District with the SUV. They were caught up in a heavy traffic. One of the trucks from the digging yard passed by with a police escort, returning to site. Frema sat quietly between the two security men. They looked straight and stiff. She looked at them from left to right. She wondered where she was taking them. She knew it was all a hoax and could not believe that Abdul Ali had bought into it so easily. She had hoodwinked the boss. Her aim was getting herself out of that pit into the open where she could call for help and be rescued. By that she thought she could foil the greatest robbery in the world. So far it had worked. But she had been warned not to try to play heroine. What should she do? People were passing by the vehicle. Should she scream she had been kidnapped? Who would come to her rescue? Her worry and anxiety grew as all these thoughts ran through her mind.

What a stupid decision she had taken following the trucks; getting caught; making the wild promise; and there she was, sitting in between those mercenaries with a promise she was going to provide a better solution for that thief in order to gain her freedom. Who was she going to get? What if the person refused to cooperate? She would have done her part, anyway. Would they let her go? It suddenly dawned on her that she had taken a big and dangerous gamble. Try to escape? That did not seem possible. Unable to think of any escape plan, she gave up the effort. Then she remembered one of the chiefs in Otumfour's palace, the Sumankwahene. She had interviewed him when she was doing a story on a chieftaincy dispute in one of the Asante divisional areas where two royals in that division were battling for legitimacy. They can't do anything to her if she returned empty handed, she thought. "I will do this," she said to herself and turned to the driver. "Please, do you know Ala Bar?"

"Yah," Agyei responded.

"That's where we are going." She directed.

Hawkers and other traders walked by. The Central Business District was bustling as usual. They followed a go-slow traffic behind two taxi cabs. Ahead, two young men pushing a heavily loaded cart appeared at the corner of the street. The taxi driver leading the traffic attempted to speed past the cart before it would come to the intersection ahead. In the process, his cab scraped the cart slightly, tipping the load off the cart, sprawling it in the middle of the street and blocking the small lane completely. The cab driver drove away after causing the mess. The traffic came to a sudden halt. A long line of cars formed behind, tooting their horns. The SUV was stuck with no way to exit.

"What the f..k! Hell!" Tango exclaimed

"How could he do that?" 1st Security said venting his frustration: "Go. Help them out to clear the road," he implored 2nd Security who immediately obliged. 2nd Security opened the door to his side and dropped out to go to assist clear the blocked road. Tango immediately recollected a similar situation that got them to lose Kofi Nsiah on the Kakum road. The incident was too fresh in his mind. He turned to look but the second security man had already descended from the SUV and was on his way.

"Get him back in the van, right now!" Tango screamed at 1st Security who had sent his colleague out of the vehicle.

"He is just helping clear...." 1st Security tried to justify his action.

"I said get him back in the vehicle!! Now!!" Tango screamed back at him.

By then, 2nd Security was already close to the boys with the cart. 1st Security also got down in an attempt to get the 2nd Security back. "Hey, Get back inside!" He called his colleague back.

Tango saw 1st Security had also got out of the vehicle. Incensed, he screamed at him to get back into the vehicle.

Frema immediately sensed there was something amiss. She wondered why Tango was irritated and vehemently trying to prevent them from getting out of the vehicle. For a few seconds she saw that both security men guarding her had left her alone in the vehicle and Tango was frantically twitching and turning. The idea flashed through her mind that it could be her chance to escape. She waited till the 1st Security man got closer to the door. With a hard kick, she pushed the vehicle door which was not shut, hitting the 1st Security. The impact sent him sprawling on the ground. With lightning speed, Frema dashed out of the vehicle into the milling crowd.

"Hey! She is escaping," Agyei said as he saw her running into the crowd. Tango cursed himself. He also dashed out of the vehicle after her. How could he be so naïve to have underestimated Frema.

1st Security recovered. "Where is she?" he inquired. Agyei pointed at the direction she had taken. 1st Security saw Tango as he pursued Frema. He signaled 2nd Security who also joined him to follow Tango. She crossed a street. A car missed her narrowly. She ran in between cars around Kejetia and then turned off into Kumasi Central Market. She ran in between stalls. The two security men had caught up with Tango who had slowed down, strategically assessing the direction she might take. They searched frantically for her. Tango gave a signal to 1st Security to take a lane to his left to see if he could cut her off ahead. He followed the directive and moved ahead. Tango again directed 2nd Security to take the right lane. He also followed. Frema quickly dashed into one stall and begged the owner for a place to hide.

She squeezed herself into a corner in the stall when the lady obliged. Tango appeared in the lane.

The two security men also appeared from the opposite direction. It only meant that she could be in the lane between them. From her hiding place Frema picked her phone to make a call. She turned the phone on; it immediately triggered a signal in the communicator Tango wore in his ear. Tango pulled from his top breast pocket a detector and flipped it on. It was a small GPS device with an LED screen. There was no signal coming to show where Frema was. But as soon as Frema's phone got activated Tango's detector picked her signal. His detector began to beep indicating how far away Frema was from him. He signaled the two men to come towards him in order to close in on her. As they did, the detector beeped louder.

Hiding in a cloth seller's stall, Frema saw 1st Security go past the stall. Tango and 1st Security met. He signaled she was closer, pointing to the stall. The stall owner sat completely composed, looking away as if nothing had happened. Tango pointed to her stall. 2nd Security turned to the stall and pulled the stall owner away from the entrance sending her sprawling to the ground. She began wailing and called for help. 2nd Security popped into the stall for Frema. She emerged holding a can containing some stinking concoction. She splashed the concoction on Tango in the face, with some entering his mouth and nostrils.

"Ouch! Huff." Tango lost hold of the scanner detector letting it crash on the ground. The other men took cover from the concoction.

"Piss and shit!" 2nd Security indicated. Frema threw the can at 2nd Security. With the men off guard Frema took to her heels again. Some people, responding to the wailing of the stall owner, trooped in.

"After her!" Tango ordered and 1st Security raced after her. Tango picked up his detector. It had gone off and therefore he could not track her immediately. 2nd Security pulled one of the cloths hanging in the stall and tossed it to Tango. He wiped his face clean of the concoction and cleaned up the detector. Before they could follow up to chase Frema a group of young men gathered around them with cudgels and other offensive weapons. Sensing the imminent attack on them, 2nd Security pulled out an identity card from his top breast pocket and flashed it.

"National security! National security!" 2nd Security shouted, pulling out his rifle from under his jacket. The massing crowd immediately succumbed and gave them way to pass. Tango looked again at the detector to track Frema. It was off. As they ran, they met a young girl carrying a bucket of water on her head. 2nd Security lifted it off her and handed it over to Tango who washed his face and turned the rest on himself to wash off the concoction and to douse the stench. He threw the bucket away and ran along.

The poor girl realizing she had lost her water dropped to the ground, rolling and wailing, "My water, my water!"

Frema bumped into a couple of hawkers, spilling their wares they carried on their heads. 1st Security was getting closer. She pulled some table top stalls down behind her. They fell in the way of her pursuer, impeding his movement in the process. Soon, she made up some distance. She crossed a busy street with heavy and fast-moving traffic and disappeared. 1st Security reached the roadside and could not cross because of the vehicles speeding on the road. By the time it eased up for him to cross, he was joined by Tango and 2nd Security.

"I've lost her." 1st Security told them, helplessly looking at his colleagues. Angry Tango hit the detector in his palm with the effort to get it back on. The device was not responding. He asked his men to call the driver to pick them up from where they were. 1st Security called Agyei to pick them up.

In his house, Nana Sumankwaa was seated on a kitchen stool

behind a small table with lunch spread on it, yam *ampesie*(boiled yam) with *kontomire*(spinach) and palm oil stew. He put his final morsel in his mouth. Attaa walked in with a bowl of water and soap. She pulled away the food tray and placed the bowl on the table. Nana Sumankwaa washed his hands.

"Attaa," Nana Sumankwaa called his house help. "Tell your mother I am going to the University to see your uncle Kofi. I will come early for supper. Tell her the food must be enough for the two of us. He will be coming home with me."

"Yes, Nana. I will tell her." Attaa responded and curtsied.

Nana Sumankwaa picked up a top hat hanging on a stand and wore it on top of his partially bald head as he walked out of the compound.

Frema appeared at a corner near Nana Sumankwaa's house. A handful of boys were playing soccer nearby on a small dusty and grassless pitch. She stopped one of them and chatted him. The boy pointed the direction of Nana Sumankwaa's home.

From the house, Nana appeared and hailed a taxi. The boy noticed Nana Sumankwaa and indicated to her that he was the one by the roadside. Before Frema could turn to see, however, Nana Sumankwaa had boarded the taxi which had begun to move away. Just at that time, the football rolled towards Frema. She picked up the ball and gave it a big kick. The ball flew in the air and dropped on the bonnet of the taxi. The sudden and unexpected bounce startled the driver and caused him to bring the car to a sudden screeching stop.

"Kwee!" the boy exclaimed while his colleagues clapped and cheered in amazement at her performance. The taxi driver stepped out of the car and angrily rushed towards the boys with a rod he had pulled out of his cab.

"Who did that? Who did that?" the driver asked angrily as he rushed in with the rod to strike at the culprit.

Frema owned up, "I did."

The driver turned to confront her. "Why? You could have broken my glass!" "No. I wanted to stop you. I am looking for the man in your car." She said boldly as she strolled past him towards the cab. The taxi driver shook his head in disbelief and followed her. Nana Sumankwaa had gotten out and was standing by the car. He asked who the culprit was.

"Nana, I did." Frema said as she curtsied. "I came to you. You were moving away and there was no other way to stop you."

"You could have caused a terrible accident, you know that." Nana Sumankwaa chided.

She apologized. "But I am here to... to see you."

"I am sorry, too." Nana Sumankwaa sat back in the vehicle and spoke to her with the door ajar. "This is a wrong time, as you can see. I am on my way out on a serious appointment. You can come back later or early tomorrow morning. Driver, let's go." Nana Sumankwaa attempted to close the door. Frema held it and drew closer.

"Nana, this can't wait. I must talk to you at once."

Nana looked at her. He was getting irritated. Frema looked at the driver as he sat in the vehicle. She drew closer to Nana Sumankwaa and spoke in a suppressed tone, "I have very vital information for you. You are the only one who came to mind as I got to this vicinity."

Nana *Sumankwaa* rebuffed her loudly. "That's what they all say when they are looking for favours. Who are you? And who sent you?"

"My name is Frema. You should remember me. I am a journalist with the Ashanti Pioneer."

"What did I say? You all are the same. You are here to blackmail me. You are rather looking for something from me to make your news, aren't you? You want me to spit so that you will publish me in your newspapers that I had spat and blow me up on your many radio stations, not so?" Nana said, getting angry with her. "Driver, take me away." Nana Sumakwaa shifted and shut the door.

"Please, Nana," she frantically pleaded, speaking through the window. "This is a serious matter. I can't tell you what I have been through before getting here." The driver ignored her as she continued to talk and took off. She strolled along as the cab started moving. "The survival of *Asanteman*…" she muttered. The cab left her speeding away, disappointed. But her last words were sufficient to catch the attention of Nana Sumankwaa. He heavily tapped on the back rest of the driver's seat, signaling him to stop. The driver pounced on the brakes and brought the cab to a screeching stop. Tears from her eyes dropped as she stood crestfallen. But her sad face suddenly warmed up with a slight smile as she saw the cab reverse towards her.

With a curious face Nana Sumankwaa peeped through the window at her. "Did you say the survival of *Asanteman*?" he asked.

"Yes, Nana," she said nodding.

"Sit down." Nana Sumankwaa moved aside to allow her to sit by him and the cab took off.

Tango and his team joined the SUV as it arrived. He picked up his communicator which he had left in the vehicle as he jumped out to chase Frema. He called for support. "Tango calling base."

"Yes, Base. Come in Tango."Jim responded.

"We've lost hummingbird. Tracking device is malfunctioning. Please help to locate hummingbird."

"Alright. Just a minute." Jim searched on his scanner and saw the icon of Frema moving on a street map. "Hummingbird current loco: Ashanti New Town. On the move on the… 2nd Avenue, heading eastwards towards the…… Accra road."

"The lady has been located. She is on the move on the 2nd Avenue towards the Accra road. Quick let's go." Tango relayed the direction. "You know it?"

"Yes, sir." Agyei made a quick manoeuvre and sped off towards the Accra road. "Base, track hummingbird and give us minute by minute update. We are rolling."

"What is wrong with your device?" Jim inquired "You're live here; how come you cannot track her?"

"Don't know"

Jim instructed him, “Restart your device. It should be able to work.”

Tango restarted the tracker and it began to work again. “Bingo! We are on again. There she goes. She’s on the Accra road. Hurry up.”

“Good luck.”

“Thank you, Base.”

“You’re welcome,” said Jim as he signed out.

Agyei sped up overtaking all vehicles in front of him.

Chapter Thirteen

NOWHERE TO PERCH

A few of hours earlier, Kofi Nsiah had sat behind his computer in his sitting room, part of which he had set up as his study at his University bungalow. He had connected to the internet searching for information about Abdul Ali. He wanted to know who he was, how well connected he was, whether he was worth the bother at all, now that he was no more in his hands. A few days had passed and he had not heard anything about him and his dramatic arrival in Ghana. The constant fear that Abdul Ali could spring a surprise on him to grab him at some dark corner or even at his home lurked in his mind; the thoughts frightened him. He felt he must be on constant alert. He also searched for news about what happened in the USA, particularly, the murders at his hotel. Then he checked about himself and the exhibition he had done.

He was alarmed by the results. Yes, there was news about his exhibition and lectures. It had had extensive coverage and reviews from authoritative and credible sources. All agreed that the programme had been very successful. To his astonishment, his search drew blank regarding his involvement in the crimes at the Grand Hotel and associated events, and also anything about Abdul Ali. The murders were reported alright but no links were made to him.

It was as if he was never involved in them. Try as he did, he could not track anything connecting him to the murders.

However, he saw pictures of the blast at the NYPD 5th Precinct, the damaged façade and tributes paid to Lt. Croffy whose body was recovered from the wreckage at the safe house. Cause had been attributed to gas leakage that blew up the safe house when Lt. Croffy and a couple of officers had gone there for a retreat. There was nothing said about him and no link to him, Saah or Coy. That disturbed him greatly and made him feel as if he never existed and had never gone to the USA. He touched his body; he went to the fridge and drank some water. He hit his fist against the wall. He felt the pain. Is he alive, he thought, or dreaming? He wondered. He did everything he could to convince himself that he was awake, not dead and was not dreaming either. After a couple of hours battling with himself, he dropped back in the chairs in front of a computer. He felt exhausted, dropped his head on his folded arms on the desk and fell asleep. He began to dream. He had entered a wild and weird forest. He was being chased. Next, he was fighting with some unidentifiable assailants who had caught him and thrown him into a river attempting to drown him. He struggled with them. As he lay there, he breathed heavily; his contorting face expressed how he struggled in the dream, submerged under water, drowning and swallowing water. With one big effort he pushed himself out of the water, freeing himself from the grip of his assailants. His effort in the dream was expressed out by throwing his forearms which hit hard on the monitor in front of him.

Sweating and panting, he was awoken by a heavy knock on his door. He was disturbed. He rushed to the window, pulled aside the curtain slightly to peep to see who it was. Nana Sumankwaa and Frema were waiting at the door. He quickly opened the door into his living room. He checked from outside to see if they were not being followed. Nana Sumankwaa looked at him and instantly noticed his unsettled demeanour. "You seem like you've seen a ghost," he asked.

"You can say that again," Kofi responded as he rushed back.

"What's happened to you?" the worried Nana Sumankwaa asked further.

"Nightmares and horrible dreams, one after the other." Kofi confessed. "Come in. Sit down. Who is she?" he asked on seeing Frema entering behind Nana Sumankwaa as he shut the door behind him.

"A journalist. I think she has something to say."

Frema stretched her hand to Kofi in introduction. "My name is Frema. I work with Ashanti Pioneer."

"Nice meeting you. Please sit. And what is your story?"

"I stumbled upon a group of people who are digging a huge tunnel under the city."

"A tunnel?" Kofi exclaimed, cutting in.

"Yes, a tunnel," she continued. "I saw it myself. What I gathered from them was that they were looking for the ancestral tomb of *Asanteman*. I got suspicious. I needed someone from Manhyia to tell."

"Her story seems to tie in with what you had told me a few days ago," Nana Sumankwaa added.

"Abdul Ali. Abdul Ali. Wofa, the guy is in town and is already digging to the Golden Stool!" Kofi was quite convinced and terribly disturbed.

"Why are you bothered? He cannot lay his hands on the Golden Stool. He cannot."

"Don't underestimate this man. He is capable of anything. He is an international thief, specializing in looting ancestral relics of high value. He is like a colossus. He strides the world and commands immense power and wealth. He can buy his way through anything anytime. He will stop at nothing to achieve whatever he sets his mind to. That is the kind of person we are talking about. No one can stop him."

"I will." Nana Sumankwaa said, very confident of himself.

"He is a part of an international cartel or mafia, spread all over the world." Kofi added.

Frema asked, "You seem to know him pretty well?" Then she

looked sternly at Kofi and recollected what Abdul Ali had said about Kofi. "You must be the Kofi! He spoke to me about you."

"You talked to him?!

"Yes I had a good chat with him."

"What did he say about me?" Kofi asked.

"Well, he said he was bringing you down so that you could take him to the tomb but he lost you on the way. He is convinced you had died."

"He thinks so?" Kofi added. "He wanted me to walk him to the tomb so he could pick the Golden Stool like some trophy or fleece. I got away. I lost him, or did he lose me? And just three days after, he is already digging close to the stool. I am not surprised he has come this far."

All this notwithstanding, Kofi was taking a good look at Frema and seriously assessing her. Her demeanour and her story did not convince him. He felt very suspicious about Frema. He did not mince words and went straight at her. "Lady, I don't trust a word you have said here." Kofi got onto his feet. "I think you are a fraud or a nosy journalist. Better still, you could be a paid spy sent here by Abdul Ali to track me down."

"Why, don't you believe anything I have said?" she asked with great shock and disbelief.

"Yes. Wofa, how could you entertain and bring her to me?"

"What is your suspicion? What have you seen about her?" Nana Sumankwaa asked.

"How could she have found nobody else under the sun except you to come to just when you were on your way here? Coincidence?"

Nana Sumankwaa looked at Kofi, dumbfounded. Could he be right?

"Why do you say that?" Frema burst out. She blinked and tears rained down her cheeks without effort. With great pain she narrated how she stumbled on Abdul Ali and what she had seen and gone through; the equipment that had been commandeered; the unimaginable sizes and the fleet of earth moving equipment; the sophisticated and high technology he has employed, accompanied by the high level of technical expertise of the personnel engaged and the speed at which the process was running. "He caught me when I went nosing around his tunnel. I wonder how he managed to raise equipment of such magnitude and personnel in Ghana within such a short time that he has been in the country. I saw he was very serious and well organized.

I could not imagine any way to get out of there. I feared he would kill me. I feared I might die without seeing my sick daughter again." She broke down but immediately recomposed herself. "So, I tricked him. I was able to convince him he needed some people who could lead him to the stool through the main entrance to the tomb. He bought the idea and sent me out to bring someone. Strangely, I got a rare opportunity to escape when we came out and I took it. I was looking for someone in Manhyia with authority to alert. I ran into your uncle by accident." Frema became very emotional. "I have risked my life escaping from men chasing me in the streets of Kumasi, wielding guns, to bring this information and you insult me and handle it with such scorn and affront. I am very disappointed. I have nothing sinister. No one sent me there. I am here alive just because I used my brains to get out of that den and you could at least credit me with a little intelligence." Frema turned to the door to leave.

Nana Sumankwaa rushed on her and stopped her. "Wait, your coming to me was no accident." He dragged her back. "The guardians of our ancestral stools led you to us."

"You believe me then. I am not lying." Frema wiped her wet face with tissue paper from a box on the centre table. She blew and wiped her nose too with the tissue.

"I saw it in your eyes when I first met you today. You are sincere and truthful. Let not your heart be troubled. On account of Professor's suspicion, for what he had also been through, I would not blame him." His words brought some comfort to Frema. She sat down in a sofa near her. Nana Sumankwaa walked to Kofi and held his hand to calm him down. Kofi obstinately walked away to his computer. Nana Sumankwaa again turned to Frema. "We are the custodians of the stool. In fact, I always lead the team which visits the stools, personally. Nobody knows the way to stools. Even I do not know where it is. I do not go to the tomb by myself. It is spiritual. We are led there by the spirits of our ancestors. In a few days, it will be Akwasidae. The Golden Stool and other stools will be cleansed, purified and our ancestors fed. This is the power and strength of the stools and by then all the ancestral spirits will be awoken to come. They will feed and bless *Asanteman*, the great warrior kingdom.

And you say this is the time someone wants to walk into the ancestral tomb to steal the Golden Stool? It takes only a crazy mind to attempt this. Then he should be prepared for war. The British attempted centuries ago. They failed. None has succeeded since. This is a joke. Let no one try."

Kofi felt embarrassed though he strongly believed his instincts. He looked sternly at her. He could not accept her reason. He knew Abdul Ali. He was a gambler, a smart one who would latch at any lead. He felt letting Frema out was a plot, part of his game plan: set her as bait, let her loose and she is likely to lead you somewhere. He also suspected she could be bugged too, but could he dare calling a lady with the physique Frema had, to frisk her, running his hands around her. He did not have the courage to even suggest a search on her.

As she sat down Frema was slowly getting angry. She looked at Kofi. She angrily wondered why he should suspect her as a spy for Abdul Ali. Then she remembered Abdul Ali's instructions to her: "Yes, your phone. My number is first on fast dial. Call me immediately you come by anything. Don't disappoint yourself." Frema brought out her phone from her pocket. She tapped dial key; an international number appeared. She attempted to dial. She raised her head and saw Nana Sumankwaa looking at her. She stopped. She was pensive. After all Kofi did not seem to appreciate what she had brought and thought she was a fraud, playing to give him away. She looked again at Kofi, then turned to Nana Sumankwaa. She thought of what she had been promised by Abdul Ali, her freedom and reward. She also thought of what her action to give these men away too could bring. It will lead to this thief, Abdul Ali, stealing the heritage of a great people, the consequences of which will be to bring down this great kingdom with the possible attendant fall of a nation, its history, its glory, pageantry and the lives of its people. The burden of guilt, she thought. The unimaginable consequences weighed against her conscience and petty little interest, her freedom and reward. Abdul Ali, could she trust he would keep his word? She looked again at the number on the phone screen. Her thumb went to the call key. In a flash her thumb shifted to the stop key; and she pressed it to cut the call.

"So, Wofa. What do we do now?" Kofi asked after a brief period of silence. "It seems only the three of us, beside the thief and his gang, know what is going on. We can't stop them by ourselves. It will be a poor attempt at committing suicide."

"Left to me, I will say we should not worry ourselves. Down there, it is a spiritual world. No one with royal blood can get in." Nana settled in a chair close to him.

"I saw Ohenenana with them; and, another woman." Frema added. "Ohenenana?" Kofi asked.

"Yes. The one Manhyia arrested dedua the other day." she confirmed. "It was reported he escaped." Nana Sumankwaa chipped in.

"He escaped?" Kofi asked

"No, they rescued him." Frema corrected Nana Sumankwaa. "He is in league with them. Well, that is what I thought I saw."

"But I tell you, no one not led there by the ancestral spirits can even see the entrance to the tomb, let alone see anything else."

"Nana, they have reached the caves and tunnels."

"The tomb would cleanse itself of any sacrilegious entries. You will need a code to break in. Ohenenana does not have the codes. No matter how hard he tries he is bound to fail. I assure you."

"What codes?" Kofi asked.

"You would know when it is your turn to lead. The spirits of our ancestors will dream you the codes." Nana Sumankwaa got to his feet. "In the meantime, we need to inform, *Ɔte kɔkɔɔso, Asanteman wura* (The King of the Golden State, Lord of *Asanteman*). We shall cleanse the Golden Stool with their blood, use them as sacrifices to the ancestors and their spirits shall live forever as slaves to the kings in the life beyond! My throat is parched." Nana Sumankwaa cleared his throat. Kofi rose to the fridge to fetch a drink for his uncle.

It was getting dark and by the help of the tracker, Tango and his team had located Frema and were closing in. They reached the University campus and followed the indication towards Kofi Nsiah's bungalow. Tango picked up a high-powered binoculars when they reached the bungalow. By that he was able to see infrared images and movements of those in the bungalow. Inside the SUV one of the security men who had a sniper rifle with a telescope and a silencer fitted set it up. Through the window he could also see Nana Sumankwaa, Kofi Nsiah and Frema.

Kofi brought in a bottle of wine to serve Nana Sumankwaa. Frema expressed fears of any attempt that may accede to a possible attack on Abdul Ali to dislodge him. "Talking of attacking; Nana, he is armed, the kind of arms and ammunition he is holding is no joke. His fire power is sufficient to resist any attack on him."

Her fears were affirmed by Kofi. "Besides, the tomb is right underneath the city. Any explosion down there will bring the whole city to rubbles like a tsunami."

"And the casualties." Frema added.

"So, what do I do?" Nana Sumankwaa asked. "Sit with my hands clasped in my *damirifa* (between my thighs)? Manhyia must know."

Inside the SUV Tango asked if the sniper had any of them on his target. For fear of panic and losing them, Tango ordered that the sniper should take the shot. The 2nd Security who was on the sniper rifle took a shot. The bullet passed through the window and hit the glass which Nana Sumankwaa held right in front of Kofi Nsiah as he poured the drink.

"What was that?" Nana Sumankwaa exclaimed as the glass shattered in his palm.

"Shit." The 2nd Security swore as his shot missed the target. "What? You missed?" Tango queried.

Inside the bungalow, Kofi was greatly alarmed, "Shit! They are here!"

Kofi burst out as he fell to the ground. Frightened "Who?" Frema asked unconsciously.

"Everybody down on the floor! Follow me!" Kofi screamed as he rolled on the floor and crawled away.

"Fire at random" Tango ordered. "Get them out into the open." The sniper fired several shots into the house hitting anything in sight through the windows.

Kofi turned angrily at Frema. "You see what I said! They sent you so they could track you to us. It is a set up." he said as he and his company began to crawl on their bellies to the back door. "Don't follow us, you traitor!" He barked harshly at Frema.

"I have no idea what you're talking about" Frema vehemently protested.

"Don't follow us!" Kofi attempted to push her away with his foot as they crawled on the floor.

Nana Sumankwaa restrained him. "Allow her, Kofi. We cannot leave her to the dogs. They will kill her." Nana Sumankwaa pleaded for her.

Kofi stretched to reach for the key and the knob of the door and opened it. They exited the house and crossed the compounds of adjoining bungalows through their hedges. The darkness of the evening had began to fall. They ran as fast as they could.

Tango and his men dropped off the vehicle and ran on foot to chase them. They went round the house, searched but could not find anyone.

Nana Sumankwaa could not run. He was slowing them down. "Kofi, My leg is heavy. I can't lift it." Kofi observed that Nana Sumankwaa was bleeding from his rib and thigh. He had been hit by some of the bullets. He went to his aid and they entered a colleague lecturer's bungalow.

Professor Osei was alarmed to see them.

"Osei. Osei," Kofi pleaded. "I need help. My uncle is wounded. I must get him to hospital at once."

"Gosh! He is bleeding. What happened?" Prof Osei rose to meet them.

"Your car? Where is it?" Kofi enquired.

"The key? Where is the key?" Frema demanded.

Prof. Osei was confused and could not decide what to do immediately. Then he remembered they were asking for the keys to his car. He fetched the keys. "Here. Get him into the car while I go round to open the garage door." They entered the garage through the hall as Prof. Osei went out through the kitchen. They heard running footsteps approaching the house.

"Quick! Get him into the car!" Frema screamed at Kofi as he assisted Nana Sumankwaa into the car and joined him at the back seat. Frema ran into the driver's seat. She started the car and moved without waiting for the door to open. She reversed and took away the wooden garage door. Prof. Osei was brushed away by the door. He fell and collapsed. Out of the garage Frema quickly turned the car around and sped away.

Tango and his team appeared from inside the house. They fired at the car as it sped away. He called in their SUV to pick him and his men up. By the time they got on the way Frema had gained some distance in traffic. Tango checked and he could track the car. They followed them, about two minutes away in traffic.

Frema meandered through the night traffic with terrific speed. She informed them that the Sofo Lane Interchange was ahead which was not too far away from the Komfo Anokye Hospital. Kofi asked his uncle to hold on as they were getting him to the hospital for medical attention.

Nana Sumankwaa rejected this proposal and insisted they head for Manhyia instead. He insisted he wanted to speak to the King before he was taken anywhere.

"You are bleeding. Let's get you medical attention first." Kofi tried to persuade him.

"No. Take me to Manhyia," he insisted, straining in pain.

Kofi directed Frema to do so. As she slowed down and indicated to exit, they felt a big bang and a jolt on the car. The SUV had caught up with them and had rammed into the back of the car. The impact swerved the car left and right and Frema struggled with the steering. The car climbed the embankment on the left. She brought it back onto the road, manoeuvred and brought it under control. Frema was about stop to check the impact the band had caused.

"Go! Go! Go! Don't stop!" Kofi screamed. Frema hit on the accelerator speeding as fast as she could with the SUV pursuing. They ran in front of the Komfo Anokye roundabout and down towards Kejetia. She made a right turn to Pampaso with SUV at her tail. She entered the CBD. The streets were empty of the usual heavy human and vehicular traffic. She made a quick turn into another lane. The SUV attempted to follow but ran into an oncoming car. As Agyei extricated the SUV from the jam, it gave Frema a few seconds to break away.

Ahead, in front of Hotel de Kingsway, vehicles were parked in such a way that the available space was too narrow for a vehicle to pass. Frema turned into the lane, brushed through two cars and burst a tyre in the process. The car was unable to move again. The SUV driver missed the turn and zoomed past the Hotel de Kingsway turn.

Frema parked and descended. She ran round and came in to help Kofi pull Nana Sumankwaa out. He was going cold as he had lost so much blood. He was feeling drowsy.

"He is going cold. We must get him to the hospital. Quick, find a taxi." Kofi asked Frema to look for one. Frema ran off for the taxi. One zoomed pass but did not stop when Frema frantically flagged it down. Nana Sumnakwaa beckoned Kofi closer. His voice was fading. He was growing weaker. Kofi Nsiah drew closer as he held Nana Sumankwaa in his arm.

"Kofi, come." He spoke in his faint voice, Kofi strained to listen. "The task in the tomb is an arduous one and must not be taken lightly. Your companions to the *ban mu* (ancestral tomb) will refresh you with what you have to say each time you have to go there. First, know that the threshold of the ladder of death, once ascended, there is no turning back."

"Wofa, don't talk like that. You will be okay."

Nana Sumankwaa coughed and continued. "Know also that each departed king has a name, *nton* (a clan) and *ntam* (a taboo or sacred oath). You can only pass him if you can cite his names and accolades, *nton* and *ntam*." Nana Sumankwaa coughed again and continued, "Appellations appease. Rain appellations on them and you'll get an easy passage to the stools. This is the clue to your code to the tomb. Don't forget the *busummuru,* the sacred sword, your sword of authority. I wish you luck. Call the young woman too for me. She has a good heart. Don't leave her to the scoundrels. They will kill her. Call her; I must tell her something too.

Kofi gently lay Nana Sumankwaa on the seat and exited the car to call Frema.

Nana Sumankwaa dropped his head and fell unconscious. Kofi returned with Frema to the car. He tried to lift Nana Sumakwaa but he did not respond. "Wofa, wofa!" Kofi frantically shook him to try to revive him. He gave him artificial respiration and a life kiss to revive him but to no avail.

"Oh no.!" Kofi turned to Frema looking distraught. "Oh. Gracious!" Frema sighed.

The bright lights of the SUV turned on them as it appeared at the corner and turned into the lane. "They are coming!"

"How did they find us again? Go! Go! Go! Into the club!" Kofi abandoned Nana Sumankwaa's lifeless body in the car and ran after Frema into Hotel de Kingsway club.

There was a live band playing music, when they entered, with the dancing floor filled with people. They milled through the crowd. Tango and his men dropped off the SUV and also entered the club concealing their weapons. Kofi and Frema sneaked through a door that led them to the kitchen and exited at the back door. Tango and company followed them into the club. They looked round to find them. They followed through the door to the kitchen when he saw some of the attendants of the club moving to and fro.

Kofi and Frema appeared on the High Street in front of the post office and raced to a dark corner beside the Military Museum. They hid behind the parked disused armoured vehicle in front of the military museum. They checked to see if their pursuers were behind them. The way seemed clear. They ran from the military museum to the cenotaph and then to the statue of Prempeh II standing in the middle of the roundabout at the end of the Prempeh II Street. Their pursuers appeared near the Military Museum and saw them as they sneaked behind the statue. They fired a few bullets, hitting the statue. Kofi's heel accidentally stepped on a lever concealed at the base of the statue. A ten-inch thick slab on which Frema was standing behind the statue began to slide away. She tried to jump aside but slipped, lost her balance and fell into the opening. She grabbed at the edge of the opening to break her fall. Kofi rushed in to save her from falling into the hole. He grabbed her hand but he was unable to pull her up. Frema's hand, therefore, slipped through his palm, dropping her on steps that went down deep into the hole. She fell, tumbling down a stairway of about three yards to a landing area. It was dark in there.

Frema tried to get up. She tried to grab something to rise. Then she felt a piece of metal sticking out on the wall. She held it to pull herself up. By so doing it engaged the mechanism that operated the opening and closing of the slab. After a few seconds the slab began closing again. Kofi turned and saw his pursuers running in. Without any further hesitation and thinking, he jumped into the hole after Frema just in time before the slab closed the entrance again, crashing himself down on to the stairs.

"Where are you? Are you okay?" she asked.

"Yes. Yes. I am here. It is dark in here." Kofi lamented.

"I've got light on my phone." Frema pulled her phone and flicked its light on to illuminate the surroundings. Kofi tried to rise up. "Auch! My arm." He had bruised his arm when he rushed to drop in and tumbled down. With the phone light they could see themselves and immediate surroundings. Frema examined his hand. It was not a serious abrasion but he was bleeding. Kofi tore off one of the sleeves of his shirt. Frema assisted him to use it to tie his bleeding arm.

Up above they could hear the footsteps of their pursuers. Tango's detector beeped heavily indicating that she was close by as they ran in. Then suddenly the beep cut as the slab closed firmly; no signal was coming in again. They searched frantically for where they had disappeared to. Tango saw the lever Kofi had stepped on to open the entrance to the tomb. He concluded that could be the key to the escape for the two they were pursuing. He held it, heaved on it to tried to use it, turning in all directions. In his anxiety he exerted too much force on it; the lever yanked off. He threw away the piece in anger and frustration. He picked his communicator.

"Come in, Base. This is Tango," he called in to Jim.

"This is Base, Tango. What's up?"

"Info Number One that the hummingbird has flown out of the nest. We've lost signal on her. We are returning to base."

"Roger, Roger!"

Kofi Nsiah and Frema heard footsteps up above them move away. With the aid of Frema's phone light they surveyed around to check their new location. By the wall they saw a traditional torch and pieces of flint stones. Down below them they saw the stairway going into the hole. Kofi cracked the flints to light the burning torch. The illumination there improved.

"Are you thinking what I am thinking?" Frema asked Kofi as she critically examined their surroundings and what was being revealed to them.

"I'd be damned."

"The entrance to the ancestral tomb of the great kings of *Asanteman*. Wow! We've found it," an excited Frema exclaimed. "The steps go deep down. Come." Frema followed down the steps.

But Kofi held on, "Wait, wait, wait. We cannot go in there. We are not qualified to enter there."

Frema was defiant, "Who said that?" "What are we going to do down there."

"Your uncle said no one can find the entrance unless he is led by the spirits."

"He also said only those of royal blood are qualified to go in."

"What do you think you are? How could we have found here if we were not being led here by the spirits. This is no accident." Frema turned and with her phone light she began descent down the stairs.

Kofi hesitated but decided to follow her. "I am a royal, what about you?"

"I am, by association. The only thing you need now are the codes."

"Stop!" She turned to face him. Kofi held Frema by the shoulders.

"What are we going to do down there without them?"

Frema turned to him as he stood holding the torch. "Those up there with their rifles are after our blood, waiting to pounce on us. Are we going to sit here, waiting for how long, for them to find us? While we wait, it will be good fun, excursion tour or sightseeing for me." She turned and resumed her descent. "I'll write a book of it. Don't forget, I am a journalist, an inquisitive one at that. I am going down."

"Your inquisitiveness is what has brought us to this," Kofi said.

"I thought you were the researcher in Anthroplogy and this should have tickled your fancies."

Embarrassed by her words of admonition, Kofi reluctantly

followed her down. As they descended, they saw more torches fixed to the wall. He lighted them as they came by. And on the walls were well-carved akan adinkra symbols.

"Look, Kofi," Frema pointed the phone light to a symbol.

Kofi rushed in with the torch. "What is it?"

"Look, *Gye Nyame*. The other, *Adinkra* symbols. They are on the wall going down." Frema descended further. "*Sankɔfa*, *Nkɔnsɔn Nkɔnsɔn*, Come."

Kofi's curiosity was aroused and got drawn into what they were seeing, "Wow! *Fi hankra, dɛnkyɛm*. These are about three centuries old. I've never imagined these were here."

"I know the meaning of a few of these symbols: *Gye nyame* – except God; *Sankɔfa* – picking up from the past; but these I don't know," she said pointing her light on them.

"Oh," this was Kofi's territory of knowledge. "This is *Fi hankra* – safety and security lie in the brotherhood of man. That is *Akoma ntoasoɔ*, solidarity and unity. *Nyame bewu ansa na m'awu* meaning God will not die for me to fear death; *Dɛnkyɛm* is crocodile, spirit of resilience. This here is *Aya* –the fern, meaning I am not afraid of you; and that is *Nkɔnsɔn kɔnsɔn*, we are each a link in the cooperative success."

They descended deeper where stairs ran down by the wall on one side and a vast open space on the other side, about five or six floors deep. They followed till they got to a large landing area that ran into a cave-like structure. The granite interior supported the superstructure of some parts of the city of Kumasi. It was so solid that the tomb underneath did not seem threatened at all. They arrived at a point where they saw two tunnels, one to the left and the other to the right. They drifted slowly to the right tunnel as they observed more adinkra symbols and the torches. They began to feel some vibration in the tunnel and an unfamiliar sound. As the vibration got stronger, the accompanying sound also grew louder.

Kofi Nsiah did not feel comfortable. He was not afraid; he just felt it was not proper or right to intrude into the sacred tomb when they were not assigned to be there. He looked around and listened. He called Frema's attention. "Woman, I think we have come far enough. It's time to go back."

Frema ignored him and followed the exciting scenes being revealed to her with every step she made. With her phone camera she took some photos of the objects and herself and of Kofi as well.

At the other side, the Worm bore through the granite rocks. Abdul Ali watched the operation with keen attention. Ohenenana and Pommaa stood behind him. Kruger sat on the Worm while Don supervised the conveyor belts which carried the dusty waste on them into the open space. The rest of the men carried some of the debris farther away, making a big heap.

The noise and the vibrations of the Worm drilling grew louder and louder where Kofi and Frema stood. They had moved quite a distance from the landing area where they took the right tunnel. Kofi felt more and more uncomfortable with every step they took into the belly of the tunnel. Farther away they went.

"Maame Frema, I am beginning to think this is a good signal that we have come far enough and the spirits do not want us here. These vibrations are unusual. And they are growing stronger by the second. Let's go back before the roof caves in on us." The vibration caused some rock particles to drop from above them. She ignored all the signals until a bigger rock dropped from above, missing her narrowly. She backed away. Kofi turned to run. Frema followed without any more prompting. As they ran back, the sound and vibrations grew louder and stronger. Suddenly, the Worm popped out, perforating the wall into the tunnel in front of Kofi and Frema before they could reach the stairway to climb up. It rolled forward over the gravels and rocks till it came to a halt. The lamps fitted on the Worm blinded them. The sound went down as the drill part of the Worm was turned off.

"My God, what is that?" Kofi nearly shouted in astonishment. He could not imagine anything like that.

"Your digging friend is here too." Frema answered. "Oh, no!" Kofi exclaimed in great disappointment.

"Another tunnel!" Kruger shouted as he stepped off the Worm. He noticed Kofi and Frema as they began to back away. "Stop there, you two. Don't move or I will shoot you." Turning the direction, he had come from, he shouted, "Boss! We have a surprise company." Kofi Nsiah could not identify the speaker. Then Abdul Ali emerged from behind the lights.

"Well, well, well. Prof. Kofi Nsiah, I was told you had joined your ancestors. I never thought I was going to find you with them here in their tombs. He, he, he, he," he laughed more out of excitement than shock. "This is a small world."

"The dead can't speak. I did not die, as you can see." Kofi replied arrogantly. He had picked up a little courage and decided to stand up to Abdul Ali.

"I am glad you didn't. You are like a cat, you know. You have more than nine lives. Well, we are going to finish what we started, together. It is becoming more interesting. He, he, he, he." he laughed again. "And you, Miss Frema. Thank you for bringing him where I wanted him. I thought you would bring him for your reward. Never mind. I am a gentleman. As we agreed, you shall receive it and your freedom. You want it now or later?" Frema did not answer. Kofi looked at her, confirming his earlier suspicion of her as part of the grand scheme of Abdul Ali who had used her as a bait. "Forget about all that happened before you got here. It was all part of the plan. The end justifies the means. You both are here. That is more important. Now, let's get to work. Where are the embalmed bodies of the kings and the golden stool?"

"There are no tombs of kings and no golden stool." Kofi replied sharply. "Don't waste my time. What are you doing here then?"

"Running away from your goons."

"You can run, but you can never hide. You've run from the frying pan into the fire, from them to me. Lead us to the tomb and the golden stool." Abdul Ali stepped forward towards Kofi.

Kofi backed away. Frema followed him, but Kofi screamed at her. "Don't come near me!" Frema jumped with fright, surprised by Kofi's sudden change of attitude towards her. Kofi had got enough of her. "You tricked us, you snake."

"I did not trick you." Frema tried, pleading her innocence.

"You, double-faced, double-tongued liar. Because of you my uncle has died! What do you want from me again, you evil one? Go for your reward now that you've brought me to him, the thief, so he would steal our heritage and destroy our kingdom."

Frema, breaking down in tears continued to persuade him to understand her. "I was also running for my life, didn't you see? Yes, Nana died. It could have been me or you. How could I have risked my life running to Nana if I was faking it?"

She tried to hold Kofi's hand but he broke off and backed further away. "Please, believe me," she followed him. "I am not lying. I am sincere in my call and I am standing by you to the end, whether you believe me or not, to fight these evil vampires. I promise you, they will not lay their hands on the stool. If they have to get you to succeed, they will have to come through me first." She turned and stood in front of Kofi ready to face Abdul Ali and his men. Kofi backed down in his hostile attack on Frema. Perhaps if he had any fight, he had better direct it at the real perpetrator rather than on to the poor woman who had so far shown some courage before Abdul Ali and his men. It was dawning on him that she was not a willing bait.

"Don't waste our time." Abdul Ali interjected. "Stop the comedy and get on with it. The stool, I am only here for the stool. Take me to it. I want to sit on it and also acquire the power of immortality it possesses. I want also to show the world how easy it is to possess this well protected treasure, the stool, the all-famous Golden Stool, the soul of *Asanteman*, the same way as I have done to the Great Mask of Alata and the Stallion of Yenega of the Mosiland. I do not need to wage useless, relentless and senseless wars with your kingdom as the British did with your ancestors. We are in a new age now, the new age of science and technology; advanced technology. The wars we fight now are technological wars; wars of the mind and intelligence. You must be smart, otherwise you cannot survive."

Ohenenana appeared with Pommaa following him. They stood beside Abdul Ali. Don also appeared carrying a sub-machine gun in his hand. Behind him appeared over one hundred other men and women, those Abdul Ali had recruited: professionals, engineers and other workmen and artisans.

Kofi turned to Ohenenana and addressed him: "Oh, you? So you're behind this sacrilege, the invasion of the ancestral abode of our departed kings? This abomination?" Kofi changed to his native language and spoke in *Twi* to him: "*Sɛn na w'aton wo man ama akronfoo yi agyeɛ? W'agu wo ho anim ase wɔ wo ne wo manfoɔ anim. Wo nananom animuonyam na w'ama no ahwe aseɛ. Wo yɛ hohwinii paa.*" Translating: "For how much have you sold your kingdom to these thieves? You're a traitor and a disgrace to yourself and your people. You've brought the dignity of your ancestors into disrepute. You should be ashamed of yourself."

Ohenenana rushed past Abdul Ali and Kruger towards Kofi. "Hei, hei, hei. Mind what you say to me." He grabbed hold Kofi by the throat. "You and your fucking kingdom. What respect have you shown me, huh? You've banished me from your kingdom, haven't you?" He also turned to speak *Twi*: "*Berɛ a me hunuu wɔnnom adwene no, mede mmirika ntɛntɛ baa ahenfie se merebɛbɔ Otumfour amaneɛ. Deɛn na moyɛɛ me? Mo kyeree me dedua. ɛnyɛ saa akronfoɔ yi a, anka sesɛɛ mo de me ayi mmusuo*" Translating: "When I realized what their intentions were and I ran to Manhyia to alert the king, what did he do to me? I was arrested for contempt. But for these thieves who came to my rescue, I might be dead by now, used as blood sacrifice." He turned to English again, "They've shown me love while you sent me to the gallows. They showed me kindness where you condemned me. All that you've done for *Asanteman*, what do you have to show for it? You are pathetic." He pushed Kofi away. Kofi staggered back. Frema helped him to stand steady. In the process Kofi lost hold of the burning torch he had been holding all along, dropping it onto the ground. He charged back on Ohenenana and grabbed him too by his shirt at the torso. "You don't insult me! You don't insult the king! You don't insult *Asanteman*!" Frema tried to restrain him.

"Enough! Enough!" Abdul Ali shouted to bring order. "Break it up!" Kruger shouted at them.

With a big heave Kofi Nsiah hit Ohenenana hard on the head with his forehead, sending him dizzy, reeling backwards to the ground. He rose quickly to his feet, wobbled and fell again. He got up again and charged on Kofi Nsiah. Kruger restrained him as Pommaa also went in to pull him aside. Frema pushed Kofi further away. She turned round holding Kofi behind her.

"You stay back!" Kruger took control of the situation.

"What do we do next?" Frema whispered to Kofi. He then realized she was the only one on his side. Seeing that she was the only comfort he could have, Kofi decided to concede to her as half a loaf was better than none. Your enemy's enemy is your friend.

"Any ideas?" Kofi whispered back.

"We run."

Kofi turned, dashed and picked up the torch from the ground, following Frema as she ran deep into the belly of the tunnel. Kruger, Don and Abdul Ali holding flash lights pursued them. Ohenenana and Pommaa followed them reluctantly. Hired workers, locals and expatriates also followed, some carrying their tools and other accoutrements. The way ahead was covered with cobwebs, indicating that it was a dead end. Kofi Nsiah turned to face his pursuers, waved hard the torch in his hand as a weapon to ward off anyone who tried to approach them. "Stay back. Don't come near us." Frema stood behind him.

"Well, well, well. Have you run out of ideas?" Abdul Ali said laughing at Kofi's seeming infantile effort at warding off his assailants. "Put that thing down. You've got spirit, but it won't help you here."

"Stay clear!" Kofi warned again.

"Kruger, seize him!" Abdul Ali ordered.

Kofi took a step back. Frema stepped forward and swung her foot in a karate kick. Kruger caught her foot and threw her away like a light rug. Kofi threw the burning torch at Kruger and ran to Frema's aid. Kruger parried the torch, dropping it in a pool of oil on the floor by the wall. The oil lighted up in flames and began to burn. Like a lighted fuse, the flame ran along a duct filled with oil which went behind the cobwebs. There was a light explosion and a thick smoke puffed up engulfing Kofi and Frema. Abdul Ali and the rest took cover as no one knew what had happened behind the cobwebs.

THE GOLDEN STOOL

The Golden Stool, known as Sika Dwa Kofi, is the soul and spirit of the Asante Kingdom, symbol of unity, being carried on Akwasidae, celebrated every six weeks, the traditional Asante calendar month.

Central to the story captured in this book, Sika Dwa Kofi continues to be a mysterious artifact that has featured in every attempt to subjugate the warrior empire.

Otumfuo the Asantehene, becomes the physical manifestation of the soul of Asante once he occupies the Golden Stool.

Otumfour Osei Tutu II, Asantehene sitting in state in full regalia with the Golden Stool, flanked by the Mpanpansuohene, okra and his swordsmen.

Nana Afia Kobi Serwaa Ampem II, Asantehemaa, Queenmother of Asante, pays homage to her son, the Asantehene on Akwasidae.

Otumfuor Opoku Ware II, (1970 - 1999) fifteenth occupant of the Golden Stool, sitting in state in full regalia at Manhyia

Otumfuor Nana Sir Osei Tutu Agyeman Prempeh II (1931 - 1970) sitting in state at Manhyia. During his reign the title Kumasehene was changed to Asantehene on 31st January 1935.

Otumfour Agyeman Prempeh I, Asantehene (1884-1931), the 13th occupant of the Golden Stool of the Asante Kingdom.

Otumfour Opoku Ware II, Asantehene (1970-1999) 15th occupant of the Golden Stool the Asante Kingdom

Otumfour Nana Sir Osei Tutu Agyeman Prempeh II, Asantehene (1931-1970), the 14th occupant of the Golden Stool of the Asante Kingdom

Otumfour Osei Tutu II, Asantehene (1999 - to date) 16th and current occupant of the Golden Stool in full battledress - Batakarikesie

Chapter Fourteen

THE TOMB OF THE KINGS

As the smoke settled, they saw an opening like a big crater in the wall.

Abdul Ali and Kruger went in on Kofi. Kruger picked him up, raising him to his feet. Abdul Ali pointed to the crater. Kruger pushed Kofi towards the crater. Frema followed Kofi and the two entered the crater.

Like the crossing of the Rubicon, Kofi Nsiah's entry through the crater kicked in the spiritual awakening of the ancestral burial place. To the utter amazement of Kofi Nsiah and Frema and Abdul Ali and his gang, the tomb was revealed! It was very cold in there as a breeze blew across the vast area.

"Oh. So, it is real!" Kofi whispered in acknowledgement at what had manifested.

"Wow!" Frema exclaimed in a mixture of fright and amazement. She drew closer to Kofi and grabbed hold of his hand. She shivered. Kofi stretched his hand over her back to the other shoulder and pulled her closer. He felt goose pimples on her as he ran his hand around her upper arm.

"We are there!" Kruger announced.

"Yes!" Abdul Ali burst into uncontrollable laughter: "Ha, ha, ha, ha. At last. Ha, ha, ha!"

A great spectacle unfolded; an open field about the size of a football field opened before them. It was misty and one could barely see beyond ten to twenty metres away. The first thing that attracted any entrant was the busumuru which lay across and supported by two forked stumps in front of the first cubicle. The busumuru was an afena, an Asante traditional sword that looked more like a matchet with a broad blade, curved at the tip. It was made of gold and sheathed with a fury hide or an animal skin, mostly that of a wild beast like a leopard or a lion. On top of it was fitted a ferocious reptile, like a snake, designed in pure gold. On the right side of the tomb, there was a line of cubicles or tombs where the departed kings had been embalmed and kept. The walls of the cubicles were made of mud with wooden scantlings as pillars. They were colourful and neatly decorated with traditional adinkra symbols. The roofs were thatch, made from leaves and grass, neatly cut and trimmed. The entrance to each tomb or cubicle was closed with an *aserɛnɛ*, a mat of woven strips of raffia palm branches. By each door, outside, were bottles of schnapps which were used for libation.

Inside, the King's embalmed body, though emaciated, was seated in his state chair known as *kɔdeɛ* or *kɔtɔkɔdwa* in the same manner as he used to sit in state while alive; his chair was a wood frame patched with gold plates at its joints and corners; he was dressed in his full war dress, a parchment kilt called *batakari tuntum,* a black smock or gown, with decorative accessories, ornaments, amulets and talismans; in his right hand, each king held a sika *afena* or a golden sword, and in the left, a small-size shot-gun made of gold; a piece of gold pendant or nugget was stuck between his lips, and, for a head-gear, an elephant-hide cap in black, called kropɔn kyɛ, also decorated with parches of gold; his legs were exposed from below the knees and he wore a pair of golden sandals and anklets; over his head was spread a large umbrella.

Behind him stood a number of emaciated embalmed bodies of persons who had traveled with the king to the other world as his servants and warriors; to the left and right, as he sat in state, were smaller stools, though not occupied, representing those of his sub-chiefs (Abrempɔn) and courtiers who sat in state with him when he was alive.

Kruger was stunned by the sheer magnificence of the spectacle. He gently stepped aside to allow Abdul Ali in. Ohenenana and Pommaa also followed him observing the spectacle, stunned and amazed. Abdul Ali felt emotionally satisfied, knowing very well that the stool was within reach.

Kofi Nsiah tugged Frema and whispered to her. "Let's get out of here." He grabbed hold of Frema's hand and pulled her away. They turned straight away but walked into Abdul Ali who stood directly behind them.

"Where do you think you are going?" Abdul Ali accosted them.

Kofi brushed him aside and walked on. "I can't be part of this, the desecration of the tomb of the kings of *Asanteman*. Come away, Frema." Kofi boldly pulled Frema along.

"Stop wherever you are." Kofi stopped but did not turn to look at him. "You are not leaving here; not until I have the stool in my hands. If you attempt to leave or do anything to sabotage me, I will shoot you, this time." Abdul Ali pulled out his pistol and pointed it at him. "Where is it?"

"I don't know."

"Don't waste my time. Where is it?"

"I don't know!" Kofi turned. He was frightened to see Abdul Ali holding a gun pointing it at him. Holding Frema's hand, he nonetheless began to walk briskly towards the crater through which they had entered the tomb.

Kruger cocked his sub–machine gun and so did all the armed men who were following them. Kruger fired at a spot near Kofi's feet. Kofi backed away. Instantly, there was a slight tremor. The *aserɛnɛ* mat at the first door rattled. Frightened, the other workers who had joined them into the tomb began retreating towards the exit. The dummy of the last king, Opoku Ware II rose; stout and strong. Like a zombie, the king walked out, tearing off the mat and exiting the cubicle, in search of the intruders to the tomb. Seven other dummies emerged from the cubicle, holding various cudgels and weapons. The frightened men and women ran and hid behind the armed men.

Ohenenana and Pommaa were frightened too. They began backing away slowly towards the exit. The zombie king and his men moved towards Kofi who was closer to them. As he had turned with the intention to leave, Kofi did not know what was happening behind him. The screams and the movement of the people alerted him that something was going on. Abdul Ali was astounded by the appearance of the dead king and his entourage; he started moving back slowly.

Kofi Nsiah turned round only to realize that the zombies were closing in on him. He was bewildered, and Frema too. Kruger, Don and the other gunmen took positions and fired their guns at the zombies. The bullets dropped off as they hit them, and without any impact. The zombies advanced. A state of pandemonium broke out. The frightened workers dashed off in various directions. Some of them who were closer to the entrance of the tomb bolted in fright; the others crammed at a corner in the tomb, screaming.

Abdul Ali, moving away, ordered the gunfire to cease as the zombies drew closer to Kofi for fear Kofi could be hit by friendly fire. They all paused, waiting to see what he would do. Frema, frightened to her bones and dumbfounded bolted towards where Ohenenana was. Kofi had gone blank in his mind, totally confused. Then, it suddenly came to him what Nana Sumankwaa had told him just before he passed out. He started getting quick flash backs:

"…the threshold of the ladder of death once ascended, there is no turning back."

"Don't forget the *busumuru*, your sword of authority."

"Know also that each departed king has a name," "*nton* (a clan)," "*ntam* (a taboo or sacred oath)" and "*mmranee* (appellations)"

"You can only pass him if you can cite his *nton* and *ntam* and *mmranee.*"

"Rain appellations on them."

"...to get an easy passage to the stools,"

"...the clue to your code to the tomb".

These recollections ran very fast in his memory as his uncle's voice reverberated in his ears. He panted and breathed heavily. His heart throbbed hard in his chest and so loudly in his ears.

Suddenly, like a possessed man, Kofi yelled and dashed towards the king. He ducked under, as the king swung the golden sword, passing it over his head within hair's breadth. Sliding on the ground, he whisked past the king till he grabbed the busumuru which was resting in between the two forked stumps. He turned round swiftly, holding the busumuru in both hands. Then he rose to his feet and stretched his hands towards the king. Immediately, he recognized the king and yelled:

"Opoku Ware Ababio!
Ɔware Katakyie! Mefrɛ wo, ebru!"
"Opoku Ware II!
Ware, The Great one! I call you thus, Sire!"

{Opoku Ware II (1970 – 1999)}

Kofi quickly turned into *kwadwom*, a type of poetry of appellations and praise songs he had worked on with a former head of his department, his former lecturer and professor in anthropology, Emeritus Professor Kwabena Nketia. He tried to recollect the sequences of the words and rhymes of the abodin and mmranee (appellation and accolades) of kings, usually chanted with *mmɛnson* and *atumpane* (seven horns ensemble and talking drums) and also by the *abrafoɔ* (the king's executioners):

"Opoku Ware, Ware Katakyie...
Opoku Frɛfrɛ...Opoku Tenten eeeeiiiiiii!
Hwan na ɔbɛnya sɛ Akyiaa Ayikwan awo no?
Obi nyaa saa bi a, anka obɛyɛ bi.
Krɔbea Asante Kɔtɔkɔhene,
Asanteman Wura.
Opoku Tenten, wo firi he ni?
Hwan na obɛnya sɛ Gyaakye Opoku Panin ne
Akyaa Ayikwan ba ne no?
Opoku Ware, Katakyie,
Me mmɔ wo din nwe, awisi oo!"

"Opoku Ware, Ware, the Great One,
Opoku Frɛfrɛ, Opoku Colossus!!
Whose wish is it that Akyiaa Ayikwan is his mother?
The wish many envied.
King of Krobea Asante Kotoko, Lord of Asante.
Opoku Colossus, where do you come from?
Whose desire is it to be the offspring of
Gyaakye Opoku Panin and Akyaa Ayikwan?
Opoku Ware, Katakyie!
I do not call your name in vain, Sire!"

The zombie king, Opoku Ware II, stopped its advance. He whirled round and began walking backwards toward his tomb, as if some force was pulling him back; his seven other zombies similarly walked backwards to the tomb, to the astonishment of Kofi and the rest of them. Kofi continued:

"Merema wo Krɔbea Yirefi Anwoma Asante Kɔtɔkɔ.
Asante atwa ntire agu oo!
Twum Akyampɔn nofonbo.
Asante asiesie bo o suman-titi eei aayi!
Krɔbea Asante Kɔtɔkɔhene.

Merema wo due awisi o!
Opoku Ware, me mmɔ wo din nwe awisi oo!
Hwan na obɛnya sɛ Gyaakye Opoku Panyin ne
Akyaa Ayikwan ba ne no?
Obi nyaa saa bi a anka Ɔbɛyɛ bi.
Opoku Tenten, Opoku Tenten!
Yɛbɔ wo din a, yɛnto wo so.
Yɛbɔ wo din a, yɛnto wo so, Ɔkɛseɛ."

"I salute you with the accolade of
"Krobea Yirefi Anwoma Asante Kotoko"
The bravery and valour of Asante.
Twum Acheampong, succulent breasts that feed multitudes.
O you, great ancestral warrior spirit of Asante!
King of Krobea Asante Kotoko: Condolence!
Opoku Ware, I beseech you with great reverence…
Who won't desire to be the son of
Gyaakye Opoku Panyin and Akyaa Ayikwan?
The good fortune many yearn for.
Opoku the tall,
Opoku Colossus!
When we call your name, we do not flatter.
When we call your name, we mean it, Great One."

Kofi Nsiah chanted with the sword still pointing at the king, Opoku Ware II, until he and his zombie warriors were all back in the cubicle. He rushed to the door of the cubicle, picked up and placed back the *aserɛnɛ* at the door. The place went totally silent; the men and women there were awed. In their various places of hiding, they held their breath.

Then Don yelled in jubilation, "Yeah! He did it. Hoo ho!" raising his weapon in the air. One after the other, they sighed with relief, feeling the end of an unexpected ordeal. They came out of their hiding places, suspiciously looking round to see if it was really over.

Meanwhile, Tango and his colleagues arrived at the top of the tunnel. They saw the drilling area was deserted. “What’s up? Where is everybody?” He spoke to Jim through his communicator.

“Down there. We’ve lost eyes down there. Don’t know what is going on there. No video or audio.”

“And what are you doing sitting up here? They probably may be in some trouble.” Tango rebuked them. “Let’s go check up on them.”

Jim and his colleagues in the ops room joined Tango. “We’ll need these.” Tango pointed to two boxes containing ghost buster weapons lying there.

They unpacked two weird-looking weapons, looking more like a laser torch. They strapped them on the back of Tango and Sam, Jim’s co-pilot, like a backpack with a pointed nozzle held in the right hand. They were sophisticated, having electronic settings and requiring specialist handling. The two men carrying the weapons, assisted by their colleagues, were lowered down the tunnel. They followed the trails towards Abdul Ali and the rest. They walked past the bodies of the operator of the Worm and the others who fell in the tunnel with Kruger.

They heard footsteps of men running towards them. They took cover and aimed their guns, thinking they were adversaries. When the running men appeared, they identified them as part of their team but, their demeanor, frightened faces and shivering suggested something was wrong ahead. Tango grabbed hold of one of them. “Where are they?” he inquired. And with his hand, the frightened man pointed the direction. He wrestled himself out of Tango’s hold and took off with his colleagues at his heels. “Come on, let’s go.” Tango leading, they ran past the Worm as it parked, with its engine still running and lights on. They carefully inspected the Worm and followed on ahead.

The men who were running out of the tomb got to the base of the mechanism they had designed to lower them into the pit. They engaged it to climb out of the pit. They followed closely behind the first. In their anxiety and haste they exerted a lot of pressure on the mechanism. A metal bar which held the system in place began to give way. A knot made to hold the bar slipped loose and dropped them a few metres back into the pit. In panic, they struggled and rushed up on the ropes. The weakened mechanism collapsed as they exerted much more pressure on the system. The men dropped and crashed on to the precipice of mud and rocks below, dying instantly from the impact of their fall.

The mist in the tomb had slowly receded a little to reveal the second cubicle. The expedition team thought perhaps what they had just experienced was the only spectacle. They gradually began to gather; they had moved far off from the entrance, so they walked cautiously lest they stir awake yet another dead king. Nonetheless, with a loud pop, the *aserɛnɛ* at the second cubicle door blew off. The next king in line bounced out. Some of them, frightened, screamed at the sound.

{Osei Tutu Agyeman Prempeh II (1931-1970)}

"Kofi, they are coming again!" screamed Frema, trembling and frightened to the core of her marrow, yelling and pointing. She could not come out of her hiding corner.

Kofi was also startled and fell to the ground. The busumuru fell from his hand. He quickly grabbed it and ran off to a little distance away from the entrance of the cubicle. Seeing them, he faced the new zombie king and warriors, pointing the busumuru at King Osei Tutu Agyeman Prempeh II, he yelled again calling and singing appellations in *kwadwom* as he did the first. He called:

"Agyeman Prɛmpɛ eeei!
Me mmɔ wo din nwe, awisi oo!
Ɔsɛe Tutu Agyeman Prɛmpɛ Ababio, wo no no!
Kwame Kyeretwie! Agyemang Prɛmpɛ!
Okaakyire, Woyɛ barima, Woyɛ katakyie!
Krɔbea Asante, Asante Kɔtɔkɔhene, Merema wo due, awisi Ɔsagyefoɔ, Okoduo Asante Na'Adu, yɛma wo damirifua!

Kɔtɔkɔhene, damirifua! Krɔbeahene, damirifua!
Merema wo Krɔbea Yirefi Anwoma Asante Kɔtɔkɔ.
Asante atwa ntire agu oo, Twum Akyampɔn nofonbo! Asante asiesie bo oo, suman-titi!"

"Agyeman Prempeh eeei!
I beseech you with great reverence,
Osei Tutu Agyeman Prempeh II,
Kwame Kyeretwie (the captor of the leopard!)
Agyemang Prempeh.
Youngest One,You are viral and strong,
You are fearless and brave!
King of Krobea Asante Kotoko:
Condolence
Great Conqueror, Victorious Nana Adu of Asante: Condolence!
King of Kotoko: Condolence;
King of Krobea: Condolence!
I salute you with the accolades
"Krobea Yirefi Anwoma Asante Kotoko!"
The bravery and valour of Asante,
Twum Acheampong, succulent breasts that feed multitudes! O you, great ancestral warrior spirit of Asante!"

Kofi chanted on but the zombie king and his warriors kept coming. He felt he was not making the required impact so he began to yell louder.

"Krɔbea Asante Na'Adu merema wo due awisi oo!
Onyankopasakyie bɔmmɔfoɔ.
Kurotwiamansa, wo ho baabi yɛ kakapempen!
Kwame Kyeretwie! Agyeman Prɛmpɛ Ababio!
Me mmɔ wo din nwe, awisi oo!
Owusu Akyeao, Ɔberempɔn ba,
Ɔsei Tutu Bɛdiako, Ɔkronkron,

Abɔ-wo-din a, abɔ-kyɛkyɛ!
Hwan na obɛnya sɛ ɛdweso Owusu Panyin ne
Akua Bɔkoma Sikapɔ ba ne no?
Obi nyaa saa bi a anka obɛyɛ bi.
Kwame Kyeretwie! Agyeman Prɛmpɛ Ababio!
Busumuru! Yɛbɔ wo din a, yɛnto wo so
Yɛbɔ wo din a, yɛnto wo so, Ɔkɛseɛ!"
"King of Krobea Asante Nana Adu: Condolence!
The mysterious hunter!
The mesmarising, fearful leopard of mysterious nature!
Kwame Kyeretwie! Agyemang Prempeh II,
I do not call your name in vain, Sire!
Owusu Akyeaw, son of a Mighty One!
Osei Tutu Bediako, You are sacred,
Men shudder at the mention of your name!
Who would not desire to be born
As the son of Ejisu Owusu Panyin and
Akua Bokoma Sikapo, The nugget.
The privilege many yearn for.
Kwame Kyeretwie, Agyemang Prempeh II, Busumuru!
You are the true one,
When we call You by Your name, Great One, we are sincere!"

At this point, the *kwadwom* kicked King Osei Tutu Agyeman Prempeh II and Kofi pursued him with the appellations till the king also retired. He ran to the door of the cubicle and placed the *aserɛnɛ* on the door. He moved away to stand at a distance to look, waiting to see what was going to happen next. But almost immediately and instantly the next king popped out.

{Agyeman Prempeh I (Kwaku Dua III) (1884-1931)}

It had become obvious Kofi was getting the way the whole

scenario was panning out, yet he sighed with frustration. It looked as if he would have to go through all the fifteen kings in reverse order. If only he could remember their names and he would know their appellations! He wished he knew them off-hand, judging the number of years he had worked on them. Kofi commenced the *kwadwom* for this next one and ran to face him with the busumuru before the zombie king could exit his cubicle.

"Agyeman Prɛmpɛ eeei!
Me mmɔ wo din nwe, awisi oo!
Agyeman Prɛmpɛ, Krɔbea Asante,
Asante Kɔtɔkɔhene, Merema wo due awisi o!
Osagyefoɔ, Okoduo Asante Na'Adu,
yɛma wo damirifua!
Wo na Kwasi Kɔkɔɔ twaa wo asuo;
Kɔtɔkɔhene damirifua!
Na wo san begyee w'adwa bɛtenaa wo kɔkɔɔ soɔ.
Krɔbeahene damirifua!
Merema wo Krɔbea Yirefi Anwoma Asante Kɔtɔkɔ.
Asante atwa ntire agu oo, Twum Akyampɔn Nofonbo!
Agyeman Brempɔn se
Ofiri Kumase Adu Ampɔforo Antwi.
Okumase Adu Ampɔforo Antwi hene,
Krɔbea Asante Na'Adu, mmerema wo due awisi o!
Otumfoɔ Agyemang Prempeh, me mmɔ wo din nwe, awisi oo!
Kurotwiamansa da kwantempɔn mu Asamoa.
Ɔbanin a, ɔbanin suro no.
Ɔbanin a, yɛn nyinaa suro no.
Hwan na obɛnya sɛ Ɔbrempon awo no?
Obi nyaa saa bi a, anka ɔbɛyɛ bi!
Ɔsagyefoɔ Agyeman Prɛmpɛ,
Me mmɔ wo din nwe, awisi oo!
Yɛbɔ wo din a, yɛnto wo so;
Yɛbɔ wo din a, yɛnto wo so, Ɔkeseɛ."

"Agyeman Prempeh eeei!
I beseech you with reverence,Sire.
Agyeman Prempeh, Krobea Asante,
Asante Kotokohene: Condolence!
Osagyefoɔ, Okuduo Asante Nana Adu; Condolence!
You, though exiled by the white man;
King of Kotoko: Condolence!
You returned on to your Golden Stool.
King of Krobea: Condolence!
I honour you with the accolades
"Krobea Yirefi Anwoma Asante Kotoko"
The bravery of Asante, Twum Acheampong Nofonbo.
The Great King Agyeman says he is from Kumase
Adu Ampoforo Antwi
He is the king of Okumase Adu Ampoforo Antwi.
Krobea Asante Adu:
Deepest Condolence!
Otumfoɔ Agyemang Prempeh,
I do not call your name in vain, Sire.
Asamoa, The Great Leopard that has seized the highway!
The man feared by many a man.
The fearful!
Who would not desire to be the offspring of someone great.
The good fortune many yearn for!
Osagyefoɔ Agyemang Prempeh,
I call your name with deep reverence, Sire.
You are the true one,
When we call your name, Great One, we are sincere!"

Kofi pounded the zombie king so forcibly that he could not exit from the cubicle. King Agyemang Prempeh I retired. Kofi quickly placed the *aserɛnɛ* at the door.

Kruger and Don had gone closer to Abdul Ali. They stood by

him and gave him protection holding their weapons at the ready, as he watched on. What Kofi was doing with the kings looked more interesting than frightening to the crowd in there, men and women; they watched with keen enthusiasm and anxiety. Abdul Ali observed the unfolding phenomenon and at every moment he became more convinced that his decision to choose Kofi as the right person around whom his expedition could succeed was correct.

Tango and Jim and the rest appeared at the entrance of the tomb. Tango yelled, "What's going on here?" His voice and their unexpected entry startled a couple of the spectators, scuttling them. They pushed their way through the little crowd of frightened, yet anxious visitors of the tomb, to reach Abdul Ali. They were amazed at what they saw.

"This is a spectacle, you won't believe," Abdul Ali uttered. Seeing the ghost busters he said, "Glad you brought these. Good thinking. Set them up quickly before we are surprised again."

"We lost the lady out there."

"And she appeared here with Kofi, where we need them!"

"You don't mean it!" Tango chuckled. He craned and saw Kofi.

"It was a good bait. Hurry up before we are overwhelmed again. Kruger, help them out. It looks like we have a long battle to run."

Kruger joined Tango and Jim to set the weapons.

Kofi momentarily got distracted by the equipment and how they went about setting them up as the fourth king appeared with a jolt. It was obvious the rest of the fifteen departed kings were bent on making an appearance. The way they would deal with them, they had no clue. But from what Kofi had done with the first three, he could come to a simple conclusion that he had to continue the way he was going till he had retired all the remaining twelve kings. He was already exhausted and it did not seem he would endure to the end.

They all reacted spontaneously, some screaming as the fourth king appeared. This king had a large number of zombie warriors following him.

}Kwaku Dua II (1834-1867)}

Kofi saw the king appear but went totally blank again. He just could not remember which king in line had appeared, his name and the appellations for him. He stretched the busumuru towards the king but could not utter a word. He started to shiver and began backing away from the king.

Frema yelled to alert him: "Kofi, the king is out!"

"Who is he? I can't remember who." He responded, completely bereft of any clue.

"Who is this?" Frema yelled to Ohenenana and Pommaa, each suggesting possible names.

Ohenenana shouted the name: "Kwaku Duah … the first!" "No, the second!" Pommaa countered to correct him.

"Yes, the second! Kwaku Dua, the second. They seem to be coming out in reverse order!" Ohenenana confirmed. But Kofi was overwhelmed and could not speak. He pointed the busumuru at the zombie king, he pointed again and again as it approached him. He came face to face with the zombie king. The king raised his sword to strike Kofi. He moved backward, tripped and fell to the ground. The zombie king struck at him with the gold sword. Kofi raised the busumuru to block the swift drive of the sword and engaged the king in physical combat. He rolled away on the ground and rose to his feet. Antonio and some of the men around, with tools joined in to assist Kofi in the fight, attacking the accompanying zombies who carried various weapons: spears, swords and cudgels. They could not stand the strength of the zombie warriors. Their guns had no effective impact on them. The zombies dispatched them off with ease, killing and injuring some of them.

"Fire the weapons. Fire!" Abdul Ali ordered Tango and Sam to engage their weapons to support Kofi seeing the zombies had subdued and massacred his men and were turning towards them. Their weapons failed to function. They tried again, but again the weapons would not function.

"Mine is not working." Tango said, as he fidgeted with it. Sam confirmed his had also malfunctioned.

Abdul Ali became paranoid and screamed at them. "I said fire the weapons!"

Kruger quickly opened a section of the back pack and inspected a control panel. He touched the cables, making sure all were fixed correctly. Abdul Ali also called for Tango's. They fidgeted with the weapons trying to cue in a code. Suddenly the one Kruger was working on responded unexpectedly. It went off with a blast, discharging a high voltage flare of fire just when a couple of the zombies turned their attention on Abdul Ali. The fire hit the roof of the cave, bringing down a large rubble of debris, some crashing on the approaching zombies. A large amount of the debris fell at the entrance, blocking the only exit to the tunnel, thus completely trapping them all in the tomb. Some of the frightened intruders who had turned towards the exit meet the rubble from the roof coming down to block the tunnel, crushing some to death and wounding some. Kruger fired at one of the zombies. It disintegrated the zombie warrior.

"It worked!" an excited Kruger yelled. Abdul Ali was still fidgeting with the weapon and couldn't get it started. Some zombies got closer from behind him. Fearing a shot at them may hit Abdul Ali and those around him, Kruger left the laser weapon to Tango and with Don; they dashed in to fend off the zombies.

Kofi was subdued by the zombie king, Kwaku Dua II. He fell. The zombie king raised his sword to strike. There and then, Abdul Ali got the weapon started. He turned, just in time, to see Kofi was under pressure and, fired at the zombie king. The zombie king was blown off by the high energy discharge. By that, the remains of king and his zombie team were sucked back into their cubicle. Kofi got to his feet and ran there to seal it with the *aserɛnɛ*. He heaved a heavy sign of relief but quickly recomposed himself, ready with the busumuru in his hands. A number of them who got injured during the bout were carried aside, and their wounds attended to.

Frema kept away fearing she might distract Kofi if she drew closer. She perceived what he was doing needed all his attention and therefore kept herself at bay. She had joined Ohenenana and Pommaa who had by then realized and recognized that at that moment, it would be in their common interest to work together, if they should survive and come out of the tomb safe and sound.

The mist receded far deep; but instead of the next king, four of them popped up simultaneously in reverse order.

{Kofi Karikari (1867-1874)}

{Mensa Bonsu (1874-1883)}

{Kwaku Dua I (1834- 1884)}

{Osei Yaw Akoto (1824-1834)}

There was quite a crowd of zombie warriors which overwhelmed the already dwindling numbers of the intruders. This gave Kofi no chance to chant any *kwadwom*. The zombie kings and their warriors attacked and engaged the intruders in a fierce battle, fighting everybody. The intruders in turn stood their grounds and defended themselves with all and any tools or weapons they could lay hands on. The Security men engaged by Abdul Ali fought with riffles, sub-machine guns and pistols. Notwithstanding the fire power of arms and ammunitions they possessed, they did not make much impact. The bullets could only destabilize and distract them momentarily, but the zombies got back into action and pursued the intruders. The workers used their hand tools and head pans to fight and defend themselves. Some more got injured and others, killed.

Those with the laser weapons strategically sought the zombie kings out and eliminated them one after the other. And any particular king that was taken out by the ghost buster was sucked away with his bunch of zombie warriors. Kruger and the laser team succeeded in eliminating the four kings, and their warriors disappeared with them back into their cubicles. The surviving intruders stayed alert with weapons and implements in their hands, ready to face the next batch. Kofi quickly rushed in and with the assistance of some of the handymen, they fixed the four *aserɛnɛ* at their respective cubicles.

Since Frema, Pommaa and Ohenenana had no weapons and could not fight; they found an obscure corner to hide, away from the combat zone, discussing and debating among themselves which next kings were due to appear. They tried to identify the next King in order to alert Kofi if he could remember the appellations.

"The last one was Kwaku Dua I," Pommaa suggested.

"How do you know?" Frema cut in. "Four kings came out. There were four *aserɛnɛ* on the floor. If you count from the first king, seven have come out so far. So if you check who is the eighth king? Osei Bonsu."

"Yes, the next king will be Osei Bonsu." Ohenenana confirmed. No sooner had Ohenenana mentioned the name than the zombie king and his warriors popped out. "Osei Bonsu!" he shouted to Kofi's hearing. Kofi waved the busumuru in the air to confirm he had heard the name.

{Osei Tutu Kwame Asibe Bonsu (1800-1823)}

Kofi picked the cue and began to chant the appellations as the king approached him with his attendant warriors:

"Wo no no! Ɔsɛe Bɔnsu!
Ɔsɛe Tutu Kwame Asibe Bɔnsu!
Ɔsɛe Bɔnsu a, ɔko-kyere-ahene,
Bɔnsu, Wokum Adinkra Kwadwo Kɔsompire.
Wokum Akwasi Nyirenyire,
Bɔnsu a, Oko-tu-broni, Oko-gye-aban,
Oko-to-ɛpo, Oko-dware-ɛpo
Obi gye wo akyingye a, twa ne ti ara. Tin!
Kukuru-butu. Kon!
Bɔnsu, Oko-dware-ɛpo
Frempɔn, dammirifua! Dammirifua! Damirifua!
W'aku no! W'aku no!

Wokum nnipa ma nnipa ye mmɔbɔ.
Boafo ako-ako, Ɔbanin twerɛboɔ a, ne ho bon atudro!
Bɔnsu, Ɔko-dware-ɛpo eei!
Kɔtɔkɔhene damirifua, Krɔbeahene damirifua
Merema wo Krɔbea Yirefi Anwoma
Asante Kɔtɔkɔ Asante atwa ntire agu oo!
Twum Akyampɔn nofonbo. A
sante asiesie bo o suman-titi aayi
Krɔbeahene Ɔsɛe Kwame Asibe Bɔnsu,
Me mmɔ wo din nwe awisi oo!
Yɛbɔ wo din a, yɛnto wo so;
Osei Bonsu, oko-kyere-ahene eei!
Yɛbɔ wo din a, yɛnto wo so, Okeseɛ."

"All hail! Osei Bonsu!
Osei Tutu Kwame Asibe Bonsu.
Osei Bonsu, conqueror of kings.
Bonsu, you slayed Adinkra Kwadwo Kosompire.
You slayed Akwasi Nyirenyire.
You fought the whiteman, deposed him and
threw him out of power and authority.
You captured lands and Castles as far as to the coast
And waded the stormy sea.
You decapitated anyone who dared you. Kukuru-butu. Kon!
Bonsu, the whale, Frempong,
Condolence, condolence, condolence!
The ruthless brave warrior
Who slaughters with no pity.
The pellet that smells of gun powder.
Boafo, the great warrior.
Bonsu, the whale!
King of Kotoko: Condolence;
King of Krobea: Condolence!

I salute you with the accolades,
"Krobea Yirefi Anwoma Asante Kotoko".
The bravery of Asante, Twum Acheampong Nofonbo
O you, great ancestral spirit of Asante
King of Krobea, Osei Kwame Asibe Bonsu,
I beseech you with reverence, Sire!
Osei Bonsu, Deepest Condolence!
You are the true one
Osei Bonsu, the great conqueror.
Great one, You are the true one!"

But before he could complete the appellations for Osei Bonsu, the next king appeared. "Opoku Fofie!" Ohenenana shouted again.

{Opoku Fofie (1798-1799)}

"And Osei Kwame!" Frema yelled as the next king also appeared.

{Osei Kwame (1777-1798)}

Two more zombie kings and warriors popped out. with a host of zombie warriors following.

{Osei Kwame (Oko-awia) (1764-1777)}
{Kusi Obodum (1750-1764)}

"They are coming." Don yelled. "More of them!"

"Guys get ready! And fire indiscriminately!" Abdul Ali ordered. The army of the zombie kings and a host of their warriors charged in, launched and ran riot on the human intruders, and they in turn engaged them in a fierce battle from all fronts with all weapons and implements, with Kofi in the center. Those with rifles and pistols reloaded their weapons and fired at them but could not eliminate the zombies. When they ran out of bullets, they used their guns in combat with the zombies until the laser weapon could come to their aid or they were over-powered and killed by the zombies. Those with the work tools could only use them as shields; no matter where they ran the zombie warriors chased them and attacked, wounded or killed those who could not defend themselves.

One zombie warrior strayed towards where Ohenenana and the ladies were. It struck its spear at them; they ducked; Frema picked a stone and hurled it at the zombie hitting it in the head, breaking it off the loose neck. The skull fell, the rest of the frame rose without the head. The hands holding the spear swung it wildly in no particular direction and at nobody. It lost its bearing and wandered off in the opposite direction. Zombie warriors which had lost parts of their frames still struggled on to attack the intruders.

From another angle, Abdul Ali and his crew encountered difficulties with their laser weapons from persistent and continued use. The fire power was dwindling. It sent out fire but was not effective. The energy storage had reduced considerably. After every, shot it took some time before it could reboot to fire again. This gave the zombie kings and their warriors some advantage over the intruders who kept running and shooting intermittently. In between the laser shots they used other weapons to ward off the attacking warriors. Kruger and his team adopted a strategy of seeking out only the kings to make the battle easier for them. They tried but missed them narrowly on one of them.

Kofi was cornered by zombie kings Osei Tutu Kwame Asibe Bonsu and Opoku Fofie. He fought bravely and extricated himself from their hold. He ran to a safe location. They chased him and attacked him there. With the busumuru Kofi could face the kings. He fought fiercely with them but he could not contain them for long. He was overrun by them. Kings Osei Tutu Kwame Asibe Bonsu struck Kofi down; he fell and lost hold of the busumuru. Sam attempted to shoot his laser to support Kofi; it malfunctioned. He tried to restart it. He was attacked by a zombie from his blind side. He was struck on the head, sending him crashing to the ground. A huge and fiercely looking zombie turned onto Abdul Ali who was standing by Sam and attacked him and knocked him down. The zombie raised his weapon to strike him again. He rolled aside. The zombie missed. Kruger saw Abdul Ali was in difficulty and rushed in on the attacking zombie and hit it with a plank, disintegrating it into pieces. Kruger quickly pulled the nozzle of the weapon from under the lifeless Sam, aimed and took out zombie Kings Osei Tutu Kwame Asibe Bonsu and Opoku Fofie who had overcome Kofi as he crawled helplessly on the ground away from them. The remains of the two kings and their accompanying warriors, simultaneously, were swiftly sucked back into their respective tombs easing the pressure on Kofi. He dashed for his busummuru.

Kruger sought and took out the remaining Kings Osei Kwame, Kusi Obodum and Osei Kwame (Oko-awia). Consequently, they were all sucked back, they and their warriors, into their tombs.

The misty atmosphere cleared further leaving some small portion still covered. This misty area had divided the tomb into two. On the right side were the tombs and to the left, a woodland forest. Ahead, the landscape graded into a rocky hill of some sort; a stream flowed from the top of the rocky hill in a waterfall down into a pool below the hill. There was a big log, the stem of a big fallen tree, about thirty feet long, lying half on land and half in the water with its branches submerged in the pool.

The Golden Stool was still not sighted. There were heavy casualties on the intruders. They assisted the wounded quickly to safety. Some tried to clear the rubble blocking the exit. Frema rushed out from her hiding area to check on Kofi as he and his team moved quickly away from the cubicles.

"Are you ok?" Frema asked, anxiously. She was very nervous and worried. She knew it was not over. Kofi tried to persuade her to move back to the safe area where she had been hiding. "I am scared. I am afraid for you."

"Don't worry. I'll be fine. I am not doing badly at all." Kofi chuckled, as he breathed heavily, trying to regain some strength.

While they counted their losses Kruger approached Abdul Ali: "But where is the Golden Stool? We've been fighting, yet we have not sighted it."

"Let's sort the battle out. The kings are the guardians of the stool. When we clear the guards we shall figure out the next line of action." Kruger looked at Adbul Ali and shook his head, frustrated. It felt like "time out" for them as there was a long break in hostilities. But it was not for long.

Opoku Ware I popped out, throwing them back into panic again. The warrior zombies accompanying the king were numerous; those with weapons reloaded bullets and magazines to resume firing. Frema was frozen, scared and could not move away.

{Opoku Ware I (1720 -1750){

The zombie kings leapt forward and soon reached Kofi to engage him. Kofi quickly raised the busumuru to the king. He fell into a frenzy as he started chanting his appellations.

"Wo no no!" Kofi began. "Opoku Ware!.......
Opoku tenten, Opoku Kɔkɔɔ,
Ataapu Akwa;
Anyemadu Kɔkɔɔ ba Opoku Kɔkɔɔ
Krɔbo Adusɛe Bogyabene Berempɔn ba
Opoku Tenten, Hwan na obɛnya sɛ Ɔberempɔn awo no?
Obi nyaa saa bi a anka obɛyɛ bi Opoku Tenten, wo firi he ni?
Wofiri Kwabre Wonoo.
Wo firi Amakom nnuadewawaase.
Opoku, Asafodeɛ.
Kyere me na menka Asafodeɛ."

"All hail!
Opoku Ware!
Opoku Ware
Opoku, The tall one,
Opoku, the light-skinned one, Ataapu Akwa;
Opoku, the fair one;
Son of Anyemadu the light-skinned one
Opoku the gallant,
the prince of the hot-blooded Krobo Adusei,
What a privilege to be given birth to by someone great?

The good fortune many yearn for.
Opoku Tenten, what is your ancestry?
You hail from Kwabre Wonoo;
From Amakom, under the Mahogany tree.
Opoku, the legend
Alert me! And I'll tell you tales of great warriors!"

Frema felt uncomfortable and unsafe staying behind Kofi and so close to the engagements. She decided to move back where she was hiding with Pommaa and Ohenenana. Just then, Osei Tutu I Opemsuo, the first king of Asante, creator of the kingdom, popped out with a larger number of warriors following. He uttered a battle cry. He looked fierce.

"Kofi!" Frema screamed as she noticed Osei Tutu I approaching. "Another one is coming!" She bolted farther away from Kofi as he concentrated pressing on Opoku Ware I.

King Osei Tutu I observed the scene briefly and then slowly charged with his men into battle. The warriors attacked Abdul Ali and his men. As they rushed in, Kofi Nsiah continued with his appellation on King Opoku Ware I whom he held in frenzy, pushing him towards his cubicle.

"Ɔbɔɔ nnipa Bɛdiako Kyere Ampɔforo Adu Kwa.
Tweneboa Adu Ampɔforo Berempɔn ba
Opoku Tenten. Opoku Tenten,
Me mmɔ wo din nwe, awisi oo!
Opoku Ware, merema wo due,
Awisi o Yɛbɔ wo din a, yɛnto wo so
Yɛbɔ wo din a, yɛnto wo so, Ɔkɛseɛ."

"Creator of man, Bediako Kyere Ampɔforo Adu Kwa
Opoku Tenten, Son of Tweneboa Adu
Ampɔforo Berempɔn Opoku Tenten,
I do not call your name in vain, Sire!

Opoku Ware, Deep Condolence!
When we call your name, we do not flatter.
When we call your name, we mean it, Great One."

{Osei Tutu I (Opemsuo) (1680-1717)}

Osei Tutu's warriors were ruthless as they joined the battle. They attacked and butchered several of the already dwindled numbers of the intruders but the king directed his attention to Kofi. It seemed that the busumuru tended to attract them to it and the holder. He rushed on to Kofi.

Kofi saw Osei Tutu coming but kept pressing on, intensifying the appellations on Opoku Ware I, repeating and running it over and over, pressing on Opoku Ware I.

Frema saw King Osei Tutu I was slowly warming up to Kofi although he had not dispatched King Opoku Ware I. Kofi needed concentration for a few seconds more to get rid of it. Realizing that if King Osei Tutu I got to Kofi, he would not be able to send King Opoku Ware I away and also that it would be too difficult for him to deal with both Opoku Ware I and Osei Tutu I at the same time, Frema decided to wade in with some distraction by drawing the in-coming king towards her. She picked up a broken piece of a weapon on the ground and hurled it at King Osei Tutu I in an attempt to thwart its approach towards Kofi. The king stopped, looked at her and sneered at her. His crystal-like eyes glowed, sending cold chills through her spine. Though Frema got frightened, she took off thinking the king would be lured to pursue her. Instead, one of the fiercely looking zombies took off after her. She tripped and fell on her belly. She turned over only to see this zombie warrior standing on top of her with its weapon ready to strike. She closed her eyes as the zombie raised its weapon. The die was cast, she thought she was going to receive the blow that was going to dispatch her into eternity. From where he was fighting Kruger saw Frema was caught in a difficult situation. He aimed and fired his laser at the zombie from that distance. The laser caught and consumed the zombie. Its remains crumbled on Frema. She screamed as she felt the cold ashes on her body. Kruger then rushed to her. Eye closed, she screamed when she felt a hand touched her. It was Kruger's.

"Hey, you're ok?"

Frema opened her eyes and saw it was Kruger. She quickly pulled herself up onto her feet. "Thanks, man." She looked at him with eyes of gratitude, panting profusely. Kruger did not wait but passed on to dislodge other zombies. She sighed and rushed away.

King Osei Tutu I got closer, sneered at Kofi in an attempt to call his attention to engage him. Kofi ignored and concentrated on what he was on.

He pushed harder and harder till he succeeded in sending King Opoku Ware I back into his cubicle just in time before King Osei Tutu I could strike him. Warriors of King Opoku Ware I, swiftly, got whisked away with their king. King Osei Tutu I swung his sword. Kofi ducked and sharply turned, pointed the busumuru on him and engaged King Osei Tutu I with his appellation.

"Wo no no! Ɔsɛe Tutu, Opemsoɔ!" Kofi ranted. "Kɔfabae a, wo na wokɔfaa *Sika Dwa* Kofi baae. Me fre wo, eburu…"

"All hail! Osei Tutu, The sovereign, The creator, through whom the golden stool came. I beseech you with reverence, Sire."

Osei Tutu was instantly kicked into frenzy and began backing up to its cubicle.

"Ɔsɛe Tutu eei!
Asanteman Wura. Ɔpemsoɔ!
Wo yɛ Ɔbrempɔn! Wo yɛ Ɔhene!
Wo yɛ Awirade!
Ɔbrempɔn Nana 'Sɛe fata Awirade!
Korɔbea Yirefi Anwoma Asante Kɔtɔkɔ!
Ɔsɛe Tutu, Wo na wode Asanteman baaeɛ.

Ɔsɛe ntutu brɛbrɛbrɛbrɛ, w'asi ta!
Ɔsɛe eeei, Ɔsɛe damirifua! Damirifua!"

"Osei Tutu eei!
King of Asante, the sovereign!
You are mighty, You are king
You are lord.
The sovereign lord, Nana 'Sei
Krobea Yirefi Anwoma Asante Kotoko
Osei Tutu, You created the Asante kingdom.
Osei, step gently, walk majestically!
Osei eeei, Osei condolence! Condolence!"

Kofi held and contained Osei Tutu with appellations. He flowed fluently and persistently while the combat went on with Abdul Ali and the rest of his crew and the other zombie warriors. Kofi continued:

"Wo nono! Wo na wode baaeɛ.
Yirefi Ankomaguo a ɔne Amansan baaeɛ.
Yirefi Ankomaguo a ɔne Anɔkye baaeɛ
Maa Anɔkye kɔ yii Sika Dwa Kofi baaeɛ.
Ɔma wo kyɛm a, wɔ ma wo kyɛm-takyi.
Asante Kɔtɔkɔ!
Obuabene Akuampɔn ɔne wo regorɔ ne 'Sɛe Tutu e!
Ababerɛ a ebare nnua,
Asantewaa a ɔbɔɔ akofena ba 'Sɛe Tutu
Ɔsɛe Tutu se ofiri Asumegya Gyamkɔbaa
Gyebi Kaakaamotobi Berempɔn ba.
Ɔsɛe se ofiri Santemaso
Ɔsɛe se ofiri Kokofu Adu Ampofro Antwi.
Ɔsɛe Tutu se ofiri Kokofu Nyinahenase.
Ɔmaanu Berempɔn ba.
Abrankese Aniapam Owusu Akwasi Berempɔn ba.
Ɔsɛe Tutu se ofiri Abrankɛse Nyameani.

Ɔsɛe se ofiri Kumase Adu Ampɔforo Antwi.
Okumase Adu Ampɔforo Antwi hene 'Sɛe Tutu e!
Me mmɔ wo din nwe awisi oo!
Ɔpemsoɔ, merema wo due awisi o!
Ɔsɛe Tutu, yɛbɔ wo din a, yɛnto wo so.
Ɔsɛe Tutu, yɛbɔ wo din a yɛnto wo so,Ɔkɛseɛ."

"All hail! The creator.
Yirefi Ankomaguo, (Sovreign Lord) who led multitudes.
Yirefi Ankomaguo who brought Anokye
For Anokye to conjure the Golden Stool.
When you are honoured, You are honoured graciously.
Asante Kotoko, the porcupine.
Akuampon, the slayer of colossal giants
Are your contemporaries, 'Sei Tutu e!
The creeper that binds the mighty oak,
Asantewaa, who fashioned the sword,
Is your mother, 'Sei Tutu.
Osei Tutu says he hails from Asumegya Gyamkobaa.
Prince of the fearful lord monster of Gyebi!
Osei Tutu says he hails from Santemaso.
Osei Tutu says Kokofu Adu Ampoforo Antwi is his ancestor.
Osei Tutu says he hails from Kokofu Nyinahenase.
Her Royal Princess Omaanu is your mother!
You are the prince of
the Lord Aniapam Owusu Akwasi, the gaint.
Osei Tutu says he hails from Abrankese Nyameani,
the abode of giants.
Osei says, Kumase Adu Apoforo Antwi is his ancestor.
'Sei Tutu e! Lord of Okumase Adu Ampoforo Antwi.
I beseech you with great reverence, Sire!
O, you sovereign king, Deep Condolence!
Osei Tutu, You are the true one.
Osei Tutu, the Great one, You are the true one"

With every line of the appellation King Osei Tutu I was whipped into deeper frenzy and Kofi kept the pressure on him. Kofi had succeeded in taking the great warrior out of the combat area and slowly pursued him towards his cubicle.

Abdul Ali and his crew also fought on and did not give the warriors any quarter. Ohenenana and Pommaa who were close by had their own skirmishes. They had been routed out of their hiding place into the mainstream battle, showing a few bruises and bloody clothes. Pommaa was struck down by a zombie warrior. As she lay on the ground helplessly, she closed her eyes waiting for the final blow by the zombie warrior. Frema bravely dashed in and with a weapon, blocked the zombie warrior and dislodged it away. Frema gave Pommaa a hand and quickly pulled her up to her feet. In the process Frema noticed Pommaa had blood wetness in between her thighs. She drew Pommaa closer in a friendly hug and whispered to her.

"You had a heavy thud when you fell. You're bleeding?"

"Yes. But it is the time of the month, you know," Pommaa replied.

Frema eyed her as she wandered away. She wondered what further implication that was going to add to their already gargantuan battle they were embroiled in. Pommaa was not a royal, and as a female, it was forbidden for her to enter the tomb in the first place. Worse still, she was menstruating, one big abomination and taboo where they were. Customarily, women who are allowed into the tomb are matured older women, mostly those who had reached menopause. Frema could only pray for divine intervention.

The battle continued relentlessly with many dead and wounded bodies strewn all around. Kofi had almost succeeded in sending Osei Tutu I packing with his appellation when he was suddenly distracted by a bright light accompanied by a thunderous sound coming from the mist with a whirling wind. It drew close till it swept him off his feet. An image appeared out of the light. It was Okomfo Anokye, the high priest who conjured the Golden Stool, a great friend of Osei Tutu I

Opemsuo, with whom - and with the Golden Stool - the Asante kingdom was commenced and built! He was by his side at every battle and it was obvious the current battle in the tomb could not have ended without him. He had come to aid Osei Tutu I, his friend, as he had always done in times of old.

Kofi had lost the busumuru as he fell. He struggled to pick it up. He was unable to reach it quickly enough. Okomfo Anokye stamped on it as he held the handle. The busumuru broke into two, throwing Kofi off balance. Osei Tutu rushed on him to strike.

Kruger, from where he was, saw that Kofi had run into trouble again.

He fired the laser weapon at Osei Tutu I. Okomfo Anokye's image trans-positioned itself and went in to block the rays of the laser. The white aura around him made it impervious to any physical elements. He turned and pointed his *bodua,* the cowtail, his wand that seemed to hold his spiritual powers, at the laser light. With supernatural power, he deflected the laser light, sending the deflected energy into the woodland, which brought down some trees with thunderous explosions! Kruger fired again. Okomfo Anokye repelled it. Kruger tried to fire; the weapon would not respond. He threw it aside and snatched the other weapon in Abdul Ali's hands. He fired and the shot was again deflected. The deflection brought down some boulder on the rocky hills. Kruger fired again and held a sustained beam on Okomfo Anokye who also held the beam with his bodua. They held each other until the laser machine in Kruger's hands blew up, throwing him some distance away. Tango rushed to his aid. He was hurt and could not raise himself and stand up on his own. Abdul Ali ran in too to check on him. He shook his head, his eyes sunken and desolate. It was obvious the die was cast. The battle was over. His greatest fighter has been felled. His laser weapons were all damaged and ineffectual. Kofi too was having a hard time with Osei Tutu I and Okomfo Anokye. There was no way he could defeat the warriors in the tomb. Kruger looked at his boss and groaned in pain. Abdul Ali turned to look at Kofi.

Kofi picked up the broken busumuru and pieced it together. With his two hands holding the pieces he resumed the appellations on Osei Tutu 1. It kicked him and threw him into frenzy again. Kofi held him, pushing him. Osei Tutu slowly receded, with Kofi at him towards his cubicle.

Meanwhile, as the others were fighting the zombie warriors, Frema, Ohenenana and Pommaa got separated as they ran away in different directions. Okomfo Anokye then turned on Kofi again. With his bodua he whirled Kofi off his feet. Kofi lost his hold on Osei Tutu I bringing him back into combat again. Okomfo Anokye pointed his bodua at Kofi. He was thrown to the ground again. Osei Tutu I rushed on him. He struck with his sword, Kofi ducked, picked up the pieces of the busumuru and fought his way with the pieces until he got to the edge of the pool of water.

Kofi realized he was no match for Osei Tutu I and Okomfo Anokye combined. He knew he had to look for other strategies if he was to make any gains to overcome Osei Tutu I at all. Then a thought crossed his mind. He recollected that one other thing that could defeat the king was what sent him to immortality. What killed him? Yes, Kofi remembered. The greatest ntam, taboo, of the Asantes. History had it that King Osei Tutu I died in an ambush while crossing river Pra in a battle with the Akyems. He concluded the king was so fortified that no weapon made by man could defeat him. He deduced further that the great King was riding in a palanquin when he ran into that fatal ambush. When his attacker realized their bullets could not fell him, they turned their guns on the men carrying him. In the process, they succeeded in hitting the carriers who lost their hold of him and dropped him in the river. Thus, the king died drowned.

Armed with this knowledge, Kofi taunted the king and got his attention. He abandoned the busumuru and made for the log lying in the water; he climbed on to it. Osei Tutu I chased him there and jumped onto it too, followed by Okomfo Anokye. Kofi stopped, realizing he had gone far enough on the log in the water. He turned and waited to engage Osei Tutu I. But before Osei Tutu I could strike, Kofi dashed into him with all the strength he could muster and grabbed him by the waist. The impact sent the two into the pool of water. Kofi Nsiah held his breath and struggled with the zombie king under the water. Kofi realized he gained advantage on the zombie king in the water but he lost his breath and therefore had to surface. The zombie King struck twice at him but missed. Kofi grabbed him again and pulled him into the water. They resurfaced again. Kofi quickly grabbed him the third time and pulled him back into the water. After sustained pressure in the water, the Osei Tutu I zombie figure blew up in a big bubble under the water throwing large volume of water cascading into the sky. The zombie image of the king in a smoke silhouette leapt out of the cascading water into its cubicle. All the remaining skeletal beings were swiftly drawn back into their cubicles. The image of Okomfo Anokye with the aura around it which hovered above as Kofi engaged Osei Tutu I in the water spun swiftly away, disappearing into the misty area. It was clear the battle was over. Kofi had defeated the kings, guardians of the Golden Stool. Abdul Ali rose to his feet. All the others watched the spectacle as the rest of the zombies were whisked away. They all cheered at their victory, congratulating themselves.

Frema who had watched from a distance, anxiously waited for Kofi. He surfaced, floating in the water, Frema cheered as she saw him struggle to keep afloat. The misty area had cleared, revealing a platform like a *pato* (patio or podium) set deep in the area. It was a shed with wooden scantlings as pillars and roofed like the kings' cubicles.

There were three identical stools lying on three short pedestals or stumps, each with a small pillow, on which the three stools lay. The first stool from the right was glittering gold. The second was a similar stool in silver and the third was dark black-like lead.

"Stools! The Golden Stool." Pommaa screamed as they appeared, drawing everyone's attention to it.

Abdul Ali and his remaining men eased towards it to have a look, even the wounded. They rushed, though cautiously lest they stir up any surprises. "Here we are!" he exclaimed almost silently to himself.

"Yes!" Don leapt in excitement. "Bingo!" Tango yelled.

Ohenenana strolled reluctantly with Pommaa towards the stools. Curious ones of the few men that were left standing on their feet ran past them shoving them aside. Frema had divided attention; one on the stools and the other on Kofi in the pool of water. She settled for Kofi and went to him. Kofi swam swiftly out of the water. By the time he got to the edge for Frema to help him out, however, Abdul Ali was almost by the stools. "I'd be damned," he swore.

Ohenenana suddenly hurried up towards Abdul Ali and with all his strength pushed him aside, restraining him from moving forward towards the stools. A few armed men remaining cocked their weapons one after the other. Kruger shouted and waved them to stand down from where he was resting.

"This is as far as you go," said Ohenenana.

"What is the meaning of this, partner?" Abdul Ali asked.

Ohenenana pushed him back. "I am not your partner. No more. Not in this crime against my people, my blood, my heritage. Return to wherever you've come from. You will not take the Golden Stool. I will not allow you. You will have to go through me first."

"You cannot stop me. I have defeated the spiritual guardians of the stool. They could not stop me, how can you, a mere mortal?"

"You didn't stop them." Ohenenana shouted him down.

"Kofi did!" Pommaa interjected.

"And I am going to stop you." Ohenenana said as he attempted to push Abdul Ali back.

"But I have paid you for this, haven't I?"

"Here, take your money and get out of here!" Ohenenana pulled out bundles of money he had concealed in his clothes and threw them at Abdul Ali. "Get out of here!"

"Get out of my way." Abdul Ali brushed him aside. Ohenenana engaged him in a tussle. Abdul Ali pushed him aside and moved forward toward the stools. Ohenenana leapt forward, grabbed his hand and pulled him back. He ran past Abdul Ali, turned to stretch his arms across to prevent Abdul Ali from going past him. Abdul Ali's surviving men keenly watched the encounter between the two but did not intervene. Abdul Ali tried to go past Ohenenana again. Ohenenana grabbed him and engaged him in another scuffle. Abdul Ali tried to wrestle with him but could not lift Ohenenana's heavy body. Ohenenana in turn grabbed Abdul Ali by his mid-section and lifted him from the ground and squeezed him. He slapped Ohenenana with both palms. Dazed, he dropped Abdul Ali.

Tango felt he must act to stop Ohenenana before it got nasty. He picked up a broken spear lying about and hurled it towards Ohenenana as he charged on to Abdul Ali. The spear pierced him in the back as he grabbed Abdul Ali. He reacted painfully to the thrust of the weapon, tried to reach it but lost his balance. Abdul Ali pushed him away. He whirled round and fell on the spear behind him. The impact pushed the spear through his heart. He wriggled on the floor.

"Nooooo!" Pommaa screamed as she ran toward him. "Aahh! Hmm!" Ohenenana could only moan.

"I am sorry, partner." Abdul Ali said looking at him as he lay with blood oozing out of him. He jumped over Ohenenana and moved towards his trophy which was an arm's length away.

Pommaa rushed to Ohenenana's side, knelt beside him and lifted his head. He was bleeding and dying. Frema dashed there too. Kofi was stunned as he lay on the bank of the pool, half in, half out from where he had watched the encounter between the two. The warm face he showed when Ohenenana stood up to challenge Abdul Ali slowly turned sour. He was at a loss, looking at Ohenenana. He thought of the paradox of the situation. First, he had lost out on what he had himself, set out to prevent from happening but paradoxically only succeeded in bringing Abdul Ali down from the US to steal the Golden Stool, his ancestral heritage. Secondly, in trying to save his life he had succeeded again in clearing the path, leading Abdul Ali on a red carpet to the fleece. Thirdly, Ohenenana, whom he had accused as a traitor and collaborator of Abdul Ali had just turned round to resist him but lost. And now, here he lay, bleeding to death. He could only helplessly look on as Abdul Ali went to lift the Golden Stool up like a trophy. Kofi could not believe it was happening. He managed to pull himself out of the water as Frema joined Pommaa by the side of Ohenenana who was hanging precariously on to life.

The surviving security men hired by Abdul Ali took positions, cordoning off the stool area, pointing their rifles, daring whoever would attempt any opposition. Only a handful of the workmen were still alive. Some were wounded while the others, petrified into inaction. They backed away seeing the guns pointed at them. The excitement with which they had all run in to view the spectacle of the Golden Stool after surviving the gruesome battle, the catastrophic phenomenon with the guardians, the dead kings and their zombie warriors, had died. They backed away and moved closer to the blocked exit.

Abdul Ali was completely satisfied. He had reached his target and nothing was going to stop him from laying his hand on it. Getting out of the tomb was not his worry yet. He moved forward to the three stools.

Kofi ran to join Pommaa and Frema by Ohenenana. He held Ohenenana's hand when he knelt down by his side. Ohenenana was weak and could speak faintly. "*Me nua*, (My brother) I am fuck up, I am fucked up." He sobbed with tears in his eyes. "I have failed. I have failed *Asanteman*."

Kofi was desolate. He shook his head. "Nana, why did you have to get yourself involved in this?" Kofi consoled him. "*Me nua, due* (My brother, my sympathies)."

But, Ohenenana urged Kofi on, "Don't give up. The spirits are with you. Evil shall not succeed. Stop him for me. I know you can" With these words Ohenenana dropped his head and died. He lay still with his mouth and bright eyes wide open.

"Farewell, my brother." Kofi passed his palm over Ohenenana's face to shut his eyes and gaping mouth. Pommaa screamed and wailed uncontrollably. Frema held on to Kofi as he rose to his feet, but later she turned to Pommaa to console her. Kofi turned to Abdul Ali, this time fired up to face him with everything in him to stop him or die, trying. But it was just too late; it was like shouting to close the gate after the horses had bolted out of the stables or like bringing out the basins after the rains had ceased.

"Tango, Don! Help me here." Abdul Ali had reached the stools. The two went in to assist him to bring the stool, glittering in gold, down from its pedestal. It was not too heavy for one person to lift, but he felt it was so delicate that it required careful handling.

Kofi charged forward but could get only to as far as the armed men. They bounced him off and he fell to the ground. From where he fell Kofi could only watch with great disappointment as Abdul Ali and his cabal placed the stool down. Tango and Don helped him, each by each arm, lowering him to sit gently on the stool.

"Here comes the new King of the Ashanti. I am master of all I subdue, the conqueror of the Ashanti Kingdom, new occupant of the Golden Stool." said Abdul Ali as he was placed on the glittering gold stool.

"All hail the king! All hail the king! All hail the king!" Three times, they helped him to sit on the stool. Abdul Ali burst into uncontrollable laughter of joy and utmost satisfaction which reverberated in the tomb. Kruger and Jim waved from where they were, Kruger was unable to move without support and leaned on Jim.

What happened next was unexpected and sudden. Abdul Ali's laughter ceased, abruptly. A streak of smoke emerged from underneath him. He felt some heat warming his buttocks. He screamed and instantly he was engulfed in heavy smoke. He was lit up in flames. "Help me! I am burning!" He screamed for help. He could not get up from the stool. Tango braved the smoke and went in to help him off. Abdul Ali vibrated on the stool as if he was electrocuted by high voltage current. Tango touched him but the electric wave that surged through him threw Tango off some distance away. Don took off in fright, running away for dear life. He fell and struggled to get up and continued to run. The weapon-bearing men on seeing the scene also fled helter-skelter. Kofi quickly crawled away and the rest watched as Abdul Ali burned into a heap of ashes on the stool.

"No way! *Na niama!* (Serves you right!) Yes!" Kofi leapt with joy, screaming on top of his voice. The ancestral spirits of *Asanteman* had duly rewarded the transgressors with the appropriate penalty.

The rest of Abdul Ali's team, both expatriate and locals, still alive and the wounded, bewildered, frightened and petrified, fled in all directions. They converged at the exit. With everything they could lay hands on, they hurriedly began to dig away the debris that had dropped to block the entrance to find the exit out of the tomb. The wounded tried to pull themselves together, stronger ones assisting the weak.

Frema ran to Kofi Nsiah to hold onto him for comfort. As they moved towards Pommaa who was still crying and holding the lifeless body of Ohenenana, Kofi whispered to Frema, "The stool they took was not the right one."

"All that glitters is not gold, so they say." she responded.

"The real one is more or less the black stool. It is blackened out of sacrifices and libations poured on from time immemorial. Our work here is finished, woman. Let's join to dig our way out of here."

"Yes, we will tell our story another day."

When the two got to her, Pommaa had stopped crying. She slowly let go the lifeless body of Ohenenana and rose to her feet. She headed towards the stool area. They wondered what she was up to. Frema called her to join them. Pommaa did not respond but kept going towards the stools.

"I am no fool," she soliloquized. "I came in with all I had. I am not going out empty handed."

Frema sensed her intentions. She tried to persuade her that hers would be a fruitless effort and that she should join them to find their way out of there.

Pommaa turned to Frema and remarked harshly, "That man lying there was all I had. Without him my world is ended. I came into this with him hoping for some reward at the end. Who is going to pay me now?"

"Well, my dear, such is life; you win some, you lose some. Come. Let's see how we can get out of here. There is hope while there is life. You can't tell what providence has in store for you."

"No! You don't know my loss. You can't understand my pain." Pommaa harshly reacted to Frema.

"We have caused enough disturbance here already. Let's leave now while there's time."

Pommaa looked her in the face and said, "I am not leaving here empty handed. I go for my booty."

"You are not taking anything out of here, are you? "

"Yes, I am. If that fool could not find the right stool I can. And you don't try to stop me." Pommaa warned.

"Kofi, please stop her. She is gone crazy." Kofi hesitated. "Those whom the gods want to destroy, they first make mad. Stop her! Stop her before she aggravates our already compounded calamity," Frema added.

Kofi had drawn closer. He joined in. "You can't sell the stool anywhere," he chipped in. "It is a priceless, historical and ancestral relic that cannot be quantified for sale. Everything in here is of immense value far beyond any cash equivalence."

Frema realized they could not persuade her. She decided that if persuasion failed, force must be applied. She rushed in, grabbed Pommaa by the hand and tried to restrain her. "Come, come woman. You can't touch anything here, let alone take it away." Pommaa broke away from her grip. "You're forbidden! You just saw what happened to those two." Frema grabbed her again and tried to pull her away. Pommaa resisted. The two women engaged in a brawl.

Kofi Nsiah rushed in to separate them. He succeeded in pulling Frema away from Pommaa. This offered Pommaa a little edge over

Frema. Pommaa threw her arm and it hit Kofi Nsiah in the face with a hefty blow, sending him reeling to the ground. She hit Frema hard in the face and she fell beside Kofi Nsiah.

Pommaa leapt off towards the stools. She drew closer and passed the gold stool with the smoldering remains of Abdul Ali, and on to the black stool.

"Don't touch it!" Frema screamed as Pommaa stretched forth her hands for the black stool. But Pommaa grabbed the stool and pulled it off the pedestal. It was heavy, though, not so heavy that one person could not carry it. She tried to drag it off the pedestal as it was not light enough to lift with one hand. She dragged it again and it dropped off the pedestal. The bells on to the stool rattled as it hit the floor. Its impact caused a slight tremor. Those trying to dig a way out of the tomb felt it. They intensified their efforts, though they were not making much progress with the scanty tools available, against the big and heavy boulders they had to clear.

Frema turned to Kofi and asked him to do everything to stop Pommaa. She warned him of possible repercussions. "She is a woman," she added. "She is not a royal! It is a taboo for her to touch that stool. And worst still she is in her period. Jeez! Kofi, do something!" She was now hysterical.

Before Kofi Nsiah could utter a word, Pommaa dragged the stool again. The bells jingled. A severe tremor shook the tomb. It threw everybody down. A purge of the sacrilege began. The tremor continued and intensified; boulders, rock particles and sand began to fall from the roof, with quakes running continuously in ascending proportions. The ground cracked open, separating Pommaa from Kofi and Frema. The debris dropped into the abyss. There was a great pandemonium inside the tomb. They screamed at every impact and ran to where they thought was safe as the tremors intensified. The ground swallowed rocks and debris and some of the intruders, dead or alive, as they ran for survival. Droppings and debris from the roof came crashing on terrified men and women; some boulders and stones exploded, throwing away frightened intruders who stepped on them. They screamed and cried from every bit of the calamities they were enduring. Some struggled to save themselves from slipping into the gaping abyss.

The pond bubbled and exploded. Its waves flooded the area, sweeping onto the stool Abdul Ali sat on, washing off all his remains away and drained into the gaping trenches, carrying along some of the intruders alive or dead. They screamed and wailed as they endured the catastrophe, some struggling to save themselves from being swept by the waters into the open trenches. Ohenenana's body was lifted by the floods and swept into one of the trenches. Kofi and Frema were caught in one of the floods which swept them away in separate directions into the trenches. Kofi grabbed on to a protruding rock as he fell off the edge. He held on to the rock till the splashes of flowing water receded. He saw Frema also hanging precariously by her dress and struggling to save herself. She got stuck in between a small crevice in the melee. Kofi pulled himself out to safety and ran to Frema's rescue. He reached out to Frema. He grabbed her by her hand and pulled her as she also worked herself to safety. She limped along. She had had a bump with the knee. They struggled through the purge. He helped Frema at difficult areas, climbing or jumping across gaping trenches.

Notwithstanding the purge, the patio for the stools and the area of the kings' cubicles remained intact with no disturbances at all. Kofi saw an opening in the wall which also remained intact and calm. It was large enough to go and hide in there.

"Come on," Kofi urged. "Let's try and reach there. It will be safer in there."

Kofi helped Frema into the safe hole that looked like a capsule. Satisfied that Frema was safe, he returned for Pommaa. He saw her as she struggled in great difficulty with the stool, walking along at the edge of the pool of water. He worked his way carefully towards her.

Meanwhile, the attack on the remaining intruders continued relentlessly, precise and direct. Some of the frightened intruders tried to seek refuge in areas where they thought they were safe to hide, but they were eliminated one after the other. Some fell in gaping trenches; others were crushed by fallen rocks and debris while some of them were swept away with the dead by floods into the gaping abyss. A number of them who tried their luck in the woodland were whisked away and disappeared into thin air. Those who had survived up till then and could manage, came back to the digging area and continued to dig for the exit.

Kofi approached Pommaa at a point he felt was conducive to bring her to safety. He called her and tried to persuade her to abandon the stool to save her life. Kofi had reached a crossing point where with a little effort Pommaa could leap over a short stretch.

"Maame, drop the stool," Kofi pleaded. "Come over here and I will help you to safety. We do not have the luxury of time to lurk around here any longer. Come over here!"

Pommaa obstinately ignored him and held on to the stool. A boulder dropped from the roof, missing her by a hair's breadth. She screamed in fright and fell but she struggled up and went on relentlessly farther away from Kofi. The water bubbled and exploded again. The sweeping waves ran into Pommaa and carried her away. She clung onto the stool as she floated and was drifted towards a deep trench. The stool got caught up in a crevice between two rocks. With her fastened hold on the stool she was saved from falling into an abyss. Kofi rushed there when the floods had subsided. He found a rock to hold on to and stretched his hand to her. It was within reach that with a little leap Pommaa could reach Kofi's hand for him to pull her to safety. She, instead, found a position to hold and began to pull the stool which had gotten stuck in between the rocks.

"Maame, please, stop and stretch out to me, let me bring you over." Kofi called out to her but she would not budge. Watching from where she was hiding, Frema called out to her to allow Kofi to assist her to safety.

"Shut up, you bitch," Pommaa yelled at Frema. "I don't want any help from you."

Kofi came in again. "Ok. Ok. I am here. Reach out and I will bring you to safety." But no amount of pleading would persuade her. Kofi continued to inch his way gradually towards her. She kept pulling at the stool until eventually it got dislodged out of the crevice. The very effort threw her off balance. Kofi wedged one of his legs in a crevice and lurched forward for her. As her concentration was on the stool, she followed the direction the stool went and grabbed it with one hand but not in time for her to also catch Kofi's hand as well.

"Kofi!" Frema screamed as Kofi lept forward out of her view and caught Pommaa's outstretched hand while she held the stool with the other. Frema screamed and wept. Kofi grabbed Pommaa's wrist, grimaced as he strained to fasten his grip on her; but try as he might, he could not hold fast on Pommaa's hand for long. Her wet hand slowly slipped through his fingers. With the stool in hand, she dropped into the deep abyss screaming as she went down, her eyes and mouth widely open in deep fright. Pommaa let go of the stool as she fell. Frema could hear Pommaa as her shrill scream faded into the abyss. "Oh Pommaa. Kofi! Oh, Kofi," she wept thinking both of them had fallen. Then she saw kofi emerge from the abyss. He had slowly disentangled himself and climbed up to a safer area. She screamed with joy. "Kofi! Oh, thank God you are safe!" He worked his way towards her. "Where is she?" Kofi shook his head in disappointment.

A few seconds later the Golden Stool slowly emerged out of the abyss behind Kofi. Frema screamed and pointed. "Kofi, look!" They watched, as by itself, the Golden Stool flew in the air unaided till it went back to rest as it was before Pommaa removed it. The other one Abdul Ali sat on also lifted itself back to rest where it was before. The two pieces of the broken busumuru joined back together and lifted itself onto the fork where it had rested before. The tremors and the purge resumed and intensified. Kofi rushed towards where Frema was hiding. Everywhere he stepped blew up as if he had stepped on a mine.

There was a big blast and a quake causing more debris to drop from the roof. Kofi jumped fast and raced through the imminent catastrophe with debris falling all over and the blasts at his feet, chasing him out of the tomb. He jumped into the hole; Frema pulled him in just in time as debris from the roof came down crashing to seal off the area. The "capsule" in which they hid vibrated like the final spin of a washing machine. It was as if it was going to blow up any minute. The two hid in there, clinging onto each other with their hearts in their mouths. Frema kept screaming at every jolt. The tremors, quakes and floods continued until the earth swallowed all the remaining intruders and the remains of the dead. Kruger, Antonio, Jim, Don, Tango and all who followed Abdul Ali in to the tomb, they all perished. The floods swept and washed the grounds clean, sending all the debris into the trenches. The cracks and trenches pulled back together and sealed up, leaving the grounds as they were before the intruders invaded; as though no one had stepped there before. The thick fog quickly advanced to cover the area again as it was before. In fact, it was as if nothing had happened.

Held up in their safety "capsule" Kofi remembered the prediction of Nana Sumankwaa: "We shall cleanse the golden stool with their blood and bury them in the graves they themselves will dig; their spirits shall live forever as slaves to the kings in the life beyond." Kofi shook his head. "The men with evil intention entered the sacred tomb, the ancestral burial grounds of the glorious Kings of Asante, with none returning. They entered with fool-hardiness and arrogant hearts; they perished with their egos and greed, stewed in their self-conceited pride and ignorance," Kofi muttered.

Chapter Fifteen

RETURN FROM THE DEAD

Kofi and Frema hid in the tomb holding onto each other till the noises and the vibrations subsided and died out. There was calm and tranquility in the tomb area. Trying to figure out how to get out of the capsule they were held in, they saw a streak of light appearing through a little crack on one side of the walls. Kofi Nsiah traced the light source to a crack in the wall. With his foot he kicked hard, breaking a space, big enough for them to squeeze through. He helped Frema out after he exited. They were back in the tunnel with the adinkra motifs on the walls where he had lighted the burning torches. They traced their way back up to the stairway, hanging on to each other. They saw the remains of the Worm which lay buried in the rubble. They followed on and climbed up to the entrance underneath the statue of Prempeh II. Frema remembered that she had unconsciously pulled on a lever that pulled the slab to close the entrance of the tomb. She pulled on lever again. The heavy slab slid, creaking away. Kofi led the way up pulling Frema along. The sky above showed it was dawn; the statue of Prempeh II confirmed that they were back to the city which was beginning to wake up to the early morning activities in the Central Business District.

"Kejetia, Kejetia, Kejetia! Tech, Tech, Tech!" The trotro, mini commuter buses moved briskly about with their driver assistants calling for passengers. "Pee, pee. Poo, poo!" The taxi cabs honked away.

"Cling, cling. Cling, cling!" The bicycle and the motor bike riders whisked past.

"Ashanti Pioneer, Daily Graphic, Ghanaian Times, Daily Guide!" The newspaper vendors yelled as they walked away, while other sellers screamed out their wares.

Kofi quickly pulled Frema to the top. The slab slid back to close. Hand in hand they raced into the street in their dirty clothes. After a few steps Frema broke down in tears. She could not help herself. She slowed down and stopped. Kofi turned to her. In the middle of the road, with vehicles passing by them, she embraced Kofi with both hands wrapped around his neck and hugged him. She sobbed uncontrollably, shedding tears. They were tears of joy. About twenty-four hours ago, she recollected, she had woken and dressed up to visit her sick daughter; she accidentally walked into those trucks laden with earth dumping them into the Nwabe dam and the harrowing experience that ensued had now become history. She looked at Kofi in the eyes and held him warmly. Kofi slowly warmed up to her and lifted her off her feet, kissed her long on her lips and gently put her down.

Suddenly she paused. "Kofi?" she called to him.

"Frema, you're not thinking what I am thinking," he responded.

"Of course!"

They turned and raced towards Hotel de Kingsway tracing their way back where they had come from when Tango and his men had chased them. They passed the military museum and turned into the alley that got them to where they had left Prof Osei's car. It was still where they left it. All the other vehicles there were gone and the place was deserted. Kofi heaved a sigh of relief. They walked towards their car. It was just as they left it, with the damage on it. They slowly approached it; Kofi opened the door. It was empty; Nana Sumankwaa was not in it! There were blood stains on the seat.

"He is not here." Kofi sighed. He looked back at Frema. "The police might have found the body and taken it to the morgue."

"Are you sure?"

"Why not?" Kofi's searching eyes peered into her face.

"I don't think he has been taken away by the police. If they had, they would have taken the car as well."

"So who took him?"

"That's what we have to find out," Frema added.

"Then we must inform the police," Kofi suggested.

"The police? What are we going to tell them when they begin to inquisition us? What answers would we give them?"

"Simple, we left our uncle's dead body in a car and... and.... went away When we returned it had disappeared."

"And will they believe us?"

"So?"

"So, where do we begin to look for him?"

"The morgue." Kofi suggested again.

"Why the morgue?"

"That's the only place to find dead bodies."

"Alright, let's go."

Kofi opened the car door in an attempt to sit down. He looked at Frema and wondered why she was still standing and rather staring at him. With her eyes she signaled Kofi to look again at the car he wanted to sit in. It was then Kofi realized the car was not in any good condition to be moved again, all four tyres were flat!

Frema pulled her car keys out of her back pocket and waved it at him. "You have a car?" Kofi asked. She nodded. "Where?"

"On the Seventh Street." Frema led the way. They ran. Soon, they arrived on the Seventh Street. They turned on to the street. Frema's car was still parked where she left it; and with the remote control she opened the doors for them to sit in. She looked sternly at the Number 32/12, 7th Street which was two houses away. She could hear the generator purring. She pointed to Kofi. "This is the entrance. This is where Ali started the digging from."

"Where?" Kofi could not understand what Frema was trying to draw his attention to. "Do you want us to see what's in there before - ?" He moved further ahead towards the building.

Frema quickly dismissed the idea. "No, let's find Nana first. We can come back later to interrogate what is in there."

Slowly, Kofi returned to the car, looking back intermittently at the big warehouse structure. It reminded him of the similar structure in the US out of which he commenced his return to Ghana with Abdul Ali.

Frema sat in the driver's seat, put the key to the ignition and started the engine. At the start of the engine there sounded a heavy explosion from within the concealed structure that shook the grounds like an earthquake.

Kofi rushed to the car and sat down. "Go! Go!' Go!" He screamed at Frema. Frightened, Frema hit the accelerator. The car screeched away. A second explosion blasted off, blowing up the warehouse structure, sending out heavy smoke and flames with burning debris up into the air and everywhere! Some burning debris crashed into a nearby house and other structures. Those which fell around started burning anything combustible - trees and cars parked around and close by. One piece of hot burning metal flew after Frema's car, coming faster than she was driving. The red hot metal, large enough to smash away the car, missed it just as Frema turned at the corner. The metal crashed into a passing bus which also exploded into flames. Frema raced as fast as she could through the Central Business District which was virtually empty. They saw fire tenders which were rushing to the site of the explosion, blurting their siren and flashing their red and blue lights.

"Where do we go?" she asked after a while when they were far away enough and she had calmed down..

"Erm," Kofi reflected. "Nana's house. Let's first inform the family what has happened to him and explain the circumstances that led to his death. After that we can go searching for his body at any morgue. He is a chief and would have to be accorded the appropriate dignity and repect he deserves at the time of his demise."

Frema complied and drove to Nana Sumakwaa's house. She parked at the entrance of the house and the two descended and made their way in.

Kofi was apprehensive entering the house. He wondered how he was going to break news of the death of his uncle at such an ungodly hour. Knowing how sensitive it was and also how women take the death of their spouses he felt very reluctant to enter the house. Frema joined him as he stood at the threshold of the main entrance. Frema took his hand and led him in.

The gate at the entrance to Nana's house was not closed so they let themselves into the compound. Kofi saw light in the kitchen area and the hall too. "I will only ask for him and pretend as if I do not know what had happened to him," he whispered to Frema. "That will set the tone that he is missing. It would be a good beginning to commence a search for him."

"That's a good idea," she whispered in response.

Emboldened by this, Kofi ventured Nana Sumankwaa's door. He heard movement in the hall. He concluded it was Nana's wife and approached the door. He tapped gently on it. He waited pensively, tensed up and still battling in his head how to frame his sentences to address her. He heard footsteps as they moved towards the door. The lever turned and the door suddenly flung open. There, in the doorway, stood Nana Sumankwaa glowing with his grey beard and hair on his partially bald head and a big smile on his face. He wore only a pair of white shorts which exposed his bandaged thigh with a big plaster fixed to his right rib. The suddenness of his appearance at the door and his visage hit Kofi and Frema with shock, sending them fleeing. Bewildered Frema tumbled over a bench nearby, tripping Kofi as he stepped backwards. He fell on her. The two struggled to rise, pulling each other down and screaming. "Ghost! Ghost!"

"Kofi!" Nana Sumankwa called, bursting into uncontrollable laughter.

Kofi and Frema froze at his voice and slowly turned to look at each other.

"Yes, it's me. I am not dead!" Nana said. Auntie Yaa appeared and stood behind him, smiling.

They turned to look at Nana Sumankwaa and then, to each other again. "No, he died! In my arms!" Kofi said convincingly with Frema nodding in confirmation as they tried to get on to their feet, confused.

"Oh, I collapsed, I passed out. I came to, just a few hours ago. Something like a tremor shook the car. That stirred me up. I saw the whole place was deserted. I did not know where you went. I was famishing too; so, I decided to come home to find something to eat first before I go searching for you. It was not until I got home that Auntie Yaa drew my attention to my blood soaked clothes. She was shocked to see me in that condition, still alive. You know, she was a nurse. She has given me first aid. And I am waiting for the food! Come in. This was our supper prepared for us yesterday. You are in good time to join me." Astonished Kofi and Frema slowly rose to their feet, awed by Nana Sumankwaa's narration.

"You were resurrected by your ancestors," Frema muttered.

"I am glad to see you two together," Nana Sumankwaa said with a sparkle in his eyes. "I'm sure you are getting on very well.Don't worry to say anything now," he continued. "I know you have a lot to tell. I will have all the time to listen to all your tales."

Dumbfounded, they followed him into the hall to a set table. Auntie Yaa returned with a bowl of fresh water and soap. As Kofi set to wash his hands Frema walked close to Auntie Yaa. "Auntie, can I use the bathroom?" "Of course! Follow me." Auntie Yaa beckoned to Frema and led her away.

Kofi broke the news to Nana Sumankwaa, "Nana, we entered the tomb, the mausoleum!"

"You did? You found the entrance?" Nana asked, excitedly.

"Yes, we did." Kofi affirmed.

"Come, sit down and tell me all."

Auntie Yaa returned and showed Kofi where he should sit. He took the napkin and wiped his wet hands and sat down.

Kofi commenced narrating all that had happened from when they left Nana Sumankwaa's lifeless body in the car.

Frema returned to the table. She joined in with other aspects from her perspective. They concluded with the big explosion that sent them fleeing the final spot.

They ate and drank and laughed their hearts out. Nana Sumankwaa got to his feet. He reiterated his conviction: "My children, let me tell you of the reality of the power of the Golden Stool. From time of old till now, it has offered sacred protection for all its occupants and their citizens, from royalty to the commoner, including the rich and the poor, young, old, slave and master, man and woman. I told you: if you are not directed by our ancestors, you would not find the tomb. Again, anyone who makes any evil attempt on the Golden Stool, he and his followers, their blood will be used to cleanse the sacrilege they commit; they will be buried with the kings and, their spirits shall remain perpetual slaves to the Kings in the life beyond! What you have done in the last twenty-four hours, let me assure you, I have seriously taken notice!" He then raised his glass, "To the two of you: Blessings of the gods and our ancestors, for prosperous lives, good fortune; and, to a future life together, I drink."

"And it shall come to pass." Auntie Yaa concurred.

Frema sat quietly. She slowly rose to her feet and raised her glass to drink to the toast Nana Sumankwaa had proposed. They all said, "Cheers," one after the other.

Kofi and Frema bade Nana Sumankwaa farewell when eating was done. Nana and Auntie Yaa followed them to Frema's car. They waved as the two drove away till their car disappeared in the distance.

"So, what next?" Frema asked, looking at Kofi from the corner of her eye. Kofi turned to look at her but hesitated in responding. He pretended he did not hear her speak. She pressed, "Aha! You have not responded to my question!"

"Huh?" Kofi reacted as if as he had then heard her. "What was it?" he asked.

"I asked what was next to do." Frema almost screamed sensing Kofi's pretence.

"Oh, erm, I'll go back to campus to check on my house and on Professor Osei too."

"Okay." Frema said. "I'll take you there." She made a fast turn to join the Accra Road into a heavy traffic, cutting in carelessly in front of another vehicle, causing the driver to blow his horn at them as he struggled to avoid a collision.

"Careful," Kofi admonished her for the reckless driving. She defiantly ignored Kofi, showing no remorse for her action.

"This is a wrong time to go this direction," she muttered, as she pounded on the steering wheel, frustrated by the slow pace of the traffic.

Kofi looked at her as she fidgeted with the steering wheel. "Did you say you lived nearby?" Kofi asked

"Yes, Nhyiaeso Flats." She was not the least amused with the traffic; her response expressed her increasing frustration.

"Exit at the next junction." Kofi suggested.

"Why?" Frema asked sharply. "That will take us off route."

"Yes, I know. But that will take us out of this heavy traffic onto the Ridge by-pass and to Nhyiaeso. It's a much longer route but it will be far faster and less frustrating." Frema did not respond but turned off as Kofi proposed. "You can show me your apartment as we shall definitely pass by the Nhyiaeso Flats." Frema's face brightened. She turned to look at Kofi with a twitch on her lips, pretending she was not interested in the new direction she had taken.

The exit route was indeed freer and faster which soon brought them to the Nhyiaeso Flats. Frema stopped in front of one of the blocks and parked her car at her usual parking spot. The two of them got down. Frema picked her hand bag and led the way to her flat. They climbed the step up to the fifth floor. She searched through her hand bag for her keys and opened the main door. Kofi was impressed by the set up as they entered the apartment.

"Welcome to my apartment, my home." Frema said as she threw the hand bag in the settee nearby.

"Nice place you have here," Kofi commended.

She went to the fridge and opened it. "Care for a drink?" "No, not now. I am very full."

She shut the fridge without taking anything for herself either.

"Sit down. I'll quickly change into something neater; then I'll drop you off home." Frema entered her bedroom. Kofi dropped into a single seat sofa and took a good look around again. Frema took off her clothes and searched through her wardrobe for something fresh to wear. She stopped and went to the door and popped her head, hiding the rest of her naked body behind a curtain in front of the door. "You can also take a quick shower and change your clothes too," she addressed Kofi. He sat up straight, perplexed and surprised. She continued, "I have something you can wear. There is another bath room in the next room. There are fresh towels and lavatory kits." She went back into the room and shut the door.

Kofi slowly got up. He took the offer and approached the room. He entered the shower room, undressed and dropped his dirty clothes on the floor. He turned on the shower and took a warm bath. He wiped off his wet body, wrapped the towel loosely around his waist and returned to the bedroom. Just as he shut the bathroom door behind him Frema entered the room with a new pair of jeans trousers and a T-shirt, his size. "Hope these would do for you." She said and dropped them on the bed. She was in a very transparent morning coat with a towel wrapped around her head like a headgear; Kofi could clearly see her contoured body as she wore nothing underneath except a set of well-studded strings of beads glittering around her waist-line. She had a physique that could easily pass her for a beauty contestant. Notwithstanding breastfeeding after the birth of her daughter, her breasts still stood firm on her chest, and her nipples, pointed, and showing through her apparel as if they had never fed a mouth with milk before! Frema looked at him. She shied away, avoiding his eyes; yet she looked at his naked torso, spotting no hairs. She also saw he had a fine physique, not too sporty, but fairly moderate. He had no six packs, but his stomach was quite flat. Not a very handsome man, but he was a decent man, good enough for a good woman.

Kofi moved for the clothes as Frema turned to leave the room. After two steps Kofi gave an uncomfortable sigh, "Ash!" This caused Frema to also turn immediately and looked back. There Kofi stood, naked; the towel that he had wrapped around his waist got caught in the door as he shut it behind him, and had pulled off him when moved.

"Oh. I am sorry." Frema shielded her face with her hand and turned to leave.

"Wait!" Kofi gently said. She stopped short but did not turn. He gently approached her, grabbed her gently by the shoulders and pulled her towards him. For a moment she grabbed his hand and tried to pull herself out of his hold. Kofi strengthened his grip, though gently. It caused her to take in a deep breath but suddenly, she relaxed and let go of herself onto him, feeling his body as she leaned on him. It sent sweet, romantic emotional feeling through her. She turned quickly to face him, looked him in the eyes, melting into his arms. Kofi felt her well-endowed frame on him as she slowly stretched her arms to reach his neck and pulled herself up to reach his lips with hers, tenderly kissed him, rubbing her breast which had popped out her gown onto his body, melting her lips on his and her whole being into him. Kofi responded with equal emotional passionate tenderness. The sweet flagrance of the perfume she wore, a mixture of jasmine and lemon spiced the atmosphere. Then she jumped up and wrapped her firm thighs and legs around him. This sent Kofi off balance. He held her firmly with both hands around her waist, staggering to the bed with her still hanging onto him and managed to gently drop onto the bed. The two took their time holding and touching and kissing each other for what seemed to be an eternity. After passionate love making, they both fell asleep in each other's arms.

Frema was the first to wake up the next morning. Her eyes opened to see herself, naked, cocooned in Kofi's arms, her buttocks pushing against his lower belly and his thighs with his right arm running across her breasts. She could not turn herself. Kofi had collapsed on her. She slowly moved away his right arm and right leg that had virtually clamped her to the bed and slowly eased herself from underneath him. She rolled off the bed and headed for the bathroom. She sat on the toilet, and closed her eyes. Kofi still lay in bed when she returned to the bed to try to retrieve what she wore. She had nothing on except the glittering beads around her waist. She realized that the towel and her transparent dreams gown had gotten underneath Kofi's body. She tried to pull them away but they were stuck. She could not get them without waking Kofi up. Seeing how deeply he lay, still sleeping, she decided to let him be, pulled the cover cloth over his nakedness and went to her bedroom for new clothes. She chose a very skimpy jeans-shorts that could barely cover her big buttocks with her waist beads visibly exposed around her waist-line and a top that was nothing more than a transparent silky lace of about six inches wide which covered just her nipples, hanging on two strings over her shoulders. She moved to the kitchen, humming lullaby love lyrics and began preparing breakfast.

Kofi turned slowly on the bed and stretched himself. He opened his eyes slowly. He looked relaxed, the effect of a good rest. The passionate night he had spent with Frema was more than a sedative that knocked him out cold; enough to calm his nerves and anxieties from the grueling trauma he had endured in the past few days. He turned again and realized he lay in unfamiliar surroundings. He was not at home. He quickly brought himself to the edge of the bed and sat up. He saw the clothes Frema brought him and instantly remembered the story from there. He had mixed feelings. Unlike Frema who did not hesitate to conclude a possible serious relationship coming out of their encounter, he shook his head, rushed to the bathroom for his own clothes. Realizing they were too dirty to be worn again, he settled back for those Frema had given him and quickly dressed up.

Frema's breakfast was ready. She decided to get Kofi to make himself ready for it. She stretched her hand for the knob but it swung open before she could touch it. And to her surprise Kofi stood with his dirty clothes in hand ready to leave.

"Oh!" She exclaimed, more in shock than surprise. "You're ready to leave?"

"I am sorry things have turned out the way they have." Kofi's reaction took Frema aback. She was more perplexed by what followed. "Please, forgive me for taking advantage of you. It will never happen again. I'm really sorry." Frema was in shock as he walked past her toward the main door.

Without turning to him she responded, "I can understand. And you don't have to apologize. You are not obliged." Just as he touched the door, Frema turned. Very disappointed, she fetched the keys to the door. She moved in to open the door for him. Kofi stepped out and turned to say goodbye. Their eyes met. She was close to tears. "I can understand your situation. Everything seemed to have happened too quickly and I wouldn't want to hold you to anything." Kofi could feel Frema strumming him with her words. She was just saying exactly how he felt within. He did not expect to have fallen in love with her so quickly. "It's not easy to adjust to sudden encounters like these. You're overwhelmed and I am not surprised you're growing cold feet."

"I'm not overwhelmed. I am not growing cold feet. I am just – just…"

"Alright. I have made you breakfast," she said as he tried to avoid her eyes, "Before you leave, would you mind having breakfast with me?"

"Oh, really?"

"Look, after this you can leave. And I'll not bother you again."

Kofi looked down her cleavage. She turned and moved away without waiting for any response from him. He watched how her two half-exposed buttocks rattled behind her. He heard the music made by her beads. His eyes almost popped out of their sockets. He sighed and swallowed deeply. For a moment he went blank and confused, his emotions battling with his conscience. The seductive and alluring poise caught him again like magnet. He had not taken a good look at her until now. He felt a sudden urge surge through him that pulled him back into the room. He dumped his dirty clothes aside and kicked the door close with his heel and dashed after her. By the time Frema reached the kitchen he was just a step behind her. The hot wave of passion that had suddenly began churning inside him, sent him grabbing her from behind just as she picked a tray on which the breakfast had been laid. Without hesitation and any caution, Frema abandoned the food and swung herself to him with passion more than twice what they had expressed in the night. They held each other tightly, kissed and caressed. She pulled his T-shirt off while he peeled off the lacy skimpy top. They both went for each other's pants, hot short or long. She pulled down her zip before she went in for his. Kofi's thumb hooked the beads around her waist as he tried to pull her hot pants away, over her rounded buttocks. Unconsciously, his pull snapped two of the three strands along with her hot pants. The individual loosened beads pelted the acrylic tiled floor, sprawling around. Paying no attention as they got consumed with lusty passion, Kofi broke off and pushed the food tray aside to make space on the kitchen cabinet. He lifted her onto the kitchen cabinet and dashed in between her thighs. She threw her legs around him and pulled him tighter to her.

Three days had passed since Kofi and Frema entered her apartment. None of them had stepped out. Like new love birds in a nest on honeymoon, they locked themselves up and cut themselves out of the world outside and enjoyed each other. They slept and woke up together; she cooked and they ate together; they bathed together and made love. They took their time together seriously, as if to make up for lost time. It seemed they had lived in solitary lives. Indeed, they had a lot of catching up to do. Kofi had not had a real passion in his life until then. No real woman had touched his life and made him feel as real a man as Frema had.

Frema, on the other hand, had had some relationships before, very intimate and passionate, sometimes, rough and crude. She was hot but very picky when it came to men. She calmed down when she met Oduro, the father of her only child, Bibi, six years ago. Oduro was a married man, very wealthy. He had a lovely family he would not leave for anything. Yet, when they met, they got attracted to each other so much so that they could not let go of each other until she became pregnant and made a wrong suggestion that she wanted him to leave his wife for her. She was so crazy about him and she thought Oduro would prefer her as wife since his current one had not given him any child yet.

Oduro enjoyed his time with her but a child was not what he needed from her. He had had two from previous relationships before he got married. When Frema's pregnancy came in, he felt it was time to quit before he got tied up, and so he did, leaving Frema desolate. He, nonetheless, accepted responsibility for the pregnancy; settled her very well, buying her the apartment and her car and giving her some good cash in a bank and some financial investment as well. Frema had never lacked anything for herself and looking after Bibi since then, but the suddenness of the end of her relation with Oduro shook her so much that from then on, no affection from any man had attracted her until she met Kofi. She really had fallen for him. And for the three days the two had immersed themselves in passion so deep that they had forgotten anything else existed.

Chapter Sixteen

FEATHER IN THE CAP

The Asante had a calendar that ran recurrently for every six weeks or forty-two days; they called it *adaduanan*. At the end of the *adaduanan* the last Sunday was observed as *Akwasidɛɛ*, a festival which every chief, from the lowest to the Obrempong or paramount chief, would celebrate in their locality. The Obrempong would hold a durbar, sit in state to receive homage from all his citizens and subjects. The various paramountcies would celebrate this and the biggest would be what the occupant of the Golden Stool would celebrate. In the whole year, nine cycles occur. Out of these, the Obrempong or the king for that matter, would select one of them and celebrate it as the grandest for the year, which was usually called the *Akwasidɛɛkeseɛ*. There was always a weeklong schedule of activities set to precede the *Akwasidɛɛ*. These included visits to the stool house or mausoleum where departed chiefs and royals were buried. In the case of the stool house, the stool the Obrempong or departed chief used, while alive, was preserved and kept in a designated room which the family would hold as such. The Asante believe in life after death and during this period the royal family would go to commune with the departed ancestors. The gods and the spirits of these departed ancestors were fed; prayed to for protection: to guard and guide the living out of all evils and calamity; called upon to intercede on behalf of the living and toprovide good health, progress and prosperity in the land and in the state. The tomb which Kofi and Frema went to, where the kings of Asante were buried, was the biggest and the grandest mausoleum or stool house in the kingdom.

On one of the days, the Wednesday preceding the *Akwasidɛɛ* which they called *Awukudɛɛ*, the spiritual leader of the state would go to the mausoleum to perform the rituals of cleansing and purification, and also feed the departed ancestors. The rituals would include the making of libation, slaughtering of a sheep and sprinkling its blood on the stools of the states and those of ancestors preserved in the mausoleum and the feeding of the dead with mashed yams and hard-boiled eggs.

It was very late in the night, in fact, a little after midnight into Wednesday, before the Sunday on which *Akwasidɛɛ*, the biggest *Asanteman* festival, was to be celebrated. The whole of the city of Kumasi was dead asleep, Nana Sumankwaa led a small group of men and women numbering about sixteen, dressed in black. They moved in a procession towards the High Street. They included the Banmuhene, Otumfoɔ's chief responsible for mausoleums and burial grounds. They carried with them some quantities of Schnapps drinks, three huge rams and a large brass bowl of mashed yam. They soon arrived at the roundabout in which stood the statue of Prempeh II. They stopped and looked around. The whole area was quiet and deserted, with no movement of any persons, as if there was a curfew. Nana Sumankwaa approached the statue and went down for the lever that would open the entrance.

He saw the broken handle lying by. Nonetheless, he pulled a knife he carried in a sheath hanging around his waist, and stuck it into the hole where the lever to open the entrance had broken off. After a bit of struggle, he succeeded in opening the entrance. The slab shifted aside revealing the stairway that ran into the ground. Nana

Sumankwaa supervised for all in his party to descend, and he joined them. The first person to reach the first landing area took the flint in order to light and provide a burning torch, but there was no torch on the post! A spare one lying by was brought in and lighted to lead the group further down. At every post where a torch was to be lighted, they realized that they were all burnt out! Spare ones lying below each post were brought in and lighted to replace the burnt out. They followed through the path Kofi and Frema had passed a few days earlier, that had adinkra symbols on the wall. No one asked any questions. A few of the torches that could not light were dipped into a pot of oil to get them to light and burn. They walked all the way down, past the point where the Worm had broken through to give Abdul Ali and his men access to encounter Kofi and Frema, but they did not see any sign of the Worm. Instead, they saw debris from the roof of the cave in a pile, completely covering the Worm out of sight. Everything seemed alright and in place, yet Nana Sumankwaa could notice minor changes at certain points that confirmed Kofi's story that they had been there a couple of days earlier. They went further to the entrance where Kofi dropped the torch that lighted and blew up a crater which gave them access into the tomb. There were cobwebs blocking the passage. The one carrying the torch pointed it to the wall. What should have lighted like a fuse that would run along the wall to blow the passage as it did for Kofi - did not light up.

"Nana, it did not light up!" the carrier of the torch said, shuddering.

"Oh, incredulous." Nana Sumankwaa rushed past the men and women ahead to see why. It was not the first time they were experiencing such a situation. He inspected the area, touched the duct and realized there was no oil in it. A pot sitting close by had some liquid in it. Nana Sumankwaa called for it.

"Keep the fire away." Nana Sumankwaa said, and the torch bearer moved aside. The pot contained combustible liquid. Some quantity was poured into a duct. It smelled like fuel, pungent. After about three minutes, when the pot had been stowed away, the duct was lit. This time it lighted. The burning fuse ran beyond the cobwebs and after a few seconds there was an explosion and the smoke. That caused the opening of the crater. The group followed into the tomb after the smoke had died down. It was as they had left it the last time they were there, no change, just as Kofi and his intruders first came and saw it. Nana Sumankwaa looked around. Everything was intact. He burst into laughter. "Our ancestors are great! Hahahahaha!" The rest wondered what he meant. He alone knew.

They quickly settled down and set up the processes to commence the rituals they had come to perform. They started with libations and the slaughtering of the first ram. The whole tomb was revealed as far as the Golden Stool and the other stools; the cubicles of the departed kings also appeared, unlike when Kofi and his illegal visitors were there, indicating that the current entrants were legitimate. Nana Sumankwaa picked up the *busumuru* from the forks it rested on and ran through series of incantations and appellations similar to what Kofi Nsiah had done. One female in the group, a fairly matured person in her sixties, picked up the bowl of mashed yam and began sprinkling it, in a fashion very much like the planting of seeds by broadcasting. She would fill her palm with the mashed yam and sprinkle it around. Nana Sumankwaa approached the first cubicle of the ancestral king. A small brass bowl of mashed yam and eggs was placed at the entrance. A libation, appellations and incantations for the king were made, appealing to the ancestor to accept the offering and come to feed. The tedious process went on flawlessly from one cubicle to the other without incidence. This lasted for several hours till they ran through all the fifteen former occupants who had become guardians of the Golden Stool. Special rituals were performed when they reached the Golden Stool. There were the three stools: the one in black; the one in silver and the one in gold. A few more bottles of schnapps were used for libations and the biggest ram left was slaughtered. Nana Sumankwaa asked for a white calico cloth; he threw it over the stool in gold and wrapped it in the cloth. The stool was carried into a big brass bowl with a cover. When the rituals and ceremonies were over the stool was brought out concealed from the sight of all. It was not until almost midnight that Nana Sumankwaa and his team completed their mission and departed the tomb by the same entrance. The oil duct was refilled and all the lighted lamp blown out one after the other before they departed the tomb.

While Nana Sumankwaa and his ritual team were in the tomb, and while they were still in the thick of the spiritual activities, Frema had woken up early that morning and made breakfast. She brought a large tray into the bedroom while Kofi was still asleep. She stood for a while and watched him as he slept. Many thoughts ran through her mind. She had thought she was not going to fall in love with any man, at least not yet. For years, nothing was pushing her to, but there she was, falling for a stranger in less the twenty- four hours of meeting him. That was quick. There was something about him, irresistible, she could not really describe, that was pulling her to him each time she saw him.

She moved to place the tray on one side of the bed. She went to the window and pulled the curtains apart to bring in some sunlight. The sudden strong brightness woke Kofi up. He pulled the cover-cloth on the bed over his head to shield his eyes from the bright sunlight.

"Wakey, wakey!" Frema said as she drew closer to him and sat beside him on the bed. "Wake up. It is time for breakfast." She lay on him and pulled the cover from his face. "Get up, go quickly wash your mouth and brush your teeth. I have something nice for you."

Kofi stretched his arms around her, smiling. "What else is better than you? You are the sweetest thing I have ever known."

"Hm? Don't flatter me."

"It's true. I have fallen in love with you," Kofi said gazing at her. "I am glad I met you. I'll be happy to be your friend."

"You?" She remembered Kofi's violent reaction towards her the first time they met, how he was ready to decimate her for coming to them, thinking she had led Abdul Ali and his men to track him down. But could she blame him for his suspicion about her? Kofi was right, dead right. How naïve she was then and could not understand him for his reaction. Well, was it love at first sight? She looked him deep in the eyes and dropped her head on his chest. Kofi held her firmly. Frema took a deep breath, but suddenly broke herself away from him, out of his grip and got off the bed.

"Come on, get up. The meal will be getting cold."

"What is today?" Kofi asked, turning to sit by the side of the bed. He had lost count of the days as he had gotten himself immersed and consumed in the new relationship he had encountered; the first and most fulfilling time he had spent in many years with someone he had felt deep affection for. His academic work had taken too much of him denying him adequate time for his passions and pleasure.

"Wednesday," Frema responded. "Five days since we first met."

"I'll need a phone. I must check on my uncle," Kofi said to her as he headed for the wash room, naked.

"Hey, this is unpardonable." She rose and retrieved her mobile phone from her bedroom and brought it just as Kofi returned from the wash room with a towel around his waist. He took the phone and dialed Nana Sumankwaa's number from memory. Frema set the breakfast. He placed the handset to his ear. "Hello?'

"Yes, hello." A female voice responded from the other end.

"This is Auntie Yaa."

"Auntie Yaa, this is Kofi. I am looking for Nana."

"Oh, your uncle is busy today. He won't be available till tomorrow morning."

"Oh, what could he be doing?" Kofi asked.

"You know Sunday is *Adɛɛkesɛɛ*. Today, Wednesday is *Awukudɛɛ*. He will be spending the whole day at the mausoleum to perform all the rituals to purify the ancestral stools and feed the ancestral kings."

Kofi's mind immediately went to the tomb. He had quick flashes of the amazing experience they had in the tomb. "Oh, yes. But how is he?"

"He was doing pretty well before he left."

"Good. Please tell him I called to check on him."

"He was also looking for you before he left. I will tell him to call you when he returns. I am sure he will be able to reach you on this number?" Auntie Yaa added.

"Yes, Auntie. Thank you, Auntie Yaa," said Kofi and hung up. He joined Frema who had started on the breakfast.

It was not until the next morning that Nana Sumankwaa returned home. He was very tired and completely exhausted from the several activities of rituals he had had to perform in the mausoleum. His injuries exacerbated his condition. The stool they had removed from the tomb was sent to Manhyia into a special room. It was cleaned and polished before he left it. When he got home, he had a bath and a light breakfast and went to rest.

In the early afternoon, Auntie Yaa went in to wake him up. She had received a message from the Akyeamehene, the king's Chief Linguist at the Manhyia Palace that needed his attention. As part of the *Adɛɛkesɛɛ*, Otumfoɔ would bestow one of the highest state honours of *Asanteman* on one prominent citizen and the lot had fallen on Kofi Nsiah for his exploits in showcasing the culture and tradition of his people abroad. The official announcement was going to be made in his family house and since Nana Sumankwaa was his head of family, it was proper that he hosted the ceremony. Auntie Yaa was very efficient. She initiated all the protocols while Nana Sumankwaa was resting. She immediately called in Nana's personal linguist and with him they informed and invited all prominent personalities in the family, the Abusuapanyin, Obaapanyin and other elders of the family. When all was set, she was going to call Kofi on the number she had spoken to him previously.

Frema had driven Kofi to his bungalow at the university. They entered the house and saw the damage that was caused when the savage men of Abdul Ali pursued them. With the house phone he called the university estate department to come in to see and fix the damage. It was not long before a group of men arrived to assess the damage and prepare a report. Frema followed him as he went about the inspection. Frema's phone rang. She picked it out of her bag. "Hello," she answered.

"Hello. Erm, er-," Auntie Yaa hesitated. She was surprised and taken aback on hearing a female voice instead of Kofi's, she was lost on what she had to say.

Frema recognized her voice and could sense her confusion and apprehension. She immediately intervened. "Auntie, it's me, Frema, the lady who came to the house with Kofi that morning."

"Oh, dear me. Forgive me, my dear. I am so sorry."

"Never mind, Auntie. Kofi is here. Would you like to speak with him?"

"Yes, I do. Thank you"

"Kofi, phone." She ran to Kofi and handed it over to him. "Auntie Yaa."

"Hello, Auntie Yaa." Kofi took over the phone and spoke.

"Kofi, there is an emergency. You are required to attend a ceremony here right now. Your uncle, the Obaapanyin and Abusuapanyin, together with all the family elders, will gather here soon and they are expecting you to be here too."

"What is happening?"

"Oh, nothing serious," Auntie said, "you will know the details when you get here. Kofi, when you're coming, bring your new friend, eh," she chuckled.

"Okay, Auntie." He turned to look at Frema who was eavesdropping but pretended she was not listening. "We will be there."

After the call, Kofi went to talk to the head of the team of workmen and handed him the keys to the bungalow. He joined Frema who was then waiting in her car. Just as she moved the car, Kofi prompted her to turn into Prof. Osei's house immediately. That is when it dawned on her how they had completely forgotten him. She parked by the roadside. They walked into the compound and to the front door. They saw the garage door which had been patched and fixed. They knocked at the door and waited.

Prof. Osei appeared at the door with a bandaged head and his right arm in a plaster of paris up to his shoulder. He was a very pitiful sight. He helped himself with a walking stick as he managed to inch his way to the door. He slowly opened the door.

"Oh my God!" Frema exclaimed on seeing him.

"Jeez! Prof." Kofi could not believe that this was what happened to him when they left with his car. Frema grabbed on to Kofi's arm, distraught.

"What do you want here?" Prof. Osei yelled when he recognized it was Kofi. "What do you want from me? Get out of my house! Get out!"

"Please, Prof…" Kofi attempted to give some explanation but he was instantly shouted down.

"I don't want to hear anything from you, you rogue! Where is my car? Where is my car? You knocked me down and did not care to check on me for five days. Are you now coming here? To my funeral? Get out! Get out of my house!"

Embarrassed by the encounter, Kofi and Frema turned and retreated away from Prof. Osei.

"I've reported to the police! You have stolen my car! They are looking for you! You will go to jail! I have reported you to the University Council! They will discipline you!" Prof. Osei yelled after them as they rushed into their car, ashamed, and drove away. They left the university campus for Nana Sumankwaa's house.

Nana Sumankwaa and his elders were getting ready for the ceremony. Some of them were seated in the courtyard on traditional stools in a horseshoe formation. They were dressed in simple colourful traditional apparel. Nana Sumankwaa sat in the middle of the horseshoe; a young man held a small umbrella over his head with his Obaapanyin to his left and Abusuapanyin to his right. The other elders and invited members of the family sat to complete the horseshoe.

Kofi entered the courtyard with Frema following him closely. They went round, shaking hands with the elders as they sat. He was ushered to a seat set for him in between Abusuapanyin and Nana Sumankwaa. Since Frema was not known to the family and was not expected at the function, no seating arrangement had been made for her. But as soon as they saw her as the guest of Kofi's, a quick adjustment was made to accommodate her. A stool was placed to Kofi's right for her.

The emissary of Otumfoɔ arrived at the assemblage just at the time the seating arrangements were completed. Akyeamehene, head linguist of the king, carrying his staff, akyeame poma in his hand led the delegation. He was accompanied by the Mpumpunsuohene, head of the royal courtier and Chief of Protocol who bore on his left arm the *mpumpunsuo*, the king's sword of authority, and two other elders. The *mpumpunsuo* was an exact replica of the *busumuru* Kofi used to repel the warrior kings in the tomb a few days ago. A small group of *kete* drummers and courtiers followed them, beating the drums and singing. After a short welcoming formalities, the entourage was sat near the pile of rocks or the house shrine, which was across and directly opposite where Nana Sumankwaa sat, underneath a large umbrella. When the drumming stopped, Nana Sumankwaa's Okyeame rose and requested, on behalf of his boss, the mission.

Akyeamehene rose to his feet and addressed the gathering. "Nana Sumankwaa, Obaapanyin, Abusuapanyin and all you, elders here assembled, I come as the emissary of the owner of the land, *Asanteman Wura, Ote- kɔkɔɔ-soɔ,* Otumfoɔ Osei Tutu II with pleasant news for your family. Is the Professor here?"

Kofi, surprised, slowly rose to his feet, wondering what it was about.

He turned to look at Nana Sumankwaa.

"Your son and nephew," Akyeamehene continued, "Professor Kofi Nsiah who is the head of Department of Traditional Studies at the Kumasi University has been cited by Otumfoɔ for his exemplary work in the promotion and advancement of the traditions and culture of the Kingdom of Asante. For this reason, the king has nominated him for *Asanteman's* highest honour of the season. The honour will be conferred on him on Sunday at the *Akwasidɛɛ* durbar." He paused and turned to Kofi, "Professor Kofi Nsiah, by the powers vested in me as Otumfoɔ's Akyeamehene, and by the authority of this staff in my hand, I invite you to make yourself available on that day to receive the honour. Congratulations, Professor! Otumfoɔ ma wo amo! Congratulations!" Akyeamehene sat.

Nana Sumankwaa, elders and all present responded cheerfully with great excitement and applause. The drumming resumed. Some of the family members danced to the music.

The Mpumpunsuohene ran in with the *mpumpunsuo* sword and whirled it over Kofi's head as a sign of congratulations from the king. *"Mo, opeafo!"* he shouted to Kofi.

Kofi was totally overwhelmed by the news. He turned to look at Frema who sat next to him. Unable to control herself, she rose and hugged him with tears in her eyes. Some members of the family ran in to congratulate him. While some shook his hand, others embraced and hugged him.

Nana Sumankwaa led the family to thank the king's emissary and to send the family's gratitude to the king for the honour. Kofi and Frema joined them to express their thanks by shaking hands with them.

Two bottles of schnapps and a bottle of whisky were presented to the Akyeamehene and his entourage. This was a token to confirm that the family had accepted the honour bestowed on them and would present Kofi to receive the honour. Other drinks were also brought in as refreshment for the occasion. Everyone at the ceremony was served.

When the king's emissary and his entourage had left and the fanfare had died down, Nana Sumankwaa and his Ɔbaapanyin and Abusuapanyin moved into his sitting room with Kofi to plan for the ceremony. They advised him on the choice of clothes to wear and gifts he would need to bring as presents to the king to thank him for the honour and also to congratulate him for the celebrations of the

Akwasideɛ. Frema and Auntie Yaa sat a little away from them, listened and took notes. They conferred and decided on a list of things to do and where to get what.

Kofi and Frema returned to Nana Sumankwaa'a house the next day. They joined him at table in the hall for breakfast. When they were done, Auntie Yaa and Frema left the two men and went shopping. They visited the kente weaver's shop. They saw some of the weavers on the loom weaving intricate designs and colours, synchronizing the movements of their feet with their hands, throwing the shuttles to weave in rhythm. They checked through the finished kente strips and full cloths; they picked very colourful cloths for themselves and their two men, Nana and Kofi. Auntie Yaa reached into her bag to pay for the items.

"Allow me, Auntie." Frema said, holding her hand to restrain her. "Allow me to pay for them. Please."

"Oh, Nana has already given me money for all we would purchase." Auntie Yaa lamented.

"Yes, but with all due respect to Nana, please allow me as a gesture of sincere gratitude to him."

Auntie Yaa was dumbfounded. She reluctantly conceded to Frema and allowed her to pay for all the purchases. From there, they went to the sandal designers and selected the appropriate slippers to match the cloths. The wine shop was their next location where they selected and bought a classy assortment of alcoholic beverages appropriate for the presentation.

They returned home in the evening. Auntie Yaa related Frema's gesture to Nana Sumankwaa. "Nana, you have to thank your "in-law". She paid for all the purchases we made."

"She did?" Nana Sumankwaa asked, surprisingly, impressed.

Frema was perturbed. She least expected Auntie Yaa to broach the matter. "Oh, Auntie Yaa," she protested. "I thought we were going to keep this a secret between us."

"Oh, I am sorry for your discomfiture. Such a wonderful gesture must not go without appropriate appreciation," Auntie Yaa insisted. Frema was discomforted. She moved closer to Kofi and held onto him, shying away. "Don't shy away, my dear. Nana, please thank her."

"You can trust my Auntie Yaa to give you away at a time like this," Kofi remarked, teasingly, as he pulled Frema towards Nana Sumankwaa. "Such benevolence deserves the requisite gratitude."

"Thank you," Nana Sumankwaa expressed his gratitude to her with a handshake. Then he gave Kofi two special passes that would give them access to seating at the durbar.

When all was done, Frema drove Kofi back to his bungalow at the University. Kofi got down and walked round to Frema's side. She also got down and met him and gave him a hug.

"Come early to dress up at my place." Frema said as she disengaged from him.

"Yes, yes." He looked at her and said: "Thank you."

She sat down but just before she moved, she remembered. "Yes, about Prof. Osei's issue. I've been thinking. We must find someone to intercede to resolve the problem we have with him."

"Yes, we'll tackle it after the celebrations."

"Ok. I'll see you tomorrow." She took off waving her hand out of the car.

Kofi stood and watched her disappear in the darkness before he went to his bungalow.

Frema was tired but she felt very satisfied with what she had done. She arrived at the Nhyiaeso Flats and parked in the lot. She slowly dragged herself up the stairs to the fifth floor. It was not quite bright as she approached her floor. She noticed something like luggage in front of her door. She hesitated and observed carefully, slowly getting close. Then she recognized that it was a human being lying by the door, asleep and covered with a cloth.

She was disturbed and wondered why someone would come to sleep at her door.

"Who is there?" She asked as she got closer. Then she saw and identified the cloth. It was her mother's. She lay asleep at her doorstep. Her heart began to throb. "Maame! Maame!" she called out.

"Huh?" Maame responded as she stirred out of her sleep. "Oh, Maame? What are you doing here at such a time?"

"Where have you been all day?" She lifted herself off the floor trying to shrug herself out of her sleep.

"Where is Bibi?"

"She is here." Maame lifted the cloth revealing a sleeping Bibi covered by the cloth to protect her from the mosquitoes. She stretched herself and scratched her arm to sooth the itches from mosquito bites.

"Oh, Maame." Frema dropped the things she was carrying and rushed in to pick up Bibi. She lifted her up into her bosom. "Is she alright?"

"Yes, she is. We are all alright."

"When did you arrive here? Why didn't you call me before coming? Why haven't you called since you arrived?"

"I left my phone back at Nwabe. I don't know your number off-hand."

"Have you eaten?" Frema turned Bibi in her arm and looked at her as she still slept.

"Yes. Bibi has eaten biscuit and drank some juice."

Frema was very upset but could not blame her. "Ah, Maame, you did not try at all. Don't take yourself and my baby through such drudgery again.

Call me, if you want to come here. I'll come for you. Haven't I told you this before? Please lift my bag for me. No, the hand bag." She asked her mother to bring her hand bag. Still carrying Bibi she searched for her keys. She found them, opened the door and entered. Maame collected the rest of the things Frema had dropped and her own stuff and followed her closely into the room, shutting the door behind her.

Maame realized Frema was upset but why should she blame her? She poured her heart out as she followed her. "Don't blame me, my girl. When was the last time you visited us? I called to tell you Bibi was unwell. You drove all the way there. You did not even go in to see her to check how she was doing; you flashed through and left in a hurry as if the devil was chasing you. You have disappeared since. I called many times; your phone did not answer. I waited; you did not call. What did you expect me to do? If you do not care about us, I care about you. So, we came to check on you. I knew that no matter where you had gone you would come back home to sleep."

Frema realized she was to blame for the unfortunate situation; she felt too embarrassed and remorseful to give any response. She took Bibi into the bed room and lay her on her bed. Maame settled in the sofa. Frema returned quickly and went to the kitchen to prepare something for them to eat. Maame joined her. They chatted while they went about it. Frema tried to brief Maame of her new experience and encounter over the last week or so, within the short time they had before they retired to bed. She told her about the most wonderful man who had come into her life. What she made clear to Maame was that she was happy to see them. "And most importantly, Maame," Frema added, "Otumfoɔ will give Kofi the highest *Asanteman* State honour. I am honoured to be his chaperon at the ceremony. I am also glad you are here to be part of this great event. Kofi is a nice man and I am glad to be the woman by his side at this time."

Maame was overjoyed and thanked her stars and God for the turn of events. She was excited to be part of the ceremony. Deep inside her, she was most elated that at last, Frema had found a man in her life.

Chapter Seventeen

AKWASIDƐE KESEƐ

The Sunday morning for the ceremony broke with bright sunshine. All Kumasi was bustling with activities for the Akwasidɛe keseɛ, the biggest ceremony on the calendar for the people of Asante to showcase the tradition and culture of the Asante Kingdom and to celebrate the Golden Stool. The eventual grand durbar commenced. At the grounds, Otumfoɔ, the occupant of the Golden Stool which is the soul of the Asante Kingdom, would sit in state to receive homage from all and sundry. Very prominent people from far and near and from home and abroad were invited. Every household, whether related to the Kingdom or not, but which felt obliged to participate, feverishly prepared for it.

They prepared: men and women, young and old, the rich and the poor, the noble and commoner, people from all walks of life. They came out in their best, in different forms, shapes and colours.

"Adɛe tɔkye oo!!" One could hear the festival greeting being shouted to celebrants meaning: "pleasant *Akwasidɛe* to you." And they would in turn respond, *"adɛe ntɔ yie!"* meaning, "pleasant *adɛe* with good tidings."

Kofi got himself ready from his University bungalow in a simple outfit, a shirt made of local fabric and a pair of shorts. He took a taxi and went to Frema's apartment. On the way, he saw a number of bus-loads of celebrants being transported to the center of the city where the grand durbar was going to take place. He dropped off in front of Frema's block. He looked up and viewed the fifth floor. He ran into the building and up the stairs and rapped at the door. Bibi went in to open the door. Kofi was surprised to see her. "Hello, how are you?"

"Mummy, there is someone at the door!" She yelled out.

"My name is Kofi. You are Bibi?"

She nodded.

Kofi squatted and looked her in the eye and said: "Next time, do not open the door when you do not know who is knocking."

Bibi nodded again and ran off to Frema as she emerged from her bed room. She was preparing. Frema passed her and went to Kofi, hugged him and gave him a light kiss on his lips.

"You are here in good time. Come," Frema pulled him in and closed the door. "This is my Bibi. Bibi say 'hi' to Uncle Kofi."

"Hi, Uncle Kofi."

"Hi, Bibi."

"My mom is in there." Frema gestured with her head to the second room as her hands were engaged trying to tie her head-gear to cover her dreadlocks.

"You did not tell me you were inviting them," Kofi expressed his surprise to her. "When did they arrive?"

"They came in to surprise me too. I did not invite them." She turned to Bibi, "Bibi, go to Maame for her to dress you up. We are going out with Uncle." Bibi obliged and joined Maame in the other bedroom. Frema stopped tying the head gear and pulled Kofi into her bedroom where they passionately embraced each other. They broke off and resumed dressing up. Frema brought out Kofi's kente cloth, jewelry and sandals. He took off his shirt and adorned himself with the kente as Asante men do - wrapped it around his back through his right armpit, exposing his right arm, flowing down to his feet and tossed both stretched ends together over his left arm and shoulder, and finally locked it tight by tossing the stretched left end back unto the left shoulder. He completed with a gold chain around his neck and a bracelet. He slipped his bare feet into a pair of sandals and felt it fitting perfectly. Frema fitted into a beautiful attire, long tight skirt and blouse made out of a colourful kente. Her make-up was resplendent. They stood side by side and looked at themselves in the mirror and they were satisfied. Frema took out a bottle of perfume and sprayed some on to herself and on Kofi as well.

Maame was ready. She had also dressed up Bibi. They came out of the bedroom at the same time as Kofi and Frema. Her first encounter with Kofi overwhelmed her. The first impression on an in-law, they say, must be impactful, and Kofi made more than enough of an impression. She stood and looked at him in his beautiful kente. "Is he the one?" she asked.

"Yes, Maame. This is Kofi. My friend." Frema brought Kofi to meet Maame.

"Are you the man who has stolen my daughter's heart?" Maame asked as she shook his hand.

"If she says it so, then it is so," said Kofi. "I am glad to meet you. I am glad to know your wonderful daughter. And Bibi."

"Maame, we must be going now. We are getting late." They picked up what they would need from the room and headed downstairs to the car.

The traffic was heavy on all the roads that led to the Kumasi stadium, venue for the durbar. There was a big carnival of traditional rulers. The multitude that had descended on the streets of the City of Kumasi was unimaginable. From about a kilometer or more to the stadium, the streets were filled with human traffic. There were those who were trooping to the stadium to participate and others who were going there to watch the proceedings. There were also others who had come out of their homes as spectators; they stood by the road sides to watch those on their way. They hailed and cheered the many participants. Many Abrempɔn, paramount chiefs who had jurisdiction over traditional areas also elegantly came and passed by, and people watched from their rooftops, from their windows and balconies, cheering and waving at all of them. They trooped with their elders and subjects in processions, dancing to the music performed by the drummers who accompanied them, under their colourful large umbrellas. There were also those who commented and criticized what they saw as unpleasant or funny. Once in a while one would hear, "*Adɛe tɔkye oo,*" screamed out of the crowd and followed by its response, "*Adɛe ntɔ yie!*"

Frema managed to get as close to the stadium as she could. She got to a point where there was a police barricade which did not permit vehicles to go beyond. No matter how hard they tried, showing their official passes as special guests, the police would not allow them to drive beyond. She managed to squeeze her car into a small space nearby and parked. They made the rest of the way on foot just like the others. They joined the fun of the cacophony of music and drums of various types and sizes, and the singing and cheers of the many that followed and danced. It was a pleasant sight to those who understood but a crazy melee of confusion to the uninformed.

Over seventy paramount and divisional chiefs known as Abrempɔn participated. Each divisional, paramount chief or Ɔbrempɔn arrived with his sub-chiefs, elders and subjects. They were also accompanied by their queen- mothers and their courtiers.

The Ɔbrempɔn trooped in a particular form. He was led by the executioners of his court and warriors who, as it were, were to clear the way for him and his entourage. The Ɔkyerɛma, the divine drummer, who carried a small drum which he beat to announce the coming of the Ɔbrempɔn, led the main procession, followed by stools carriers and then seven horn blowers called mmɛnsɔn to herald the Ɔbrempɔn. Behind them were the linguists or Akyeame carrying in their hands their staffs of authority; the chiefs or Ahenfo and elders also followed with smaller umbrellas over them in an order of authority and relevance, each of them accompanied by one or two personal aides. There were relatively smaller chiefs. They did not have umbrellas over them.

Right in front of him, as he walked, the Ɔbrempɔn was escorted by six courtiers or nhenkwaa who bore, each in their hands, traditional swords called *afena,* made of steel or iron with a long broad blade with gold plated handles and wore on their heads a black cap made of hard leather decorated with gold called kropɔnkyɛ. The nhenkwaa carried the *afena* by the blade; the handle was reserved for the Ɔbrempɔn only. The Mpumpunsuohene, the leader of the nhenkwaa and also chief of protocol for the Ɔbrempɔn, carried a special *afena,* the sacred sword called the mpumpunsuo, sheathed in leopard skin, or the skin of any wild ferocious beast, for that matter, with a huge gold ornament on it. Its handle was made of or decorated with gold meant to be handled by only the Ɔbrempɔn in whose court it served. All who bore it, carried it by the blade end and would present it to the Ɔbrempɔn who should take it by the handle.

The only time someone other than the Ɔbrempɔn was allowed to hold this unique afena by the handle was a time when the person permitted so to do was going to swear an oath to the Ɔbrempɔn. The Mpumpusuohene who always carried this special sword also wore a cap made of hard leather and gold, decorated with unique gold ornaments or turkey tail feathers or those of a peacock set in the form of an arc. He controlled the movement of the procession. At certain points, the Mpumpunsuohene would stop the procession for the Ɔbrempɔn to dance to the music of an ensemble of drummers of fɔntɔmfrɔm, mpintin, ntahra or kete which accompanied the entourage. The Mpumpunsuohene carried all communications between the Ɔbrempɔn and his elders and subjects.

Each Ɔbrempɔn's status was known by how he was decorated with ornament of gold from rings, armbands, bracelets, necklaces and head- gear to the size and number of umbrellas he would be permitted to use, his Ɔhemaa and Ahenfo, accompanying elders and subjects. The size of his total entourage also showed how powerful or influential he was. The Ɔbrempɔn could carry in his hands a white silk scarf, white cow tail or other ornaments decorated with gold.

The Ɔbrempɔn's ensemble of drummers followed closely to provide music for him and his entourage to dance. The warrior squad which sported and displayed their weaponry of guns, knives and other implements, followed behind the ensemble, firing muskets as the entourage moved along.

The Queenmother or Ɔhemaa and her retinue followed closely behind the Ɔbrempɔn. She was led by her elders who were her Sub-Queenmothers, Mmaampanyinfoɔ of the various chiefs of the Ɔbrempɔn. She also had her own ensemble behind her.

The Ɔbrempɔn, his Ɔhemaa and Ahenfo were dressed in full regalia of rich fabrics or kente cloths of different types and colours, gold ornaments of chains, necklaces, rings, head-gears, anklets and armlets and so on. Whatever they wore they made sure that their appearances would not match up to or compete with those of Otumfoɔ, the king, in style and richness.

Kofi held Bibi's hand, closely followed by Frema and Maame. They meandered through the resplendent pomp and pageantry of the many Abrempɔn that had arrived.

From their paramountcies, the Abrempɔn arrived one after the other: first was Mampong; the occupant of the silver stool, second in command to the overall king, but not a direct successor to the king. And so were Sekyere, Nsuta and Offinso, showing off what they were made of in power and authority and in history. From Ahafo: Bekyem, Kukuom, Tepa and Goaso, they trooped and danced in pomp and pageantry. Slowly and patiently, they all, Dwaben, Edwiso, Agogo, Dwaaso and Konongo arrived at the durbar grounds in rich regalia and prestige; and so also from Baantama, Nkawie, Esumengya and Fomena and from all the corners of the Asante Kingdom the Abrempɔn continued to arrive for the durbar and headed towards the arena.

The Kumasi Sports Stadium was filling up in the stands and on the main field. Each ɔbrempɔn arrived and was shown to his designated spot. They settled in and sat in state - Adansi, Bekwai, Manso and Kokofu - to wait for the arrival of Otumfoɔ, the king, ruler of Asante Kingdom and occupant of the legendary Golden Stool. There were also ally chieftains from Duayaw Nkwanta, Dormaa, Gyaman, Techiman, Nkoranza and Denkyira; from Akyem, Akuapem, Ga-Adangbe, Anlo, Akwamu, Fante and Nzema and as far as Gonja, Dagomba and Mamprusi, the Mosiland and Alata, in their splendour. The kings of the Swazis, the Zulus and Bugandas were invited and they arrived in majesty.

The participation of Otumfoɔ in the Akwasidɛɛ festival was of a different order altogether. It had its stature and drive completely different from that of all the Abrempɔn, though, they represented a miniaturized replica of that of Otumfoɔ. Earlier in the day, Otumfoɔ brought to the Apagyafie to prepare for the ceremony. He arrived in his Rolls Royce, flying the *Asanteman* flag of yellow, green and black with the dɛnkyɛmkyɛ, the state emblem fitted in front and behind the car. He was casually dressed though, but one could see the depth and quality of his appearance. He was ushered into the safe house to prepare for the ceremony.

Apagyafie was about a kilometer away from the stadium. Otumfoɔ's protocol and handlers had had to find, as was the norm, a nearby safe house that Otumfoɔ and his entourage would move to, the morning of the ceremony, from where the king would prepare and start his triumphant majestic and kingly palanquin ride to the durbar grounds. The host for this purpose would be a noble of good repute, a prominent member of society of good standing with Manhyia or one of the royal houses of the kingdom. So, this time the lot fell on the Apagya royal house or Apagyafie and the Apagyahene was to host Otumfoɔ.

The security of the house was checked for the safety of Otumfoɔ. All the regalia of the king were brought there: his umbrellas, palanquin, a large round mat made of pieces of leather like a parchment kilt, the king's stool and another stool for the *Sika Dwa*, the Golden Stool and foot rests. One significant object that came in was the big brass bowl that Nana Sumankwaa and his spiritual team brought out from the bane mu. It was carried carefully into the safe house. Each and every member of the king's retinue who attended on him also came with their accoutrements and properties required at such a ceremony. From the ordinary ahenkwaa (courtier), obrafoɔ (the executioner), Ɔkyerɛma (divine drummer), carriers and sword bearers with all their respective chiefs or commanders, the royals, sons and daughters, grandsons and granddaughters of the king, to the elders and senior chiefs or Abrempɔn and the Otumfoɔ Mpumpunsuohene, the chief of protocol, who were all part of his immediate entourage were all assembled.

They all went about their chores and prepared, individually, as a member of a team and whichever role they would play to present the king in a resplendent way, worthy of the rich culture for which the Asante Kingdom was noted.

Kofi and Frema arrived at the durbar grounds through the VIP gate. They were allowed through when they presented their invitations. From where he stood, a large balcony with steps that went down to the center of the playing field, he could see the whole stadium, the stands from left to right and the main playing field below him. For a moment, he took a panoramic view. The stadium was filled to capacity. All the stands were full with tens of thousands of anxious spectators.

The playing field was filled by a sea of colourful umbrellas of various shapes and sizes, spotting at the top of each or most of them, many different shapes and types of totems, exhibiting a very colourful scenery. A long series of canopies had been raised in the middle of the near side and directly opposite the chiefs, for the special guests and dignitaries who were attending the ceremony. On the far side and in the center, a small dais had also been raised; that spot was designated for Otumfoɔ, and to the left and right of the spot, all the over seventy paramount chiefs or Abrempɔn and ally guest traditional rulers who had been invited were arranged in their respective order of relevance and authority in reverence to Otumfoɔ.

They had all almost arrived and settled in at their respective designated spots, except for a few who were still trooping in and dancing to show off. The Mamponhene, occupant of the silver stool arrived. He and his entourage dressed in white and silver, trooped amidst music and dance and were ushered to their designated spot.

The Bantamhene, one of the prominent and powerful Abrempɔn in the kingdom, the one allowed to ride in a palanquin to a function Otumfoɔ would attend, arrived. He arrived in his palanquin, dressed in black with his hard leather head gear, a cap, kropɔnkyɛ, not decorated with ornaments, but he wore amulets instead of gold trinkets and ornament. The Bantamhene, the warrior chief was the only one in his stature allowed to carry weapons with him to ceremonial grounds like Akwasidɛe. Frema was surprised to observe him in black for such a joyous festive occasion while his courtiers and retinue appeared in rich festive clothes. She asked Kofi why.

"The Bantamahene is the commander or sahene of the royal armed forces," Kofi explained. "That is his official ceremonial uniform, if I may say so. He is in charge of Otumfoɔ's security and wherever Otumfoɔ would appear in public like this. He rides his palanquin to signify his stature, command and authority in the kingdom. You see, he is the only Obrempɔn who had come in a palanquin. He is also holding a weapon. He is very important in the scheme of things, particularly for today."

An usher arrived and invited Kofi and his company, interrupting the discourse. They were escorted to a reserved area. Auntie Yaa had arrived earlier and had been seated. There were only two seats available on the front row next to her. Kofi and Frema were given those seats. They were excited seeing her. After exchanging pleasantries with Auntie Yaa, Maame was sent three rows behind them. Kofi insisted Bibi stayed with them in the front row. He raised her on to his lap. She was so mesmerized that she could hardly take her eyes off the spectacle that was unfolding, turning left and right in utter bewilderment, the streaming of the Abrempɔn and their entourages, drumming and dancing, receiving cheers and encouragement from the guests and the spectators as they filed past. The intermittent firing of muskets startled her each time there was a bang, and she would grab hold of Kofi for comfort but would almost immediately return to look as soon as the sound of gun fires died away.

The traditional cloth for the Asante male was worn wrapped around the body over the left shoulder and exposing the right arm. All men wore their cloths over their shoulder as noble men or royals with a pair of oversize knickers or shorts to match. The Queen mothers or Mmaa mpanyinfo or other royals and noble women also wore their cloths the traditional way called dansinkran. Theirs was a two-piece attire. One, worn like an under- cloth, mostly a white material for ceremonies like the Adɛe, they would wrap and tie the under-cloth firmly at the torso over the breast, flowing down to just below the knee, with a second band tied at the waist like a sash to give it the waist-line shape. The second cloth, a ceremonial cloth which was a little smaller than that of the males was worn the same way as the men's, wrapped over their left shoulders, exposing the right shoulder.

Dress code was very restrictive and strict. Apart from chiefs and those designated as chiefs, linguists, elders and those with command to responsibilities, all the men and women, all others who served in the king's palace and court as servants and courtiers were not permitted to wear their cloths over their left shoulder. These included members of the royal family. Once activities for the celebrations kicked in, all who called in to serve, wore their cloths below the shoulders. No matter the size or quality, the cloth was wrapped and tied, exposing both shoulders or torsos, as in the men, in reverence to the king. In the case of their female counterparts they also kept their shoulders bare even if they came in a two-piece attire. Some wear footwear; others, lower in responsibility do not. Those who had the right to wear their cloths, male or female, always had to part their left shoulder bare whenever they appeared before the king. The Abrempɔn, royals, noble men and women, chiefs and elders and all, gave the king that reverence. None of the servants were allowed to wear footwear before the king. Those permitted to wear slippers would slip their right foot out of the slipper, bare their left shoulder and bow before the king.

The time to move to the durbar grounds arrived. The Mpumpunsuohene, the chief of protocol, the commander of the courtiers of the king's palace, the chief who wore his ceremonial cloth below his shoulders and walked barefooted, holding the mpumpunsuo on his left arm and in his ostrich feather hat set in an arch form, made the announcement. The mmɛnsɔn blowers sounded the alarm as the servers closer to the king began exiting from the room he was preparing in. All the musical ensembles began to sound, fɔntɔmfrɔm, mpintin, kete and so on, each in their own beat, form and rhythm. Each group of courtiers assembled to play their roles in service to the king and lined up one after the other.

Nana *Sumankwaahene* and his spiritual group took the lead with the *samanka*, a brass bowl, *yaawa*, which had some ritual artifacts of some carving and fresh leaves in it, carried on the head by a male ahenkwaa, closely guarded by his colleagues. The presence of the *samanka* symbolized the approach of the king to a public function and the *samanka* was to lead, cleansing the way of all evils. The king's state chair, the *kɔdeɛ* or *kɔtɔkɔdwa* and the hwɛdom, the stool for the Golden Stool, a pitcher of water and other accoutrements used to set up and decorate a palour for him at the durbar grounds appeared and were taken in to join the file. A silver vase known as *puduo*, draped in a silk net, carried on the head of a man, appeared. The *puduo* held the king's personal imprest, out of which he made generous donations or presentation of gifts to deserving citizens and guests.

The Golden Stool, the sacred stool, *Sika Dwa* Kofi; a small stool, made of gold, shining with two golden bells chained to it, the soul of the kingdom emerged, heavily guarded by a couple of abrafoɔ. It was designed like the *asesedwa,* an akan traditional stool, normally carved out of wood. It was carried on a pillow on the back of the two shoulders of a man who had a white calico cloth wrapped around his waist. He was assisted by two other men each by his sides to help him carry. They were also dressed in white wrappers. The bells clung to the stool jingled as they walked along.

Immediately after the stool, the King appeared to tumultuous cheers and applause with a small umbrella over his head. He strode gently in a colourful kente cloth, a mixture of red, gold, green, black, purple and white, intricately woven into a rich and beautiful pattern. He walked in majesty, graciously as the king that he was, adorned with jewels and ornament in gold, from his fingers up to his shoulders. Laced around his neck were loads and piles of necklaces and large pendants, in a beautiful array, spreading across his shoulders. From his feet, his toes, his ankles to his calves, all decked in gold trinkets and rings. His underwear, though not visibly exposed, was a colourful and beautifully wrapped loin cloth from around his lower abdomen down to his mid-thigh. A strip of purple velvet cloth, about two inches wide, had been designed into a head-gear, decorated with gold artifacts, served as his crown which he wore on a well-shaven head. Also, across his left shoulder down to his belly, he wore strips of gold chains designed into a sash. He wore a pair of beautiful black sandals also decorated with gold. All who had gathered there in cloth bared their left shoulders and bowed, with the right foot out of their slippers or sandals as the king passed. Others raised their two fingers, fore and middle of the right hand, to him as a sign of encouragement, loyalty and reverence.

The seven horn blowers, the mmɛnson went up in praise, heralding the king, owner of the kingdom, the custodian of the traditions of the people of Asante and true occupant of the Golden Stool. He stopped, looked left and right and listened. After the appellations, Otumfoɔ was slowly ushered from the Apagyafie into the street where the palanquin had been prepared, decorated and laid for him. The various strands of vast and diverse families of royals, extended relations of children, grandchildren and great grandchildren of the king had converged in their numbers to support and serve their king. He waved and received more cheers from the several hundreds that had thronged there, including the ordinary citizens, the noble, the rich and the poor, who had gathered in the vicinity, to catch a glimpse of their king. raised their two fingers, fore and middle of the right hand to him.

"*Mo, Ɔpiafo!*" The crowd cheered, meaning: " Well done!"

"*Ɔhene, nya nkwa daa*!" Many more yelled: " May the king live long".

"*Nana, wo tri nkwa o*!" "Congratulations!"

"Ɛsɛ wo; ɛfata wo!" "It is yours! You deserve it!"

"*Ohene, wo ho ayɛ fɛ*!" "You are handsome, you look resplendent!" Such were some of the many praises and adoration rained on him.

The several royals and servers who had called in to serve and the on-lookers cheered, sang and danced in paying obeisance to him. As soon as the king reached the frontage of the house, about six large umbrellas were immediately brought in to replace the small one that had been held over his head to shield him from direct rays of the sun.

The mass procession began to move slowly; each and everyone knew the task assigned them as individuals and as groups; they went on steadily and smoothly without any stampede. It showed the meticulous and systematic thinking that had gone into the planning and the execution of activities of such gargantuan magnitude, that had to go on that day. Twelve young men who carried ɛkyɛm, rectangular shields made out of furry animal skins, held them high in the air and rattled them in honour to the king as he walked. At a point they would throw and whirled their ɛkyɛm high into the air and grab them again in a spectacular acrobatic display.

The Golden Stool moved into position front of Otumfoɔ under the umbrellas.

The king's procession was ready to move. Otumfoɔ mounted the palanquin and settled in comfortably on a short padded seat, spreading his legs forward to fit into the well stuffed couch. From the four corners of this cylindrical trough were handles by which the palanquin was to be carried. The carrying crew, the *asoafoɔ*, gently lifted the king and raised him till the handles reached their shoulders. A pad or *kahyire*, as it was called, made from dried plantain leaves, tied into a thick stuffy disk of a cushion was placed on each of the *asoafoɔ* shoulder, on which palanquin handles were rested and balanced steadily. As soon as the palanquin stabilized, twelve sword bearers in their krɔpɔnkyɛ decorated with pieces of gold, placed their twelve junior mpumpunsuo on the edge of the palanquin. Each of these minor mpumpunsuo was known by the design of the gold ornament set on it.

All the divisional chiefs who constituted the Kumasiman Council, the Abrempɔn of Kumasi, the immediate councilors or elders of Manhyia Palace and Otumfoɔ Akyeame, formed up in a file ahead and led the procession on the street in front of Apagyafie. They fitted between Nana Sumankwaa and his spiritual group and immediately before the Golden Stool and the King's palanquin. Some had small umbrellas over their heads and were moderately dressed up for the occasion.

"*Animu nkɔ!* Move ahead!" the Otumfoɔ Mpumpunsuohene shouted, ordering the movement of the procession to commence as soon as he noticed the king was comfortably raised in the air. In precision and order, like a military regimental movement, the procession commenced. The executioners, the abrafoɔ, the security of Otumfoɔ, who carried in their hands, thin swords in metal sheaths, these swords were more like those used in fencing, slim and pointed at the tip, unlike *afena* with a broad blade, blunt and curved at the tip, these men ran along the procession and made sure it moved on in order and precision, clicking and brandishing their swords, gnashing their teeth, warning people as they passed by. The abrafoɔ wore short skirts, some made of jute sacks, leather or untreated animal skins; disguised by painting their faces in black and white clay, covering their heads with caps made of animal or human skulls. Their fierce and fearful appearances, as they ran along, shouting and screaming in frenzy scared onlookers who may have strayed into the procession. They did not give any quarter to anyone in the performance of their duty, such that, sometimes those in the procession who strayed off into their way, fell victim to their ruthlessness and got manhandled by these abrafoɔ, all in making sure nothing came to disrupt the smooth movement of the procession.

The *mmɛnsɔn* players blew along to herald the king as he passed; the *fɔntɔmfrɔm* ensemble followed behind him, beating for him to dance. At a distance behind the king, two men carried two young girls of about twelve years old, each on the shoulders. They sat with their thighs wrapped around their carriers' neck. The girls in colourful kente and dansinkran hair style, decorated with gold ornament from the head, around the neck, arms and finger to the calves and ankles. In their right hands, each girl carried a long furry white horse tail that rested on the left shoulder and often, after every short moment, they whirled the tails over their heads, ostensibly, to drive away all evil that trailed the king from behind him.

Behind the girls, four sizeable chests containing treasures of the king were carried on the head by a group. Otumfoɔ's entourage was completed by the royal guard made up of twelve men, heavily armed with traditional weaponry of shut guns, daggers and other implements.

The Asantehemaa, Queenmother of the Asante Kingdom, by the practice of the matrilineal inheritance system, is not the spouse of the king. She is a direct relation of the King's. The King is either her son, brother, uncle or her sister's son. Although she had overwhelming powers in the chieftaincy set up, her authority and powers rested in the King. Yet, the fate of the king's stay in office rested in her bosom: she appointed or approved the nomination of anyone who must ascend the throne and by extension would be responsible for his removal whenever the need arose; a chicken and egg situation.

She appeared, resplendently dressed in the fashion of the female royalty, baring her right shoulder and decorated with jewelry and ornaments, with a neat dansinkran haircut. She had also been prepared from a similar safe house close by and followed the king's procession at a short distance. She was led and accompanied by a bevy of women, her royal companions, made up of female complements of Abrempɔn and elders of the King's courts. There were also handmaids, maidens and servant. The Asantehemaa was carried in her special chair by four men. She was shielded with large handheld flat fans instead of umbrellas. She was also followed by her musical ensemble of drummers to which she danced and received cheers from her subjects and many that had thronged the route.

All the invited guests, dignitaries and the very, very important personalities (VVIPs) had arrived at the durbar grounds and taken their seats. It was not long before Otumfoɔ's procession took the last bend off the road and approached the precinct of the durbar arena with the beating of drums and dancing and responding to the cheers of the teeming crowds, accelerating the festive mode to a very high point. The procession advanced on till it arrived at the edge of the inner perimeter of the stadium where the Abrempɔn, the high dignitaries and VVIPs were seated.

The stadium which was filled to capacity erupted into deafening cheers when the king was sighted with his array of colourful umbrellas. He danced and waved towards the cheering crowds. Bibi spotted the courtiers leading the king's procession who carried long pipes and drew Kofi's attention to them. "These are the king's pipes and tobacco," he told her.

"The king's procession is long." Frema remarked.

"Indeed. It even includes those who handle the king's wardrobe and each individual property required for his use, such as his slippers, his cloths, his ornaments and so on and so forth; his state chair, cushions and foot rest. Those are in charge of setting up his palour when he sits in state." There was a firing of muskets that frightened Bibi. She grabbed hold of Kofi.

Otumfoɔ was taken along the edges of the canopies where the dignitaries were seated. He greeted them by waving his raised right hand as he was still being carried in his palanquin. The VVIPs rose to their feet and waved back in acknowledgement. Often, his ride would be halted; he would dance towards some of the dignitaries and they in turn would cheer him in appreciation. Some of the dignitaries were called up to him, with whom he had a hand shake and a short chat or exchange of pleasantries. Kofi lifted Bibi when the king reached where they were for her to have a good view. She waved. The king waved back as he was carried slowly past them in his palanquin. She giggled excitedly.

Finally, Otumfoɔ was brought to the dais where he was to be seated, after he had made a full tour of the guests and his Abrempɔn and royals who had responded to his call to come and celebrate the auspicious day with him. Otumfoɔ's palanquin was finally lowered and brought to the ground. Four men who were part of his courtiers came forward, removed their large cloths and spread them out to conceal Otumfoɔ from public view as he descended from the palanquin and prepared himself to sit in state. The palour was quickly set and decorated with *kɔdeɛ* or *kɔtɔkɔdwa,* his State Chair placed on the large mat made of parchment of leather. The *hwɛdom,* was placed to the left beside Otumfoɔ's stool on which the Golden Stool was rested on its velvet cushion. He was ushered to his seat, the palanquin was removed after which the cloths were also removed for Otumfoɔ and the Golden Stool to be revealed, seated as they were to be presented to the world. He was decorated with his cloth spread to cover him neatly, his legs exposed from just below his knee, showing his calves and ankles decorated with gold ornaments. His feet, nicely pedicure, fitted in his beautifully designed traditional footwear, rested on a foot stool. The golden weapons he carried in the palanquin were taken away; and in their stead he was given a white horse tail to carry in his left hand.

The Kumasi Council or the immediate Councilors of Otumfoɔ who had come along with him to the durbar sat in an assemblage around him in a horse shoe formation, replicating the larger set up of the *Asanteman* Council, comprising the various divisions or fekuo as they are called, namely, Krontre, Akwamu, Nifa, Benkum, Adonten, Gyaase, Ankobea and Kyidom with their courtiers who sat in front of them on the floor or on small stools called adamadwa bearing whichever implement, property or accoutrement of service to the King at the edge of a red carpet walkway laid up to Otumfoɔ's dais. The most significant were the twelve sword bearers who sat lined up in front of Otumfoɔ, six aside facing each other, crossing the swords they bore in pairs to form a barrier.

Just as Otumfoɔ settled in, the Asantehemaa arrived at the palour after she had also gone round to greet the gathering as her king had done. She was also lowered down from her ride in front of Otumfoɔ. She made her way to Otumfoɔ walking on the red carpet. On sighting her, the mmɛnsɔn blowers heralded her in as she walked in. The Mpumpunsuohene announced the Asantehemaa to Otumfoɔ and led her to the presence of the King. The sword bearers lifted the barrier they had made with their swords and allowed her through. She walked in, closely escorted by a male attendant who had wrapped his cloth to his waist, bearing her right arm decked in gold ornaments from her fingers to her upper arm in his palms. With the support of her hand bearer she greeted Otumfoɔ by stretching forth her right hand, congratulated him and wished him well. As Otumfoɔ took her hand, two praise singers standing behind him broke into *kwadwom* or songs of praise, extolling the virtues of the king.

"Ɔsagyefoɔ gye adwa gu ase
Okuduo Asante Na'Adu tena ase aayi
Kɔtɔkɔhene tena ase, Krɔbeahene tena ase aayi
Merema wo Krɔbea Yirefi Anwoma Kɔtɔkɔ aayi
Asante atwa ntire agu oo Twum Akyampɔn nofonbo aayi Asante asiesie bo o suman-titi aayi
Krɔbea Asante Na'Adu ee tena ase aayi
Ɔsɛe Tutu meremɔ wo din nwe awisi o

Hwan na obɛnya sɛ Edweso Owusu Panin ne
Akua Bakoma Sikapɔ ba ne no

Obi nyaa saa bi a anka obɛyɛbi
Maanu Atie Dufie ba, Dammirifa nyane aayi
Kyerewa Nintofie mmɔdwee nna

Osodofoɔ dade eduru Twum Akyampɔn nofonbo aayi
Osi ani kurowi oo suman-titi aayi."

The reverberating voices of the praise singer said:
"Osagyefo, a seat for you,
Descendant of Okuduo Asante Nana Adu,
a seat for you, King of Kotoko, be seated,
King of Korobea, be seated.
I am handing over to you
Korobea Yirefi Anwoma Kotoko Asante,
Noted for deeds of bravery,
Twum Akyampong Nofonbo
Asante is ready for your arrival, O powerful spirit.
A seat for you, Nana Adu descendant of Krobea Asante.
Osei Tutu, permit me to call you thus
Who would not like to be the offspring of
Owusu Panin of Edweso and Akua Bakoma
renowned for the gold nugget?
The wish many yearn for.
Child of Atie Dufie, Dammirifa,
that keeps vigil, wake up
At Kyerewa Ninto's house, jaws do not rest
Love that climbs over iron,
Twum Akyampon Nofonbo
When he steps, his feet fall gently
and noiselessly, powerful spirit."

He held onto her till the praise song ended before he released her. She was then directed to her seat placed beside the Golden Stool.

When all had settled down, the lead linguist, Otumfoɔ Akyeamehene stood up with his staff of authority in hand. The Mpumpunsuohene picked a microphone, craved the silence of the gathering and all cacophony of music playing came to a halt.

The Akyeamehene took over the microphone and announced the purpose of the gathering. "Otumfoɔ, Nananom, Special Guests and very important personalities here assembled, you are all here because Otumfoɔ has graciously invited you to bring your honour and dignity to grace this auspicious occasion of Akwasidεεkesεε today. Otumfoɔ welcomes you all individually and collectively. You are all Otumfoɔ's guests and by the power vested in me as his chief linguist I shall personally see to your comfort and hospitability. Otumfoɔ will now receive homage."

The Akyeame sat down. The Mpumpunsuohene, carrying his mpumpunsuo on his left arm went to Otumfoɔ, ostensibly to seek his permission. He went on one knee before Otumfoɔ. Otumfoɔ nodded in consent to him and with that the Mpumpunsuohene rose and headed for the VVIP canopy. The special guest of honour was invited to approach the Otumfoɔ. The Mpumpunsuohene led him and his immediate entourage and one after the other they walked directly up to the king who remained seated with his right arm, decorated in gold trinkets, resting in the palms of an attendant seated on an adamadwa next to him. The guests were heralded in with fanfare by the mmεnsɔn players as they approached the king. With the assistance of the attendant, Otumfoɔ raised his arm to the special guest of /honour and as soon as their hands clasped, the two praise singers broke into their *kwadwom* again. He held on the hand of the guest in silence till the appellations were over, after which they exchanged pleasantries. This gesture was extended only to special guests and dignitaries identified and acknowledged for the honour of state salute, like heads of delegations and prominent personalities. The accompanying members of the delegations, although were allowed handshakes with the king, they were not honoured with such a salute. There were yet others who were allowed close but not close enough to earn a handshake. They were made to bow at a distance, to which the king nodded in recognition. Men in traditional cloths who were allowed bared their left shoulders and walked, barefoot, to the king and took their handshakes. Those dignitaries in traditional cloths allowed to approach the king in their footwear were made to slip their right foot out of the slipper, bared the shoulder and bowed to take the handshake.

When the batch of the special guests and dignitaries were done with, a large quantity of assorted drinks and gifts, neatly wrapped and packaged on large trays were brought in, carried by a group of young women on their heads. The young women were lined up, some distance away, before the king. The gifts were announced as presents from the guest of honour to the king.

"Nananom, Otumfoɔ Akyeame," the Mpumpunsuohene addressed the linguists of Otumfoɔ, "this is what the guest of honour for this Special Akwasidɛɛ says: He says he is highly honoured to be the Special Guest of Honour for this occasion. He is therefore making this presentation to congratulate His Majesty the King for this wonderful celebration. It comprises assorted drinks and a special donation of one hundred thousand dollars cash contribution to the Otumfoɔ's Education and Development Fund." There was thunderous applause by the gathering. He continued, "He wishes the King, God's blessings, long life in good health and a peaceful reign. He also wishes Otumfoɔ's Abrempɔn, his Queenmothers and all the elders and great citizens of the *Asanteman* a joyous celebration. Three hearty cheers. "*Mompene won ɛɛ*!"

"Yeah!" the gathering yelled in response

"*Mompene won ɛɛ*!"

"Yeah!" the gathering yelled again.

"*Mompene won ɛɛɛɛɛɛ!*"

"Yeaaaaaaah!" The gathering gave a thunderous yell with the mmɛnsɔn players also giving off a fanfare presentation. The gifts were received and stowed away.

The Abrempɔn of his majesty were called up. They approached the king one after the other. The Bantamahene was first to pay homage to the king. At a distance, his personal attendants were stopped;

he handed over his weapon, removed his head-gear and all amulets and talismans and handed them to his attendants; with his umbrella removed from over him and closed up, he was then allowed to move forward alone. At a point, one of the king's abrafoɔ jumped in front of him; pointing a rusty afena he carried in his right hand, placing it on top of his fisted left hand and stretching it towards the king, then he began yelling out appellations.

Otumfoɔ!
Wo yɛ ohene ampa, woyɛ kokroko!
Ɔte kɔkɔɔ soɔ
Asanteman wura, Asanteman, wodea
Abɔ-wo-din-a-abɔ-kyɛkyɛ
Hwan na wo suro no?
Obiara hyɛ w'ase.
'Sɛe Tutu se, Wo tumi nyinaa wie ne nan ase
Ne sika dwa Kofi anim

Otumfoɔ!
You are king, you are supreme!
The occupant of the Golden Stool
The overlord and owner of all Asanteman
and everything there in your territory;
Men shudder at the mention of your name
You fear no one
All are but subordinates to your authority
No matter whom you are, no matter your authority
Or how much you are revered,
Your power, authority and reverence end
At the feet of his majesty and the Golden Stool,
Osei Tutu says.

The appellation ended, the Bantamahene continued his approach to Otumfoɔ. He was stopped yet again by another Ɔbrafoɔ who ran another verse of appellation of Otumfoɔ before he was finally allowed to get to His Majesty. The sword bearers lifted their barrier and allowed him through. With about a few steps to the King, Bantamahene stopped and adjusted his cloth. Baring his left shoulder slightly, he took a couple of steps towards his king, stepped forward with his right foot, slightly slipped his right foot out of the traditional sandal he wore and bowing before him the Bantamahene stretched forth his right hand. Otumfoɔ's hand-bearer lifted his hand and when Otumfoɔ took his ɔbrempɔn's hand the praise singers broke in again. The handshake froze for the praise singers to run their verses through after which the Bantamahene gave the King hearty congratulations and wished him well. Bantamahene turned away from the presence of his supreme lord, readjusted his apparel to normal position. When he got to his attendants he collected the properties he left behind and redecorated himself with them. His umbrella was restored over him and he went back to his seat.

The Mamponhene who is the Adontenhene of the kingdom, followed immediately after the Bantamahene. In the same fashion he removed his ornaments from his arms and fingers and handed them to his attendants and approached Otumfoɔ. Similarly, the abrafoɔ interrupted him; patiently and courteously he endured the abrafoɔ as a sign of respect and reverence to his king and lord. He was allowed through to Otumfoɔ. As soon as their palms met the praise singers broke in with their *kwadwom*. They paused and waited till the *kwadwom* was ended and exchanged pleasantries. After a short 3moment they were done and the Momponhene departed the king's presence. And so followed the rest of Otumfoɔ's Abrempɔn.

The Akyeamehene rose to his feet when the Abrempɔn completed their turns paying homage to the king. He asked that other dignitaries who had lined up to take their turn to pay homage to the king be suspended for a short ceremony. He announced the next item on the activity of the day: the conferment of state honour on Professor Kofi Nsiah.

The Mpumpunsuohene yelled, "Conferment of State Honour on Professor Kofi Nsiah. May the good Prof approach the presence of Otumfoɔ." Kofi Nsiah lifted Bibi off his lap and rose to his feet. Holding Bibi's hand, he beckoned Frema to join them. As they walked to Otumfoɔ's palour Nana *Sumankwaahene* rose from his position in Otumfoɔ's entourage and joined him. Auntie Yaa and a couple of his family members joined them, standing behind them. Maame got up from her seat and ran in to join them. From where she sat, it took her a while to get close. Suddenly, a security man stepped up and stopped her when she tried to break through a barrier. Try as she might to convince him that she was part of the delegation, it did not appeal to the security man to allow her through. She waited there and watched the ceremony from that distance.

Kofi and his entourage were brought closer by the Mpumpunsuohene to the presence of the king. The entourage had grown bigger as other members of the family run to join in. The party was stopped in front of the Akyeame. Kofi and Nana Sumankwaa and his Abusuapanyin and the Obaapanyin were made to step forward. He turned to look back at Frema who had taken hold of Bibi by the hand. Frema winked at him and he winked back while Bibi smiled and waved at him too. Kofi was made to bare his left shoulder and face the Akyeame. All the Akyeame rose to their feet, holding their staffs of office.

"Professor Kofi Nsiah," the Akyeamehene addressed him with a citation. "Your singular efforts in promoting the name and image of *Asanteman* and the Golden Stool in far-away lands have brought honour and prestige to the Kingdom. Your great contribution, unparalleled in our recent history, has also brought honour to your family and to yourself. News of your exploits have reached His Majesty, your King, for which he has decided to honour you today as: 'Special Ambassador of the Asante Kingdom and the Golden Stool'. In this light, it has pleased Otumfoɔ, *Asanteman* wura, ɔte kɔkɔ soɔ, to honour you today by conferring on you a special title, Busumuru. You shall enjoy full

protocol of Otumfoɔ and all benefits that come with this honour. Otumfoɔ wishes to encourage you to continue and do more in the coming years. He wishes you well and the blessings of the Almighty Creator, the guidance of our ancestral gods and the fortitude of our great ancestors." The family members cheered and applauded:
"*Mo, ɔpiafo!*....Congratulations, brave one!" they yelled.

Kofi was asked to follow the Mpumpunsuohene to the sword bearers. He was made to tie his kente cloth firmly around his waist, exposing his torso. He complied. When he was done he, was asked to remove his foot wear and move through the sword bearers who had then parted their crossed swords.

The Mpumpunsuohene handed him the mpumpunsuo when they reach the king and was asked to swear an oath of allegiance to him, the Golden Stool and *Asanteman*.

Kofi held the mpumpunsuo sword by the handle. Suddenly, a quick shivery feeling ran through him bringing quick flashes of his encounter with the busumuru in the tomb. He immediately recomposed himself and raised the mpumpunsuo, pointing it to the sky and then brought it down to point it to the earth. He then pointed it to Otumfoɔ and said; "I swear by Almighty God, by Mother Earth, by the Golden Stool, by the King and the great Oaths of *Asanteman* that I, Kofi Nsiah having been elevated to this high position of honour, will do well to respect the honour done to me. I shall respect and honour the King and the sanctity of the Golden Stool; show due honour to Otumfoɔ's Abrempɔn and elders of the land. I shall honour the dignity of the spirit gods and of our forebears. I shall be true and do well to *Asanteman*. Whenever I am called, I shall respond, rain or shine, day or night, save in death or infirmity; I shall never turn my back on my lord Otumfoɔ, the Golden Stool or *Asanteman*; nor would I ever speak with water in my mouth. I break the great Oaths of *Asanteman* if I fail and shall subject myself to suffer the penalty thereof."

The family and the gathering cheered and applauded while the *mɛnsɔn* players blew a fanfare interlude. Kofi handed the sword to the

Mpumpunsuohene. He took a few steps towards Otumfoɔ and stretched his right hand to him. Otumfoɔ took his hand, and the praise singer raised a *kwadwom* verse after which Otumfoɔ spoke and congratulated him. Kofi turned and shook hands with Asantehemaa who had watched the proceedings admiringly. Nana Sumankwaa followed Kofi to thank Otumfoɔ. Kofi moved to the Mpumpunsuohene and whispered into his ear. They turned and looked at Frema. Kofi beckoned her. She approached them and was directed to go for a hand shake with the King. Accompanied by Bibi, Frema moved to the King. She curtsied as the king took her hand and shook it warmly. Bibi broke her hold from her mother and stepped back and held the edge of the flair of her dress band bowed to the king. This attracted the attention of the king and caused him to burst into laughter. He stretched his hand to her. Bibi dashed forward and took the king's hand. The king gave her a warm handshake too. Frema and Bibi were excited for the opportunity as they were escorted from the presence of the king.

Kofi called for the packages and parcels they had brought as gifts for the king. The Akyeamehene received them including a cash donation and announced them to the King.

"The ceremony is ended. Take him, decorate him with white clay and show him to the people." The Akyeamehene ordered. The rest of the family who were waiting for their turn with the King were halted and asked to bow from wherever they were.

When Kofi returned to his family the anxious men and women pounced on him and sprayed his face, head and his body with talcum powder in jubilation. They lifted him up on their shoulders, singing and drumming and dancing. "Oseeyie ee! Yee yie ee!" They carried him away. Frema and Bibi trotted behind them.

Maame looked at the security man who stopped her. He was distracted by the scene as Kofi rode on shoulders past him. Seeing his attention was off her, Maame quickly whisked past him unnoticed and joined the jubilant crowd shouting and cheering. Soon, she joined Frema and Bibi as they cheered from behind the main crowd.

"Oseeyie! Yeeyie, yeeyie!" the crowd cheered as Kofi rode on their shoulders and was taken away from the precinct of the durbar. As he sat up on the shoulders of his kinsmen, the noises of singing and drumming and dance faded into oblivion for a moment. Flashback flashes of his experiences in the last few days came to him, so strong that the he felt like he was in a trance. Firing of musketry shook him awake. Then he turned and saw Frema and Bibi, following. He suddenly came back to himself. Tears began to drop from his eyes as he rode away out of the celebration of the *Akwasidɛɛkesɛɛ*. Then he suddenly tapped heavily on the men who carried him and vehemently demanded that they set him down.

The joyous celebrations drums, music, dance and cheers suddenly came to an abrupt halt and end. Frema and Bibi also halted. Frema was confused as she saw Kofi struggling to free himself from his carriers who were also bemused by his understandable conduct They grabbed and held him, preventing him from escaping. After a bit of struggle with Kofi, the men backed down. When he was freed of their hold Kofi pushed his way through his astounded kinsmen, brushing them aside. He stopped at a short distance from Frema who was equally confused and awed just like his kinsmen. Kofi then dashed towards her with his arms stretched out. Frema let go of Bibi's hand in her hold and also dashed toward Kofi. The two ran into each other's embrace. Excitedly, he lifted her off her feet and whirled her around, set her down and gave her a passionate kiss on her lips. Frema equally responded to his expression of affection. Maame who had then gotten closer took hold of bewildered Bibi as she had been abandoned by Frema. The kinsmen who were left perplexed suddenly got rekindled and rushed on Kofi again, grabbed away from Frema back onto their shoulders with their music, drumming, dancing and cheers. And away, they took him. Together, holding hands, Frema, Maame and Bibi followed the jubilant crowd of Kofi and his kinsmen also cheering: *"Oseeyie ee! Yee yie ee! Oseeyie ee! Yee yie ee!!"*

THE END

Lightning Source UK Ltd.
Milton Keynes UK
UKHW012207250220
359315UK00001B/128

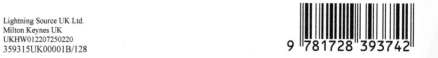